Power

Play

The
Jared Russell Series

Book Two

Power

Play

Cover design by Bryan M. Powell

Interior design by Bryan M. Powell

Published in the United States of America

Action - Fiction, Adventure – Fiction, Contemporary – Fiction, Romance – Fiction, Islam – Fiction, Suspense – Fiction, Father and Son – Fiction, Women's – Fiction, CIA - Fiction

15.03.22

Cast of Characters

Ayatollah Abdullah Bashera – Prime Minister of Lebanon

Amil Abdullah Bashera – the eldest son of Abdullah

Rajeed Ishmael Bashera – the second born son of Abdullah

Anita Sumira Bashera – Abdullah's only daughter

Jared and Fatemah Russell – Founders of the Harbor House

Richard and Mindy Owens – Missionaries with Campus Bible Association

John Xavier – Senior Partner with Xavier and Wright Architectural Design Firm

Jimbo Osborne – head of hotel security

Belinda Turner – the Grand Hotel's head of housekeeping

Uncle Abbas – taxi driver

Habib Teriek Hanif – Uncle Abbas' nephew

Captain Ali – skipper of the el Labrador

President Susan R. Ferguson - America's first female President.

Andrew Kelly - the President's Chief of Staff

Larry Morgan - Head of the President's Security Detail

Ms. Rachel Anderson - fifteen-year veteran in the Secret Service

Leah Clark – part of the Presidential Security Detail

Mr. Stephan Von Janson, Head of the Green Peace Movement

Amil Bashera – Diplomatic Attaché with Green Peace

Dr. Richard C. McMillan – Head of NOAA

Iris Didion - Secretary of NOAA – envious, jealous, vengeful

Farooq-e-Azam (aka) Kaleel Bashera – undercover CIA agent

Prime Minister Shimer ben Yousef

Teriek Azar – leader of The Sons of Thunder

Prologue

Beirut, Lebanon

"Allaaaaah . . . "

The morning air crackled with the first of five daily prayers from a nearby minaret calling the faithful to assemble and pray. The scuffle of leather sandals on pavement broke the sacred moment as a young boy raced through the crowd stumbling over the kneeling men.

"How dare you refuse to pray," a man cried. His angry words, laced with vulgarity, flew like shafts of lightning bolts. A gnarled hand stretched out, barely missing the youth's shirttail as he darted in and out of the assembly.

"If you don't give me that Bible, I'll kill you, I swear," the father said, his words coming between gasps of air.

"No! It's mine and you can't have it," cried the boy and took off across the piazza.

Pulling a gun from his waist, the boy's father took aim and squeezed off a round. The shot went high, and the boy ducked. Knowing he had moments to live, he turned right and headed for the open market. Clambering through the narrow street, chased by his irate father, the boy scattered a flock of chickens, knocked over a basket of fruit, and overturned a cart filled with vegetables. Another shot rang out and the shoppers parted like the Red Sea.

Panting for breath, yet unyielding, the boy sprinted down an alley which opened up to a major freeway.

With his father close behind, the youth paused a moment letting a semi-truck pass, then darted across the northbound lanes of Al Akhtal Al Shaghir Boulevard. Another wild shot whizzed through the sultry air, driving the boy for cover behind a palm tree. With seconds ticking, he scrambled to his feet and charged across the highway. A moment later, a white Chrysler convertible appeared in the center lane, catching the boy like a dear in its headlights.

As if in slow motion, the driver cut his wheels and slammed on his brakes. Amid burning rubber and squealing tires, the boy stood, frozen in place.

Another shot rang out.

Chapter 1

Beirut, Lebanon

Jared and Fatemah stepped from their honeymoon suite on the fourth floor of the Sheridan Coral Resort and into the waiting elevator. He tapped the button marked 'Ground Floor', and the doors silently slid shut. Wrapping his arms around his bride of nine days, Jared watched the view through the glass-enclosed elevator as it made its slow descent. Her perfume wafted around him, captivating his attention, intoxicating his senses.

"Don't you love this place?" he whispered in her ear.

Fatemah sighed heavily and turned to face her husband. "I do and I can't wait to get back here to begin our ministry. I already miss the place."

Moments later, their descent ended with a gentle bump and the doors receded out of sight.

"After you, my dear," Jared bowed slightly at the waist.

Releasing a giggle, Fatemah stepped into the spacious lobby. "Oh Jared, you're such a romantic, just like your father."

Not able to resist, Jared returned the comment with a light swat which drew an adoring glare. Together, they strode through the crowd greeting the friendly bell-hop on the way to the parking deck.

As they stepped into the warm Mediterranean breeze, the valet brought Jared's rented white Chrysler convertible to a gentle stop along the curb and jumped out. Jared handed him a five-pound note and helped Fatemah into the car. He skipped around to the driver's side, got in, and with the flick of a button, lowered the convertible top.

Jared inhaled, "Don't you love that salty air?" he asked, revving the engine.

Fatemah returned a Cheshire-cat grin and tugged a broad brimmed hat over her head. "Yes, it makes my skin tingle."

Heading south on Al Akhtal Al Shaghir Boulevard, Jared tried to absorb the pristine beauty of the well-manicured lawns and luxurious homes. A flash of movement caught his eye as a boy with his shirt torn and his hair disheveled dashed across the highway, followed by an older man carrying a gun.

Jared slammed on the brakes and swerved barely missing the youth. The car jumped the curb, smashing into one of the palm trees lining the road. The salty air was replaced with the pungent stench of burnt rubber and steam from its radiator.

Over blaring horns and screeching tires, the man's voice assaulted Jared's senses.

"Get back here you filthy infidel," the man screamed, as the boy tried to scale the concrete buffer. He raised the weapon, took aim, and fired. The bullet whizzed past him striking the wall and chipping out a piece of concrete.

The report of the pistol sent a jolt of adrenalin coursing through Jared's veins. He jumped from the smoking car with Fatemah close on his heels and ran toward the man as he leveled the gun again. Like a defensive linebacker, Jared lowered his shoulder and bowled him over sending the gun in one direction and the man in another.

Fatemah raced to the fleeing boy's side, her breath coming in short snatches. "Here, hide behind me," she said in Farsi, wrapping her arms around him.

The man leaped to his feet, fists clinched. The veins of his neck bulged as he hurled a string of expletives at Jared. "Why have you interfered; you fool?" he spat, then swung at Jared barely missing his chin.

Jared, being a full six foot two and a hundred ten pounds heavier than the smaller Arab man, held him at bay with an outstretched arm.

"Hold on now buddy, what's this all about? You can't go around shooting children," forgetting he wasn't in America.

"This is a domestic issue. You have no right. This boy has renounced Islam and converted to Christianity. It is my duty to kill him. Now let me go," he demanded.

"Sorry, no can do. I can't let you murder an innocent child." With that, Jared scooped up the weapon, flipped open the cylinder, and emptied it. Then he disassembled the gun and tossed the parts in three directions.

The man's dark eyes glowered with unchecked anger, his fists clinched, "I'll have you arrested and condemned as an enemy of the state, you filthy—"

"Ah, ah, ah, no racial slurs allowed here."

Crack!

Jared upended the man with a right hook, sending him sprawling.

A horn blared as a taxi skidded to a stop. "Get in, get in!" demanded the taxi driver, his voice filled with urgency.

Jared held his position.

"Do what he says," Fatemah ordered shoving the boy inside.

Before the man could recover, Jared pivoted and dashed to the side of the taxi, "Come on, let's get out of here," the driver said, his voice laced with tension.

As Jared slammed the door shut, it became obvious why. A large crowd of onlookers had gathered, shouting, "Death to the traitor!"

The elderly man, his knuckles white from gripping the wheel, floored the taxi. Its tires spun, sending up a rooster tail of stones and debris as he fishtailed from the mayhem.

A moment later, a rock struck the back window of the fleeing vehicle as it swerved through the crowd.

"Where are you taking us?" Fatemah asked, her eyes wide with fear, still clutching the trembling child.

Staring straight ahead, the older man said, "Out of the city. It's the only way you or this boy will survive," his gruff voice made worse by the racing engine.

"But sir, you don't understand. We are tourists from America, and we are scheduled to leave tomorrow," Jared pleaded, leaning forward.

The driver's eyes flashed. "No, you don't understand. This is Lebanon, a Muslim country. That father has every right to maintain his family's faith. By interfering Mister American, you have brought great harm to our cause," he said with controlled anger.

Jared tried to absorb the implications of what the man said. "Your cause?" he questioned. "I don't get it."

The taxi driver slowed his speed and softened his tone. "My cause is to rescue children. Children who like this young child have trusted Christ as their Savior. It is my duty, my responsibility, yes, my calling is to help these new believers. I would have stopped his father, but in my own way. You, by your actions, will give the Imams and Ayatollahs reason to overreact. The next thing you know, they will be declaring a fatwa."

"A what?" Jared asked as the adrenalin rush throbbed in his temples.

Fatemah, who had been sitting quietly, stroking the young boy's head, looked up. "It's like a law, a moratorium against all evangelistic activity. Violators could face imprisonment, exile, or in some cases, execution."

Jared turned to face his wife, "But I couldn't allow that man to kill his child. I couldn't live with myself had he succeeded."

Looking down at the shivering boy, Fatemah forced a ragged smile. "All the more reason for us to hurry back and establish the Harbor House," she said, patting her husband on the shoulder.

He winched at her touch. "Still tender?" she probed.

His fingers touched the scar where a bullet had passed through. "Yeah, I think it will always give me trouble." Bitter memories of Ahmad's lifeless body in his arms scraped across old wounds and he bit back a tear.

The taxi driver made one last turn, and the Sheridan Coral Resort appeared in the distance. "I'm going to drop you two off at your hotel. Report the accident, pack your bags, and be ready to leave Lebanon as soon as possible. Do you hear me?"

Jared rubbed the back of his neck. "Yes sir." Handing him the fare along with a sizable tip, Jared leveled his gaze. "Sir, we believe it is God's will for us to come back to your country as missionaries."

Shaking his head, the older man squinted in the rear-view mirror. "You Americans, always so confident. I certainly hope you have counted the cost."

Chapter 2

Ayatollah Abdulla Bashera's Office

With his fingers knit behind his back, Ayatollah Abdullah Bashera paced the Persian carpet like a wild bull. His black beard splayed wildly over his robust chest giving him the appearance of a modern day Black Beard. A light knock on his outer door brought him from his musings.

"Come!" His voice bellowed.

Silently, the heavy oaken door swung open and Amil entered.

The Ayatollah pivoted on his heels and released an impatient huff. He was not accustomed to waiting, especially for his son. "Good, of you to come. Sorry about having to disturb your prayer, I'm sure Allah will understand."

Amil stood, back straight, wondering if Allah was as capricious as his father. He had never seen him so agitated. Ever since his mother died, his father had been a different man, a driven man, an evil man, blaming his younger sister Anita for her death. At the end of the day, however, Amil wondered if he didn't blame Allah.

"Have you read about the American interfering with a Muslim father executing judgment on his son?" the Ayatollah asked.

The air grew thick with tension, "Yes, I have, Father."

"It is for such foolish actions Allah the merciful will pour his wrath upon that infidel nation without measure."

"And how do you suppose he'll do that, sir?"

The older man strolled to his palladium window and gazed over his vast estate. "In two weeks I will speak with Prime Minister Rashad el Zanainullah and insist that he enforce the Fatwa. If he does not comply, I will seek to have him removed from office and declare myself the supreme leader of Lebanon." His smooth tones masked slightly the hatred he held for Christianity, and its intrusion into his country.

"Do you have the support in the parliament to ram it through, Father?"

Cocking his head, a cruel smile escaped his lips. "More than enough support in both houses of parliament. I could be sworn in by week's end, if it weren't for that namby-pamby vice prime minister. Once installed, I will enforce a no-tolerance law against all proselytizing. Anyone caught trying to convert a Muslim will be prosecuted, expelled, or executed. We must stop this attack upon Islam once and for all."

Amil, the twenty-seven-year-old, first-born son of the Ayatollah, took his place next to him. Though only an inch taller than his five foot three-inch father, his white teeth, quick smile, and amiable personality made him every girl's desire. Amil stroked his goatee and searched his father's face. The man's eyes glowered with unchecked anger.

"And what would you have me to do, Father?" Amil asked, snatching a hand full of dates. He popped one in his mouth and chewed, then popped another.

"Those are a gift," the Ayatollah said, stepping from behind his desk.

"Oh? From whom?"

An evil chuckle percolated in his throat. "From Sheik Ishmael? al Hussar."

Amil gasped and nearly choked. "Are you sure these are not poisoned?" he asked, spitting out the date.

The Ayatollah scooped up a hand full and shoved one into his pursed lips. "I assure you, they are not poisoned."

"But why would you trust anything Hussar gave you? You know the man is a lying, thieving—"

"That's enough Amil," he said with a wave. "I have my reasons."

He lifted a large envelope and handed it to Amil, "Here, read this and prepare to leave immediately."

Amil lowered himself into a chair. Its lamb skin surface felt cool and soft to his touch. After pulling back the envelope flap, he poured out its contents onto the desk. His fingers trembled slightly as he inspected the diplomatic papers, visa, passport, and a badge stating that he was a diplomat with the Greenpeace Movement.

"What is all this?"

His father plopped heavily on his chair and crossed his arms. "Amil, you have been given a great honor. If you show yourself faithful, you will earn a rich reward from Allah the merciful."

Great reward, he gritted his teeth. "Yes, Father, as you wish."

His father held up his hand. "I wish you to be quiet and listen. This position will give you a free pass inside the Great Satan. Use it wisely. Already, there is a sleeper cell making their way to a secret location. Their instructions are to wait, be ready to strike when the moment is right. You, my son, must be ready too. Remember the training you received in Mogadishu."

Flashbacks of hot desert training, forced marches, shooting ranges, and hours spent studying technical manuals of satchel bombs skittered across his mind like wind-driven leaves.

"So how does being assigned to the Greenpeace Movement advance our cause of spreading Islam, Father?"

The Ayatollah stood and stepped in front of his desk. Placing a fat hand on his son's shoulder, he looked him in the eyes. "Son, all in good time, all in good time. Your job is to gain the infidels' trust, their confidence, and their secrets. Only then will you be in a position to spread the caliphate. Now go, you have a long and dangerous journey ahead of you."

"And what of Rajeed? Is he not going to accompany me?"

The Ayatollah's face reddened. The veins of his neck stood out. "Your brother will have his own work. I am sending him on a very dangerous mission of his own. He too will strike at the heart of the Great Satan. With Allah's blessings, both of you will make your mark for Islam. Now go!"

Chapter 3

Seattle, Washington

The lunch crowd at Palomino Restaurant thinned enough for Jared to locate his boss seated in a booth near the back. As waiters moved about the brightly lit dining room, soft music mingled amidst low conversations, and Jared wished he was meeting Fatemah rather than Mr. Xavier. It had been a week since he and Fatemah returned from their honeymoon, when he got a call from his boss's secretary. Mr. Xavier, with Xavier and Wright Architectural Group, wanted to meet him for a late lunch.

"Jared," John Xavier said, lifting his eyes from a sheet of paper, "thanks for coming." He folded the paper and tucked it into his briefcase.

It was the first time they had seen each other since Jared's wedding, and the older man extended his hand. "Congratulations on your wedding. Please, take a seat, Jared." The lines on his face gave nothing away.

The two men shook hands, and Jared slid into the booth. As he did, a waitress handed him a menu.

With a wave of his hand, John glanced at the waitress. "No need for that, ma'am, I've already ordered for both of us. It should be here in a minute or so."

The waitress nodded, took the menu and backed away.

"By the way," John said, clutching Jared's forearm with an iron grip, "that was a beautiful wedding. You tell your wife she looked absolutely fetching."

Jared smiled at hearing the turn of phrase meaning, 'good looking.' "I'll tell her."

Another young server stepped at their table and slid two plates bearing a couple of club sandwiches in front of them. John caught him by his sleeve as he turned to go. "How 'bout a refill of coffee and a fresh one for my friend here," looking at Jared. "How do ya want your coffee?"

It always amazed Jared. The man was a workaholic with boundless energy. You'd think by now he'd slow down and retire, but no, not John Xavier. His intensity and drive had no limit.

Jared's smooth face wrinkled into a grin, "I'd like it with cream and sugar."

Two minutes passed, and the waitress returned with two full mugs of the black brew. The aromatic fragrance invigorated Jared's senses as he inhaled. "Ah, I so love a good cup of coffee."

Rubbing his hands together, Mr. Xavier acted like a kid on Christmas day. "Good, and put it all on my ticket," he said, his enthusiasm bursting at the seams.

"Jared, you did a heck of a job with the Center for Islamic Studies there in Stanford, Michigan. It was completed under-budget and on time. And the way you handled all that," he lowered his voice and waved an expressive hand, "all that Islamic controversy. It was masterful."

"Thank you, Mr. Xavier, and thank—"

"—call me John, we're not at the office," his boss said, lifting his meaty sandwich.

Jared accepted the correction with a nod, "Okay, John it is. Thank you for your generous wedding gift. That will go toward our . . . uh. . . our long-range goals," Jared said, eyeing the envelope at John's elbow. "Mind if I pray over lunch?"

The question caught John mid-bite, "Yes, by all means. We could use all the prayer we can get."

Taken back by his boss's cavalier answer, Jared bowed his head and began. "Thank you, Lord, for this food and your provision. We need your wisdom. Please guide and help us, in Jesus' name, amen."

To Jared's surprise, Mr. Xavier joined the "amen."

Jared took a bite of his club sandwich and chewed it thoughtfully. *I wonder who's going to go first,* he mused. Finally, his curiosity got the better of him and he broke the uncomfortable silence. "Mr. Xavier . . . Fatemah and I have been thinking about—" A raised palm stopped Jared mid-sentence.

"Now look, Jared," John interrupted, "I gotta hunch I know what you're about to say, but before you do, I've got a proposal of my own I want you to consider."

Surprised, Jared sat back.

"You see, Jared, the Lebanese International University in Beirut is about to undertake a large expansion project, and we've bid on the job."

Jared's heart quickened and his pulse pounded in his temples. "Yes, sir?"

"And Mr. Wright, the board of trustees, and I have talked it over and feel it would only be right to offer you the first shot at being the lead architect."

Jared held his boss' steady gaze. With concern, Jared asked, "Do you think that's wise, knowing Beirut's history with the Marines?"

John pushed out a ragged breath. "I was there! I had buddies who died in the blast, you know." His eyes took on a pained stare.

"No, sir, I didn't." Jared looked away.

His boss shifted uncomfortably. "I started having nightmares … again."

"John, in all the years we've known each other, why wait until now to tell me this? I could have . . . " Jared's voice trailed off.

"I thought it was behind me, buried in some secret corner of my mind. But when Wright and I landed in Beirut, and I saw where the Marine barracks were . . ." he paused and tugged at his collar. It all came rushing back. The muffled cries of my men, the smell of sulfur, the blood, the burning flesh. It was *Hell* all over again. "You know, Hezbollah still guards the compound, and the International Airport for that matter. They won't let anyone near the place."

Jared swallowed the lump in his throat. He'd read about the bombing. It was part of his training, his heritage as a Marine. On

October 23, 1983 at 0622 hrs a large delivery truck broke through two guard posts into the lobby of the Battalion Landing Team's barracks and exploded, killing 241 U.S. Marines, sailors, and soldiers. "So, do you think it is a good idea for me, a former Marine, to go to that hotbed of terrorism?"

A labored sigh escaped John's lips and he leaned back. "Things have changed a lot since the civil war ended. Yes, Hamas and Hezbollah operate with a free hand right under the government's noses, and yes, they still have one of the largest training camps in the Bekaa valley. But I still think the university expansion bit is a good idea."

"Mr. Xavier, uh, John, I, I don't know what to say," he sputtered.

With an interesting glint in his eyes, John folded his arms across his chest. "Well, don't say anything. Not until you and Fatemah have had time to pray and talk it through."

Nearly choking on his coffee, Jared set his cup down and cleared his throat. "Mr. Xavier, you never struck me as a religious man, why the change of—"

Laying a hand on Jared's forearm, John held his gaze. "Now son," Xavier said, cutting him off with the wave, "there's a lot you don't know about me. But suffice it to say, I'm deeply religious and have a keen interest in the affairs of that country. Now, I want you and Fatemah to take a long weekend up at my cabin, enjoy yourselves, and come back with your answer."

As he spoke, he flipped the manila envelope over displaying the words, 'Do Not Open Until After Supper.' He smiled at the scribbled letters and slid it in Jared's direction. "I want you to read over the complete proposal and get back to me on Monday."

His set jaw left Jared little room for negotiation. Jared took a hard swallow and accepted the proffered manila envelope. "Yes sir.

***

After a day's drive into the hill country of Wayne County, north of Seattle, Jared turned off the country road and onto the gravel driveway leading to Mr. Xavier's cabin. A soft rain had bathed the branches of the conifer trees making them shimmer in the fading light. The air was pregnant with the fresh scent of pine mingled with mountain laurel. Jared shut the engine off. He and Fatemah stepped from their car, inhaled, and released a slow breath. "Don't you just love it up here?"

Fatemah stood for a moment and glanced at the deep forest. "Just listen," she paused. The pin-drop silence pressed in around them. "I think you could actually hear the voice of God in a place like this."

Jared wrapped her in his arms and gazed deeply into her soft green eyes. "That's exactly why we're here," he said, the lines around his eyes wrinkling into a smile. Leaning down, he kissed her warmly. After retrieving their overnight bags, he led her up the stone steps.

After a few minutes of searching, he found the key box, retrieved the key and unlocked the door. As he swung it open, a warm glow from the chandelier spilled out and bathed them in soft tones.

Stepping inside, Fatemah caught her breath. "This certainly isn't what I have in mind when I think of a log cabin," she said, as her eyes wandered from the hard wood floor to the rough-hewn railing leading up to the second story. "Just look at that fireplace, you could burn a whole tree in it."

"Yes, and would you get a look at those trophy heads lining the walls?"

Fatemah glanced around the spacious living room. "Well, you can keep them. All those animals staring at me give me the creeps."

She wrapped her arms around her waist and moved closer to her husband. Jared dropped their overnight bags and pulled her close, "Don't worry, I'll protect you from those ferocious beasts," nuzzling her with his nose.

Fatemah pushed him back with a wry smile. "Okay lover boy, but first we have dinner. Then, as promised, we can see what Mr. Xavier is offering."

Although the temperature in the area was in the low 70's during the day, the chilled air crept in like a thief in the night, robbing the mountains of any warmth.

With dinner behind them, Jared built a fire while Fatemah changed. Fifteen minutes later, she returned wearing a cozy pair of sweat pants and one of Jared's shirts. She plopped down next to him, eyes wide, "Well? Are you going to open that envelope or sit and stare at me?"

Jared suppressed a juvenile grin, and lifted the unopened envelope. With a wry smile, Fatemah snatched it from him, tore open the seal, and slid its contents onto her lap. "There's no better way to find out, than to read what they say."

Jared threw another log on the fire and settled down to study the proposal.

After a few minutes of reading, Jared glanced up, his eyes misting. "Fatemah, this is wonderful," he said. "It's like God arranged this whole thing." His hand enveloped hers. "What Xavier and Wright are proposing is: we go to Beirut, rent a large house, and I act as liaison between his office and the Lebanese International University. Meanwhile they hammer out the plans for the expansion project."

"What if they don't get the contract? Does that mean we'll have to come home?"

Jared inhaled and released it slowly. "I suppose so."

"What does liaison mean? Will you have to fly back and forth between Seattle and Beirut?"

He shook his head, "No, as a matter of fact, my job will simply be to walk the university representatives through the process and smooth out ruffled feathers."

"I don't understand, what will you actually do?"

Jared scanned the proposal again, looking for an answer. "Here it is, 'As concerning your day to day duties, you will be available to translate phone messages from English to Farsi, and to maintain a minimal presence on the campus, establishing good relations with the faculty, administration, and students.'"

"That's it? You're 'Mr. Goodwill?'" Fatemah asked, her eyes at half-staff. "Jared, you know diplomacy isn't your strong suit. One slip-up and you could blow the whole thing."

Crestfallen, Jared feigned offense. "I thought I did a fair job at keeping Jimbo from killing Ahmad."

Fatemah crossed her arms and shook her head, "Yeah, I remember, but I never will forget the look on Jimbo's face when you made him apologize to me and Shirin for calling the Arabs rag-heads."

For a moment, the two sat and laughed at the memory. An ember popped, sending a glowing piece of charred coal onto the hearth. Fatemah jumped as her thoughts returned to the present.

"But, why the large house?" she asked.

Jared lifted the sheets of papers and scanned them, "The only thing I can figure is that it's for entertaining. Look at the *budget*. We could feed scores of people on an allowance like that."

Fatemah slumped back and squeezed a large pillow on her lap. "Why's Mr. Xavier doing this? I mean, really? This sounds like a set-up."

Jared gazed into her eyes. "I don't know. He just said he had his reasons."

"Well, whatever they are, it certainly appears we have a green light on starting the Harbor House project."

The Harbor House was one of Fatemah's two dreams. Her dream of owning an art studio would wait. She fell silent as a tear cut a thin rivulet down her cheek.

"What's wrong, Fatemah?"

She played with her wedding ring, watching the light from the recessed lights dance on each facet. After a halting breath, she peered into her husband's eyes, her voice barely above a whisper.

"I've always dreamed of one day being a famous artist. Now that dream is slipping away."

Jared took her by the hand and brought it to his lips. "Mrs. Russell—"

Her index finger touched his lips. "Mr. Russell, as I was about to say, this too has been a dream of mine. Ever since I ran away from home to escape my father's abuse, I longed to establish a place where Muslims who turn to Christ could go. Sometimes you have to experience the death of one dream in order for the other one to be born. I'll never forget the fear in the eyes of that young boy we saved, and I shudder to think what might have happened had we not been there."

"So, is your answer, yes? You think we should go?"

Fatemah's chest rose and fell and she placed her hand on his cheek. "Jared, I'll follow you wherever God leads you. Of course I think we should go. God has opened the door and supplied the means all in one move." Her words, though whispered soft, solidified the decision.

***

"I'll call Dad, he'd want to know."

Thirty minutes later, Jared pushed the end button and let out a tired breath.

"I take it things didn't set too well with yo' momma?" Fatemah said in a playful tone.

Jared tugged at his collar. "Dad was okay with the idea But Momma? Um, um, um. She wants no part of you *raisin' her grandchil'rin* in some foreign land," he said, attempting to mimic his mother's black, southern charm.

Chapter 4

Beirut, Lebanon

Streaks of orange flashed across the melting night sky as the golden orb pressed closer to the distant mountains. Deep purple shadows retreated like wraiths in the advance of the coming dawn. In the city, Canadian missionaries Richard and Mindy Owens awoke with the call to morning prayers. The Bourj Abou Haydar Mosque, located a few blocks away from their two bedroom flat, sounded out the call five times a day with regularity. That was the downside. The upside was their third-floor apartment, located directly across from Lebanon International University on Msaybeth, gave them quick access to the sprawling campus.

After their arrival six months ago, they were beginning to feel more at home. Lebanon, considered to be the jewel of the Middle East, was emerging from a decade of civil war and international conflict with their neighbors to the their south and east. Strategically located along the Mediterranean Sea, Beirut, her capitol city, was a primary port for the region. Tourism and the private sector were quickly becoming the major pillars for growth and recovery. It was here Rick and Mindy began a campus ministry.

Being good with his hands, Rick endeared himself with some of the local men by repairing their aging Volvos or Volkswagens. Mindy, on the other hand, held a nursing degree and had already dispensed dozens of Band-Aids and twice served as a mid-wife. Word was getting around that these Canadians were good people.

***

A warm breeze swept across the campus of the Lebanon International University making the palm trees sway with a gentle rhythm. Habib Teriek Hanif stepped from his computer science class, placed a pair of Izod sun shades on his face, and walked along the well-groomed sidewalks. Having recently transferred from a small college in the Bekaa valley, Habib, meaning true believer, wasn't quite sure what he believed. He took a seat on one of the benches shaded by an old olive tree. *This is a good place to sit and meditate on Allah the merciful . . . or God, if there is one!*

Out of the corner of his eye, he caught sight of three classmates cutting across the campus. Their body language alone told him the man behind the literature table was in trouble. When they got closer, Habib watched their animated conversation. *This isn't going to be pretty,* he surmised. Even though he'd never met the man, the few times they'd crossed paths, he seemed like a nice enough guy. He didn't know why these guys were accosting him, but he didn't like it.

Standing, Habib picked up his pace, but before he got very far, the three guys flipped the table over, scattering pens, pencils, and stacks of literature to the wind. Shouts arose as the man protested. One of Habib's classmates threw a punch, doubling the man over.

"What are you doing?" Habib demanded, pushing one of the guys off the missionary.

"Stay out of this! He is an infidel, and he's spreading lies," he said, pushing back.

Habib, though smaller than his classmate, was not intimidated. "I haven't heard him spreading lies. This literature," he picked up a pamphlet and shook it in his face, "whether it's true or not, it can't stop the spread of Islam. Why not simply ignore him, and he'll go away."

"You're an American sympathizer," the shorter of the three sneered.

"Yeah? Tell that to my Hamas commander," Habib fired back, then glanced around. He hoped no one else heard the comment.

After giving Habib a shove, the taller classmate turned and stomped off stiff legged, his face twisted with rage. The one nearest

Habib, spit at his feet, then backed away.

"Are you okay?" Habib said, picking up the table.

"I'll survive, thanks, but you didn't—"

"Yeah, I did. Prejudice is ugly no matter who is guilty of having it."

Rick struggled to his feet and brushed the dirt from his knees. "Well, I appreciate it. My name is Rick, by the way."

An alarm sounded and Habib glanced at his watch, "Look, I must be going, my class starts in five minutes. I do not think they will be back," he said, looking over his shoulder.

"That's alright; I'll know better than trying to argue with them next time."

Habib gave him a quick nod. "That is probably a very good idea," he said, then snatched up his backpack and took off across the lawn before his next class started.

***

The following week, Habib came by the literature table, slowed his pace, and nodded.

"Aslama salami," Richard said, in an attempt to reach out to Habib in his own language.

A choir of pearly white teeth appeared as Habib returned a quick smile. "Wa 'alaykum assalam. And upon you be peace," he answered, keeping his voice low.

"I really need to work on my Farsi, don't I?" Rick asked, his eyebrows rose into a question.

Habib fought back a chuckle, "Yes, well that was pretty pathetic, but I appreciate the attempt." Glancing over his shoulder, he continued. "Actually, you would be surprised how many students on campus speak English. Since it is the language of commerce, it is a required class on most international universities now."

"Your English is certainly very good. Did you pick it up in school?"

Habib's face reflected an inner pride. "Yes and no, my family lived in a Sunni village named Hadeth El-Joubbeh, a rather small, but very beautiful resort town in the northern part of Lebanon. A lot of tourists go there from all over the world. As a boy, I picked up a little English, French, and even some German." A distant gaze filled Habib's eyes as he thought of his home.

"Tell me more about it. I've not had a chance to do much sightseeing yet," Rick said, trying to get Habib to let his guard down and talk.

"Hadeth sits on a hill about 1450 meters above the sea level and overlooks the famous forest called the Cedars of Lebanon. It has about 500 residents during the winter and about 8000 throughout the summer. There is also a Catholic missionary school run by a group from Great Britain. That's where I received my formal education and learned most of my English."

"Your local mosque didn't prohibit you from attending a Catholic school?"

Shaking his head, "No, the high school wasn't quite that religious. It wasn't a threat to Islam at all."

Rick's eyes widened, "So that's why your speech has a bit of a British lilt to it."

A whimsical smile brightened his face. "Yes, that's right."

Rick shifted to see if anyone was walking nearby, then lowered his voice, "Look Habib, I noticed you took some literature from the table the other day. Have you had a chance to read over it? Do you have any questions?"

Glancing at the literature, Habib nodded, "Yes, I did read some of it, and frankly, I have lots of questions."

"Well, I'd be happy to spend as much time as it takes to answer them. Is this a good time to meet? I mean, is this a free hour?"

As if not sure, Habib pulled a notebook from his backpack and scanned his class schedule. "Let me see. Splendid, this hour is free. I can meet here if that works for you."

Relieved, Rick pulled out his IPad and tapped in the

appointment. "Oh, yes. That's why I'm here, to be your friend and to answer any questions you have."

For a moment, Habib's dark eyes bore a hole through him. The idea of a westerner becoming his friend hit him like a sand storm. He'd never thought of becoming friends with an infidel. He simply wanted to practice his English, get some answers, and move on with his life. Yet, the offer appealed to him. He was a bit of a loner, though extremely handsome. He knew no one on campus, and at the time he really needed a friend.

"Okay, then I'll see you next Tuesday afternoon at one o'clock."

"Great, I'll be here." Richard stuck his hand out to shake Habib's.

Reluctantly, Habib returned the gesture and shook hands. His heart raced. *What would my Shi'a father think if he found out that I'd shaken hands with the enemy?*

Chapter 5

Beirut International Airport Border Security

Officer Ameed el Quatari sat staring at Jared's passport, taking his eyes off of it only long enough to glance at Jared and return to the passport. He and Fatemah were prepared for this type of interrogation, being warned by the American embassy.

After taking Mr. Xavier's offer to be the liaison between his company and Lebanon's prestigious international university, Jared found himself sitting in the Lebanese Department of Customs, answering some tough questions.

"You say you are coming into my country to do what?" the customs agent asked for the third time.

The aluminum chair which held Jared's weight, groaned as he shifted positions. "As I told you two previous times, I represent Xavier and Wright Architectural Group. I am the liaison between them and the Lebanon International University. They are about to begin a massive expansion, and if I leave soon, I might get there in time for the ribbon cutting."

Officer Quatari remained aloof despite Jared's sarcasm.

Knowing the interrogation room was bugged with video and audio listening devices, Quatari had to put on a pretty good show of reluctance.

"Please excuse me. I must check with my colleague." The metal chair scraping across the concrete floor, reminded Jared of the night Rashad was abducted from the police department and killed. His palms slicked, and his pulse quickened as he broke into a cold sweat. Glancing at the one-way mirror, he prayed he wasn't being observed.

Lifting his face to the steel mesh enforced window, Officer Quatari watched as Fatemah, dressed in her most colorful burqa, succinctly answered the border security agent's questions.

"So you say you're an American, why are you coming to my country?" The customs agent pressed.

Before she could answer for the inth time, a knock on the door, echoed into the small interrogation room.

"Please excuse me for a moment, Miss . . . uh . . . Miss Russell."

"It's Mrs. Russell. I am married," she reminded him, her patience wearing thin.

He nodded, "Yes, of course."

After a quick consultation with his counterpart, Officer Nadar returned and pounded the stamp on her visa. "Welcome to Lebanon, Mrs. Russell, enjoy your stay, and please obey all the laws of my country."

He stood and escorted Fatemah from the room.

Outside of the Lebanese Consulate, Fatemah paced, waiting for her husband to arrive. Fifteen minutes later he emerged. The strain around his eyes melted into a warm smile as they hugged.

"I'm glad that's over," she said, looking rather fatigued.

"Me too, but just think," Jared fingered the paperwork, "God is already at work." Pointing to the little sign of the 'Fish' on the lower left of his visa.

"Let's find a hotel and see what else God has for us," Fatemah said as she flagged down a cab.

An old yellow taxi cab pulled alongside the curb, and the elderly driver hopped out. With more agility than Jared expected, the man jumped from behind the wheel and helped them with their luggage. As Jared pulled the cab door shut, a wave of recognition swept over him. Had he met this man before?

"Where to my children?" the taxi driver asked.

Taking Fatemah by the hand, Jared peered ahead. A pair of dark eyes waited with anticipation. "To the American Embassy, north of the airport. I want to visit the Marine Memorial."

Nervous eyes glared in the mirror. "My son, are you sure you want to go there? It's not safe."

An ice cold hand gripped Jared's and gave it a gentle squeeze. "Driver, I understand the place is crawling with Hezbollah. For that matter, you may be a member of Hezbollah, but my brothers in arms are memorialized there and I have to see it. It's my duty."

The taxi driver gave him an understanding nod. "I assure you my son, I am not a member of Hezbollah." The words rolled thick off of the driver's tongue. "I will take you there, but you must not take any photographs, no pictures. Do you understand?"

Jared felt the whites of Fatemah's eyes widen. "I understand. I just need five minutes."

The taxi pushed through several narrow streets until it came to a halt in front of two flag poles standing silent vigil over a memorial bearing the names of the two hundred seventy two Marines killed in the blast. Jared got out and stood for a moment. Overhead, the American and Marine flags hung loosely, undisturbed as if they held their breath. Jared gave them a crisp salute and walked to the wall which was etched with the names of the victims of that fateful day. He scanned them, looking for one name. Near the last column, he stopped and fingered the impression. A lump formed in his throat as salty moisture gathered and ran down his cheeks. "Thank you John for your sacrifice," he croaked. His voice sounded strange to him and he was glad he was alone.

A slight wind picked up and the flags rose and fell as did his heaving chest. Jared glanced up and squinted. A ray of sunlight danced on the mast-head making it appear gold, while a lone seagull spread its wings and soared higher. He released a labored sigh. He'd paid his respects, now it was time to make a difference. With renewed vision, he walked back to the taxi where Fatemah and their driver stood in low conversation.

"We need to find a hotel and a good Realtor, can you help us?" Jared asked, streaks of moisture still glistened on his black cheeks.

The crow's feet around the old man's eyes wrinkled into a smile. "Yes, of course. I just so happen to know a very good Realtor, very honest. You will like him very much. Let me take you there now." He gunned the engine.

"Whoa, hold your horses now buddy. Let's start with the hotel and maybe tomorrow we could meet your Realtor friend."

The old cabbie smiled and flipped on the occupied light. Then, grinding the gears, he put it in first and accelerated into traffic.

Chapter 6

Ayatollah Bashera's Office

Anita, the third born child of Ayatollah Bashera, stood, hands folded behind her back, her chin buried in her chest, her lip quivering. "But Papa, that wasn't me—"

"It wasn't you?" he boomed. "The electronics store has video surveillance cameras all over the place, of course it was you. By rights, you should have that dainty little, thieving hand of yours chopped off along with your lying tongue. The only reason it hasn't happened is because of me." He paused for effect. "For *that* you should be grateful."

"I am Papa. I am. It will never happen again. I promise—"

"It should never have happened in the first place, you little thief. You brought disgrace on my name. What would your mother think? Why you did it in the first place is what I want to know."

"I … I wanted to give you a birthday present."

"My birthday was weeks ago, don't add more lies to your already long list of sins. Allah will not be pleased."

"I'm sorry Papa. It will never happen again—"

"And that reminds me," he stood and began pacing the floor of his office. His sandals left deep impressions in the plush carpet. "I've been getting calls from your school. It seems you've been caught cheating, skipping class, and being disruptive."

Anita shrank under his withering assault. "Guilty; but I hate that school. Why can't I go where all my friends go, instead of that stuffy old finishing school?"

"It is because of your friends you are acting out all this bad behavior in the first place." His fat index finger jabbed the air.

Anita wrapped her arms around her slender body and swirled in a circle. A dreamy smile defined her lovely features. "Papa, I just want to be free, free like a bird. Is that too much to ask?" Arms outstretched as she pretended to be a ballerina.

"Would you please stop dancing around and listen. Have you forgotten you are a Muslim. You live in an Islamic state, and you're a female. You'll never be free. Do you hear me, *never*," he said, emphasizing every syllable.

"You're just saying that because you hate me," Anita fired back, tauntingly. To Anita, the conversation was all a game. She loved matching wits with her father, and she especially loved pushing his buttons. "Ever since Mom died, you've treated me like it was my fault. Well, it's not—"

"If you weren't out sneaking around, you could have called the doctor as soon as the seizure began, but no, you were where? with your friends." His voice reverberated.

"Yes, and where were you? Building your harem! What would Mother say to that?"

Before Anita could duck, her father swung.

Crack!

Falling backwards, she tumbled over a winged back chair, tasting iron. The floor rushed to meet her. *I guess I pushed him too far that time,* her hand touched her cheek. *But at least I know he still cares for Mother.*

"Don't you ever speak of your mother again. I am the next great Ayatollah, it is only fitting that I have a harem."

Anita pulled her knees to her chest and pushed out a crocodile tear. Except for her burning cheek, she was enjoying the time she had with her father. At least, she had his attention, even if it meant being slapped.

"As for you, young lady, I have arranged for you to be married to Sheik Ismael al Hussar on the day of your sixteenth birthday."

Jumping to her feet, Anita clenched her hands into two tight balls. "Me, marry him? He's your arch-enemy. You hate him," she fired back.

Bashera retook his seat, his rotund belly oscillating as he laughed at his daughter's reaction.

"Correction, was my arch-enemy." Popping a date into his mouth, he continued. "I decided to make peace with him, and he asked for a token of my sincerity." His voice was tinged with insincerity. "So I offered you."

"But Papa, you can't do this—"

"Oh, I already have, so enjoy your freedom." He chomped another date into his mouth and spat out the pit. "You've got eleven months."

"Nooooo!"

Chapter 7

The Harbor House

"Look Fatemah . . . there is a house for rent," Jared said as they and their real estate agent drove through an upper class neighborhood.

Leaning forward, Fatemah placed her hand on the real estate agent's shoulder and asked, "Mr. Hamid, would you mind turning around and going back to that house with the For Rent sign in front of it?"

The realtor's bushy eyebrows met into a question, and he applied the brake. After a quick U-turn, the car came to a gentle stop in front of the gated house. Balancing his laptop on his knee, he typed in some numbers. A moment later he smiled and said, "Ah, here it is." He adjusted the screen so Jared and Fatemah could see it. "This particular property is a rent-to-own single-family dwelling. I know the owner, and he is very reasonable."

"What's the square footage?" Jared asked, his pulse quickening.

"Give me a moment," Mr. Hamid said, scrolling further down. "It is a Mediterranean style, five bedroom, three bath, situated on a lot and a half. It is 7,363 square feet with arched openings, a balcony, walk-in closets, an art niche, built-in cabinets, and shelves. It even has a large butler's pantry. Do you want to go inside?"

With a quick jerk of the handle, Fatemah leaped from the car and began racing toward the house. "Open the gate, open the gate!" her hands rattled the bars as if it were the Bastille.

Jared stood next to her and craned his neck, looking in. "Hold your horses, Fatemah, give the man a chance to find the lock-box.

A moment later an electronic snap jolted the barrier to life. "Watch out," the real estate agent said, as the gate began to retract. "Just a safety precaution, all homes are gated," he assured Jared's suspicious expression with a weak smile.

Once inside, Mr. Hamid opened the sliding glass door which led to the rear patio. A warm breeze freshened the house's stale air.

"There, that's better. Follow me," he said over his shoulder.

After viewing the rooms, they gathered in the open living room.

"This is beautiful. It will be perfect for the Harbor House," Fatemah said, her wide eyes scanning the FAQ sheet.

"And it is located just two blocks from the university," the realtor added, knowing about Jared's job.

Using his tape measure, Jared measured the hall and a couple of the bed rooms. Then he checked the breaker box and the home's security system. Satisfaction registered on his face as he returned to the living room. "It looks like a sound house, structurally. The question is, how much is my boss willing to pay?"

Fingering the FAQ sheet the real estate agent had given her, Fatemah quipped, "This is the nicest one we've seen."

"Yes, Mrs. Russell and with it being fully furnished, it won't last very long on the market. Are you ready to sign a contract?"

Jared pulled his cell phone from his pocket and speed dialed his boss. "Here, you guys work out the details, I want to check out the attic," he said, handing the phone to the agent. "Be sure to ask the owner if he'd mind me turning this place into a hospitality home when you talk with him."

The agent nodded and held up an index finger. "Hello?"

By the time Jared returned, he found the agent and Fatemah staring at a stack of papers. "It looks like you have your Hospitality House, Mr. Russell. Now, if you will sign a few papers, we will get the ball going."

Unable to restrain a grin, Jared said, "You mean, 'get the ball rolling.'"

"Yes," the agent's face colored slightly and he lifted his shoulders uncomfortably. "Please, sign here," pointing with his monogrammed pen.

Chapter 8

Lebanon International University

As the September morning expanded, a brilliant, shimmering sun peaked through the branches of the olive tree. Rick greeted a few students who passed by, then took a seat at a concrete table. He prayed for wisdom as he scanned his New Testament for a special word from the Lord. A shadow crossed over him and he glanced up, squinting.

"Aslama alakim my friend," Rick said.

Habib returned a weak smile before answering. "Wa 'alaykum assalam." His dark black eyes spoke of concern, of fear, of pain.

"Habib, what's wrong? You look like you've lost your best friend."

Handing him the morning newspaper, Habib asked, "Have you seen the paper today?"

Rick took the proffered page and scanned the headline. It read: **Shi'a Family takes Fatwa Seriously!**

The story went on to give the gruesome details of the last hours of the Waseem family. The rambling, bloody murder/suicide note that said much, but told little.

Habib took a seat, clearly shaken. "If my Shiite father ever finds out that I have even spoken to you, this will be my fate." His finger tapped the newspaper Rick held.

Rick laid it aside, his mind racing. "Habib, I thought you came from a moderate Sunni family."

Shaking his head vehemently, Habib said, "No, I came from a Sunni village, but my family is Shi'a. Either way, both take it very seriously if you dare to question the authority of the Imams or the Qur'an."

After taking a quick scan of the newspaper article, a picture formed in his mind. "Well Habib, how can I help?"

"Why are you talking to one of my children, you western infidel pig?" The authoritative question interrupted him mid-sentence.

The voice was that of Ayatollah Bashera. His looming frame blocked out the sun and cast a long shadow across Habib and Rick, as a group of curious onlookers gawked.

Rick's heart quickened as he stood, hands extended. "This university gives me the freedom to have general conversations with anyone who is willing to talk. They encourage freedom of thought and expression."

The veins of Bashera's neck bulged. "Well, I do not, and you are in violation of my Fatwa," his throat tight with rage.

A moment later, three of the Ayatollah's followers grabbed Rick by the arms while another slapped him across the face. Other angry thugs grabbed Habib and began to beat him, while the frightened onlookers gathered. None from campus security showed up, and no one intervened. The beating, which lasted only a few minutes, seemed to go on for hours. Finally, the Ayatollah lifted a hand.

"Enough, I think I have made my point."

The two men holding Habib released their grip and dropped him in a heap next to Rick.

"Don't talk to this man again or the next time, I will not be so merciful. Remember! I never forget a face."

As the crowd cleared, Rick lay in a tight ball. His stomach ached from being kicked and his head throbbed. This wasn't what he'd expected when he volunteered to be a campus missionary. Yes, they told him there were risks, and yes, he knew there would be opposition, but he never dream he'd get beaten for talking to a student about God. Anger surged through his veins as he tried to understand.

"Habib, are you going to be okay?" he asked, shaking him gently.

Habib moaned, and Rick rolled him over. Blood and dirt were smeared across his face from a lacerated lip. A large knot swelled on his forehead, and his white shirt was ripped open.

"I don't know. I think they broke one of my ribs." Habib said, holding his right side. His left eye was swollen, and he appeared disoriented.

"I can't believe that man would have his thugs beat us up just because we were talking." Rick said as bitterness spilled out.

Habib took a pained breath. "Believe it. That man enjoys making other people suffer. He is a very dangerous man," he said, as he leaned forward.

Rick pushed himself to his feet and placed his hands on the concrete table. It didn't make sense. "Can I take you somewhere? The university clinic? The hospital?"

A moment passed, and Habib lifted his arm. His trembling fingers touched the knot on his forehead, and he grimaced. "I will be alright. I just need to walk."

"No Habib, you can't do that. You probably have a concussion. Lie still and let me get you something to drink." Rick grabbed a bottle of water from his backpack, twisted off the cap, and tipped it up to his friend's lips.

Habib let the cool water run down his throat. "I think I will be alright, so long as it does not happen again."

After a minute, he blinked and squinted up at Rick. "There is something I do not understand."

"What's that, Habib?"

"I do not understand how my religion can be so brutal. Would your god require a man to kill his family if they converted to Islam?"

Shaking his head, Rick reached out and helped Habib to the bench. "No, Habib, my God would not. He is long-suffering, not willing that any should perish, and He does not force anyone to believe in Him, but neither does He condone beating those who reject Him," he said, looking at the receding men who had beaten them.

"What would happen if someone turned from your God?"

Rick steadied himself on the table. "Look, Habib, that's a very good question, and I really want to answer it, but first we need to do a couple of things."

"What's that?" his eyebrows met.

"First, you need first aid and second, I need to teach you a few things about the nature of God. Then you will better understand the consequences of believing in Him or rejecting Him. That will take time. After you get feeling better, would you like to meet again?"

Habib's eyes darted from side to the side and he licked his lips. Nodding, he tried to smile. "Maybe next time we can choose someplace less conspicuous."

"Yes, that's a good idea. How about my apartment next Thursday evening around 7:00 p.m.?"

Habib's shoulders rose and fell and he leaned heavily on the table to keep from toppling over. "That's fine, but where do you live?"

Pointing with his chin, Rick continued, "In those high-rise buildings across the street. My wife is a registered nurse. How about I take you there and have her apply first aid on those lacerations. That way, you'll know where I live."

"Good, but I don't think I can walk far."

With a light pat on the back, Rick helped his friend to his feet. "Don't worry; it's not that far, just across the street from the university. We can get there in a few minutes."

"Okay, but keep a look-out for the Ayatollah and his thugs."

Traffic was light, and the two men left the campus without anyone noticing. As they trudged along the shaded street, Rick asked, "Did you know my Holy Book has something to say about Lebanon?

Keeping his eyes on the sidewalk, Habib continued his halting gait. "No, I had no idea."

"Yep, I've done a lot of research about your country," Reaching into his back-pack, Rick produced a small Bible.

Clearly interested, Habib gazed at the tattered leather cover.

"What does it say?"

Without missing a step, Rick thumbed through his Bible until he found the place he sought. "From the top of the Cedar, from the highest branch I will take a shoot and plant it myself on a very high mountain, this branch will bear fruit and become a noble Cedar."

"Please explain what that means?" he asked, straining to see the words.

"It means that God will take special interest in Lebanon and will personally see to it that the best trees of his creation are growing in your country."

Habib winced as he tried to smile.

"It sounds like your God is a good God."

"He is Habib. He is, but he hates cruelty and injustice."

As they walked along the sidewalk, Rick noticed a man bent over, looking under the hood of a broken-down Volkswagen.

Chapter 9

The Harbor House

Fatemah stood, hands on her hips eyeing the stacks of empty boxes which littered the garage. She had worked all morning and yet the task of emptying boxes showed little progress. Heaving a weary sigh, she lifted the next box and carried it into the living room, leaving dozens yet to wait their turn.

Between trips to the university and talking with Mr. Xavier, Jared worked on altering the floor plan to accommodate mixed-gender residents. By the end of September, they hoped they could be ready to take in their first guest.

After emptying the box Fatemah returned from the garage, brushed aside a web of hair, and plopped next to Jared at the dining room table. Picking up the newspaper, she scanned it with a frown. "I don't see my ad for a housekeeper again," letting out a frustrated breath. "That's the second time in as many weeks I paid to run an ad, and it didn't make it in time." She folded the paper and tossed it into the trash. "Are you even listening, Mr. Russell?"

Jared, who'd been pouring over the latest proposed changes by Xavier and Wright for the last hour, glanced up. "Did you say something?" a crooked smile tugged at the corner of his mouth.

"Jared Russell, you haven't been listening to a word I've—"

Buzz.

"Now, I wonder who that could be," she said, her eyelids at half-mast.

Jared breathed a sigh of relief and feigned wiping his brow.

Slipping on a pair of sandals, Fatemah covered her head and stepped outside. She squinted in the bright sun light as she paced across the circular driveway. A light sea breeze fluttered her burqa, but she didn't mind. It was the first time she'd been out of the house all day. Approaching the gate, she noticed a young girl, her head covered, standing, glancing around nervously.

"Can I help you?" Fatemah asked, expecting the stranger to extend her hand and beg for money or food.

The young girl jumped, her hand to her chest. "Oh, hello." Pulling her head-covering tighter, she took one last glance over her shoulder. "Uh, ma'am, is the house-keeper job still available?" her eyes wide with hope.

Surprised at the young girl's boldness and use of proper English, "Why, yes, yes it is," she continued. "Please step in and let me get you some hot tea and we can talk about it."

Taking one last look over her shoulder, she cleared her throat and slipped through the open gate. Confident she'd not been seen, she gave Fatemah a shaky smile, lowered her chin, and followed her into the house. Only then did she relax.

"Please take a seat in the parlor, and I'll be with you in a minute," Fatemah said, as she pointed to the sitting room and disappeared into the kitchen.

A few minutes later, she returned with a tray of fruit slices, crackers and cheese, and a pitcher of hot tea. Setting it on the coffee table, she took a seat and studied the young lady's features.

Raven hair cascaded over her shoulders while two dark orbs mounted in almond sockets glanced around the room, taking in every detail. A whimsical smile danced on her moistened lips as if guarding a secret, and a pair of dainty hands, like playful children, rested on her lap.

"There now, allow me to pour some tea and let's talk." Fatemah hadn't met any of her neighbors since moving in and was craving a little female chatter. "My name is Fatemah Russell, what's yours."

Hand to chest, the young lady straightened. "My name is Anita, it means 'favor and grace'."

Giving her a knowing look, Fatemah suppressed a smile and continued, "Yes, I knew that. My father immigrated to America from Lebanon when I was a child. I learned Farsi from him."

"You speak it very well," she said, fingering the china tea cup.

"Thank you Anita. Now tell me, how did you find out I needed a house-keeper? The paper hasn't run my ad for the last two weeks."

Anita pinched back a smile and avoided eye contact. Using her father's connections, she scuttled Fatemah's efforts to run the ads.

"Uh, well, I read it in the paper a couple of days ago and was hoping the position was still open," she lied.

Nodding, Fatemah narrowed her eyes. "Well, how much experience do you have at being a house-keeper? You seem quite young."

The clock on the wall tapped out the seconds as Anita took a sip of tea and dabbed her lips with a napkin. "My father occasionally teaches at the university, much like a professor. Our home is very large, much larger than this one," she said, letting her eyes wander. "It is often used as a meeting place for dignitaries and heads of state. I am responsible for the servants, who keep the house spotless."

"So you manage the house-keeping. How many servants are there?"

Index finger to her chin, her eyes scraped the ceiling as she tried to sound confident. "I'd say about twenty, sometimes more if we have a big event scheduled," she prevaricated.

"Well, how do you propose keeping our house spotless if you have so much to do at yours?"

Anita took a final sip of tea and set the cup down. "I said, I manage the house-keepers, I don't do the work myself," a wicked chuckle percolated in her throat.

Clearly intrigued, Fatemah was impressed by her class, her poise, the way she carried herself. This was a well-cultured young woman. *I wonder why she wants to work for me.* She breathed in slowly and held it a moment. "Tell me again why you want to clean our little home?"

The young lady's face darkened as she searched the floor with her eyes. Honesty was not her strong suit. She'd become so good at her little game of deceit that at times, she had trouble discerning between her reality and the truth. Finally, she released a long sigh and leaned forward, "Oh, Mrs. Russell," her voice broke with emotion, "how I long to be free, and having financial freedom seems to be the fastest way to get it. You see, I am betrothed to a much older man who already has five wives. I loathe the man. I want to earn enough money to run away from home before I'm forced to marry him." Her eyes pled for understanding.

The flash of memories long forgotten roared back, and Fatemah caught herself reliving the past. The fear, the pain, the loneliness she'd thought she'd buried, reared their ugly heads. She pinched her eyes shut, trying to chase out the demons, and caught herself not breathing. Finally, she pulled herself free and gave Anita a weak smile.

"How long do you have before you are to be married?"

Anita did a quick calculation, "I am to be married on my 16th birthday. That's eleven months from now."

Reaching out, Fatemah took Anita by the hand. It was soft, but firm. "I will be praying that God will intervene. By the way, I'd feel better if you'd call me, Miss Fatemah. I'm still getting use to Mrs., oh and, you've got the job. You can start tomorrow."

Anita clasped her hands under her chin and pranced up and down. "Oh thank you Miss Fatemah," her voice rising with glee. "That is so kind of you, both to hire me and to pray for me. I have often prayed to Allah, but he has never answered my prayers, not once. Does your God answer your prayers?"

Fatemah's face brightened. It was a delight to talk about God, especially to one so eager to listen.

"Oh yes, Anita. He answers all the time. Sometimes He says, 'yes,' sometimes He says 'no,' and sometimes," she paused, "He says 'wait.'"

Anita gulped at her last statement. "How do you know what to do when he answers in so many ways?"

"Well, when the answer is yes, it's pretty clear. For example, I prayed that God would lead just the right person here to be my housekeeper, and you showed up, even though my ad didn't run," her eyelids lowering.

Anita fanned herself, and she nuzzled the floor with the toe of her sandal.

"Now, if the answer is no, that's pretty clear as well. The other day I prayed that God would provide us with a nice new car, and my husband, bless his heart, came home in an old VW Bug, which has broken down twice already this week."

Anita giggled at her new employer's candor. "How about when your God says wait?. What do you do then?"

"That's the hardest thing I've had to learn, but I wait. I wait until God shows me what to do next."

"Wow! Your God is very interesting. I would like to know more about him," she said, eyes wide as saucers.

Fatemah chuckled, "I would love to tell you all about him."

"Miss Fatemah, are you aware my country is considered a Christian country?"

Hands on her hips, Fatemah's voice grew dubious. "Oh? I thought it was predominantly a Muslim nation."

"Yes, it is, but there are more and more Christian churches popping up all over the city. As a matter of fact, I heard there was a small Baptist church just three blocks from here," she said, retaking her seat.

"Why Anita, what gives you the idea we would be interested in going to a Baptist church?"

Glancing at a picture of Mr. Russell, Anita said. "Oh I don't know, don't most Americans go to the Baptist church, especially, you know, black Americans?"

Amused, Fatemah lifted Jared's picture and smiled.

"Girl, you make too many assumptions. All Americans don't go to church, and no, just because one is black doesn't mean one goes to the *Baptist* church. But we would be interested in going and checking it out."

Chapter 10

Lebanon International University

The car Jared purchased was truly a vintage automobile, a 1968 Volkswagen Bug. It had five on the floor, no air conditioning, and came complete with a cracked windshield, much different from the spacious Land Rover he'd gotten used to back in Michigan. The little VW could only carry four passengers at most compared to the Land Rover's space for six.

Jared finished another stressful negotiation between his office and the university administration when his car sputtered to a stop at the corner of Michal Abi Chahia and Msaybeth streets. Frustrated, he got out, lifted the rear hood and began looking in the engine compartment.

"Do you need some help?"

Startled by someone behind him speaking in Farsi, Jared raised his head, knocking it on the opened hood.

"Ouch," he muttered, rubbing the back of his head. Turning, he faced two men staring down at him. The first was a young Arab man who stood, holding his side and looking like he had gotten into a fight with a bear. The other was a white man dressed casually in a golf shirt and khaki slacks. His pant leg had been ripped, and he appeared slightly disheveled.

"Do you need some help?" he repeated.

"Yes, I bought this thing a few days ago and it just quit running," Jared answered in his best Farsi.

Realizing he was speaking the wrong language, Rick quickly shifted gears. "Hi, my name is Richard Owens, and this is my friend Habib."

Jared glanced from one man to the other wondering if their presence spelled trouble.

Rick stepped closer and lowered his voice. "Uh, it's a long

story."

Palms held up, Jared smiled, "That's okay. I don't need an explanation."

Rick nodded and glanced around Jared's sizable frame. "Well, let me take a look at this thing, they're not that tricky to work on, and I can usually spot the problem pretty quickly."

Jared stepped away as his new acquaintance squatted down and reached into the engine compartment. Rick grunted and twisted his arm around to get a better position. A few minutes later, he stood, pulled a white handkerchief from his back pocket and wiped the oil from his arm.

"My wife, Mindy, will shoot me for doing that," he added with a wry smile. "Okay, now, try starting your engine."

Jared climbed in and tried the key. To his surprise, the engine sputtered and started.

"It was pretty simple; the ignition wire came off of the solenoid. It needs to be tightened better, but that should hold for the time being," Rick said over the hum of the motor.

"I sure do appreciate your helping me. Could I take you some place?" eying Habib's wounds.

Rick took a quick glance at his friend. "Yeah, sure, why not. I have some tools at my house. I can tighten up that nut in a jiffy."

The two climbed in with Habib still holding his side.

"We aren't far, just around the corner," Rick said, pointing at the next intersection.

Jared put the car in gear and pulled away from the curb reflecting on the day he and Ahmad had been beaten up by a gang of Muslim youths back in Michigan.

"Rick, are you sure I can't take you guys to a hospital or a clinic? You look pretty badly beat up," Jared asked after hearing Rick relate the story.

"No, the more we say, the more we'll have to explain," he said. "Anyway, my wife's a registered nurse. She'll take good care of Habib and me.

A few turns later, Rick pointed to a cluster of buildings. "Pull up there, that's my high rise just up ahead."

Jared pulled to a stop and glanced into his rear-view mirror. "Rick," he said, as the two got out of his car, "my wife and I have recently moved to Beirut, and we're opening a hospitality house. It's a cross between a shelter for homeless and abused, and a bed and breakfast. Would you have any ideas on how to get the word out?"

Rick stood for a moment rubbing his chin. "I might. I'll do some checking around and get back with you. Can I call you?"

Relieved, Jared jotted his new cell phone number on the back of an index card. "Yeah, sure. Here's my cell number, call me when you can," he said.

Rick tucked the card in his pocket and helped Habib up the stairs to his apartment.

Chapter 11

Beirut Baptist Church

A wave of excitement swept over Fatemah as she and Jared pulled in the parking lot of Beirut Baptist Church. Dressed in the traditional Arabic clothing, they got out of their Volkswagen, walked to the front doors, and paused. "I wonder if their service is in English," Fatemah mused.

Jared gave her a reassuring smile, "English, I checked. Now quit worrying, it will be fine."

She released a tense breath and followed his lead. Already a group had gathered outside its doors and were filing in. When Jared and Fatemah stepped inside, Jared stopped short. "Man, does this remind me of a few years ago."

Fatemah turned, "Oh? And when were you here? Is there something you're not telling me?"

Shaking his head, "No, it's just that—"

"Assalamu alaikum," said a lady greeter dressed in a colorful burqa, interrupting him, "welcome to Beirut Baptist Church, are you new to Beirut?"

Jared accepted her extended hand and shook it lightly. Then the greeter took Fatemah by the shoulders and placed a kiss on her cheeks.

"Yes, we are. My name is Jared Russell, and this is my wife Fatemah. We've recently opened a new hospitality house called Harbor House."

"Well it's nice to meet you. We hope you have a blessed day," she said as she ushered them to a seat.

"Oh by the way, we have a special speaker this morning." Jared's head whipped around expecting the same man who'd spoken back in Stanford, many years ago, to step from behind the lady.

"He's an evangelist to the Muslim people, and he's here to share his testimony."

They took their seats and soon were surrounded with people from all over the world.

"I hope I'm not tested on all of your names," Jared quipped, as he shook yet another hand.

The church service began with everyone joining hands and singing the Doxology, then prayer. At the conclusion of the prayer, the pastor encouraged everyone to turn around and greet the folks behind them. A wave of laughter scattered like a bevy of quail. Apparently, this was not the first time he'd made such a request.

In the confusion, Jared turned, expecting to meet another strange face, but instead he heard, "Fancy meeting you here Mr. Russell, is this your wife?" It was Rick, the man who'd fixed his ailing vehicle.

"Rick," Jared sputtered. "Yes, yes, this is my wife, Fatemah." She extended her hand which was readily received.

"Nice to meet you Fatemah. Now, is your name Arabic?"

"Actually no, it is Lebanese, my parents immigrated to America when I was a pre-teen."

"I see. Well, it's very nice to meet you."

After a momentary pause, Jared turned to the woman next to his friend. "And this must be Mindy." The two greeted each other as the pastor took to the podium.

"I had no idea we'd be meeting so soon, Rick." Jared said.

Rick nudged his wife. "Mindy, why don't we have Mr. and Mrs. Russell over for Sunday dinner?"

She'd already taken her seat, but looked up, "That would be great," she said with a sharp nudge to the ribs.

"Why'd you go and do that?" she asked through tight lips.

"I don't know. I thought it would be the hospitable thing to do."

"Well, it wasn't, I think they're trouble makers," she whispered.

Rick cupped his hand over his mouth, "Look, give me a break. I was just trying to be nice."

"Nice to who, me or them?"

"We'll talk about it later, now hush." Glancing up, he caught Jared's eye and shrugged.

"Look, if this isn't going to work out—"

Rick cut him off with the wave of his hand. "No, we're fine. It's just that," he paused uncomfortably.

"What he's trying to say is, having an American come to our house might send the wrong message to our neighbors," interjected Mindy.

Jared rubbed his chin, "I see," doing some quick thinking. "How would they know we're Americans? As a black man, I could be from almost anywhere, and Fatemah, well, she's from right here?"

Mindy's face reddened, "Well, I hadn't considered that."

"So are we still on?" Jared pressed.

Reluctantly, Mindy nodded.

Jared caught Fatemah's eye, she nodded her assent.

"Okay, we'll follow you there after church, and I promise to speak in Farsi the whole time," Jared added.

The statement brought a weak smile to Rick's face.

As Jared returned to his seat, Habib stepped up.

"Well, hello Habib, I didn't know you attended this church"

With a nervous glance around the room, Habib lowered his eyes, "I don't. This is my first time here. I've never been in a Christian church in my life. I just hope my family doesn't find out, or I'm in big trouble."

"Well you are in good company here, young man." It was the guest speaker. "I have been in your sandals. I know what it is like to be rejected by my family and friends." He stepped up and greeted Habib with the traditional kiss to both cheeks. Taking him by the shoulders, he held his gaze. "I hope you will listen carefully to my testimony. What is your name?" he asked, taking a seat next to him.

Uncomfortable with such attention, Habib's face reddened, "My name is Habib."

"Well Habib, I will be praying."

"Thank you sir, no one has ever prayed for me. What is your name, sir?"

The demure man with piercing eyes smiled, "My name is Omar Ben Ali. In a few minutes I will be asked to speak, but let me tell you, I know what it's like to have questions, to search, to hunger for the truth. You see, I am an Algerian by birth, born in a Muslim home. My father was a Muslim imam, a sheikh, and he taught Islam in Cairo, Egypt until his death. My family took pride in their Islamic heritage. Almost all my forefathers were Muslim clerics."

Habib's face brightened into an unusual smile, "I am from the Bekaa valley, but my parents weren't so devoted."

Omar waited for Habib to relax and open up. "Well, in the early years I was looked upon as a future Muslim priest. My parents even sent me to a Qur'anic school from the age of seven or eight."

"Mine sent me to a Catholic school, and that created many questions on my mind."

With a knowing smile, Omar continued, "I, too, had questions; questions about God — His judgment, His truth, man's eternal destiny. My questions brought mockery from others. I lived in despair and hopelessness because I was seeking something Islam did not provide. My father made me memorize almost all the Qur'an, and I became a mechanically religious young boy, while my heart was dry, like the desert."

Fatemah leaned close to Jared and whispered, "That sounds just like the home I was brought up in, very rigid."

The guest speaker shook his head, knowingly. "I lived in a Muslim neighborhood, hearing the thundering calls to pray five times a day. I was taught that Islam was the final religion, which canceled Judaism and Christianity. When I reached my teens, I wanted to know which religion is true. But as you know, Habib, questioning Islam is not tolerated, so my investigations had to be done in secret."

Habib shook his head. "I know about getting caught asking questions," rubbing his still aching ribs.

"Yes, my young friend, all I wanted to do was learn the truth, and for my trouble? I got this." He rolled up his sleeve and displayed a large scar across his wrist. "They tried to chop off my hand, but this only made my search more intense. The questions I kept asking myself were: Where will I go after I die? Don't I have the right to know? Why do Muslims so strongly reject discussing their own religion? How can I know that Islam is the only true religion?"

Habib nodded, "Yes, sir. I've been asking those same questions. It bothered me to realize that I was considered a Muslim just because I was born to Muslim parents and lived in a Muslim nation. No choice was given me; no chance was offered me to examine and find the truth."

"I understand, my son, believe me when I say, I know the ache in your heart. While I was reading a certain book, I ran into some verses from the Bible which greatly attracted me. These verses spoke with authority about Jesus Christ. They say, 'I am the way, the truth, and the life, no man cometh unto the Father but by me'."

Rick patted Habib on the shoulder. "I shared that same verse with him not long ago."

A crooked smile parted Habib's lips, "Yes, I remember. And I also asked you, 'What about the prophet of Islam? Why do Muslims only speak of the prophet of Islam never of Jesus Christ? Islam claims to be the ultimate truth, but what about the Bible'?'"

Omar touched his arm, "Young man, many of your friends have those same questions but are too afraid to ask."

"So did you find the answer to your questions?" Habib asked, clearly interested.

Leaning in closer, Omar said, "Yes, while reading, I came to other statements by this same Man named Jesus Christ. He said, 'Come unto me all ye that labor and are heavy laden, and I will give you rest.' I had sought rest for many years, and this man named

Jesus claimed to be the source of rest and invited others to come to Him. At that time, I had never had a Bible; I had never seen one. Then secretly, I asked a professing Christian to lend me a Bible so I could read more about this Man who claims such authority."

Habib glanced at Rick, "He gave me a Bible written in Farsi."

"Have you started reading it?"

"Yes, I have read all of the Old Testimonials and am working on the New."

Omar lifted his hand to correct him when the pastor stepped to the wooden podium and announced the guest speaker.

The humble man's dark eyes showed sadness as he excused himself.

For the next fifty-five minutes, the former Muslim turned evangelist mesmerized the audience with his passionate rhetoric.

"In the past, I'd read and memorized passages from the Qur'an. But God never spoke to me through its teachings. When I read the Bible, there was a different voice speaking, a different message with a different authority. I gathered the courage to go forward and asked the preacher if a Muslim could also have access to the heavenly Father," he continued.

"The preacher shared with me the most precious verse I'd ever heard. He said, 'For God so loved the world that He gave His only begotten Son, that whosoever believeth in Him should not perish, but have everlasting life'."

Habib's eyes misted. He hung on every word. "Mr. Rick told me that verse, too."

"This verse alone has the answers to all religions." Omar's voice resounded. "God sent His Son to die on our behalf because of the sin of all mankind. It takes only believing this truth to escape eternal hell. God did that out of love and the goodness of His heart; but also because He is a righteous judge. The judgment of God requires a penalty for sin. For the wages of sin is death, but because God is also merciful, he offers us the gift of eternal life through Jesus Christ our Lord. The simple truth seemed too good to be true, but it is. I could not ignore God's call to me, 'Come.' The more I read from the Bible, the more I became convinced that God was speaking to me personally. Finally, after years of agony, I was led to the truth that the Lord Jesus Christ is God; He is the truth; He is the giver of life; He is the only way of salvation."

Omar scanned the crowd as if he could see into men's hearts. "Habib, won't you join me in the spiritual freedom I have in Christ our Lord?" He called as the organ played softly.

Hearing his name, Habib tensed. He wasn't used to such attention, especially in a Christian church. In a panic, Habib bolted for the exit with Rick close behind.

"What happened?" Rick asked, hand on Habib's heaving shoulders.

Bending at the waist, Habib steadied himself against the corner of the building, "I don't know. The walls seemed to close in, and I felt like I was going to pass out."

Rick cast a glance in the direction of the door. People were already spilling out. "Yeah, that got a little intense. Maybe you should take your time and think about what he said before jumping into things."

After a few labored breaths, Habib straightened and looked into Rick's eyes. "I don't like to be pushed, not by the Mullah's, not by the Ayatollah, and especially not by some converted Muslim. This is too important a decision for me to rush into."

Chapter 12

The Owens' Home

Amid the tinkle of flatware on Correlle plates, several buoyant conversations bounced around the table.

Lifting his plate, Jared asked, "Mindy, this meatloaf tastes great, mind if I have seconds? It's been weeks since I've had an American meal."

"*Jared Russell*," Fatemah blurted, "you love my cooking. What are you saying?"

Hands held in surrender, the twisted expression on Jared's face was priceless. "I was just saying—"

"I know what you was 'just saying," Fatemah said, hand on her hip.

Mindy passed him the meatloaf, then turned a condescending gaze at Fatemah. "Well, if it's all the same, this isn't American food, it's Canadian."

"You don't say," Jared said. "I didn't know there was a difference." Scooping up another portion, he passed the dish to Fatemah who'd been eyeing him warily. Unnoticed, he reached down and rubbed his shin where she'd kicked him. She smiled demurely, took a slice, then asked for the gravy.

"So Jared, tell me more about this Harbor House. Is it a type of bed-and-breakfast or something?" Rick asked inquisitively.

"No" looking at Fatemah, "actually, we got the idea from Fatemah's background."

Mindy allowed surprise to register. "Why, what happened to you Fatemah?" Mindy asked, her voice softening.

"To start with, my father emigrated from Lebanon, from the Bekaa Valley. As I said in church, he was a strict Shi'a Muslim. He raised his four boys and two daughters to adhere to the Shia theology. My father demanded complete obedience to the teachings of the Qur'an. It was a living hell. I often questioned the logic of the Qur'an which only infuriated him. He said if I didn't stop asking such questions I would burn in Hell with scalding water being poured over my head."

"That sounds like the testimony of our speaker today," Habib observed.

"You're right. Much of what he said brought back painful memories."

"So what did you do?"

Fatemah took a sip of tea, set down the glass, then continued. "As a teenager, I met a neighbor, and we became good friends. The only problem was that she was a believer in Christ. I often asked questions about my friend's faith and the Bible. I began reading the Bible for myself. God began to work in my heart. It wasn't long before I too placed my faith in the Lord Jesus."

Rick laid his fork down and stared at Fatemah. "What happened when your father found out?"

The corners of her mouth turned down, and she let out a labored breath, "When he learned of this, he made several attempts at killing me. Once he threw a hair dryer in the bath-tub when I was taking a bath. Fortunately, the cord wasn't long enough, and it unplugged before hitting the water. Then he pushed me in front of a moving car, but it swerved before hitting me. In order to stay alive, I ran away from home. My pastor and his wife took me in until I turned eighteen. By then I had graduated from high school, and I immediately enrolled in Junior College in order to get training for a job."

Rick shifted uncomfortably. "That's terrible, Fatemah, God was certainly watching over you. Is that what gave you the idea of providing a safe house for endangered and abused Muslim converts?"

Shaking her head, "No, not really. I got that idea after working with Jared in the construction office. He came to Stanford, Michigan to build a Mosque, and I was hired as one of his secretaries." Smiling and taking Jared by the hand, she continued. "As the Lord drew us together, He began using us to win Muslims to Jesus. We became aware of the persecution of Muslim or Arabic believers. Jared had the great idea of making our honeymoon a mission survey trip as well. We actually came here to Beirut for our honeymoon."

Jared related the story about the young boy he and Fatemah had rescued. "That was all the confirmation we needed," he concluded.

Rick's eyes shifted between Jared and Fatemah, "Wow, that's something! But why were you building a Mosque?"

With a shrug, Jared held up his hands, "That's a long story. Maybe we should save it for another day."

Mindy stood and began collecting empty bowls and plates. "Well, now that you're here and have the Harbor House, how do you plan to deal with long term guests?"

"Yes, that is a problem. We can't keep them indefinitely," Fatemah said with candor.

"I've been thinking about that, Fatemah," Jared said as he rubbed the back of his neck nervously.

"We need a system of getting these people out of the country. In your case, you went to your pastor's house. But here in Lebanon, they wouldn't be safe. We need to get them out of the country."

Jared shifted his gaze to Rick. "Would you have any idea of how to go about that?"

Shaking his head, Rick shifted uncomfortably. "Now you're talking about smuggling people out of this country. That's illegal, and I don't want to have anything to do with it," he said, his jaw set.

Mindy released a controlled huff. "See, I told you they—"

Rick silenced her with a raised hand, "Now Mindy—"

"I think it's a good idea," Habib chirped, after watching Mindy's reaction. "It's risky, but a good one. I've heard of it being done in other countries. What makes it a little easier here is the fact that this is a port city. Fishing boats are coming and going in and out of the harbor at all times of the day and night."

"Habib," Rick cautioned, "don't encourage them."

"I'm not encouraging them. I'm just making a suggestion."

Releasing a frustrated breath, Rick pushed back from the table and stood. "These people don't have any idea what they're getting themselves into."

In the distance, the call to evening prayer broke the uncomfortable silence. Jared's eyes cut in Habib's direction. "Do you need time alone? I mean, you know…"

Habib's face darkened, and he shifted uncomfortably. "No, I think I will be okay," he answered unconvincingly.

"Well Jared, if it's all the same to you, I'd feel better if you'd drop the subject and not discuss it in my presence again." By Rick's set jaw and unflinching eyes, Jared knew the conversation was over.

"Good idea," Mindy said, trying to change the subject, "how about you go out on the deck while I fix some coffee."

As the sun set on another beautiful golden sky, Jared and Fatemah rehearsed the colorful story of how they met, about their friends Ahmad and Shirin and the whole mosque debacle.

"Well, Fatemah, what was your maiden name?" Mindy asked.

Fatemah smiled, "It was Bashera."

The smile on Mindy's face evaporated and she stiffened, looking ill. "Please excuse me, I feel sick," and headed to the bathroom.

Habib grabbed his stomach as if he felt sick.

Rick placed his hands on the corners of his chair and pushed himself up. "Well it is getting late," he said. "Maybe you should be going." His voice sounded flat, without emotion.

Jared sensed the tension, but was at a loss for its source. Glancing at his watch, he tried to sound conversational. "Yes, we had better get going. Thanks so much for the nice dinner and fellowship. We'll have to do it again."

Rick frowned with a baffled expression, but made no commitment.

Chapter 13

Xavier and Wright Architectural Group

"Mr. Xavier," Jared said in his weekly update, "are you sure you want me here? I mean, there is nothing to report. The university's Board of Directors are dragging their feet. The city is doing nothing but throwing up roadblocks, and I don't seem to be making much progress at being a liaison." His wide hand rubbed the crown of his head and came to rest on his hip.

"Now son, you need to learn a little patience. All good things come to those who wait. You are exactly where God and I want you. Just keep doing what you're doing—"

"But sir," Jared interrupted.

"John, you can call me John," Mr. Xavier fired back, his voice remained unflappable.

Jared released a slow breath, "But John, I'm not doing anything, that's the point."

"How's Fatemah doing?"

Stunned by the abrupt change of direction, Jared wondered where he was going with this question. "She's adjusting."

"And this Harbor House of yours? How's that working out?"

Jared rubbed the nap of his neck, "It's working out just fine, sir, ah, John. Why the sudden interest?"

The ticking of the wall clock marked the silence in measured beats. "John, are you still there?"

"Yes, I'm here. Look Jared, you and I have known each other for what, five years?"

"Six."

"Okay, six. In the six years we've known each other, have I ever not supported you?"

"No." *Except for the time I brought the Christmas tree into the construction shack, but who's counting.*

"Well, you need to trust me when I say, you are exactly where you need to be. Now I have my reasons, but you must stay the course. Do what you do best and get ready."

"Ready for what, sir?"

"Get ready to be used in ways you've never expected."

Jared leaned back in his chair, "Sir, you're talking in circles, I, I—"

"All in good time, now you give that lovely wife of yours my love and let's stay in touch."

The line went dead and Jared sat, wondering what just happened. ***

"He's a good man," Xavier said, looking at Jimbo Osborne. Jimbo was a highly trained operative with the CIA, and John was his field director.

As senior partner of Xavier and Wright Architectural Group, a front company for the CIA, it afforded him the ability to cross international boundaries without raising suspicion. Their last project, the construction of a Mosque in Michigan, netted them Imam Fahad, a man ranked high on Interpol's most-wanted list.

"Look Jimbo, we are developing an asset inside Lebanon. I mean that *I* am developing an asset. It's a pilot program I pitched a year ago to the Director. The program involves recruiting and nurturing young people from Arab countries. It's called the Young Arab Recruitment and Development Program, or Yarad for short."

Jimbo leaned back and crossed his arms over his barrel chest, "Aren't we already doing that?"

The lines on his face deepened. "No, Jimbo, not exactly. When I say young people, I mean, young. We're talking about teens here."

"Isn't that illegal or something?" Jimbo asked, his eyebrows knit.

John picked up a pencil and began writing the names of the children he knew Hamas and Al Queda had blown up on buses in Israel, Spain and a dozen other countries. He handed the list to Jimbo, who began skimming over it. Half way through, he sat straight up like he'd been poked with a hot iron.

"Some of these children have the same last name as you, John."

Xavier slowly nodded his head. "That's right. That bus in Israel," his throat closed with emotion, and he paused to take a sip of water. "They were my nephews, my brother's kids. I loved them like my own, if I had some. As a matter of fact, they were my only family. And some child, strapped with a bomb vest, was coerced into getting on that bus, and some Jihadist detonated it." His lip trembled in a poor attempt to control his anger.

He was a professional, this wasn't personal. He couldn't get emotionally involved ... but he had.

"The way I look at it, you gotta fight fire with fire." He leaned forward, his eyes burned with a fire Jimbo hadn't seen before.

Jimbo ran his hand through his thinning hair. "All right, you sold me, but what's that got to do with Jared or me for that matter?"

John stood and came around his desk. Crossing his arms, he propped his hip on its corner. "Nothing and something. The last bomber we discovered was trained in Lebanon. That's the one who blew up the bus my family was on. Word on the street has it that Ayatollah Bashera was somehow involved in the bombings."

"So, what's that got to do with me? You're not planning on sending me over to Lebanon to supervise the construction of that university, now are you?"

Xavier released a tense chuckled and shook his head. "You gotta admit, sending Jared to oversee that project was a last minute stroke of genius on my part. But no, I have other plans for you," he said, patting Jimbo on his rounded shoulder. "I understand you like cold weather."

Chapter 14

The Harbor House

The clock in the living room struck 2 a.m., and Jared threw the covers off. Restless dreams plagued his sleep, and he got up and began to pace the floor.

"Honey, what's wrong? Come back to bed," Fatemah mumbled.

"I can't sleep."

Sitting up, Fatemah screwed her knuckles into her eye sockets. "Why can't you sleep?"

Jared slumped on the side of the bed next to his wife. "It's Rick and Mindy. I can't figure out why they turned to ice. First, we are laughing and cutting up, then they turned us off like a spigot. Was it something I said?"

Fatemah flicked on the light next to the bed and brushed a bird's nest of hair from her eyes. "No, it wasn't something you said. It was something I said. I knew it the moment I said it."

Shifting his position, Jared held her gaze, "What did you say?"

Fatemah leaned forward and wrapped her arms around her husband. "Remember what we were talking about just before they changed?"

Jared searched his memory. "Yeah," a light coming on in his head, "we were telling them about how we met."

"And Mindy asked me what my maiden name was. I told her it was Bashera. That's when it happened."

For a moment, the ticking of the clock in the other room marked the only passage of time. "What's so significant about your last name? It's pretty common around here, isn't it?"

She stood, pushed her feet into a pair of silk slippers and headed to the bathroom. "I don't know, maybe Bashera is the name of a major crime ring."

Jared perched a hip on the corner of the bed. "Well, tomorrow I'm going to find out."

"Tomorrow? How about doing it today? The sun will be up in a few hours," she said, returning from the bedroom. "Now with your permission, I'm going back to sleep." She flipped the switch, and the room went dark.

***

By the time Jared made the short drive to the campus, the sun had already blazed a trail halfway across the sky. Forcing a smile, he neared the literature table where Rick sat. A quick glance at the display, and a dozen images scalded his memory— images of handing out literature and drinks, of being beaten up by a group of young Arabs, and of having long discussions with his pastor. He deeply missed him and his friend Ahmad. Right now he needed both. Reluctantly, he pushed himself forward.

"Hey Rick! So this is where you hide out during the day?" Jared said, searching his face for any clues.

"Oh, hey Jared, good to see you." He stood, forcing a weak smile. The two men shook hands warmly, but there was something in Rick's angular movements that told Jared his friend was bothered.

"Say, I need to apologize for the way we treated you guys last night, we had no right to freeze you out like that."

Jamming his hands in his pockets, Jared breathed a sigh of relief. Finally, he was going to get to the bottom of it. "That's okay, was it something we said or did?"

The pained expression on Rick's face replaced his forced smile, "Well, yes and no."

"What do you mean by that?" Jared said, pulling his hand out.

After a moment of reflection, Rick found the words he sought. "It's your wife's last name . . . Bashera."

Jared stiffened, the hair on the back of his neck bristled. "What about it?" he prompted dubiously.

"I guess you wouldn't know this, but there is a very prominent cleric who happens to share the same last name as your wife. His name is Ayatollah Abdullah Bashera. He recently declared a Fatwa, putting a moratorium on any evangelistic activity."

Jared shifted his weight from one foot to the other as he digested this new information. "So you think what? That we are somehow related to him and are infiltrating the Christian community?"

Hands raised, "I don't know what to think, but the fact that her father came from Lebanon, that she speaks Farsi, and has the same last name is a bit coincidental, don't you think?"

A group of students walked by the table chatting and laughing. One stopped and picked up a pen and kept moving, while Jared looked on in silence.

"Well, that explains your reaction, but I assure you, we are not in cahoots with the Ayatollah. Fatemah may not even be related to him. Heck, there's a whole page of Basheras in the phone book. One thing I will do though, I'll go directly home and find out." His eyes glowed with determination.

***

"He's what?" Fatemah's voice rattled the china in the dining room.

Jared stepped back, hearing her reaction. "Like I said, he's a prominent religious cleric. As a matter of fact, Rick told me the Ayatollah declared a Fatwa against witnessing. Now, I gotta know, is he related to you or not? Is he your uncle or cousin or something?"

Fatemah slumped to the couch, her head buried in her hands. "My father said very little about his family. Only on rare occasions did he even mention having family in the Bekaa valley. It was a secret he didn't want to talk about. I don't even know if mother knew his secret." She paused and glanced up, her eyes widened with realization. "Wait a minute." She stood and marched into the bedroom.

Jared could hear her rooting around in a box and throwing things around. She emerged victoriously holding an old leather-bound book.

"This is a record of my family's history. Mother sent it to me after Dad passed away. This is the first I've even thought of it," she said, eying its dusty cover.

Jared took a seat next to her. "Well, let's open it and see for ourselves."

Fatemah gently lifted the cover and began paging through the family history. There were yellowed pictures of family gatherings and celebrations. Hers was a large family, and she guessed these were her distant relatives from the old country. One page revealed a family tree. At the root of the tree were two names which were faded with time. As her finger traced the branches, she suddenly stopped and took a sharp breath.

"Oh my," her hand covered her mouth. "My father was a sheikh, a teacher of Shari'ah Law before he left Lebanon."

Jared leaned closer to get a better look. "Why did he leave if he had a following and was gaining in popularity?"

Fatemah shook her head, "I don't know." Her finger traced the lines. "Look, Father had a younger brother. His name is Abdullah. According to Muslim tradition, my father was the successor to the prophet Mohammad."

Curiously, she turned the page and a photograph fell out. Fatemah lifted it and flipped it over. Hand to mouth, she took in a sharp breath.

"What is it," Jared asked, concern deepening the lines around his eyes.

With trembling fingers, she handed him the photo.

"It's Imam Fahad, the man who tried to kill me," she said, her voice growing husky.

Jared wrapped his arm around her and gave her a reassuring hug. "Well, he won't be bothering you any longer. But who is that other man in the picture?"

Shaking her head, she pushed his hand away from her. "I don't know, but I never want to see that face again."

"No wonder Rick and Mindy had such a reaction," Jared said, flexing his neck.

A dish crashed to the kitchen floor, and Fatemah jumped. "Anita, is everything all right?" she called, looking in her direction.

Sheepishly, Anita stepped around the corner, head down and her eyes searching the floor. "No Miss Fatemah, everything is *not* all right," her fingers playing with the tassels of her apron, nervously. "I've got a confession to make. I haven't been completely honest with you."

"Oh? How so, Anita?" Fatemah asked with growing suspicion.

Her small frame shook, and she began to sob. Between halting breaths, she spoke, "When, when I applied for this job, I, I didn't use my real last name."

Fatemah jumped to her feet. "Oh? And what is your last name, Anita?"

The young girl bit the edge of her thumb nail. "Well," she paused haltingly, "it's Bashera." The name tumbled from her lips like a curse. "You see, I've been listening to you talk about your family, and I think I'm your cousin."

Mid-stride, Fatemah paused, staring. "I'm not believing this, you're the daughter of the Ayatollah? The man who hates Christians? And you're working for me? Are you here to spy on us? To report on us?" Fatemah's voice ratcheted up an octave.

Anita fell on her knees, her hands folded under her chin. "Oh Miss Fatemah, I know that's what it looks like, but it's not so. I had no idea that we were related, or that you were a Christian. As I told you before, I just want to be free. I would never tell Father about you. I'm so sorry for lying to you." Her airy voice cracked.

Warmth streaked down Fatemah's cheeks and she sank to her knees. Lifting Anita's chin with her fingers, she locked onto her eyes, "I believe you dear, and I forgive you for lying, but you must never lie to me again. Do you understand?"

Anita pinched her eyes shut, squeezing tears down her cheeks. She nodded, "Oh yes ma'am, Miss Fatemah, yes ma'am." The two women hugged as Jared watched in amazement.

As they stood, the picture Jared had been examining fell to the floor. Instinctively, Anita picked it up. Her face clouded and she repulsed.

"What's wrong Anita?" Fatemah asked, seeing the young girl's countenance fall.

"Miss Fatemah, what are you doing with this picture?"

Fatemah felt the blood drain from her face. "Why Anita, whatever do you mean? I just found it in this family album. Besides this man," she pointed at Imam Fahad, "I am not familiar with who the other man is."

Anita gently lifted the picture from her mistress's fingers. "That's my father. He and Imam Fahad were very close. Did you say he tried to kill you?"

A sharp pain stabbed at Fatemah's heart as she replayed the scenes of the night Fahad attacked her and strapped a bomb vest on her, threatening to squeeze the trigger if anyone tried to stop him. She unpacked the story to Anita while she sat, wide eyed, taking it all in.

"So that's what happened to the Imam. Several years ago, he disappeared and hadn't been heard from since. Speculation was that he had been caught up to paradise to prepare for the coming of the Mahdi."

Jared shifted to face Anita. "The truth is, one of Michigan's finest sent him out of this world, but I don't think it was to paradise." A dry chuckle escaped his lips.

Following a nudge to Jared's ribs, Fatemah continued, "He kept ranting about a blood curse. Do you know anything about that, Anita?"

Anita lowered her eyes and played nervously with the hem of her apron. "Yes ma'am. I was hoping you'd not ask."

"Why Anita?" Fatemah's voice grew tense.

Biting her lip, Anita looked up. "It was about five years ago. I overheard my father and Fahad talking. You see, my father hated your father. He was extremely jealous of his popularity and would have killed him had not Imam Fahad insisted on going to the president of Iran and declaring him an enemy of Islam."

Fatemah's mind raced as she tried to absorb this new information. "That must have been why my parents left the middle-east."

Anita continued, "My father got very angry with Fahad and years later went to the president of Iran and convinced him to send the Imam to America to spread Islam and finish what he called it, the blood curse."

Jared took Fatemah by the hand and gave it a gentle squeeze. "So now you know the answer to all the questions you've been having all these years."

For a few minutes, the three sat in silent contemplation. Finally, Fatemah pushed herself up and offered her hand to the young lady, "Anita, you wouldn't believe this, but you have a cousin living in America."

"I do?" she asked, wiping her eyes with a tissue Fatemah offered. "What's his name?"

Chapter 15

Mackinaw, Michigan

The summer sun had already reached its zenith and began its race for the distant horizon as Kaleel Bashera, aka Farooq-e-Azam, finished another grueling day of training.

Ever since the sleeper cell was discovered in Sanford, Michigan, the CIA, FBI, and Homeland Security had aggressively recruited young people of Arab descent to work in counter intelligence and surveillance within the Muslim communities. Kaleel was recruited by the CIA and excelled in his training. After seeing radical Muslim fundamentalism up close and personal, he knew what they were capable of doing. Within the year and a half, he'd achieved what no other Arab young man had. He was now a full-fledged operative, embedded in the Jihadist sleeper cell called, The Sons of Thunder. Along with rigorous physical fitness training, he had a crash course on bomb making, security diversion and money counterfeiting.

"Farooq, come over here," Teriek Azar, the leader of The Sons of Thunder said.

Kaleel checked his weapon after completing another close-quarters drill, holstered it and jogged to where his trainer stood. Teriek leaned over the hood of a jeep, studying a floor plan.

Having grown up in Mogadishu, Somalia, Teriek was no stranger to violence. His father was involved in the 'Black Hawk Down' incident. He'd witnessed the killing of his uncle by rival tribes and was forced to choose between Hezbollah or death.

"Are you familiar with The Grand Hotel on Mackinaw Island?"

"No, for the last five months, you've had me so busy I've had little time for sightseeing. I seldom even have time to eat," he kidded.

A crooked smile parted the man's black beard, "Good, idle' hands are the work-horse of the devil."

Kaleel pinched back a tight smile at his leader's faux-pas. "So, what are these floor plans?"

Teriek flipped them around so Kaleel could read them. "These are the floor plans of The Grand Hotel. This is level one, this is the second floor and up. Floors two and three are pretty much the same, but the fourth floor spreads out and has larger suites. You can see here," he pointed to the penthouse suite. "These are all named after US presidents rather than being numbered."

Kaleel raised his hand. "And why are you telling me this?"

It took all of Kaleel's resolve to keep from shooting the man in the head where he stood. He'd read his dossier, he'd studied Teriek's background, his modus operandi. This man was a cold, calculating killer and deserved to pay, but his handlers ordered him not to make a move against him until he knew the full plan, so he waited.

Teriek peeled back one more page. "This is the kitchen, study it well." Then marched away without giving him the answer he sought.

A moment passed and Kaleel glanced around to see if there was anyone watching. At the time, his team was rehearsing the room to room, close-quarters drill like a troop of dancers with Teriek observing each member closely. As the rhythmic double taps resounded, Kaleel quickly pulled a small camera from a secret pocket and began to snap multiple pictures of each page. When he'd finished, he glanced around.

In the corner of his eye, he caught Ben-ali, a recent addition from Syria, watching him. *This is not good.* Kaleel did some quick math and knew if Ben-ali turned up missing it would raise suspicions. He had to be eliminated without implicating himself, and before he could report what he saw. Seeing a training bomb vest, Kaleel grabbed it and quickly bared two wires, then called to Ben-ali.

The man looked surprised but obeyed without question. "I need you to take this and put it in the back of my truck, but be careful. This thing is dangerous." Speaking authoritatively for the benefit of all to hear. Kaleel hoped Ben-ali got far enough from him and yet not close enough to his truck before it blew.

The man gave a weak salute and trudged away in the direction of Kaleel's truck. As if on cue, Ben-ali shifted the bomb vest causing the two wires to come into contact. That was all it took. The explosion shook the jeep and blew out the windows of the training house.

"What happened?" demanded Teriek, picking himself up from the ground.

Kaleel lay, covered in debris. The self-inflicted cut above his eye provided an ample amount of blood to convince anyone he'd had a close brush with death. Feigning a concussion, Kaleel lifted his face and wiped the blood with the back of his hand. "I, I don't know. I told Ben-ali to be careful and not mess with that bomb vest, but he treated it like it was a toy."

His explanation seemed to have satisfied his leader. "Get someone to patch you up before you bleed to death. I don't want to lose two men today," then he stomped off. "Men, get this mess cleaned up and let's get out of here before anyone comes," he ordered.

A bevy of activity defined their movements, and soon they high-tailed it back to their safe house, one man short.

After Kaleel finished his duties at the training camp, he washed his hands several times, and sent the pictures he'd taken to his handler.

Chapter 16

The Harbor House

"His name is Kaleel and he's my younger brother," Fatemah said proudly.

"Where does he live? Is he a Muslim? What does he do?" Anita asked wide eyed, hands under her chin. "I've never known anyone who lived in America."

Fatemah leaned back, a wispy smile tugged at the corners of her mouth. "Let's see, Kaleel is about 5' 4'', short-cropped hair, with a goatee and the brightest smile you've ever seen."

Anita clapped her hands and beamed, "Is he as handsome as Justin Bieber? I mean, uh." Her face colored and she began fanning herself.

"Well, he's definitely not Justin Bieber, but he is the kind of guy every mother wants their daughter to marry."

"I bet you miss him," Anita said, shoulders slumping.

Nodding, "Yeah, I miss him. I miss his smile, his piercing eyes." Fatemah chuckled at her memory. "He used to drive me nuts, always washing his hands. He had a phobia about germs, which by now, he's probably outgrown."

Anita leaned over and embraced Fatemah, "When was the last time you spoke to him?"

Fatemah thought a moment, "It's been a while, but I got a letter from him the other day, would you like me to read part of it to you?"

Anita was on her feet, prancing like a Russian race horse. "Oh yes, Miss Fatemah, would you?"

"Simmer down now Anita, you're about to give me hives," Jared said, watching her agitate.

Side stepping the broken glass, Fatemah maneuvered her way into the kitchen, grabbed the opened envelope from the counter and returned. She took her seat, and pulled the letter out. Anita acted like a child at Christmas time as she began reading.

"'Dear Fatemah and Jared,

How are you guys doing? I sure miss you and Jared. It just isn't the same around here without you guys to kick up some excitement. I'd love to come and visit you all. Maybe I could arrange to come this fall if my field director doesn't have me out on some secret mission, ha, ha.'"

Fatemah paused and chuckled, "Kaleel is always kidding about being a Secret Agent, 007 guy."

The truth was, he was now a full-fledged operative, working undercover.

Fatemah brushed his comments aside and finished reading Kaleel's letter.

For a moment, Anita stood, eyes closed, a dreamy smile painted on her face, "I do hope he comes to visit you. I would love to meet him."

"Now Anita, aren't you forgetting you're a betrothed woman?"

"Oh, Miss Fatemah, don't remind me," she said and quickly scampered to the kitchen to clean up the broken glass.

Chapter 17

Vogtle Electric Generating Plant, Waynesboro, Georgia

Otis Bennett stood with his shoulder leaned against the cab of his tractor trailer smoking a cigarette, while a team of men, dressed in protective orange gear, loaded his truck. To break the boredom, he studied the myriad of insects as they swirled in the amber light of a dozen halogen globes. Below them, eerie shadows moved with a cadence all their own as men and machine worked through the night to prepare his trailer for departure.

The dock supervisor, a short, stocky man with a bad temper and language to match walked over to where Otis stood.

"She's all yours," he said, handing him a clipboard.

Otis dropped his cigarette on the concrete floor and grounded it out with his heel.

"Took ya long enough, what were you loading, fine china?" he growled.

The dock supervisor cocked his head and blessed his ancestors. "That there trailer," nodding in its direction, "has a half dozen spent fuel rods. Be careful you don't lose them or we'll have the devil to pay."

Otis scribbled his name illegibly at the bottom line on the clipboard indicating he'd received the shipment, then walked to the back of his truck to inspect the lock. As usual, it was turned inward as protocol demanded. He also took notice of the special steel belts wrapped around the lock handles. Satisfied his rig was buttoned down tighter than a drum, he climbed into the cab, cranked the Rolls Royce diesel engine, put it in gear, and pulled away from the dock.

Turning right on GA 121, he exited the Vogtle Power plant, and headed north hoping to reach the Waste Management facility located in Birmingham, Alabama before lunch. He tapped the screen on the satellite monitoring system twice. It blinked and registered his location indicated by a green dot on a red line.

The late-night run was one he'd made dozens of times since being hired by AAT Carriers. It was a good job, paid well, and gave him time for the wife and kids. As long as he didn't come in contact with his cargo, he was happy.

Twenty minutes into his journey, a set of blue flashing lights reflected in his mirror. Checking his speed, he relaxed. "Not me this time," he said to himself.

The police cruiser whipped past him and cut directly in his path. Brake lights flashed, and Otis jammed on his brakes sending rubber and smoke into the night air. The harder he pressed the closer he came to the police car. Worried he would jack-knife; he pumped his brakes. A quick glance in his mirror, and his eyes widened as another set of head lights behind him disappeared in his blind spot.

"This is not good," he muttered through clinched teeth.

The palms of his hands slicked as he tried desperately to avoid a collision. It would be his first, and he couldn't afford to get fired. With a sick child at home and an alcoholic wife, he needed this job. Gritting his teeth, he swerved hard to his left and cursed as the police cruiser mirrored his actions. White-knuckled, he gripped the steering wheel and aimed his rig for the soft shoulder. In an instant a concrete barrier appeared in his headlights. There was nowhere to go and no time to change course. The cab slammed into the railing. It flipped on its side and skidded; spraying sparks and fuel behind him. An instant later, the wounded truck burst into flames.

The other two cars screeched to a halt. A dozen men leaped from their vehicles and began running in the direction of the accident. A moment later a large panel truck pulled up. The officer set up a road block while men dressed in orange hazmat uniforms cut the lock on the rear doors of the truck. The team of men quickly off-loaded the hazardous material from the burning truck while the officer sprayed foam on the burning cab.

Once it was extinguished, he stepped near the blackened hull and peered in at the charred remains of the driver. He nodded to one of the hooded men.

"He's dead, let's get out of here before the authorities figure out one of their police cruisers is missing," Uri Kazan, an American born Turk said.

The team of masked men loaded into the panel truck while Uri climbed behind the wheel. A moment later they were speeding north on GA 121. Thirty minutes later, they reached the I-75 interchange. Taking the ramp, they blended in with north-bound traffic and disappeared.

Their trek took them to Atlanta, Georgia, where they merged with the morning commuters on I-285, north of the sprawling city. Overhead, police and traffic helicopters searched the city for any sign of a truck with a radioactive heat signature. Fortunately for the men in the truck, its inner walls were lined with a thin layer of lead. They slipped through the dragnet, undetected. Once they cleared I-285, they met a sea of red tail-lights on what Atlantans call 'Spaghetti Junction'.

Blistering the air with vulgarity, Uri pounded the steering wheel.

"I hope this in not a road block," his eyes burned with unrestrained rage.

"Relax," said one of the men in the back seat. "I've been monitoring the police scanner, and it's just a wreck involving a tractor trailer and a motorcycle. One dead cyclist and one morning commute ruined. It looks like we'll be here for a while."

Uri glanced over his shoulder. "Any chance of those fuel rods leaking?"

His partner, another homegrown Jihadist from New York, leaned forward. "No, they are packed in lead and the compartment is lined with lead. It would be a miracle for the authorities to detect our presence."

"I certainly hope so, but I feel like a sitting duck out here on the open highway."

***

Forty-five minutes later, the traffic and Uri and his men resumed their journey. It was well past midnight the next day when he exited I-95 on to Frenchtown Pike. A mile later, he brought the truck to a stop at a locked gate belonging to the Bellanca Airfield in a sleepy town of New Castle, Delaware.

Bellanca Airfield, or what was left of it, was once the home of *Columbia,* Charles Lindbergh's first choice for his trans-Atlantic flight. Since those glory days, the air field served many purposes, but now, it was the lair of Uri and his men. From here they could work undetected.

One of his men jumped from the truck and he swung the gate open allowing Uri to pull the truck around to the backside of the hanger. Another group of men stood, guns at the ready as Uri backed his truck to the rusted hanger door.

"Cut your lights," one of the men hollered.

Uri followed his orders while the moonless night blanketed them in thick, heavy darkness. One of the armed men gave a command in Arabic, and an electric hum deep within the cavernous building vibrated. With an unearthly squeak, the huge hanger door groaned, then lifted from the cracked concrete. Amber light spilled forth and spread like a golden carpet until it bathed the truck in its glow.

"Bring it back," someone on the dock ordered.

With his lights out, Uri backed into the open bay. As soon as he was far enough back, the door reversed its climb and rolled down, striking the concrete with a bone jarring thud. For a moment, the building fell silent as dust from the aging ceiling filtered down and settled on the visitors.

From the shadows, an expletive laden command echoed, and a new round of activity began. Men in orange hazmat suits gathered at the back doors of the truck. One man yanked it opened while the other looked on. A man wearing a distinctive orange uniform and a breathing apparatus revved the engine of a forklift and pulled forward. His gloved hands worked the handles with skill until he'd captured his prey and lifted the container of spent fuel rods. With care, he backed out and set the crate on the floor. As soon as the driver of the fork lift receded into the background, a team of highly trained technicians went to work removing the rods.

"Uri, your job is done for the night. Take your men over there," Dr. Jamal Karvina said, his wiry arm, draped in orange, pointed to what remained of the offices. "Get something to eat and rest up while we prepare the package."

Dr. Karvina, the lead technician, was a Pakistani nuclear scientist who had been recruited under threat of death. He knew the odds of creating a dirty bomb had a 10–40% chance of success, but despite his reluctance he was forced to continue to try.

"Is it enough?" Uri asked.

Dr. Karvina inspected the crate and nodded. "It's a moderate quantity of radioactive material, about 100,000 curies, but yes, I believe I can build a dirty bomb out of it. If successful, the explosion will throw highly radioactive material into the atmosphere. When strategically placed, its effect will cause more psychological damage than structural, but that's alright," he spoke as if teaching a class of freshmen in college. "You will have struck at the heart of the beast and hit him where it hurts the most. The economic consequences will result in significant losses in the tens of billions of dollars."

Deep lines furrowed his brow as he contemplated the result of his actions. This was his moment to make a mark for Islam. Soon the world would tremble at the thought of resisting the coming of the Twelfth Imam, the Mahdi, the chosen one. He savored the moment with a smug expression. "How long will it take to complete your task?"

The nuclear scientist rubbed his chin. "It depends on how large a bomb you want me to make." His arms extended to form an invisible shape.

Uri did some quick calculating. "I want to level this city."

Dr. Karvina rocked back on his heels, his eyes bulging behind thinly wired glasses. "Then you will need to acquire more fuel rods than these."

Frustrated, Uri crossed his arms over his chest. "Just get to work and stop stalling."

"How long do we have?" Dr. Karvina probed, his voice growing shaky.

Turning on his heels, Uri bore down upon the demure man. "Within the month. So forget all safety protocols and get this device operational as soon as possible," he said, while a dozen frightened technicians gaped.

Each had their own reasons for being there; some were forced to participate after their families were threatened, still others were paid large sums of money, not all were fully committed.

"Will my technicians be expected to transport it as well?"

"No, I'll have my team transport it once you're finished. That's all you need to know. Now get to work." Turning on his heels, Uri stomped off.

Chapter 18

The Harbor House

The trade winds shifted from the south, bringing with them dryer, less oppressive temperatures. It was October, and the Harbor House was nearly ready for its first guest. Jared hired a painting company to repaint the interior Fatemah's favorite colors; earth tones with splashes of deep purple. In between running to the university and the hardware store, Jared managed to move one wall and relocate it to accommodate mixed genders. With the added touch of new furniture and wall decor, including some of Fatemah's best paintings, the house was feeling more like a home.

Jared returned to the kitchen after sweeping out the garage and leaned against the stainless steel refrigerator. Fixing his gaze on his wife, he continued to wonder what took him so long to get up the courage to ask her out on their first date. He knew he liked her, and a little birdie told him she would entertain an offer for dinner if asked properly. So why did it take her almost getting killed to move him to action. He bit back a grin at his stumbling effort, but was pleased with the outcome.

"Honey, I'm going to be gone for a while, Rick and I want to stop by STA - 7 and thank the manager for running our ad," he said.

"Okay, but don't be gone too long, we have the pastor and his wife coming over for dinner tonight."

Snapping his fingers, Jared stuttered, "Oh man, I completely forgot—"

"Jared," her voice grew suspicious, "that's been on the calendar for weeks. We even talked about it," Fatemah said, her hand on her hip.

A toothy grin spread across his face.

"Jared . . ." Fatemah repeated, tossing a sponge at him.

Station 7 was a joint effort between the Baptist churches of Beirut and Evangelicals. It aired pre-recorded church services from Australia, New Zealand, India, Canada, and the US. Between messages, they ran commercials promoting the usual litany of items: soap, cologne, and restaurants. Occasionally, they would slip in a PSA a public service announcement.

Anita stepped in from sweeping the back porch when she heard the end of the PSA, 'Harbor House . . . a safe place!' Innocence marked her beautiful features. "Miss Fatemah, why did they call the Harbor House a 'safe place,' safe from what?"

Fatemah took a seat on the sofa and patted the cushion next to her. "Anita, please sit," her voice growing soft.

"Oh no, Miss Fatemah, a servant should never sit in the presence of her mistress. It is disrespectful."

Biting back a grin, Fatemah folded her hands on her lap. "Yes, but if one's mistress is seated and asks her young servant to join her, then it is perfectly okay." Her tones were smooth and sultry.

In an instant, Anita took her seat next to her mistress, her eyes wide with interest.

A chuckle lodged in Fatemah's throat, and she continued, "Well Anita, sometimes people make decisions that put them in danger. And they find they are no longer," she paused, "how should I say it? No longer welcome at home and in need of someplace to go until they can find more suitable arrangements. Does that make sense to you?"

Anita's forehead wrinkled, "I think so, Miss Fatemah. I hope *we* can help many people."

"Me too," Fatemah said, impressed with her eagerness to help with the rescue effort.

The gate buzzer sounded.

"Should I get it Miss Fatemah?" she said, half way across the kitchen.

Without losing a beat, Fatemah said, "Please, would you? I'm right in the middle of something."

***

Stepping outside of the Harbor House, Anita squinted in the bright sunlight. It was another warm day. Not a cloud had the courage to mar the cobalt sky. A light salty breeze ruffled her hijab as she paced across the circular drive which led to the front gate. As she approached, she noticed a young man, hands cupped, peering through the bars. His eyes, like two black disks locked onto hers as she neared. It suddenly occurred to her why he stared.

"Oh, pardon me, sir," she sputtered, realizing her oversight. Anita's cheeks pinked slightly and she immediately covered her head. "Assalamu alaikum," trying to control her breathing. She'd met many young men coming and going through her father's house, but none triggered her heart like this young man.

"Alaikum salaam, to you too," he replied, trying to suppress a grin.

Anita chided herself. He was just a guy, and probably a homeless one at that. Why did she let her heart flutter every time a guy looked at her? She wasn't of marrying age, at least not yet. She wasn't even available, and she certainly wasn't desperate, or was she?

"Is the lady or man of the house in?" His polite question brought her back to reality.

"Yes, and no," eyeing him playfully. Her dainty finger tips touched the bars and began walking upward.

The young man followed her movements, then he blinked. A confused gaze filled his eyes and he shook his head. Stepping back, he asked. "What is that supposed to mean?"

Anita always enjoyed taunting men. First, it was her father, then her brothers. Now it was time to ply her skills on this unsuspecting young man. Stroking the bars like a harp, she smiled, "It means, yes, the lady is in, and no, the man is not."

A frustrated huff escaped his lips, and Anita caught herself staring into a pair of dark orbs which seemed to pull her into his very soul. For a moment, time stood still. All was quiet, all she could hear was the distant echo of his voice.

"May I speak with the lady of the house?"

Time rushed passed, and Anita realized she'd stopped breathing. Gulping for oxygen she sputtered, "No," taking a quick glance over her shoulder, she continued, "she's busy," hoping to stall the young man long enough to find out his name. "Are you here to inquire about a room?" she asked, twirling the tassel of her hijab in her fingers.

"A room?" his voice curled up like a wisp of smoke. Giving her his best, heart-stopping smile, he glanced past her. "Oh yes, this is a hospitality house, isn't it?" His curly black hair swayed with every move, and he brushed a few strands from his eyes. "No, I'm here to help out."

Help out! That's what I'm here for. A twinge of jealousy percolated, and she was glad he couldn't read her mind.

Footsteps on concrete told her, her time was up.

"Why hello Habib, what are you doing here?" Fatemah asked, her eyes dancing between the two.

Habib managed to pull his gaze from Anita. "Oh hi, Miss Fatemah, I'm here to help Mr. Jared."

Fatemah's forehead wrinkled. "Oh, I'm so sorry. He's not here at the moment. He'll be sad he missed you."

Undaunted by this minor setback, Habib pressed on, "That's okay, Miss Fatemah. I just came by to see if you needed a hand around here. Your husband said something about a pantry?" his arms coming up as if he held a box.

Anita raised her hand in protest, but Fatemah brushed her aside and hit the gate release button.

"Oh yes, Habib, we have lots of things to do. Come in, my husband promised he'd stock the shelves before he left and conveniently forgot," she said, as she led the way to the house.

Once inside, she closed the door and paused. "Anita," she said with an impish glint in her eyes, "would you take Habib to the pantry and let him get started organizing the shelves?"

"Yes ma'am," she said, trying to control her breathing and her racing heart. "Follow me," she said, half mad at his intrusion, half glad to be alone with him even for a few more moments.

***

Habib was not prepared for the emotional roller-coaster ride he had taken. In the brief moment before she covered her face, he was star-struck. He made a mental picture of her face capturing her playful eyes, her rounded nose, and inviting lips. *Who was she? Why was she here?* He was desperate to find out.

Following her through the living room, Habib let his eyes wander around his surroundings. This home was quite different from his crowded dorm room. And compared to his parent's humble dwellings, this was a mansion. Plush couches, chairs, and end tables supporting rare vases filled the open spaces. Modern works of art and paintings with brilliant flashes of color, hung throughout the room giving him the feeling that he was in a gallery. Fresh-cut flowers sent a mixture of fragrant aromas into the air that mingled in the dancing sunlight.

Habib caught himself biting back a grin as Anita lectured him about not touching anything, as if he were a common street urchin.

When they reached the kitchen, she reached inside and flipped the light on in the pantry. With a grand sweep of her dainty arm, she showed him the boxes of canned beans, soups, cereals, and vegetables.

No wonder Mr. Jared has been avoiding it. This will take me all day to stock this room. Maybe Miss Fatemah will ask Anita to help me. He smiled at the thought.

After two hours of moving boxes around and organizing, Habib stood, his hand rubbed the kink in his aching back. A shadow appeared in the door followed by Fatemah's womanly form. "Oh Habib that's great, thank you," she paused, finger to her chin.

"There's just one little problem."

"What's that, Miss Fatemah?" his face distorted into a question.

Stepping in closer, she let her eyes scan two hours of work. Her brows furrowed contemplatively and she finally let out a puff of frustration. "I don't know where anything is." She turned and called, "Anita."

A moment later, Anita's slight frame appeared in the doorway, breathing deeply, "You called, Miss Fatemah?"

Cocking her head, Fatemah slid her eyes in Anita's direction. "Yes, would you mind helping Habib reorganize the pantry? The way he's got it set up, I can't find a thing." A slight chuckle belied her real motives.

Anita pulled her hijab over her head and smiled at Habib. He caught himself not breathing as she slipped past him. For a brief moment, the heat of her body near his, permeated his chest, warmed his soul, and penetrated his mind.

With her arms wrapped around her slender waist, she surveyed his work, "Hum, I see what she means. This will never do. Let's start all over again."

Before long, they were laughing and giggling while they shuffled things around.

"Anita?" Fatemah's voice cut through the laughter. Habib managed to keep a straight face as he watched Anita grow somber.

"Yes ma'am," suppressing a giggle.

"Nearly finished?" Her voice carried neither condemnation nor threat, but rather a slightly playful warning.

"Yes ma'am, just about." Anita's face darkened.

Habib, his hand on his stomach, burst into laughing at her contorted face.

Thirty minutes later, Fatemah returned. Nodding with a knowing smile, she inspected their work. Her fingers touched the straight rows of alphabetically organized cans of soup, beans, and other staples. "Well, now that's more like it," she said, her eyebrows knitting. "That's one more thing on Mr. Jared's to-do-list we can mark off. If you come back tomorrow, maybe we can work on my office. How are your computer skills?" her tone sincere, hopeful.

Hands in his pockets and rocking back, Habib thought a minute. "Oh, pretty good, I've done some tech work at the university in exchange for tuition."

Relieved, Fatemah stepped from the pantry. "Good, I sure could use you. Can I offer you something to eat before you go?"

Habib pulled his hand from his pocket, slid his sleeve back and checked his watch. With a quick nod, he glanced up. "No, but thanks anyway. My ride should arrive any minute now." Turning to face Anita who'd taken a seat at the counter with a heaping plate of chocolate-chip cookies and a glass of milk, he asked, "Anita, would you like a ride home? I mean I don't have a car, but my uncle is a taxi driver. He dropped me off, and I'm sure he'd be glad to take you home as well."

Biting her lip, she glanced around. "I don't know about that. I don't have the money for a taxi, I usually walk."

That was one reason, the other was she didn't want anyone to know her father was Ayatollah Bashera.

Eyeing the cookies, Habib caught his tongue licking his lips. "Well, my uncle doesn't charge me, and I will insist that he not charge you, so it's settled."

She smiled, wishing she could find a place to hide. A moment later, the muffled beep of a horn sounded outside. Puffing a strand of hair from her face, Anita set her unbitten cookie down and rushed to the front door. Outside the closed gate stood an elderly gentleman, his weathered hand beckoned.

"Abbas Taxi at your service ma'am," the taxi cab driver said.

Anita stepped back into the house, her hand over her mouth, shaking her head. "How did he know what time to show up?" she asked, wide eyes.

Pulling his hands from his pockets, Habib rocked back on his heels. "Oh, Uncle Abbas is a very Godly man. He listens to the voice of God all the time, says God tells him where to go and he goes. Most of the time he's in the right place at the right time."

"That's very interesting," Fatemah said, scooping the uneaten cookies and placing them in a bag. "Here, Habib, take these for the road. There'll be more if you come back tomorrow," she said conspiratorially.

A Pepsodent smile parted Habib's lips, and Fatemah flushed. "Thank you Miss Fatemah. I believe I will," he said accepting the proffered bag.

Mouth agape, Anita huffed, *she's a married woman, for crying out loud.* Hand on her hip she squared her shoulders, made an abrupt turn and stomped through the open gate. With a quick glance over her shoulder, she caught a glimpse of Habib's face and smiled. Confusion replaced his cavalier smile. *I hope he learned his lesson.*

Outside the gate, Anita jolted to a halt. A wash of recognition swept over her as her heart quickened and fingers of heat crept up her neck. *I know this man.* Her thoughts fluttered like moths to a flame, and she wanted to run.

From behind, a gentle hand lighted on Anita's shoulder and she jumped.

"After you, my lady," Habib said, eying the open door.

Feeling like a bird in a cage, Anita swallowed hard, "Okay, but just this once, understood?" she quipped.

An impish twinkle danced in the elderly man's eyes, and he gave a quick bow. "Oh, yes ma'am. Whatever you say. As long as you ride with my nephew, you ride at no cost."

His soft voice and gentle movements eased Anita's anxiety, and she climbed in, hoping her pounding heart wouldn't give her away.

As the tattered cab dodged in and out of traffic, Habib appeared to be in deep thought.

"Did you forget your tongue, my Son?" Uncle Abbas quipped, half smiling.

Habib roused, "Oh, I just have a lot to think about." His eyes sliced in Anita's direction.

The lovely young girl sitting next to him was all of fifteen, well educated, charming, articulate to a fault, and very opinionated. Her voice was music to his ears, the kind of music he could listen to for the rest of his life. The only problem was, she was betrothed.

His uncle returned a knowing nod. "Yes, of course."

As directed, Uncle Abbas dropped Habib off at his dorm room first, then headed to his second destination.

In order to keep things simple, Anita instructed him to drop her off a few blocks away from the Administrative Palace. She walked the rest of the way taking side streets and coming up on the west corner of the compound. Looking both ways, she disappeared through a seldom used, little known gate hidden behind a large azalea bush.

As she walked across the close-cropped lawn, she thought about the crazy conversations she'd had with Habib. He was a Shi'a, not that it really mattered to her. Like herself, he was not very religious. She also learned that he was a student at Lebanon International University majoring in economics, that he didn't have a girlfriend, that he didn't believe in multiple wives, that he loved children, and that he was open to other religious views (code words for being open to Christianity).

As she stepped through the side door of her house, her father's booming voice reverberated, "Anita?"

Her blood turned to ice as a sudden wave of nausea swept over her.

Chapter 19

The Ayatollah's Office

After another round of verbal jousting, Anita stepped from her father's presence. His continued abusive language and innuendo left her feeling empty, alone, unloved. Sniffing back a tear, she returned to her duties as household supervisor, a position she neither wanted nor enjoyed. It did, however, give her access to her father's office, and access was exactly what she needed. She fingered the cell phone her contact with the CIA's Young Arab Recruitment and Development Program had given her, and wondered why she had ever agreed to participate. It was ludicrous, but she was desperate. She had to find a way out of her arranged marriage.

With the passing of his wife, the Ayatollah relied heavily on Anita to maintain the image of piety while at the same time, adding to his harem. A loving father he was not, but she was a submissive daughter, hoping one day to win his love. That day never came . . .

***

The following day, Anita returned to her father's unoccupied office. Standing behind the heavy curtains, she watched the servants as they tended the grounds surrounding her father's estate. The house she called home had been in the family for decades. It would have been her uncle's had her father not falsely accused him of blasphemy and ran him out of the country under threat of death.

Heavy footfalls echoed, and her father's booming voice brought her from her musings. She jumped as the office door slammed, leaving her to wonder whether she should come from behind the curtain and excuse herself or listen and learn.

"I trust everything is in order, Rajeed," the Ayatollah said, taking his seat.

An uncomfortable pause stretched into seconds as Anita held her breath. Rajeed continued, "Yes Father, everything is on schedule as planned. As for—"

"—as for the prime minister, he is dragging his feet. I talked with him two weeks ago, and he rebuffed my every attempt to convince him to enforce the Fatwa. Tomorrow I will make one last plea. If he doesn't listen, I want your men ready. I will not stand for any more delays. He either obeys the will of Allah or pays the consequences. Is that understood?"

Anita listened as her brother shuffled. She knew her brother. He too suffered the same abusive treatment as she. It was obvious Rajeed was not given a choice in the matter. Finally he spoke, his voice was raspy and tense. "Yes, Father, they will be ready."

"Good. They will get one clean shot. I want no witnesses, no loose ends, no evidence which might implicate me in all of this. Is that understood?" The Ayatollah's voice crescendoed.

"Yes, yes Father, whatever you say, Father."

The Ayatollah released a string of vulgarity causing Anita's face to grow hot. She'd never heard such language and wished she'd never hear it again. A smoldering hatred for the man sparked in her heart, and she chided herself for allowing it. This was her father, for crying out loud, she shouldn't think such thoughts.

"You are a pathetic excuse for a son. Why can't you be like your brother, so decisive, so committed, so determined. Why Allah let you live, after you were burned so badly, is a mystery to me."

Anita winched. She knew her father despised Rajeed, his displeasure only made worse by her brother's scarred face. To him, Amil could do no wrong, while she and Rajeed could do nothing right. A pair of clutched fists clenched tightly at her sides and she struggled to control her breathing.

***

The following day, Ayatollah Bashera and Rajeed arrived at the front gate of the Administrative Palace. It never ceased to amaze the Ayatollah how the prime minister found a way to squander the nation's wealth on frivolous efforts to live at peace with Israel, their neighbor to the south. If he had his way, he would state Lebanon's assertion that the Blue Line, the UN established demarcation between his country and Israel, be relocated several hundred meters south of where it was. If that didn't happen, he was willing to take it by force.

Inside the prime minister's well-appointed office, the Ayatollah's meeting wasn't going as planned.

"No, Ayatollah Bashera," said Prime Minister Rashad el Zanainullah, digging in his heels, "this will upset the whole economy. We can't have you going around arresting and executing people because they want to change religions."

"Change religions!" he bellowed. "You act like people turning their back on Allah and his prophet is no more serious than changing one's party affiliation from Liberal to Conservative. Allah does not allow his followers to be capricious. He is a jealous god and must be worshiped exclusively. If you don't enforce my Fatwa, I will declare you to be an infidel and have you impeached. If you escape Lebanon with your life, count yourself an extremely lucky man."

The prime minister stood, his fingers pressing into his desk like spikes. His eyes bore into the Ayatollah with pin point accuracy. "Why Mr. Bashera, that sounds very much like a threat. I could have you arrested and thrown into prison for quite a long time." His words fell like the slow release of poison.

The Ayatollah pounced to his feet. Unintimidated, his eyes glowed with unchecked rage. "Yes, and look what that did for the Ayatollah Khomeini. That move by the Shah of Iran only helped Khomeini gain more honor and prestige in the eyes of the people. His followers numbered in the tens of thousands when he was finally released. Do you want that?" he spat.

The prime minister plopped back down in his seat, rubbed his chin with his thumb, and considered his options. After a long pause, he lifted his eyes and said, "Your recommendation has been duly noted."

Knowing the meeting was over, the Ayatollah gathered his robes around his rotund shape and marched out. As the door to the prime minister's office closed, he nodded to Rajeed. "Set our plan into motion."

***

The moonless night sent a chill through Rajeed's body as he and his spotter laid on the roof-top of an abandoned building some three-hundred yards from his target. The Russian made SV-98 sniper rifle, equipped with night scope and silencer, nestled tightly against his shoulder. His breath came in short bursts of condensation as he tried to control his breathing.

With most of his personal body-guards on break, and his wife in bed, Zanainullah's well-established routine of going to his den to catch up on some long over-due reading, played out as expected. The cross-hairs of the powerful sniper scope were fixed on the prime minister's head as Rajeed's gloved finger rested on the trigger guard.

"Target acquired," he said to his spotter.

"Take your shot, and may Allah reward you."

Sweat beaded on Rajeed's upper lip and his heart pounded in his ears. "I can't do it," he whispered.

"What do you mean, you can't do it?" his spotter's words cut through the thick silence. "If you don't your father will kill us both."

Staring blankly Rajeed's world began to swirl out of control. "I . . . I." The gun tumbled from his hands as he blacked out.

Chapter 20

The Literature Table

Mindy sat behind the literature table and watched the students lazily drift by all week. Although she'd prayed for someone to talk with, ever since the Fatwa, the chances of that happening were dwindling. Friday classes were lighter than usual as this was the Muslim's day of worship, but as usual, the university didn't always adhere too strictly with the religious life of the country.

As the less committed students drifted by, it occurred to Mindy how similar they were to their American counterparts. Many wore logo tee-shirts bearing the names of their favorite rock group, or stating a hot button phrase such as, 'We Want Peace!' Most wore tattered jeans, and except for the head covers which all females wore, she couldn't tell the guys from the gals.

Occasionally, someone would stop and pick up a free pen or slow their pace to skim the titles of some of the literature and then pass on. Amana, a tall, slender young lady in her early twenties, stopped and lingered. Mindy sensed her interest as this was not the first time she'd paused to peruse the literature.

"Assalamu alaikum," Mindy said, with a restrained smile.

The young lady took a quick glance over her shoulder, then returned a shy smile, "Wa 'alaykum assalam, and upon you be peace as well."

Following her training, Mindy sat motionless not wanting to appear overly eager. "I've seen you stop by here before, do you have any questions?"

Biting her thumb nail, she released a nervous chuckle. "Yes, I have lots of questions, but I doubt you have the answers." The young lady's honesty was both refreshing and challenging to Mindy.

Mindy inhaled and let it out slowly.

"Well, I may not have all the answers, but I know where to go to find them. You see, my Father is all wise, and he has given me a book which contains his thoughts. When I read what he wrote and, by faith, obey his commands, I gain wisdom and peace."

The young lady shifted her textbooks from one arm to the other, reached down, and touched a brochure. "I have the Qur'an, but it has never given me much hope, let alone wisdom and peace. That is what I need in my life, how can I get such a book?" she said keeping her voice to a whisper.

Sensing the young lady's anxiety, Mindy moved closer. "I can give you a copy, but before I do, I would like to invite you to a study with a group of girls such as yourself, read this book and discuss their questions."

The young lady's face brightened, but her controlled tone let Mindy know she was haunted by fear. "Oh yes, that sounds interesting, when and where do you meet?"

Leaning forward, Mindy placed her elbows on the table and kept her voice low. "We meet on Tuesday evenings at 7:00 p.m. in the Al Mattar Building in room 201. There are no classes going on at that time, and we have permission to meet undisturbed."

"Okay, I'll try to come, but no promises," she said fingering her burqa nervously and looking around.

Standing, Mindy extended a hand. "My name is Mindy, what's yours?"

The young lady's eyes widened. It was obvious to Mindy the girl had never met a westerner and was unsure how to react. Slowly, she reached out, and the two women shook hands. The warm and soft hand she held was that of a well-cultured woman. "My name is Amana," she said, doing a slight curtsy.

"Does Amana have a last name?"

The muscles in Amana's neck tensed. Fingering the hem of her burqa, she said, "I do, but let's just leave it on a first-name basis for now." Then she pulled her head covering lower and stepped away, in a fleeing gait.

As Mindy took her seat, she noticed a man sitting across the concourse wearing dark sunglasses, holding a sagging newspaper.

He stood, straightened his shirt, and stalked away.

Was he looking at me or Amana?

***

Tuesday evening two young college girls, wearing the traditional burqas, sat in room 201 waiting for Mindy to begin the Bible discussion. One by one they'd slipped in and sat down without speaking a word, not a greeting, not a hello, not a word. They were all too fearful, and yet they came. The room where they gathered, though brightly lit, contained a picture of Ayatollah Bashera mounted squarely above the white board. His dark, foreboding glare appeared to follow the movements of the girls as they took their seats. Slogans such as the Islamic creed, Allah is our God, and the Mohammad is his prophet, served as constant reminders that it was very dangerous to be discussing the Bible.

Finally, after the last girl took her seat and lowered her hijab, Mindy spoke, "Good evening girls, thank you for coming. Tonight we have two guests with us. This is Fatemah. She recently moved here from the U.S."

Heads nodded, no one spoke. "And this is Amana. She tells me she has lots of questions."

The wide-eyed group of girls smiled as they assessed Fatemah and Amana.

Samara was the first to break the ice, "Oh don't worry Amana, we all came here with lots of questions," she said, "and we still have questions." The girls giggled, "But, I have learned where to look for the answers."

Impressed by her spiritual growth, Fatemah sat back and let Mindy lead the discussion.

"All right girls, who wants to ask the first question?"

An uncomfortable moment hung in the air like a piñata. Finally, movement caught Mindy's eye as Sumaira tucked her silky black hair behind her ear and spoke. "Oh, I do," she chirped.

Mindy's expression brightened. "Okay, what's your question?"

Clearing her throat, she asked, "Does God hate the Devil?"

Amused by her question, Fatemah resisted the urge to laugh out loud. Instead, she waited for Mindy to answer.

Taking a deep breath, Mindy paused, then spoke, her voice level and sincere. "No, God doesn't hate the Devil, He hates what he is doing to his creation, but he doesn't hate him. God created him to be the most beautiful of all his creatures. But then, he became proud and led a rebellion against his creator. God had to cast him out of Heaven and create a special place of punishment for him and his followers."

The answer seemed to satisfy her.

Chloe shifted uncomfortably as she unraveled a tight ball of paper she'd kept hidden in her burqa for days and read, "Does God have a wife?"

A wave of smiles rippled around the room, breaking the tense moment. As the evening continued Fatemah was amazed with the depth of insight these searching souls possessed. It drove her to prayer.

Finally, it was Amana's turn to ask a question. She licked her lips nervously. "Does God even know I exist?" Her face bore no malice; no prejudice, no hidden agenda, just an honest quest for the truth. A truth that had long been denied them by the mullahs.

Mindy reached over and clasped her hand, her voice thick with emotion, "Oh Amana, He does, and He cares very much for you."

For the next hour, Mindy poured out her heart as she summarized the history of God's care for people. She brought the discussion all the way to the cross.

Without warning, the door burst open, and a group of hooded men stormed the room. Each man wielded a club and shouted obscenities. The girls screamed as the men began beating them.

The leader took special interest in Mindy. His words assaulted her like poisoned darts.

"Why are you here corrupting these girl's minds with your lies? It is against the law of the Holy Qur'an, you infidel." Then he backhanded her sending her across the room.

Fatemah's mind raced as she watched the scene unfold. She feared what price these women might have to pay for their interest in learning the truth about God.

Then, as quickly as it began, it ended. Having taught the girls a lesson, the men backed out of the room, leaving a group of injured, whimpering girls.

As the hushed cries of the beaten girls subsided, a faint humming penetrated Fatemah's consciousness. It began in the corner where Sumaira lay in a tight ball and grew in intensity. It was a familiar tune, one she'd heard children sing in her church in Michigan.

"Jesus loves me this I know, for the Bible tells me so, little ones to Him belong, they are weak, but He is strong."

The girls huddled together and drew strength from one another. One by one they joined the chorus: "Yes, Jesus loves me, Yes, Jesus loves me, Yes, Jesus loves me, the Bible tells me so."

Through her tears, Fatemah saw what was once a weak and convenient faith crystallize into a diamond in the crucible of suffering.

"Miss Mindy," said Amana, "I don't believe, but I want to."

Within a few minutes that classroom turned into a nursery as a child of God was born into the kingdom of God. The girls all hugged each other as the reality of what it meant to suffer for the cause of Christ settled in.

Chapter 21

The Catacombs of Dahr Al Harf

On his way home from yet another boring conference call between John Xavier and the university board of directors, Jared's Volkswagen sputtered and rolled to a stop. As he reached for his cell phone, a yellow taxi pulled up alongside and the driver called out of his window.

"My brother, do you need a ride?" It was the same elderly man who'd taken him to the airport the day he and Fatemah ended their honeymoon.

Frustrated his vehicle was so unreliable; Jared climbed out and got into the taxi. No sooner had he slammed the door, than the driver gunned the engine and took off in the opposite direction.

"Uh sir, I think we're going in the wrong direction," Jared said, after being thrown back against the seat.

Keeping his head straight, the man spoke over the sound of beeping horns and traffic as he sped east. "There is something you must see. So relax and enjoy the ride. By the way, my name is Abbas. You may call me Uncle Abbas, everyone does." The old man gave Jared a sideways glance.

Great, I'm being abducted by the geezer-squad and, of all times, I left my cell phone on the front seat of my junker.

The bitter taste of anger caught in his throat as his driver refused his commands to turn around. Finally, after several pleas, Jared crossed his arms and resigned himself to the fact that he was going to see whatever this old man wanted him to see.

Speeding east out of town, Jared watched the terrain change from urban to residential and from residential to rural. The air freshened as the mountains carried them to higher elevations, and Jared's ears popped. Goose-bumps, like hives, sprang on his exposed flesh. His failed attempts to brush them away only made his journey more unpleasant. With a quick glance over his shoulder, he caught a glimpse of the last towering skyscrapers of Beirut disappear behind a sharp curve. Moments later, they crested one peak and began their descent.

The downward climb was no better. With each turn, Jared feared the car would career over the edge, but instead, the agile vehicle clung to the winding road like a tiger in pursuit of its prey. Another sharp turn and the road ahead plateaued. Abruptly, the car swerved off of the main highway, on to a gravel lane. A kilometer later the gravel ended leaving only a sandy river bed on which to drive. As the taxi fish-tailed, it became obvious to Jared that jumping out now would be unproductive at best and very likely, suicidal.

"I hope you have enjoyed our little excursion. You will have to forgive me for having taken you on such short notice, but I thought you needed to see this with your own eyes." The older man's rich, dark eyes danced with an inner joy as he spoke. "You see, I too am a believer in the one true God; the God of Abraham, Isaac and Jacob. I worship the one who revealed himself as a servant, a lamb, a sacrifice to take away the sin of the world. His name is Yeshiva Adoni Elohim." He smiled with a warm glow.

"I have been living here in Lebanon for nearly thirty years, and have been helping the persecuted church for longer than that. Ever since I heard on the television that you were here to establish a, safe place, as you call it, I knew what you were up to. But you, my son, are thinking too small. I have been by your Harbor House. You have no idea how many persecuted believers there are and how many more are coming. I do." His voice grew thick with a new intensity. "I have been serving these dear people for years; they are my people."

The older gentleman brought the taxi to a halt in front of a rock wall. He quickly got out and stretched. Guessing they'd reached their destination, Jared opened his door and unfolded himself.

"Come . . . follow me," the older man gestured with unusual vitality.

Not knowing whether to believe him or not, Jared complied. His feet followed a well-worn path which led them past a thorn bush. A branch reached out and caught Jared by the arm causing him to winch as it bit into his flesh. With care, he untangled himself from its grip and wiped a trickle of blood from his perforated flesh.

"Be careful of the thorn bush," Uncle Abbas called over his shoulder.

Jared grimaced at his latent warning and quickened his step to catch up. Getting lost in such a wild environment was not an option.

Pausing at a small opening in the mountain wall, Uncle Abbas bowed at the waist and invited him to follow. Jared was taken aback by the temperature change. In a moment, they'd gone from the hot desert to a cool damp cave. It was dark, and it took Jared a moment for his eyes to adjust.

"Follow me," echoed the kind old man's voice as he padded down a long dark passageway. Ahead, Jared noticed lights flickering off the moist walls. The pungent aroma of human waste assaulted his nose, and caused his eyes to water.

"Sorry about the conditions down here. I've been meaning to work on the plumbing for a while now," Uncle Abbas called over his shoulder.

The constant dripping of condensation from the ceiling kept rhythm with each plodding step the older man took. He raised his hand, signaling they'd reached the end of their journey.

"What is this place?" Jared asked, his breath coming in ghostly clouds of condensation.

The elderly man spoke as if this were hallowed ground. "This is the Catacombs of Dahr Al Harf."

"You said these are your people, so, where are they?"

Uncle Abbas didn't answer Jared's question, rather, he spoke a sentence in Arabic and from the dark passages emerged frightened women holding raggedly dressed children. Most of them were in the early stages of starvation. Some leaned upon homemade crutches, while others approached him with missing limbs, teeth, eyes. Yet, at the sound of Uncle Abbas' voice Jared heard laughter.

An elderly man stepped up and greeted Uncle Abbas with the traditional kiss on both cheeks.

"What? No food my brother, just another refugee?" eyeing Jared suspiciously, he continued. "He certainly doesn't look like he suffered much for the cause of our Lord."

Jared's heart smote his conscience like a hammer on an anvil. No, he'd not suffered much for the cause of Christ. The more he thought about it, he'd not suffered at all. He wondered if the average Christian living in America could endure what these people had without losing their faith.

Glancing around at the faces, Jared stepped back. "Uncle Abbas, is this all there is, are there not any young men?"

Uncle Abbas surveyed his flock. The lines around his eyes deepened. "I have other flocks that you know not of, but these are they who have come through the tribulation."

Jared knew that he spoke metaphorically, but the point was all the more poignant. These were the survivors, the ones who escaped the persecution, and yet they suffer a persecution of deprivation, loneliness and of fear.

Leading Jared deeper into the chamber, Uncle Abbas continued his history lesson. "Over the centuries, these catacombs have been home to literally hundreds of believers who have fled here for refuge. Sometimes the suffering is less, sometimes the suffering is more, but always it is here. Here within the safety of the shadow of God's wings we find help in the times of trouble."

Abbas spoke in such gentle tones, no bitterness, no malice, no fear.

Taking a child in his arms, he stroked his face saying, "I do as much as I can to bring food and medical supplies, but I wanted to bring you here, so you could see with your own eyes the vast need of the persecuted church. It is like this," he waved his calloused hand around the room. "It might not be in catacombs, but it is like this all over the world with the exception of your country. You need to get the word out. Christians are being persecuted; they are suffering, and yes, dying for the cause of Christ. You must tell them." His throat closed with emotion.

Jared leaned against the slick walls, its icy surface biting into his thin garment. He'd seen poverty and suffering before, but none as senseless as this.

"What can I do?"

Resting his weight on an old aluminum chair, the older man's face darkened. "Pray for them, tell their stories. Let the church know that when one part of the body suffers, the whole body suffers."

"I don't know how, but I will try. Where can I start?" his hands extended.

With a steady gaze that sent a chill through Jared's heart, he replied, "You can begin by listening to their stories."

A rustling began in the back of the crowd as a young boy pushed through. At last, he broke into the inner circle and bounded toward Jared. "Mister, thank you for saving me," he cried, nearly knocking the wind out of him.

"You, you're the boy, my wife and I helped," Jared said, holding him back and looking him over.

"Yes, and if you hadn't, I would have been killed for sure." Then he slung his arms around Jared's neck as tears scalded his cheeks.

Uncle Abbas guided Jared to an old metal chair. Its cold, hard surface groaned under his weight. For the next two hours, Jared listened and documented the heart-wrenching stories of husbands being shot, sons beheaded, daughters raped and abused. The stories had a common thread, one of great suffering, of courage, of grace. Not one of the martyrs asked for mercy or recanted. They stood and took their punishment with a song or a prayer on their lips.

By the time they'd finished telling their stories, Jared's notes were blotched with tears, but he was more determined than ever to make the Harbor House a success.

Standing amid his flock, Uncle Abbas lifted his scrawny hands in prayer for God's provision and protection to be upon them.

It was in the small hours of the morning when they arrived in Beirut, and a blanket of stars watched as the old taxi rolled to a stop. "How can I reach you in the future Uncle Abbas?" Jared asked as he pushed himself out of the taxi.

"Oh you needn't worry about that, I can find you quicker than you can find me. But if you really need to find me, just pray. God will lead me right to you."

***

The old taxi darted around a corner, leaving Jared alone with his thoughts. Where would he ever start such a monumental task of telling the world about the persecuted church? With resignation, he determined to begin by going to the television station and doing an interview. Nevertheless, first, he needed something to quiet the gnawing hunger. In his rush to bring Jared home, Uncle Abbas neglected to stop for food, and he was famished, not to mention his need of sleep. His heart tugged at his conscience, and he rebuked himself for longing for the comforts of a warm bed, knowing so many slept on tattered blankets in the heart of the earth.

Jared pushed open his car door and squeezed in. To his amazement, the old clunker started with one try. Praying that it would get him home, he put it in gear and nursed it along the deserted streets. When he stepped through the door of the Harbor House, he found a nervous wife and three giggling university girls.

***

Since they were no longer welcome on campus and feared going home, Fatemah had brought them to the Harbor House. It did not take them long to settle in, shower, and change. After Fatemah had heated up a quick dinner they'd forgotten their immediate troubles and were sitting on the couch discussing the Bible when Jared came in. One look from Jared and the girls scattered like a bevy of quail. Grabbing their robes, they dashed to the bedroom laughing like hyenas while Fatemah ran into her husband's arms.

"Jared, where were you? I've been so worried," she asked, her face buried in his chest. For a moment, he held her close, thanking God for keeping him safe.

She pulled back and kissed him warmly.

"By the looks of it, I should have been worried about you. What happened?" his voice etched with concern.

Fatemah guided him to the living room and took a seat. She patted the place next to her, inviting Jared to sit. Needing no invitation, Jared plopped down, his eyes scanning the cuts and bruises on Fatemah's face.

After a brief explanation, Fatemah concluded her narrative. Jared lifted his hand and gently wiped the tears coursing down her cheeks. "I wish I'd been there, I could have stopped them."

Releasing a heavy sigh, Fatemah splashed away the remaining tears with her eyelids. "Yes, you may have, but just think of what God did instead. He brought Amana to himself through adversity." Leaning back she called, "Girls, there is someone here, I'd like for you to meet."

Sheepishly, the three girls emerged from the bedroom, heads covered, eyes wide.

"Jared, these are our first guests," she said with flair. "This is Chloe, and you remember Sumaira."

Jared smiled and nodded at the girls. They were visibly uncomfortable, wearing their new bath robes.

"And this is Amana, the newest member of our little family." Her face beamed as she spoke.

Without thinking, Jared stood with outstretched arms and pulled Amana close, "Praise the Lord. I am so happy for you." A moment later, he was encircled with Fatemah and the other girls, rejoicing.

"What about you, Jared?" Fatemah asked when they'd finished. He related the story about Uncle Abbas and the refugee camp in the mountains. "I just can't believe it. What happened to them, on a smaller scale, has happened here on the campus of LIU."

"You know these girls cannot go back to school, don't you, Jared?" Fatemah asked while fixing him a plate of food.

Nodding, "Yes, I would imagine their families have already been notified. Who knew that the government would call for a Fatwa as soon as we arrived in Lebanon? I don't think the authorities will take too kindly to us giving refuge to converts to Christianity, so we need to come up with a plan pretty quickly."

"Should you call Mr. Xavier?" Fatemah questioned.

Jared took a seat at the table and watched the seconds count down on the microwave. The sudden ding brought him from his musings. Fatemah slid a warm plate of meatloaf, mashed potatoes, and green beans in front of him. The aroma triggered his senses, and he remembered how hungry he was. After a lengthy prayer of thanks, he glanced up and looked around. "Where are the girls?" he enquired, while at the same time scooping up a fork of meatloaf.

Fatemah tiptoed into the living room, stretched on the couches were three tired girls. Rather than each sleeping in separate bed rooms, they chose to spread out in the living room.

"We'd better keep our voices down. We have some pretty tired girls in there."

Finished with his dinner, he dabbed his mouth with a napkin, and tried to relax. "Now, where were we, oh yes, you asked me a question."

The ticking wall clock marked time as Fatemah collected her thoughts. "I remember. Should you call Mr. Xavier?"

The air was thick with tension as Jared pondered his options. Finally, he released a frustrated breath. "Yeah, I suppose so. But I sure don't look forward to how he's going to react."

Chapter 22

The Prime Minister's Residence

Three weeks after the assassination, the police, acting on an anonymous tip, discovered the grizzly remains of a body on the roof of an abandoned building. Alongside the body, they found a Russian made sniper rifle and a suicide note. The alleged shooter was identified as Raul Mahmoud el Serif, a former Syrian army soldier who, according to the records, was a deserter. No further action was taken.

Following the memorial service, in which Amil, his favorite son was conspicuously absent, the vice-prime minister called for an emergency meeting with the parliament. With Prime Minister Zanainullah out of the way, Ayatollah Bashera pushed passed his rival and convinced the majority of the parliament to install him as the new leader of Lebanon. When the votes were counted, his name was at the top. Now he sat behind the former prime minister's expansive desk chatting with Prince Saud Al Rafsanjani of the United Arab Emirates.

"Yes, my friend, I plan on making it a priority. Yes, a state visit is already in the works." He paused to let the prince jabber for a moment before cutting him off. "You must excuse me, my brother, I have the Prime Minister of Turkey on the line. Yes, I'll be in touch, thank you." He slammed the phone down.

"Saudis," he cursed. "what's next?" he asked his personal aid.

Glancing down at his notes, he shifted uncomfortably. "Sir, it's the matter of the Fatwa. How far do you want to take it?"

The Ayatollah pounded the desk with the palm of his hand. "I insist the parliament move as quickly as possible and enact it as a national moratorium. Is that clear enough?"

The white-lipped aid backed away, "Yes, my lord, as you say my lord," he said, bowing. "Oh, and Rajeed is in the foyer, shall I send him in?"

"Yes, send him in." His voice went flat.

Taking small steps, Rajeed quietly entered his father's posh office. "I like what you've done to the place," he said, a crooked smile parted his lips."

"What? I haven't done anything except clean up the prime minister's blood."

"That's what I meant," he said as he slouched into a cushioned seat and propped his feet on the marbled coffee table. "I understand you have a job for me."

Bashera nodded, "Yes, I've sent a team ahead of you to do the dirty work. You will rendezvous with them in an abandoned hanger in the U.S. It's near an obscure little town called New Castle, Delaware. The warehouse is on the Bellanca Airfield. No one will even notice you if you keep a low profile. This is on a need to know basis, so you needn't ask any of your stupid questions. But just remember, Allah is our Lord, the Quran is our guide, and Jihad is our way." He slid a large manila envelope across his desk.

Rajeed swallowed hard and pushed himself up from his seat. Cautiously, he crossed the Persian carpet to pick up his instructions. Retaking his seat, he spread out its contents on the coffee table. A wicked grin creased his face. "I think I'm going to enjoy this job even better than the last one. When do I leave?"

"Tomorrow, report to the naval base. From there you will be transported by helicopter to a Russian sub. They'll do the rest. In the meantime, study those schematics until you can follow the instructions with your eyes shut. Any variation from the wiring and you will blow yourself to kingdom come. I want you to coordinate your activities with Amil's. Here," handing him a cell phone, "this satellite phone is equipped with an encrypted direct line to Amil. Use it once everything is in place. Together you will strike at the heart of the Great Satan. I, on the other hand, will be working out y own plans for the Little Satan." He turned his attention to a stack of papers indicating that the conversation was over. "Now go," he ordered. His voice bore no emotion, no love, or hatred, just finality.

Rajeed stood and crossed the floor. He placed his hand on the doorknob, and paused. He yearned to say something, to hear something; a good-bye, and I love you, anything—Nothing.

Squaring his shoulders, he stepped from his father's office. A single tear coursed down his scarred cheek and he bit back a halting breath.

Chapter 23

Jared's Home Office

Jared stepped into his home office and closed the door, shutting off the constant chatter of female voices. This was uncharted territory for him. He'd gone from one female, to two, with the addition of Anita, to five, all talking at the same time. He needed a man's den, a place to think, to pray. The closest thing he could find was his office.

Even though this was his and Fatemah's dream, having a Fatwa hanging over their heads was not. How long could he hide these new converts before they would be discovered? It would only be a matter of time. Inspecting his fingers for a fingernail he hadn't chewed to a nub, he heaved a heavy sigh.

Reluctantly, he lifted the phone from its cradle and dialed Mr. Xavier's number. While he waited for the line to connect, he prayed for God's wisdom. There was one thing he was glad to report, he'd made contact with a fellow believer who owned a fishing trawler. The captain regularly crosses Lebanon's sea boundary into international waters in order to take clients deep-sea fishing. Many of his clients were rich men who had interests in things outside of Lebanon.

The phone on John's desk awakened and he answered it on the first ring.

"Hello," his voice carried a light tone.

"Were you expecting someone else?" Jared kidded.

"Oh, no, no. I was just, well, yes I kinda thought it was your old buddy Jimbo."

Jared snapped to attention, his heart quickened, "Jimbo? Now why would you be talking with him?"

An uncomfortable silence stood between the two men, and Jared wondered if he didn't detect a slight hesitation in his boss's voice.

"Well, we had a few loose ends to clean up after he left Michigan."

Not convinced, Jared twisted the phone cord between his fingers and pressed ahead anyway, "Do you have a minute?"

"Yes, Jared, what's on your mind?"

Cradling the phone on his shoulder, he picked up a pencil and prepared to take notes. He was sure Fatemah would want to know everything. "I've got a bit of a situation."

"Oh? What kind of situation?"

Jared scratched the back of his neck with his other hand. A nervous habit he'd had for so long, he was unaware he did it. "As you know, we've established the hostel called the Harbor House—"

"Yes, and how's that working out?"

"Fine sir, I mean, we finally have some guests."

"Good, good, so what's the problem?" Xavier's voice resonated through the connection.

"Well, the problem is," he paused to choose the right words, "The problem is, Lebanon has declared a Fatwa, a moratorium on evangelistic activities. Of course we are not engaged in that, but others are, and these new converts are outcasts from Muslim society."

John's voice grew ominous. "I think I know where you're going with this. You're telling me, you have a couple of people who converted to Christianity and have become *persona non grata* you might say?"

Nodding into the phone, Jared pinched the skin between his eyes. "Three, to be exact, and with this Fatwa, they are no longer safe in the country."

Jared hesitated as Fatemah entered his office. His raised index finger, stopping the question he knew was coming. Clearing his throat, Jared pressed the speaker phone button. "You remember your offer to do anything?"

The chair squeaked as Mr. Xavier leaned forward. "Yes?"

"I seem to recall you saying something about owning a yacht. Do you still?"

"Why yes. The *Sea Queen* and boy is she a beauty. She's a 42 foot cruiser, sleeps six, and comes complete with a crew of three. I keep it docked in, uh, well, let's say I keep it fueled and ready. What do you have in mind?"

Fatemah's eyebrows rose, widening her almond-shaped eyes. "Go ahead, ask him," she whispered, nudging him forward.

"Well, I was thinking. There is a captain of a fishing trawler, and he says he'd like to meet your skipper."

For a moment, time seemed to pass at a snail's pace, as Jared waited for an answer.

"Are you still there, John?"

John coughed into the receiver, "Uh, yes, let me make a few calls and get back with you on that." His voice sounded distracted.

***

The date, November 27th nearly jumped from the calendar, as the sudden realization struck Fatemah. She'd practically missed Thanksgiving. Without the usual television and radio commercials announcing Black Friday sales events, the holiday nearly escaped her. Rather than attempt to buy a turkey, Fatemah, Anita, and the girls combined their cooking skills and created a feast of their own. With only a day to prepare, they decided to invite the Owens and Habib to the festivities as well.

When Jared returned home from running a last errand, he was greeted with the aroma of fresh-baked bread, steamed vegetables, and sweet-potato pie. Except for the Owens, none of them had ever celebrated the traditional Thanksgiving dinner. Jared took it upon himself to give a brief history lesson along with a short message about thankfulness.

After Jared finished reading a handwritten prayer, the festivities began. Within minutes, the brightly lit room was filled with chatter, covering a variety of topics from local politics to religion to sports.

By the time it ended, Jared leaned back, and rubbed his swollen belly. "Now all we need is a football game."

"I brought a soccer ball. Do you want to play?" Habib asked, his face bright with anticipation.

With a groan, Jared pushed his legs under himself and stood, "No, what I meant was watch a football game. You know, Dallas Cowboys and the Pittsburgh Steelers? That kind of football."

Rick stepped from the dining room and returned with his laptop, "I think I can solve the problem. I just need an HTML cable, and we can watch it over the Internet."

An interested glint formed in Habib's eyes. "You can get that here?"

With a condescending gaze, Rick booted up his computer. "We don't live in the stone-age, Habib. This is the twenty-first century, and I happen to be a card-carrying computer geek."

Habib appeared crestfallen, and he shrank back.

"I need volunteers to clean up. Any takers?" Fatemah asked, wiping her hands on a dish towel.

"I'll do it, Miss Fatemah, you've done enough," Anita said. Her boundless energy amazed even the most athletic in the group.

"I'll help too," Habib chimed. He gave Rick a sideways glance, not interested in the American game.

Fatemah nodded knowingly and handed him a stack of dirty dishes. "Why am I not surprised," she said, a wry smile tugged at the corners of her mouth.

Jutting his chin, Habib followed Anita to the kitchen.

***

"So what do you think of Thanksgiving? Isn't it a wonderful tradition?" Anita asked Habib, as she loaded the dish washer.

Handing her a freshly rinsed dish, Habib's head bobbed with enthusiasm, "I love it, it's a lot more meaningful than Ramadan. I would rather be feasting than fasting any day."

Anita released a throaty chuckle. "Well, I like the focus on being thankful for God's blessings rather than on the selfishness of the society we live in."

For a moment, Habib held her gaze with a quizzical expression. "I guess you're right. Maybe someday I will be a believer and can celebrate this tradition, too," he sputtered.

An uncomfortable lull filled the kitchen. In the other room, Jared and Rick screamed at the large screen TV making the moment stretch into minutes.

"Habib, what are you saying? I thought you were already a believer, why didn't you tell me?" Anita asked, her hand resting on her hip.

Caught off guard, Habib felt streaks of heat creep up his neck. The veins of his temples pulsed as the pressure mounted. "I thought you knew."

"Knew what? That you're a fake, a hypocrite, a, a liar?" her words flew at him like a thousand angry bees.

Habib slumped into a kitchen chair as if he'd been deflated. *Why the vitriol, the anger, the rejection? Can't I have my beliefs or lack of beliefs and still be friends?* His mind spun out of control.

Anita perched herself on the kitchen counter. She could see she'd hurt him, hurt him bad. It was her way of getting through the crusty outer shell of people. It worked with her father, but now she was beginning to doubt.

"Uh, I guess I came on a bit strong, Habib, I'm sorry."

Suddenly a cheer from the other room broke the tense moment. Lifting his eyes from the tile floor, Habib pushed out a weak smile. "Do you always treat the people you like, like you hate them?"

Her eyelids rose like the venetian blinds, and she blinked. "You're right. I don't know why I do that. I guess I got it from my father. Only he treats everyone that way, whether he likes them or not."

Habib ran his fingers through his black curls. "Which is it with me? Do you like me or hate me?"

Anita jumped down from the counter, her chin buried in her chest. Her eyes searched the floor, looking for a hole to crawl in. "I'm trying to be good person like Miss Fatemah and Mr. Jared, but it's hard. You have been so sweet to me, and I treated you badly. I'm sorry." Her voice softened to a whisper.

Habib took her by the hand and lifted her chin with his fingers. "The fact that you acknowledged you're wrong will go a long way toward me becoming a believer."

A labored breath escaped Anita's lungs, and she blinked away his stare. "We'd better hurry up, or everyone will think we eloped."

"Eloped? What does that mean?"

A rush of movement caught his eye as the three college girls breezed in, seeking the desserts. Turning on his heels, Habib beat a hasty retreat. "The pies are in the refrigerator," he coughed out.

Anita giggled, an impish twinkle flashed in her almond eyes. "Let's go," she said, taking him by the hand.

"Whoa, not before I get a slice of that pumpkin pie." He scooped out a piece of pie and forked a large portion into his mouth. "Umm, this is still warm," he said, savoring the moment.

Anita grabbed a plate, and scooped out a piece and slathered it with Ready-Whip, before leaving.

"What's that?" Habib asked, eying her trophy.

"Oh nothing," she said, playfully, and tugged him to the living room.

Chapter 24

The Prime Minister's Office

Light filtered through the glass panes and painted octagonal shapes on the Persian carpets strewn across the prime minister's office. An over-size desk occupied the center of the room, surrounded by plush, wing-backed chairs, mahogany end-tables, and large parlor palms. Defused light from the recessed fixtures gave the room its soft illumination.

Behind the presidential desk sat Abdullah Bashera, his rotund form pressed into the chair. "Have you heard from Amil?" the president of Iran asked over a secure satellite phone.

Bashera fingered the pen he'd been using to write some of his thoughts. "Yes, I spoke with him earlier today. He is a UN Diplomatic Attaché to the Head of the Greenpeace Movement. I am quite proud of him. He will do a great work for Allah."

"Are we on schedule?" the Iranian president pressed.

The prime minister leaned forward; his voice took on a new tone. "But of course. We are actually somewhat ahead of schedule. Everything is under control." Bashera didn't like being questioned by the Iranian president. Even though he was his only ally in the region, he hated someone looking over his shoulder.

"How are your nuclear ambitions coming along?" Bashera asked, turning the conversation around.

Without missing a beat, the Iranian president said, "We have been hampered slightly by UN inspectors and the international sanctions, but we are working around them," keeping his voice even.

Squeezing the phone closer, the prime minister continued. "Oh? Have you been a naughty boy and got some uranium from the Paks?"

"No, you fool. I wouldn't trust the Pakistanis to deliver a pizza, let alone a clandestine shipment of nuclear material. No, I have made arrangements with the North Chinese."

Bashera shifted his eyes toward the curtain. *Was that movement?* He blinked, and it stopped.

"Isn't it rather dangerous to transport uranium by freighter across the open seas? You know, with the naval blockade and all."

"Ah hum," the president said, clearing his throat. "You really are rather naive aren't you, Bashera? Of course I'm not shipping across the open sea. The U.S., the Israelis, and the Brits would intercept them before they left the China Sea. No, I prefer the old-fashioned way; to smuggle it cross country using the ancient old salt routes and in small quantities. It's taking somewhat longer to acquire it, but it's much safer by far."

"When will you have a nuclear warhead ready?" Bashera asked, trying to recover the initiative.

"We are close, my friend, very close, say sometime after the Eid al-Adha holiday? By then we will be ready to strike. So tell me, Bashera, what of your other son, what is his name?"

"Rajeed, his name is Rajeed. I have also sent him on a mission of great importance," he said with a conspiratorial tone in his voice.

"And that is?"

Sweat beaded on the prime minister's forehead. He'd not heard from Rajeed since he departed and the only way he knew he'd arrived, was the fact that the Russians told him they delivered their package. Frankly, he was worried.

"Let's just say, all the pieces to the puzzle are in place."

"And what of the rest of your brilliant plan, Bashera?" sounding dubious.

"I have men embedded in Israeli military instillations along their northern-most border between Israel and Lebanon as we speak. Within hours of Eid al-Adha, they will begin firing upon our cities to the south. We will have no choice but to protect ourselves against the Zionists. That is, of course, if you are ready."

"I said, we will be ready," his tones growing louder over the secure line. "But I need assurances that the Great Satan will be rendered impotent, Abdullah. Do you hear me?"

Sinking deeper into his seat, the prime minister glared at the dish of dates. "By the time my sons have completed their missions, the Great Satan will be totally helpless. You will then be able to move throughout the Middle East with impunity."

Satisfied, the president of Iran said, "Alhamdulillah, praise Allah."

Abdullah replaced the phone to its cradle and released a slow breath. His plan would work flawlessly, it had to. He had the element of surprise, and soon he'd have the world's support. All he needed was a few more hours, and he'd have the world eating out of his hand.

Again, movement drew his attention and he glanced to the window. The heavy curtain swayed slightly, then his phone rang.

***

The heavy curtain moved as Anita's knees buckled, but she quickly recovered. She needed to use the lady's room so badly, all she could do was to hold her breathe and try to relax. Her duties had taken her inside her father's office to inspect it when he stepped in to take the call from the president of Iran. Driven by fear and frozen by panic, she remained out of sight, not knowing whether she should run or stay hidden. She chose the latter.

Her heart pounded as she listened to her father plotting against America, Israel, and against her own country. Somehow, she had to stay alive long enough to get the word out.

She prayed to Allah, but heard nothing! But what she did hear was enough to get her killed.

From her side of the curtain, she listened to her father moving things around on his massive desk. Since his conversation with the president of Iran, he'd made and received several very sensitive phone calls. All would be considered State Secrets. It would only be a matter of time before she would have to give up her hiding place, or she would be discovered by security.

Ever since she went to work for the Russells, Fatemah had been talking with her about God's plan of salvation. She told her story after story about God's love and provision until, like a huge jigsaw puzzle, it took shape. It became obvious to Anita that Jesus Christ was the center of the picture. Bowing her head, she began to pray.

Dear Jesus, I know I have no right to come to you. I am a Muslim. For fifteen years I have worshiped Allah, but I have come to realize that he is no god, that you are the one true and living God. Beside you, there is no other. Miss Fatemah told me you are the Way, the Truth and the Life. She read from your holy word and said, all who come to you, you will in no way cast out. So here I am, a sinful, Muslim girl who desperately needs you. I accept what you've done for me on the cross; that you died for me according to the scripture, and you rose again, according to your Word. I now reject my former religion in exchange for a personal relationship with you, my Lord and Savior. I now turn my life over to your control in Jesus' name, amen.

Anita stood, wondering what might happen next. Would she hear bells ringing, angels singing, lights flashing? She certainly hoped not, at least not now.

Long moments stretched into an hour as marked by the ticking of a distant clock. Her need for relief grew to the point of desperation. *Lord Jesus? I know I just talked with you, and I have a big favor to ask. Would you help me?* she pleaded.

A great peace washed over her, and she knew God answered her prayer; even the physical need for relief subsided. In the moments which followed, she waited, listening. It suddenly dawned on her; the rough sawing which rose and fell was her father's snoring.

Holding her breath, she peeked around the curtain. To her surprise, he sat back, his head cocked in an uncomfortable position, his mouth gaped open—he was in a deep sleep. He'd been up most of the night strategizing and had dozed off between phone calls.

Still needing to use the lady's room, Anita left the relative safety of the curtain and tip-toed across the heavily carpeted floor. A flash of motion caught her eye, and she froze in her tracks. Her heart pounded like a hammer on an anvil, and sweat beaded on her forehead. Her father shifted in his plush chair, but once again resumed snoring. Inching ever so close, she reached the door. It was closed and locked on the inside.

With trembling fingers, she gently turned the dead bolt and eased the door open.

Squeak.

She stood like a wooden Indian, her heart pounding. Eyes wide, she glanced over her shoulder. Her father shifted in his chair and resumed his snoring. Pinching her lips tighter, Anita pulled the door open, and quietly stepped into the dimly lit hallway. Fingers against the frame, she eased it shut. Her lungs screamed for oxygen, and she realize she'd stopped breathing.

***

Knowing the security cameras monitored all of the halls, and that it would be impossible to avoid being seen, Anita scooped up a stack of paper and casually walked from room to room as if she had business to attend to. After a quick visit to the lady's room, she skipped down the stairs past the security desk and almost outside.

"Hold it right there, young lady." Bile crept up her throat, and she swallowed hard, eyes wide as the moon.

"Miss Bashera."

Her legs turned to water. Convinced the guard could hear her pounding heart, she turned and took a shaky step to the counter. "Yes sir?" her voice laced with fear.

"You forgot to sign out." The guard said, tauntingly, and pushed a clipboard in her direction.

The slight tremor from the adrenalin rush kept her fingers from controlling the pen. The distinct feeling of being watched made her skin crawl, and she looked up. A pair of lust-filled eyes met hers. The air in her lungs turned cold, and she stepped back.

"May I go now?" her voice husky with emotion.

The guard, a burly character with a bad temper and breath to match, stood, eyes stabbing in all directions. Seeing no one, he came around the desk and lunged for her.

"Not before you give me what I want," he said, his face growing dark with lust.

Anita skipped to her left as he grabbed for her. Missing, he cursed and lunged for her again. This time his hand found flesh and closed around her slender arm like a vice.

"Ouch, you're hurting me. Let me go or I'll tell my father," she sputtered.

"And what? That you came on to me?" His tone mocked her every word.

With brute force, he swung her around like a rag doll. But as his arm closed around her, she dipped her head and sank her teeth into his arm. The man bellowed like a wounded cow. As the bitter taste of iron stung her tongue, she tried to think of an escape. The more he squirmed, the deeper her teeth sunk. Finally, he shook her off like a viper. With fire in his eyes he grabbed her again, but before he could stop her, she kneed him in the groin. He groaned and fell to the floor. A moment later, Anita dashed through the service door on the lower floor and slipped out into the night, her skin slick with sweat.

***

A gentle rain had settled over Beirut making its streets shimmer with a golden glow. In the distance, a lone figure emerged through the haze, it was Anita. Her heavy breathing kept syncopated rhythm as her feet slapped on the wet pavement. She dashed from one street to the next, trying to put as much distance as possible between her and the palace. Pausing only to see if she was being followed, Anita leaned heavily on a signpost, her lungs screaming for relief. Willing herself forward, she forced her legs to obey.

She turned one corner and dashed behind a large date tree. A moment later, a car raced past her, its headlights cut narrow beams through the dense air. Despite her physical condition as a long-distance runner in high school, her ribs ached with exhaustion, and her legs gave way.

Gulping for air, like a fish out of water, she pulled a cell phone from her pocket and dialed a number. She waited for it to connect. When prompted, she punched in the code she'd memorized. A voice came on the line, "Read any good books lately?"

"Goldie Locks," she answered, her mouth dry as leaves.

"One moment please." The secure line went silent.

"Anita?"

"Yes, it's me. Help!" Her throat closed with a whimper.

The man's voice grew tense. "Okay, okay, we've got a fix on your location, how can we help you?"

"I think I'm being followed. I have some information."

"Okay, what is it?"

The car which drove past her made an abrupt U-turn and reappeared in the distance. She'd been spotted. Jumping to her feet, she scampered down an alley. "I only have a minute," she said in a dead run.

The muzzle of a gun extended, and a bullet exploded from its barrel barely missing her. It struck the wall sending chips of brick in her direction.

"What was that?" the voice intensified.

"Someone's shooting at me. Now listen, Greenpeace, the hit will happen—"

Anita stumbled over a trash can sending the cell phone skittering across the alley. She dove into a vacant building just as the car raced past.

Cautiously, she peeked out through a boarded window, the phone lay across the alley. It had been crushed under the wheels of the car.

Chapter 25

Jimbo's Apartment

The annoying ring of Jimbo's phone brought him to a sitting position. Muttering under his breath, he crossed his dingy bedroom and lifted the phone from its cradle.

"Hello?" irritation seeping through his one-word response.

"Jimbo, I just got a call from our asset in Beirut," John Xavier said, his voice etched with concern.

Lowering himself into a tattered seat that had seen too many bottoms, Jimbo rubbed the sleep from his eyes. "Oh? And what did your asset say?"

"That's just it, she, ur, my contact is a girl, but that's all I'm telling you."

A grin parted Jimbo's lips, "So what did *she* say?"

Xavier paused, then continued. "I'll play it for you, maybe you can make heads or tails out of it."

The CIA mid-west director clicked the play button on his computer, and the phone call replayed.

"Anita?"

"Yes, it's me. Help."

"Okay, okay, we've got a fix on your location, how can we help you?"

"I think I'm being followed. I have some information."

"Okay, what is it?"

A loud pop sounded, followed by heavy breathing.

The voice returned. "Greenpeace, the hit will happen—"

Wheels screeched and the phone clattered to the pavement, then went dead.

Jimbo swiped his hand over his face, "It sounds like your girl, Anita, was in a bit of a tight squeeze. Are you sure it was a good idea to put her in such a dangerous position?"

"I didn't, she came to us," Xavier fired back. "I can't tell you how, but just know, she volunteered for the job. We gave her a crash course, and she took it from there. So what do you make of her statement?"

Leaning back, Jimbo let the scene replay in his mind. "First of all, we don't even know it she's telling the truth. She could be using us to get out of the country."

"I've considered that. He played the last statement again . . . "Greenpeace, the hit will happen—"

"I think she was going to repeat the word, 'Greenpeace.'" Jimbo said. "A hit, that's an assassination, it involves the Greenpeace Movement. That's what I think."

"Let me check something," John said, punching in code words for the itinerary of the Greenpeace Movement. "I see there is a summit between the president of the United States, NOAA, and the Greenpeace Movement listed on their itineraries."

"When, where?"

"Let me see here," Xavier said, scrolling down the screen. "The *when* is not set, but the *where* is. That's where you're going."

"Where might that be?"

"Pack for cold weather, you're going to Mackinaw Island . . . The Grand Hotel."

***

A taxi pulled up alongside the slight figure of Anita as she ran bare-foot down the street. Shivering, Anita kept running.

"Do you need a ride my child?" said the kindly old man.

Anita slowed her pace and glanced down. It was Uncle Abbas. "Oh yes, Uncle Abbas, I am so scared," her words came in clipped phrases.

He gave her a reassuring smile. "Hop in. Let me guess, you were going to the Harbor House, but no one was home. Am I not correct?"

Still breathing hard, Anita nodded. "Yes I was, but how did you know? And why were you driving down this street? Are you clairvoyant?"

"No, my daughter, I am not, but I have my ways of knowing these things. Plus, I am in touch with the God who knows everything. When he speaks . . . I obey."

"Well you are right. I need to get to the Rick and Mindy's house quickly. I'm in big trouble," grabbing the door handle and yanking it open. An unearthly squeak sent a shiver up Anita's spine, and the elderly man gave her an apologetic smile.

"No problem is too big for my God. I don't need to know what it is, but God is in control, and he knows exactly what to do. Let us pray and ask Him for direction."

Anita, in her naiveté, expected the old man to pull over, get out and kneel toward Mecca. Instead, he began "Now Lord, you know the needs of this poor child. You know her resting places, and you know her risings. You understand her thoughts afar off. You encircle her path and are acquainted with all of her ways. Now would you give your child an answer of peace and guide her with the skillfulness of your eyes. In Jesus' name, amen."

Hand to her chest and still breathing hard, Anita looked around for someone to answer. *No one in a Muslim country prays in that name, not unless you are suicidal. We will see if God really does answer prayer.*

Minutes later, the old taxi rolled up in front of the Owens' apartment. "How did you know where the Owens lived? I didn't tell you."

"Oh, that's simple. I've been here before."

Eying him dubiously, Anita thanked him as she got out. With a wave, he disappeared into the night.

Chapter 26

The Golan Heights

The cold, moonless night in November gave Colonel Kamil Abu Hanifa and his team of commandos the opportunity they needed to penetrate the Israeli border. Their mission, to infiltrate the military base on the Golan Heights and commandeer their guns, went flawlessly.

Watch commander, Colonel Yoshi Shimon, sensed something was wrong. The movements of the new recruits under his command seemed out of place. He couldn't put his finger on it. Was it their accent, their swagger, or the hardened look in their eyes?

After a routine inspection of the perimeter, he stepped into the Petty Officer's cubical. "Sergeant Yousef, these new recruits, I don't remember them being assigned to my command."

The Sergeant returned a crisp salute. "Sir, I have the papers right here." He reached for the stack of orders. "That's funny, I could have sworn they were right there."

Colonel Shimon's body grew tense. Every muscle cried out, "*Danger!*"

As he picked up the secure phone, a uniformed officer stepped into the small office.

Shimon's hand instinctively went for his sidearm. "What are you doing—"

Colonel Hanifa's drawn weapon fired a 9 mm Micro UZI SMG at point-blank range, killing Shimon and his Sergeant instantly.

Hanifa replaced the phone on its cradle and stepped back into the command and control center. With a nod, his men displayed their guns and began firing, in crisscrossing patterns, killing everyone in the room. Before reinforcements could arrive, one of the insurgents detonated the C-4 charges and blew open the door leading to the Firing Chamber. They quickly subdued the Israeli guards and, within minutes, had taken control of the guns on the Golan Heights. They wasted no time in loading the immense weapons and repositioning them.

"Targets acquired sir. Should we begin firing?" asked Abdul Qadir, one of Hanifa's chief operators.

"Fire! And keep firing until you run out of ammunition," their commander said. Gun fire erupted outside the iron and concrete door.

The C-4 charges, which Hanifa's men planted along the narrow tunnel, exploded one after the other as the Israelis tried to retake the gun emplacements. The ground shook every time the big gun fired, sending dust particles through the underground gun emplacements. Still the insurgents kept firing as if driven by some dark force.

After hours of shelling, the Israeli military began to make headway toward retaking their guns. They had blasted large holes in the steal reinforced bunker which Hanifa and some of his men held. Knowing their time was running short, he ordered a small team to keep firing until they ran out of ammunition or were killed. He and the rest of his men took up positions and prepared to defend themselves. In the lull before the final push, Hanifa pulled a small picture of his wife and daughters from his pocket. Tenderly, he kissed it and set it on the ledge next to a row of hand grenades. His dying thoughts would be on his family.

This was a suicide mission, and they all knew it. If the ruse worked, the Israelis would be blamed for shooting first, and world support would be for the Lebanese. The next few hours would make all the difference.

***

Located along the southern border of Lebanon, Al Biqa and Zahi were the first to feel the blast of the big guns. For centuries, these two cities had been a stronghold for Christians. Muslims weren't too discerning when it came to Catholics and evangelicals; if they didn't follow Allah, they had to be destroyed.

Prime Minister Bashera smiled to himself. *I will cleanse my country of the infidels and start the war of annihilation against the Zionists, all at the same time. Brilliant!*

The incoming shells fell indiscriminately upon houses and hovels, Cathedrals and Synagogues, residences and businesses. Fires quickly spread throughout the cities as smoke filled the valleys.

As planned, calls for military support from both mayors went unanswered. Abdullah hoped to build a strong case for war in the international community as thousands of Lebanese people died, and many more were left homeless. Within minutes of the first barrage, rockets from Israeli missile batteries, which had been taken over by the insurgents, began to streak across the inky, night sky, striking eastern Beirut. Poorly constructed buildings collapsed as the ground shook. Even buildings not directly hit by the shells, fell and furthered the destruction.

Chapter 27

The Harbor House

The calm of midnight shattered as sirens began to blare. Jared bolted out of bed like he'd been touched by a bare electrical wire. Dashing to the window, his eyes stabbed the darkness and grew wider by the second.

What's wrong?" Fatemah asked, pulling the covers to her chin.

"I don't know, sounds like an air raid. I just saw a streak of light fall in the distance."

The ground shook.

"Jared, what was that?" Fatemah asked, sitting upright.

"I'm guessing the impact of a missile." Flashbacks of a war raked across unhealed wounds.

"Check the news, Jared, while I look in on the girls," Fatemah said, pulling on her robe.

Jared picked up the remote and hit the green button. Immediately, the BBC's anchorman appeared on the screen.

"We have reports that the cities of Al Biqa and Zahi, located along the southern border of Lebanon, have come under attack by the Israelis, in what appears to be an unprovoked 'Pearl Harbor' type sneak attack. The Israelis have chosen the advent of Eid al-Adha, a Muslim holiday, to begin what might turn into World War III."

Jared stood, frozen in place. Hearing the announcer, Fatemah and the girls joined him, their eyes wide with terror.

"I'm calling Mr. Xavier, pack your bags," he said without commentary.

Fatemah ran into the walk-in closet and grabbed two 'Get out of Town' bags, while the girls threw what little they owned in shoulder bags.

"You guys ready?" Jared asked, tucking his phone into his pocket.

"Yes, but where are we going?" Amana asked, her voice laced with fear.

"I'm taking you to the boat docks on Marfaa Street. I've made arrangements with my boss to give you safe passage out of the country. Fatemah, since I can only take three, I need for you to stay here, but keep out of sight. Militia groups may use this opportunity to loot Christian homes."

She nodded and brushed her hair behind her ear. Clearly, she feared for their lives.

Taking her in his arms, he kissed her as if it were his last. "I'll be back as fast as possible," he whispered. "Let's pray before we go." After a quick prayer, he helped the girls get in his tattered VW.

"Fasten your seat belts, this may get interesting," he said, as the security gate opened.

Between military vehicles and first responders, Jared picked through the narrow streets without being stopped. After forty-five minutes of playing 'hide and seek' with the roving bands of militia, they reached their destination.

One lone fishing trawler sat docked along a decrepit pier. The smell of rotting fish hung in the air like a thick blanket. The skipper of the *el Labrador,* a weathered old man of the sea, stood on her deck smoking a cigarette. As Jared and the girls approached, he took one last drag and flicked it into the murky waters of the Bay of Beirut.

"Are you Captain Ali?" Jared asked, unfolding himself from his car.

With a quick nod, he peered down at him. "I am he, and you are late," he said gruffly.

"Yes, I know. It was all we could do to get here without being shot. Are you sure that boat is sea-worthy?" Jared kidded.

Its weathered hull and peeling paint made Jared wonder.

"The *el Labrador* is as solid and sea-worthy as the day she was christened. I'd stake my life on it," the old sea captain answered, pride oozed from every word.

"Well I'm staking the lives of these girls on it so you'd better be right."

The old skipper ignored the comment and clambered down the gangplank.

"The tide goes out at five o'clock. If I am not on the other side of the reef by then, I won't make it. So you must hurry if you are to get your last passenger out of here."

Jared inhaled. The smell of rotting fish made him gag, and he released his breath. "Okay, I will hurry, but don't leave before I get back."

He jumped back into his VW and began the dangerous trip to the Harbor House. If all went according to the plan, they would accompany the girls past the barrier reef and into international waters where a private cruise ship would be waiting. Then he would turn them over to the captain's protection. The plan involved taking the girls as far as Cyprus. From there, they would take a private jet to France or Italy. The whole thing should only take a day, and the first group would be safe in the American Consulate.

As Jared raced through the back streets of Beirut, praying; *Lord, don't let this car die, not here, not now.*

Chapter 28

The Knesset, Jerusalem, Israel

The cedar paneled walls of the conference room echoed the low tones as Shimer ben Yousef, the Israeli Prime Minister, conferred with his committee. It had been another late-night cabinet meeting in which he and his party sought to work out a deal with the union bosses. It hadn't gone as he'd planned.

Shimer ben Yousef, the leader of the Likud party, was a protégé of BeBe Netanyahu. And like a Jewish version of Winston Churchill, he was a veritable rock of Gibraltar to the beleaguered nation.

An aid slipped next to Yousef and whispered an urgent message in his ear, "Sir, please excuse the interruption, but we are getting reports that some of our units along the Golan Heights are shelling the southern cities of Lebanon."

"What?" His voice, peppered with expletives, interrupted a speech by the minority leader. "I have not authorized an attack on Lebanon, why would I? We are at peace with them!"

An instant later, the room burst into a cacophony of questions, as cell phones chirped and word began to spread.

"Sir," a military aid said, as he approached the PM, "I'm getting reports that there is fighting inside a number of our military instillations. We think they've been infiltrated and the IDF is trying to retake them.

"What facilities?" Yousef demanded, his voice remaining calm.

"Sir," the aid paused, "it's the Golan Heights."

Yousef gripped the arms of his chair, "Level with me, how bad is it?"

His Defense Minister, Yuri Kasson cleared his throat. "Shimer, I just got off the phone with my field commander in the Kefar Gil

Adi region, and he believes some of our missile launchers have also been compromised. What we're looking at is World War III if we don't stop the shelling now! Even still, we'll be blamed for starting it."

The Prime Minister's brow furrowed. "What's the American's position?"

The Secretary of Foreign Affairs raised his hand. "Sir, I have been trying to get in contact with the president. It appears she is about to begin a big summit meeting between Greenpeace and NOAA and refuses to weigh in until after the summit is over."

Shimer slammed his fist on the mahogany table. "That's just great, by that time we'll be nothing but a smoking, nuclear wasteland. Put the IDF on full alert . . . Def Con 5 without delay." The PM locked eyes with the Defense Minister, "I have one question, and I need a straight answer."

"Yes sir!" Kasson said succinctly.

"Are our boys in place?"

"Yes sir, they've done a remarkable job. A team of elite Mossad performed a HALO, a high-altitude low open jump," Kasson, a four-star general, said. "I'll never understand why someone would jump from a perfectly good AC-130J at thirty-one thousand feet, travel at a hundred and twenty miles per hour down to earth just to get another insignia," he quipped. Kasson let a ripple of laughter fill the tense moment, then continued.

"Once we had boots on the ground, they quickly infiltrated the key power plants, which provided energy to the fueling stations. Under the cover of darkness, they planted explosives at strategic locations within them. As soon as the Iranians try to ramp up, 'kabang', the explosives will detonate."

Yousef's face hardened, "Hmm, the best kept secret of Iran's history since the Medes and Persians dug channels and diverted the Euphrates River, will soon be known to the world. By then it will be too late."

The prime minister shook his head. A dozen men stared back at him. "Any questions?" he asked.

Movement caught his eye as his Secretary of Commerce lifted his hand, "Yes, Isaac?"

"Sir, do we know of certainty where those missile silos are?"

The PM gave a quick nod to his Defense Minister.

He cleared his throat, "Yes. We have the exact location of the missile silos and have been monitoring their enrichment program. We've located the power plants, which provide the energy for the ICBMs. They're hidden deep within the Pontus and Taurus mountain range, and I'd bet my hat the Iranians are busy preparing the ICBM missiles for launch as we speak. It is at this time they will be the most vulnerable. The bay doors to the silo doors will be open exposing the nuclear warheads to our spy satellites. We know their capability, their technology and weaponry. We just don't know the time frame."

Yousef leaned forward catching the Defense Minister's eye, "Let's assume a worse-case scenario. Say this whole thing is a ruse to get us looking to our north, while Iran is shooting at us in the keister." His steel grey eyes bore a glint of determination. "That's not going to happen...not on my watch. Ready the southern air wing and get them in the air over Iran A.S.A.P."

Chapter 29

Rick and Mindy's Apartment

At the first sound of the sirens, Rick jumped out of bed and ran to the window. From his view, bright spotlights cut across the night sky like Light-Sabers.

"We've got trouble," he said, reaching for the phone.

"Who are you calling?" Mindy asked, clutching the covers close.

"I'm calling the Canadian Embassy to see what's going on."

Rick's face contorted as the seconds stretched into minutes. Frustrated, he slammed the phone down.

"What the matter?" Mindy's question hung in the air unanswered.

A sharp rap on their door, nearly stopped Rick's heart.

"Mindy, get dressed, this could spell trouble."

Grabbing a baseball bat, he cautiously approached the front entrance and peered through the peep hole. Outside, Anita stood, shivering and prancing up and down.

"Mr. Owens, it's me, Anita. Open up," her voice, tinged with fear.

Rick quickly unlocked the door and swung it open. "Anita, what are you doing here?"

She bounded into the apartment and slammed the door behind her, panting.

"You'd never believe it, but my father is behind the attack on Lebanon. I've got to get out of here." Her haunted eyes glanced from side to side.

Mindy stepped from the bedroom, still tucking a flannel shirt into a pair of crisp jeans, the laces of her running shoes flailing wildly.

"Wait a minute, slow down, you're talking in circles," Rick said, trying to make sense of it all.

"No, Rick, you slow down. This girl is soaked to the skin." Mindy's voice softened. "Here honey, let me get a towel and some dry clothes." She put her arm around Anita's waist and said over her shoulder, "Rick, make some hot tea before she shivers to death,"

He obeyed without comment while Mindy guided her back to the bedroom.

Outside, the siren's up and down warning continued.

"Here, put these on," Mindy said after rooting through her chest of drawers.

Anita grimaced. She'd never worn jeans, but considering the circumstances, she acquiesced. Exactly ten minutes later, the two women reemerged to a waiting tray of hot tea and sliced nut-bread. Taking their seats, Rick settled down and asked, "What's this all about?"

A labored breath escaped her lungs as Anita began. She quickly summarized the last hours of the day, while Rick tried to jot down her statement. The pencil point broke, and he tossed it aside.

"I'm going to call the embassy again," and hit the redial button. After a few minutes of hearing the same recording, he pushed out a frustrated sigh and slammed the phone down. "I keep getting the same message."

Holding the cup of hot tea between her icy fingers, Anita peered over the rim, "I tried to get to Mr. Jared and Miss Fatemah's house, but all the lights were off. I'm so worried about them too." Her voice etched with pain.

"I have an idea where they might be," Rick said as he pulled out an old city map. He spread it out on the coffee table and began to study it. "If we're going to catch them, we'd better hurry, but before we go, let me check the television."

He pushed the button and the television came on. A reporter stood in front of the Administrative Palace, microphone in hand. "The Prime Minister is outraged over the news that his country has suffered an unprovoked, relentless attack by the Zionists. He believes this is in retaliation to his insistence that settlements along the Lebanese and Israeli border be removed."

"And what are we hearing about the Prime Minister's daughter being abducted?" the BBC anchor asked.

Fingers to his ear, the reporter nodded until the anchor finished her question. Intense eyes stared into the lens of the camera. "Yes, word on the street has it that Anita Bashera, the Prime Minister's beloved daughter has been abducted by the Israelis, possibly the Mossad.

"That's a lie!" Streaks of red blotches strangled Anita's throat as she screamed at the television.

"And what, if any, are their demands?" the anchor asked.

Without missing a beat, the reporter continued. "The administration spokesman is reluctant to say, but it is believed to be just another attempt to get the prime minister to back off, but he refuses. He has, I might add, put out a one million pound reward for information leading to the arrest of her captors or her release."

Rick, Mindy and Anita gathered and watched the scene unfold.

"That's a big fat lie," Anita spat. "My Father started this war, and I've not been abducted." Crossing her arms, Anita stared daggers at the television. "We have to tell someone the truth."

"Okay, okay, simmer down," Rick said, with his hands outstretched. "First we need to find a safe place for you to hide. If this is true, you're in grave danger, and we'll have to get you out of the country."

"Rick, do you know what you're saying?"

The air scintillated with tension and Anita slumped to the couch. "It's no use. Eventually, my father's men will find me. They always do."

Over his wife's objections, Rick took Anita by the hand and pulled her up. "Let's go. Time's running out."

"But where?" Mindy insisted, "the highways will be in gridlock."

"I'm not talking about driving her out of the city."

Anita watched them banter back and forth like a pair of ping-pong players.

"Rick, what are you suggesting?"

"I'm saying, we need to get to the boat dock, pronto."

Crossing her arms, Mindy put her foot down, "Rick, you know my feelings about that."

"Yes, we've been over it a dozen times, but this is different."

"What's so different about it?" Mindy fired back.

Rick pinched the bridge of his nose, "Because this is Anita, for crying out loud, and that settles it. Now let's go."

"Rick, can't we at least check on the Russells? They may have an idea or worse, they could be in trouble, too?"

He paused and gave Mindy's suggestion time to mature. "Okay, that's a thought. We'll swing by Jared's house and check on them, but if they aren't home, well . . . " he let his voice trail off.

***

It had been half an hour since Jared left the boat dock, and he still had another twenty minutes to go.

"Oh no!" the VW sputtered and rolled to a stop.

Jared slapped the steering wheel in frustration. "Every time I need this thing to run right, it does this to me. I've had it with this piece of junk. Tomorrow—"

A set of headlights slashed across his hood, and he instinctively slouched down. An emergency vehicle sped past. Releasing his breath, he sat up and scanned the area. "I can't stay here or I'm a sitting duck," he muttered.

Jared unfolded himself from his car and began walking. Before he got half a block, a jeep boasting a 50 mm machine gun, raced around the corner. It slowed and began making long sweeps with a spotlight across the manicured lawns in search of anyone breaking the recently announced curfew.

Being a black man wearing dark clothes, he slipped into the shadow of a large date palm and waited. Despite the cold, a row of beads formed on his forehead and dripped into his eyes. After what seemed hours, the vehicle cruised out of sight. With his eyes scanning the area, Jared emerged from the shadow of the tree and began to jog home.

Ten minutes later he arrived at the Harbor House and began punching in the security code. Suddenly, a set of headlights painted his silhouette. Jared froze. *The militia.* Still holding his breath, he slowly raised his hands and turned to face the light.

"Brother, do ya need a ride?" It was Uncle Abbas.

Jared released a captive breath. "My car broke down *again,* and I need to take Fatemah to the docks on Paris Street."

Leaning out the driver's side, Uncle Abbas' brows lifted. "Oh! Are you going somewhere, my brother?"

"Yes, well, kinda. You see, we came into the possession of some very precious cargo, and I just shipped them . . . uh, it. I thought it best that we follow up to make sure that the shipment arrived safely."

Rubbing his chin, the older man nodded. "I think I understand," he said, thoughtfully. "I'll see what I can do to get you there as quickly as possible."

Jared finished punching the code and the gate groaned open. "Wait here, I'll be right back."

As he turned, the roar of an engine caught his attention. Skidding to a halt behind the little yellow cab, the car jolted to a stop and Rick jumped out.

"What are you doing here, Rick?"

Rick approached, his face pale with anxiety. "We need to get out of sight, fast. I'll explain later," he said, keeping his voice low.

Taken back at his friend's forcefulness, Jared's eyes danced between the taxi and the car. "Okay, Uncle Abbas, let's bring your car inside before someone sees us."

A moment later, Jared closed the gate and faced Rick.

"What's going on?"

***

Rick stepped aside revealing Anita, who huddled in the back seat of the car.

"She is in big trouble, Jared. She was inside her father's office and overheard sensitive information. We've got to get her to safety." The front door to the house opened casting a yellow glow on the concrete. Fatemah appeared in the entrance and rushed to her husband's side.

"Jared, what took you so long? I was so worried," she said, then pressed her lips against his. Someone coughed, and she released her grip. Uncle Abbas and Rick stood staring. "What are you doing here?"

Movement caught her eyes as Anita leaped from the taxi and dashed into Fatemah's arms. "Oh Miss Fatemah, I nearly got killed, I'm so scared."

Stumbling back, she peered down. "You poor child, come inside before you catch a cold."

Arm around her shoulders, Fatemah guided Anita back to the house. Before the door closed, Mindy pulled herself from the car and stomped after them, an angry gaze fixed on her husband.

"I take it she's not happy about your decision to bring her here," Jared said, watching Rick's pained expression. He ignored the statement and tried to explain the situation.

Jared held up a hand. "I have a plan, but it's risky. Let's get Anita to station STA-7 and video her testimony. Maybe we can have the manager program it to air at six o'clock. By then, we should be long gone."

"But Mr. Jared," Uncle Abbas laid a gentle hand on his arm, "didn't you say the tide goes out at five? That gives us only an hour."

Shifting his weight from one foot to the other, Jared acknowledged the warning. "Yes, all the more reason to hurry. If we can do this and get her on the boat in fifty minutes, we may have a chance," his voice grew in urgency.

Rick stepped in front of Jared, halting his steps. "I still don't like the idea of running a blockade. It's going to get someone killed. We should just stay out of sight and ride it out."

"Step aside, Rick. We can't keep Anita out of sight indefinitely, someone will see her and then we're all in deep trouble."

The tense moment held its breath while Rick considered his option. Finally, he relaxed, "By the way Jared, where's your car?"

The oil spot, left by his VW mocked Jared and he rubbed the back of his neck, "It clunked out again on me—left it sitting along the curb on Hallawani Blvd."

"Oh that's bad."

"Why's that, Rick?"

"Hallawani Blvd is a main corridor for moving troops from their base to the harbor. That road will be crawling with Republican Guard."

The lines in Jared's face deepened. "That settles it. Uncle Abbas, I think we are going to need your skills."

With a nod, Uncle Abbas stepped up, "I agree. It's too risky to stay here. On the other hand, the streets are crawling with armed militia. I saw several units patrolling the streets on the way over here." He paused and gave a scholarly gaze, "but I know of a better way. First we need wisdom, and that my child, only comes from God." Looking heavenward, he began, "Now Lord," he spoke as if to an unseen guest, "these whom you have given me, I have lost none, now give your servant an answer of peace, in Jesus' name, amen."

Jared cleared his throat. "What is the safest way to get to SAT-7 TV station?"

"Well, the main roads are all blocked, but we can take the back roads." Looking at Rick, he nodded, "Sir, if you will follow us with your headlight off, we can get there without being noticed. With all that's happening, someone should be at the station." A wry smile parted the elderly man's lips.

Chapter 30

The Boat Dock

Captain Ali glanced at his watch for the inth time. It was five minutes later than the last time he'd looked, and five minutes after that. In fifteen minutes, his 5 o'clock dead-line would pass. With a measured pace, he walked the deck of the *el Labrador*, smoking yet another cigarette. Time was running out. Already, the tide had begun its march to the sea. If he didn't leave soon, they wouldn't get across the barrier reef, and they'd be stuck in the harbor for another day. That meant they'd miss their connections and that, he couldn't afford.

Sucking in a sharp breath, he straightened. "Ladies, we are launching. Get down below."

With practiced skill, he unraveled the thick, hemp ropes, which bound the trawler to its moorings, and tossed them over the gun-rail. With an easy step, he boarded his vessel and cast off. By the time the *el Labrador* cleared the dock, he was in the wheel house. One weathered hand spun the helm while his thumb mashed the starter. A moment later the duel 350 hp engines sputtered, then roared to life. A column of thick, oily smoke billowed from its exhaust pipes and Ali inhaled with a satisfied expression. He loved his boat, and he loved the sea. His marriage with both of them provided the companionship he longed for and a sense of purpose. He was truly a man of the sea, the captain of his ship.

Pushing the throttle to its lowest position, he guided the trawler through the no wake zone and into the main channel, then he brought it up to cruising speed. The moonless night gave the *el Labrador* an advantage as its black hull cut the inky waters of the Bay of Beirut. Without his running lights on and only using his low level LED's to illuminate the instrument panel, Captain Ali steered the ship past the reef.

A border patrol boat appeared in the distance. Ali hoped they hadn't seen him, but even if they had, he hoped he could out run them. The captain's heart quickened as the patrol boat came about. By the size of their wake, he knew they were trying to intercept him.

"Oh shoot!" he muttered through clinched teeth.

He grabbed the throttle and rammed it wide open. The engines groaned under the strain, and the old trawler lurched forward. Wave after wave slammed against its hull as it battled the sea and time. The sleek contour of the cruiser sliced through the opposing current and quickly closed the distance. In the early morning glow, Captain Ali could see the crew readying the 50 caliber deck gun.

A nautical mile. That's all that lay between him and safety. White knuckled, he willed his vessel forward as he weaved to his star board side then back to port. In the distance, a red light bobbed on top of a buoy. *There it is. The boundary between Lebanon and international waters, if I can only make it.* He gritted his teeth and pushed the throttle harder. *It's going to be close.*

Flashes from the deck gun lit the sky. Hot lead peppered the gun-rail kicking up chunks of wood. Ali instinctively ducked as another wave of bullets raked the bow. The patrol boat was closing fast. Another minute and they'd all be dead. Desperate to avoid such a fate, he spun the helm. The engines groaned under the strain, but yielded to his command. The next burst of bullets fell harmlessly to his starboard. Out maneuvered, the patrol boat tried to regain the advantage, but was too late. The *el Labrador* cut through the fog and raced past the buoy as another burst from the deck gun reverberated.

"Yahoo! We made it," he hollered, his fists pumping the air.

Captain Ali set his craft on auto-pilot, and then climbed down the ladder. A light tap on the galley door announced his entrance. Looking into the greenish faces of his passengers, he gave the three frightened girls a weak smile.

"What was all that shooting? asked Amana.

The old captain rubbed his stubbly chin with a shrug. "Oh, twas nothing.' Just a little fanfare when we crossed the border."

An interesting glint flickered in his weathered eyes. "We'll be nearing our rendezvous point in a few minutes, so gather up your things."

Returning to the helm, he checked his radar. A red blip appeared on the screen. He pulled back on the throttle, letting the trawler drift slowly through the fog-bank ahead. In the near distance, like a phantom, the image of a vessel emerged from the fog. Captain Ali reversed his engines and pulled up close.

"This is the *el Labrador,* permission to come aboard?" his voice dissipated in the misty atmosphere.

"This is the captain of the *Pearl Lady*, permission granted." The skipper's voice echoed through the speaker system.

With a light step, Captain Ali skipped down the ladder, grabbed a rope, and tossed it to the deck hands. The CIA owned cruiser named *Pearl Lady,* held international papers and was welcomed at any port-of-call. Within a few minutes the crew helped the shaken girls from the trawler to one of the two aft cabins. Once they were below, its skipper wasted no time in getting under way. The sleek vessel's twin, water cooled, Crusader 454 engines roared to life. A moment later it disappeared in the fog.

As the girls got situated below in comfortable suites, the old trawler cranked up its engines and prepared to make its return run. For Captain Ali . . . his night of terror was over, for Jared, it was just beginning.

Chapter 31

Television Station STA-7

After twenty minutes of weaving the back roads of Beirut, the two-car caravan arrived at the television station. Jared jumped out, walked up to the door and pulled.

Locked.

Cupping his hands, he peered through the glass door. No one was in the front, and the lights were dimmed. With time running out, Jared began to pound on the door.

A shadow moved, and the large form of a man filled a door-frame. "Just a minute," the station manager called from the studio. A moment later, a large, blond headed man with piercing blue eyes approached the door. He eyed Jared suspiciously, then unlocked it.

"Under most circumstances I wouldn't think of opening the door at this hour. State your business. I got a crisis going on out there," he said, clearly irritated.

Not wanting to beat around the bush, Jared got right to the point. "You've been airing an APB for Anita Bashera, the prime minister's daughter. Well, she's with me."

Olif Sorenson's eyes bulged. "You've got to be kidding."

"Nope, now let us in, she has something to tell you about the Israeli attacks."

The big Swedish man stepped back as Jared guided Anita through the door. Fatemah quickly followed.

Jared gave Rick a wave. "We're alright now. You guys go on home. We'll be in touch."

Rick offered a weak smile and backed away.

Relieved, Jared returned his attention to the station manager. "I'll let Anita tell you in her own words," he explained.

Anita pulled her head covering back and stared and uncertainly at the manager.

"Uh, uh, I d-don't know if I can do this," she stuttered.

Olif ran a hand through his blond hair and began to pace. Minutes escaped and his patience was running out. "Go ahead young lady, what's your story."

Fatemah placed an arm around her slight frame with a supportive smile. "You can do this, Anita."

Tugging her coat tighter Anita began, "As you know, my father is the Prime Minister. Earlier this morning, I overheard him speaking to the president of Iran about the shelling."

The manager uncrossed his burly arms and began pacing the floor. "Go on, what else did he say?" his eyebrows raised.

"Well, my father got a call from someone he called, Colonel Kamil Abu Hanifa. He placed him on speaker phone, and I heard him say he and his men had taken the Golan Heights."

The big Swede straightened like he'd been poked with a cattle prod. "What did your father tell him?"

Anita bit her lip, trying desperately to control her emotions. "He told him to begin firing on the border towns of Al Biqa, Zahi and on east side of Beirut. Then he got a call from someone in northern Israel. He repeated his orders." Glancing at the clock on the wall, she cringed. "That should begin any time now."

Mr. Sorenson began pacing the floor. "Why send your military into Israel and order them to fire on your country?"

The ground shook as the second hand reached its apex and everyone ducked. Anita stared into the station manager's cobalt eyes. "According to my father, this would give Lebanon cause to retaliate and attack Israel without it looking like we started the war," she said with confidence.

"Can you corroborate your story?" he pressed.

"Sir, I am the daughter of the prime minister, you know my face, everyone does. By me stepping forth, I have committed an act of treason. They will kill me for reporting this, but if I don't tell the world, a lot more innocent people are going to die. Now, please, video my testimony?" her tone, commanding, resolute.

The station manager ran his hand through his hair as he pondered his options. "Okay Miss Anita, I believe you," his jaw set. "I just hope the world believes you. Now, we've got to act fast. Once this hits the air, the police, the militia, and who knows who else will descend on this place. When they get finished, there won't be a Station 7, so let's get started."

He stepped into the studio and rolled a camera in place. "Okay, Miss, take a seat." He nodded to an aluminum chair. Then he clipped a lavaliere microphone on to her top and checked the volume levels. Looking through the lens, he zoomed in. "All right Miss, speak slowly and clearly."

Anita bristled. Of course she knew how to speak. She was a sophisticated, cultured, young lady, thanks to that old, stuffy finishing school her father forced her to attend. The one thing she'd acquired from him was the ability to communicate. Clearing her throat, she began. When she finished, Sorenson programmed the video feed to air at 6 o'clock, then up-linked it to the satellite rotating in geo-synchronous orbit 100 miles above the earth.

"Okay, I'm getting outta here and so should you," the station manager said, zipping up his parka.

Jared reached out and shook the man's hand. "Thank you sir. You may have stopped Armageddon."

Beep, beep.

It was Uncle Abbas, "Hurry!" he said, waving his hand.

Exactly thirty minutes later, the taxi rolled to a stop at the wharf. A light fog had settled in, giving the scene an unearthly appearance. The water lapped lazily upon the shore, but other than that, all was quiet.

"Captain Ali?" Jared's voice echoed through the mist. In the distance, a lone seagull answered.

Fatemah sidled up next to him, "We're too late. He's gone."

Pulling her close, he looked down at her, and whispered, "I'm afraid so."

Chapter 32

The Prime Minister's Office

Fahid Shamoan, the prime minister's Chief of Staff, stood outside of his leader's office, clearly agitated. He knew his life hung by a thread. A tentative knock on the door brought a one-word response.

"Enter!"

His trembling fingers pushed open the door, and he stepped in. "You called, sir?"

The prime minister stood, fingers locked behind him, facing the window. He pivoted and cast an angry glare in Fahid's direction.

"Where is my daughter?" he raged.

Shamoan held his position, too stunned to answer. "We, we, can't locate her, sir. We have put out an APB, offering a reward. We are scouring the city, but to no avail. I assure you, we will find her."

The prime minister drew a Russian made Makarov 9mm pistol from his belt and pointed it at his Chief of Staff's head. "If you don't bring Anita to me today, I will shoot you myself," he screamed.

Fahid stumbled backwards and fell to his knees, eyes wide with terror, "I, I can assure you. I will personally search for her. I will not eat. I will not sleep until I have found her, but please, don't shoot me or my family. We have served you faithfully for 10 years. I trust in you."

"Shut up you sniveling idiot. One thing I detest more than the infidels is weakness, and you Fahid, are weak. Now, leave before I change my mind."

The shaken man clambered to his feet. His legs buckled, and he pushed himself back up.

"Please forgive me," he said, the whites of his eyes painted in fear, then scrambled away.

***

As the hum of the taxi's engine faded, Jared began to pace up and down the dock, unsure he was in the right location.

With Captain Ali gone, so was his connection to the outside world. There was no way out of the country, and the authorities were squeezing in like a python. A scan of the horizon told Jared dawn was less than an hour away. Anita's safety became job number one. For a moment, he considered taking Fatemah and Anita back to the Harbor House, then ruled it out. Blending among a crowd of people and hiding in plain sight made the best sense. The women drew their burqas up tighter and covered their faces with their hijabs. Jared felt like a black dot on a white sheet.

"We need to get someplace where there are a lot of tourists," he said after much thought.

"Where can we go? The city is under attack, missiles raining down all over the place." Fatemah insisted.

"The Royal Garden on Spears Street," Anita chirped. "It's always crowded, and today they're having a special dedication of a monument honoring my father. I know because I helped plan it. It will be filled with people no matter what."

"Won't your father and his body guards be there?" Jared pressed.

Shaking her head, "Nope, he hates those kinds of gatherings. Plus, he has a war to manage. He won't come out of the bunker for anything."

Fatemah's face brightened, "Is it far?"

Anita tugged her by the hand, "No, it's within walking distance. Come on."

By the time they reached the gardens, the first rays of golden sunlight filtered over the jagged mountains to their east. The gate to the Royal Garden was locked, but a small army of North Koreans, armed with cameras, gathered outside the ticket office chattering wildly. Fatemah stepped to the window and purchased three tickets. When she returned, the entrance was open, and they followed the group into the gardens. Had it been a day for sightseeing, Jared would have enjoyed the walk, but this was no holiday. He pulled his cell phone from his belt, and called Captain Ali.

"Captain Ali, where are you? I came back, and you were gone."

"Yes my friend, I had to depart before the tide went out, or I wouldn't have gotten over the reef. I must wait now until the next high tide before I can return," he said in broken English.

"When will that be, Captain?"

"About two o'clock in the morning. Can you wait 'til then?"

"I don't know. I don't have a lot of options. Got any suggestions?"

"The blockade is getting tighter. I may only have one more chance to get through. So lay low and call me around one o'clock tomorrow morning."

Jared tucked his phone back in its pouch and leaned heavily against a palm tree.

"What's wrong, Jared?" Fatemah asked, keeping her voice low.

Glancing around at the chattering North Koreans, he beckoned for Fatemah to step closer. "Our ride can't make it until around one in the morning."

Fatemah's shoulders slumped. "Oh my, that is a problem. Maybe we should find a hotel and stay there until things cool off."

"That's a good idea, Fatemah, but where?"

"I know of one," Anita volunteered. "It's not far, and I don't think they'll ask any questions."

"How do you know so much about this area? You're only fifteen."

Anita's eyes narrowed, "Yes, I'm a teenager, but I get around. Papa brought me there once for a state visit. So, are you coming or not?" she asked, giving them little choice, but to follow her strident gait.

Thirty minutes later they stood outside of a hotel that had seen better days.

"This is it?" Jared's eyebrows rose questioningly.

Anita's shoulders slumped. "Well, it's not as I remembered. We could be in the wrong one."

Scanning the area for another hotel and seeing none, Jared shook his head. "No, it's the right one, so we better make the best of it. Let's go."

Following his lead, the two women gathered their burqas close and stepped into the crumbling lobby. To his relief, the clerk accepted Jared's Master Card and handed him the key to a second floor room. Keeping their heads covered and avoiding eye contact, Fatemah and Anita followed Jared to the elevator. Only when they were safely inside did either of the women relax. Fatemah perched on the bed, while Anita slumped on a thread-bare couch that had seen better days.

As the doors to the only working elevator slid shut, the hotel clerk picked up the phone and made a call.

***

A flock of pigeons scattered as the last member of the parliament marched past them. He and the other members had been called by Vice Prime Minister Faheem ben Assam to convene in an emergency meeting of the Lebanese Parliament. Having been out maneuvered, Assam, a moderate Sunni, was more than happy to bring charges against Prime Minister Bashera.

In the well of the chamber, Assam waxed eloquent, "Ayatollah Bashera is a traitor to Islam and I demand his immediate arrest and reparations from the Bashera Foundation."

The Bashera Foundation was a shell organization set up to hide the Ayatollah's wealth.

"I further move that we sue for peace with the Israelis and call for UN sanctions against any nation that perpetuates or attempts to prosecute a war with our friends, the Israelis—"

Before he could finish his comments, the assembly shouted him down.

"Death to the Zionists," the minority leader's face grew a deep shade of purple as he repeated his cries for Assam's ouster.

Reluctantly, Assam withdrew his demands, and the parliament quickly passed a watered down apology to the Israelis and the residents of southern Lebanon.

***

Precisely at six o'clock in the morning, Anita's video hit the airwaves and was soon carried by every major news agency around the world. Prime Minister Bashera, fearing he'd be arrested within the hour, slipped past his guards. Using a little known panel in an anti-room, he squeezed down a narrow flight of stairs which opened in the pantry. From there he made his way to a black limousine. Unnoticed, he got in without a word and the car quietly pulled away from the curb. Thirty minutes later, he leaned forward.

"Pull up as close to the helo pad as you can get."

The limo driver did as he was ordered and came to a halt beside the door of the stealthy black *Versace* helicopter, its blades already turning. A single shot to the back of the head and the driver slumped to one side. The forged suicide note explaining the debt, the multiple affairs, the drugs, was all it took to cover the Ayatollah's tracks. The same fate awaited the two-man helicopter crew.

The Grand *Versace,* with its top speed of 177 mph, lifted off and headed east, then north over the Bekaa Valley. Its flight path took them 80 miles to the Hadyah Forest. In less than an hour the sleek black helicopter dropped through the clouds to a landing zone near the base of the Al-Mouzeina mountain range. Its only occupant stepped out. Ducking his head, Abdullah Bashera lumbered out of the helicopter and was greeted by his longtime friend and ally, Colonel Ishmael el Jahja.

"Greetings in the name of Allah the Merciful, my friend," the Colonel said as he slapped the Ayatollah on the shoulder.

Colonel Jahja, the leader of the Hamas militia, and Abdullah traced their history as far back as the 1976 Syrian-Lebanon war in which he led the Arab Deterrent Force. Under his command, they caused significant damage to the strength of the Leftists and their Druze allies, a move that placed the Bashera family at the top of the political food chain.

"Is everything ready?"

Jahja shifted his AK-47 from one shoulder to the other. "Yes Abdullah, everything is as you requested. We await your orders."

"Good, now send your best men and find my daughter. I want her here without delay, but I want her intact, if you know what I mean. Tell your men not to abuse her until I'm finished with her. Then they can do with her as they please," he sneered.

As they climbed into the colonel's personal jeep, two shots echoed in the distance. No one even took notice.

Chapter 33

The Grand Hotel, Mackinaw Island, Michigan

With the president's arrival on Mackinaw Island uncertain, Jimbo found himself becoming a people watcher. He'd just taken a seat beside a large parlor palm in the spacious lobby of the Grand Hotel and began skimming the newspaper when the first wave of guests arrived. Across the open space stood a rotund man fumbling with his oversized suitcase.

"May I take your luggage to your room, sir?"

Dr. Richard C. McMillan, Director of NOAA, National Oceanic and Atmospheric Administration, handed him a crisp twenty-dollar bill. "Yes, keep the change. Now, where do I go?"

The bellhop gulped and recovered quickly. "Thank you, sir. The front desk is right over there," he said, pointing.

McMillan nodded, "Don't mention it."

From his vantage point, Jimbo could observe the new arrivals unnoticed. Not impressed with the way Dr. McMillan threw money around, Jimbo turned his attention to his secretary, Miss Iris Didion. Her petite form and short choppy gait communicated there was more to her than met the eye. Following her, came three men in suits. Like the Pep Boys, each displayed a unique personality, yet there was a commonality between them. Their thinning hair, wire-rimmed glasses, slumping shoulders, along with their ashen tones were only a few of the markings of men who'd spent their lives in a laboratory. *Lab rats,* Jimbo mused, as he watched the interplay between the three. He'd studied their dossiers, now he began to put faces with names. Not seeing anyone on his watch list, he relaxed as the group disappeared in the elevator and went back to the paper.

An hour later, Jimbo roused as the second group of arrivals entered the lobby.

Their leader, Mr. Stephan Von Janson, clearly had more on his mind than the summit by the way his secretary, Heidi Stromberg, clung to his arm. As they disappeared down the hall in search of their rooms, a timid woman by the name of Andrea Williamson approached the concierge's desk and asked for her key. By the look she gave Von Janson, it was obvious to Jimbo she was not too happy about the arrangement. In a move that caught Jimbo by surprise, Andrea cocked her head and locked eyes with him. *This woman is extremely observant. Interesting.* The moment passed leaving him with the deep impression she was not to be taken lightly.

"Good afternoon, sir. I am Amil Bashera, the UN Diplomatic Attaché with Greenpeace. May I have the key to my room, please?" he said in a soft tone.

His polite demeanor spoke of class, of well-breeding, of culture … nothing like what Jimbo expected.

Reaching into his briefcase, Jimbo lifted a file. At the top of the dossier it read: Amil Bashera, 27 years old, Lebanese born son of Abdullah Bashera, holds a Doctorate in Political Science, is fluent in Farsi, Arabic, German, Italian, English and Spanish.

Jimbo pulled the small picture from its paper clip and studied it. He glanced at his subject and then at the photograph. Amil's distinctive black eyes and neatly trimmed goatee made him an outstandingly handsome man. His well-built, 5' 8'' frame spoke of hours working out in the gym, and his movements were that of an aristocrat: well-bread, well-read, and well-financed.

After reading the thin information the CIA had collected on him, Jimbo caught himself wondering if, under different circumstances, he could have been a movie star rather than an assassin.

***

The serene afternoon was broken by the drone of four engines. In the distance, a giant C-17 Globe-master III aircraft made its final approach to the matchbox size landing strip on Mackinaw Island. At 174 feet long, and a wingspan of 170 feet, The Beast, as it is called, could land and take off from runways as short as thirty-five hundred feet.

Its arrival marked a historic occasion. For the first time in its history, the island of Mackinaw had an automobile on it. The presidential limousine, called Cadillac One, rolled down the ramp of the C-17. Built on a GMC frame, the heavily armored vehicle featured bulletproof windows, a state-of-the-art communication and protection system, and traveled wherever the president went.

Thirty minutes later, Marine One, lifted off from the mainland and carried the presidential entourage across the bay. It touched down yards away from the limo in a carefully coordinated plan to limit the president's exposure to unwanted eyes. President Ferguson, code named Debutante, and her entourage stepped off and into the awaiting vehicles.

Within fifteen minutes, the six vehicle caravan snaked through the narrow streets of downtown Mackinaw. Crowds of well-wishers, supporters and non-supporters alike, lined Main Street waving American flags. Many held banners and cheered as the fifth president and the first female president to visit their island, rode slowly down the tree-lined street.

President Ferguson waved back at the adoring crowds. She was in full campaign mode even though it was the second year of her administration. It truly was a historic occasion, not just because of the obvious headlines, but because of the significance of her visit. This was a summit meeting between her, the head of NOAA, and the head of Greenpeace Movement. The purpose was to sign the Kyoto Protocol.

Due to a massive weather system rapidly approaching the island, rather than delay the meeting, President Ferguson had her arrival moved up a day. Being alerted of the change, the Grand

Hotel contracted extra cooking staff to relieve their usual kitchen crew.

The presidential motorcade rolled to a gentle stop where normally horse-drawn carriages delivered their passengers. Lining the iconic, white columns were red and blue bunting, punctuated with American flags, which flapped lazily in the breeze. Rows of servants dressed in black and sporting white aprons awaited the moment. On cue, they began clapping and cheering as the president stepped from her limo. The General Manager, Mr. John Torazino, stood at the head of a red carpet, hand extended.

"Welcome to the Grand Hotel, Madam President," he said with a quick bow.

President Ferguson scanned the view. "Wow, this is even better than Mt. Vernon. It's a wonder George Washington didn't claim this first."

Thanking the president for her comment, Torazino bowed at the waist again and ushered her into the lobby.

"As per your request, Madam President, your entourage is assigned to the fourth floor. The Millikan Suite, with its two spacious rooms, will be dubbed the Presidential Suite. I trust it will serve you well during your visit."

"I'm sure it will, thank you," the president answered condescendingly. "And I'm positive my Chief of Staff, Andrew Kelly, will enjoy sleeping in the Teddy Roosevelt Lodge." Her eyes wandered in Andrew's direction.

***

President Susan Ferguson had run her campaign primarily on an environmental platform and won the election with the backing of the Democrats, liberal Republicans, the feminists, and the Greenpeace Movement. She made it clear from the outset of her administration she was concerned with women's issues and the environment. However, her passion was to reduce the number of nuclear weapons in America's arsenal.

Taking her seat behind a Victorian desk, Susan met with her advisers and went over the last-minute details for tomorrow's meeting. Dressed in a dark navy blue pinstriped pantsuit which accentuated the curves of her body, she was as much a fashion statement as a political leader.

"Madam President, here is the DTB," Larry Morgan, her Chief of Security said, handing her the 'Eyes Only' document.

Daily Threat Bulletin – January 12th Primary threats:

1. **Israel has launched an attack on her peaceful neighbor to the North - Lebanon.**

2. **Lebanon is calling for UN sanctions against Israel.**

3. **The Arab League is ramping up their defenses and preparing to go to war with the Zionists.**

4. **Russia has promised to step in if Israel does not cease her war of aggression.**

5. **The President of Iran states categorically that he has no interest in the development of enriched nuclear material for military purposes.**

6. **With the Mid-East heating up, OPEC oil prices have skyrocketed.**

7. **Large weather system making its way across the mid-west could affect summit meeting.**

The list continued with several more entries the president was well aware of, but there was one new one . . .

20. Israel is denying all charges and is looking into the matter.

Slamming the paper down, Susan pushed her chair back and stepped around the desk. "That's just great! Leave it to the Zionists to mess up my big plans." Pressing a button on her phone, she leaned closer, "Mr. Kelly, would you step in here, please." Her last word sounded more like an addendum than a courtesy, and Larry wondered if his old buddy was about to get the boot.

"Larry, get my Press Secretary on the line. I want her to draft a statement condemning Israel's' actions and demanding Israel to cease all hostilities. Let's get ahead of this thing and put some distance between us and Israel," the president said, "oh, and put a call through to the Prime Minister of Israel, A.S.A.P."

"We have Madam President."

"And?"

"And he's not answering, seems like the prime minister's handlers are stalling for time."

"Hmm," the president mused. "This is no time for gamesmanship, not when we are their only allies in the world." She released a pent-up sigh. "Okay, get that statement ready for my eyes as quickly as possible."

"Yes, ma'am, will there be anything else?" His question hung in the air like a dark cloud. Time passed in frozen animation, until he gave a light cough.

The president looked up from the DTB with a sharp glare. "Mr. Kelly, why are you still here? I thought my instructions were clear."

Andrew cut his eyes to the right. Larry stood, arms crossed, a Mona Lisa expression painted on his face. White-lipped, he backed out and closed the door behind him.

"A little rough on the old boy. Aren't you?"

Susan lifted her eyes from the sheet of paper, "I hate weakness, and that, is one weak man."

Larry felt his face grimace at her description of his friend. "With all due respect, I think you're reading him all wrong."

"Wrong? How so?" she asked, tugging on her diamond pendant earring.

With a glance at the closed door, Larry chose his words carefully. Returning his gaze, he took a slow breath. "You might be confusing meekness with weakness. The two are exclusively different."

The president's eyes narrowed, "Larry," her voice was firm, and low, "I don't need to be given instructions on how to pick my advisors. If there's one thing I'm extremely good at, it's reading people, and that man reads like a Sunday School teacher." Her dislike for all things religious was legendary.

"Now, what about those stolen fuel rods, I didn't see it on the DTB. Have they been recovered?"

A slow nod preceded his answer. "No, Madam President. They haven't. The FBI, Homeland Security, and state officials have scoured the entire southeast and have come up with nothing. They've simply disappeared."

"Do you think whoever stole them got them out of the country before we could close the gate?"

Larry let the possibility roll around in his head a minute. "My opinion Madam President? In my opinion, they are somewhere within the continental United States being assembled into a bomb."

The president's eyes bulged. "You mean to say, we could be facing a home-grown nuclear attack and not even know it?"

"Oh, we'll know it, if it happens, Madam President. Believe you me."

President Ferguson stood, and ran her hands along the sides of her body, accentuating her form and fashion. "Look, Larry, you know my position on nuclear weapons. I am committed to a fifty percent reduction of our arsenal by the end of my first term. Something like that could embolden our enemies, confuse our allies, and strengthen the minority party. I want those spent fuel rods found, now." A tinge of desperation escaped her normally controlled voice.

"I'll get right on it, ma'am. But first, let's get through this summit."

Susan's expression softened. "Yes, let's just get through the next twenty-four hours, and then we'll address nuclear disarmament."

Larry stepped from the Presidential Suite and let the door close behind him.

"What are you doing here?" nearly running into Andrew. He leaned heavily against the paneled wall, hands in his pockets, head down. "Didn't the president give you something to do?"

A nod was all he got.

"Look man, you gotta pull yourself together. The president's counting on you."

Andrew lifted his head, his eyes narrowed. "She hates me. I can feel it."

An impatient breath escaped his lungs before he caught himself. He jammed his fists into his pockets and narrowed his eyes. "Susan doesn't hate you." A smirk parted his lips. "She may not like you, but hate is a bit strong. I've spoken to her."

"And?"

"And," he paused, "and what she admires most in a man is strength."

Andrew let out a frustrated smirk. "And I suppose you're the prime example of it?" Sarcasm etched his voice.

Hands raised in surrender, Larry stepped back. "Hey, I was just saying, do a little push back, you know, don't be so—" Larry cut his eyes in both directions, then returned to meet Andrew's, "so meek."

The shock of the statement had its intended effect, and Andrew gave his friend a crooked grin.

Chapter 34

The Israeli Command Center

Seven floors beneath the Knesset, Prime Minister Shimer ben Yousef took his seat and picked up a telephone with a direct line to the Minister of Defense.

"Yuri, the time has come, send your best to our neighbors to the east," and hung up the phone.

Within one minute, another phone rang. The commander of the Ramat, Israeli Air Force Base, one of Israel's three principal airbases located southeast of Haifa, took the call. With over 1,100 soldiers, flying the F-161 Sufa (Storm) and the F-151 Ra'am, it was the second-largest base in the IDF. The airbase boasted one-third of Israel's planes and nearly fifty-five fighters to support the Northrop Grumman B-2 Stealth Bomber. Their mission was to give protection for the 1.25 billion dollar bomber as far as the Iranian air space. From there, the B-2 would carry out its bombing run unseen and undetected at an altitude of 50,000 feet, nearly in outer space.

Having taken off hours before, the pilot of the B-2 Stealth Bomber, radioed in. "Sir, we have a lock on the targets," Colonel Shimer ben Reichmen said to his commanding officer in Ramat.

Colonel Reichmen, his name meaning the man who reigns, was a twenty-year veteran pilot. During his stellar career, he'd flown countless sorties during the 2006 Lebanon War. Now he faced his greatest challenge.

"You have permission to fire, Colonel Reichmen. Baruch Heshem Adonai, Blessed be the name of the Lord.'"

Reichmen and his co-pilot had trained for this moment, had lived for it, had prayed for it. Now that it had arrived, he paused, took a deep breath, and said the *Shema*:

"Hear, O Israel! The Lord our God is one Lord!"

Looking to his right, Reichmen nodded. His copilot lifted the green cover from a toggle switch and flipped it up. Immediately, the belly of the huge bomber opened, exposing two of its 16 two thousand pound, GPS guided J Dam bombs. With mirrored actions, the two men punched in a code. The aircraft vibrated slightly as it dropped its payload.

From their altitude, which scraped the fringes of outer-space, they watched and waited. The seconds stretched into minutes. An instant later, two flashes streaked across the sky. Had the pilot and his copilot not been wearing protective glasses, they would have been blinded as two small suns erupted, forming the familiar mushroom clouds.

Being the professionals that they were, Reichmen and his copilot avoided giving each other a high-five. Having completed their mission, he punched in a new set of coordinates and the giant plane tilted its wings and headed for home. Their only concern was bringing the big bird safely to their base. Four hours later they crossed into Israeli airspace and Colonel Reichmen breathed a sigh of relief and held up an open palm.

***

Colonel Benjamin Nystrom in his F-151 Ra'am and his wingman, flying an F-161 Sufa, streaked across the Sinai Desert 100 meters above the earth. Using laser guided rockets, they performed a surgical strike, incinerating the power plants and fueling stations located in Darkhovin, Iran, rendering Iran's nuclear capability useless.

Having successfully completed their mission, the two jets turned south and headed for Jordanian airspace hoping to go undetected.

Chapter 35

Israel's Command Center

The encrypted phones between Prime Minister Yousef and the U.S. president hissed with static, then synced. Shimer ben Yousef drummed his fingers as he waited for President Ferguson to pick up.

"Mr. Prime Minister, so good to talk with you," her smooth tones painted a thin veneer.

"Yes, Madam President, it is good to talk with you as well. Now I know this is not a call to wish me well on my 73rd birthday. I'm confident that it is related to our actions in and over Iran, is it not?"

The president's voice grew somber. "Your actions over Lebanon and Iran have placed me in an untenable position."

The prime minister of Israel fully anticipated such a statement. "Yes, Madam President, and we share your concern. My government is willing to make a full disclosure of the events which took place on the Golan Heights and in the northern territory. We have documented proof corroborating the fact our military bases were infiltrated."

A long pause held Yousef in suspended animation.

"We are encouraged that such documentation will be forth coming. My administration would welcome the opportunity to authenticate your claims. Would it be permissible to send a team of military experts to assess your military protocols and procedures?"

Prime Minister Yousef bristled at the implications. "That won't be necessary. You are aware that our IDF is the most highly trained military on the planet—"

"Yes, we know, but by your own admission, you were infiltrated. I was just making a—"

"Yes, yes, you want to appear non-partisan with your friends at the UN. Speaking of which, what position will you take today when the UN convenes?" Yousef held his breath, expecting the worst, hoping for the best.

"Well, officially yes, and we will have to join the Security Counsel of the UN in lodging a formal complaint against the state of Israel for your actions. But you know as well as I, that, that is just a slap on the wrist"

"Yes, Madam President," sounding like a school teacher. "I am not new at the game of politics. With the right hand you shake hands and with the left hand you stick the knife under the fifth rib. I'm quite aware of how the game is played."

"Yes sir, no disrespect, but that *is* how it is played. But off the record, I congratulate you on a mission well done. You have eliminated a huge threat to the region. With those nukes off of the table, Iran may be more reasonable to deal with."

"And with all due respect, Madam President, you have no idea the complexity of dealing with the Arab and Persian mind. They are probably the most treacherous military strategists in the world. They have been doing it for millennia. Even I, who have been dealing with them for 55 years of my military career, don't trust a thing they say, especially if they are smiling. It is more than 'trust and verify,' as my friend Ronald Reagan said. It's 'don't trust and still verify.' I'm not completely convinced we got them all."

"Well, I can't think of a better birthday gift."

Chuckling, "Yes, it was nice of Commander Shimer to handwrite happy birthday on those bombs."

"You know, Mr. Prime Minister, nature abhors a vacuum. Someone will take their place on the nuclear stage. Do you have any idea who it might be?"

"Well again, we Israelis have been at this for quite a while, we have our ideas."

President Ferguson's tone lightened, "We may be new at the art of gamesmanship, but we are fast learners. We also have the assets in place to keep us in the loop on an international level. In my morning up-date I was handed a list of two hot spots to keep our eyes on. One is the North Koreans and the other is the Chinese. The only thing standing between you and a couple billion Red Chinese is a few million angry Muslims. So watch your back."

Yousef smiled at the phone, "Yes Madam President, we have been monitoring those two situations and frankly, we have our concerns for America's safety as well."

"No need to worry about us. Our border security is doing a fine job of keeping out the bad guys, but thank you for your concern, Mr. Prime Minister and happy birthday."

The pencil Prime Minister Yousef had been playing with snapped in two, as his fist closed. "Thank you Madam President, good-bye."

Chapter 36

The Lebanese Parliament

The minority leader of the parliament, Sheik Zacchaeus Yakim rose to his feet to address the emergency meeting.

"After hours of searching for the former prime minister, and having not found him, are we to assume that he has fled the country, Mr. Speaker?"

A hush filled the gallery as the gavel cracked. "At this time, neither he nor Anita has been located. His security detail admits they have no clue as to their where-a-bouts. However, his limo driver has been found. His body was discovered with a single bullet hole to the head and a suicide note. Without disclosing its contents, let me say, we are looking into its claims."

Yakim continued his inquiry. "Do we have any verification of the claims by his daughter that this war was initiated by Hamas infiltrators sent from our country?"

A murmur, like wind driven sand, scattered across the assembly.

"The Israelis have supplied us with audio and video footage of the fire-fight within the Golan Heights military installations and on the missile launcher sites—"

"How do we know this is authentic? Why, the whole thing could be a fabrication," Yakim said.

Then the Speaker of the House cleared his throat, looking over his wire-rimmed glasses. "It is clear from video footage and eyewitness accounts they were taken over by a foreign insurgency. Who actually sent them has not yet been confirmed, but suffice it to say, according to Anita's testimony and the actions of her father, by all indications, it was initiated inside the prime minister's office."

The divided assembly began shouting, each side accusing the other of a cover-up. Again, the gavel fell, silencing the Parliament.

"Then, Mr. Speaker, I move we immediately fill the vacancy, at least temporarily, with the appointment of the Vice Prime Minister, Sheik Faheem ben Assam."

The Speaker of the House asked for and got a second. According to parliamentary procedures, he opened the floor to questions. After many hours of heated discussions, a vote was taken. Faheem ben Assam was elected Prime Minister of Lebanon, by a narrow margin.

***

By morning, news that Prime Minister Bashera had been ousted overshadowed the reports of the Israeli attack on the Darkhovin Nuclear Power Plant and unspecified targets within Iran. Like wildfire, fear spread throughout Beirut as expectations of an Israeli invasion grew. It was not safe for a Westerner to be seen in public.

As news agencies began broadcasting the Emergency Broadcast Signal, crowds of frantic Lebanese took to the streets chanting.

Fatemah awoke from a fitful sleep to the sound of the klaxons. Bleary eyed, she squinted at the clock. It screamed 9:05 a.m. The sudden realization struck her in the gut—they'd missed their appointment.

"Jared. Honey, wake up. We've overslept."

He snapped awake and leapt from the bed. Peering through the curtains in his rumpled slacks, Jared shielded his eyes from the sudden burst of light. With a quick jerk, he pulled them shut and leaned against the wall.

"What's wrong?"

"The streets are filled with gun toting Muslims."

Fatemah clutched the sheet to her mouth, "What do we do, if we are seen together we will have no hope of getting Anita out of the country," she said, glancing at Anita, who sat, curled on a sofa like a kitten.

"I may have to call Uncle Abbas and ask him to take her to the catacombs until things cool off," Jared said, eying Anita.

"Jared, you know how bad it was. She'd never make—"

Jared cut her off with a wave of his hand. "Then we'd better pray for wisdom."

Taking her hand, Jared bowed his head. "Now Lord, we are thankful for watching over us through the night, but, as you know, we overslept. We need to get ourselves and Anita to safety. Would you please guide us?"

When Jared finished, he stood and walked over to the dresser.

"Oh no," he muttered, keeping his voice low.

Fatemah turned to face him, eyes wide. "What?"

"My cell phone is dead."

Chapter 37

The Owen's Apartment

After leaving the television station, Rick and Mindy made their way back to their apartment and began packing. With any luck, they hoped to get to the Canadian embassy before it was overrun.

The phone rang, and Mindy jumped. Hand to her chest, her wide eyes watched Rick snatch it from its cradle after the third ring. "Hello?"

"Mr. Rick, this is Amana, I just wanted to call and tell you, we made it safely to Cyprus. I tried to reach Mr. Jared, but I couldn't get through."

Rick quieted Mindy's questions with the wave of his hand, then turned his attention back to Amana. "Uh, they ran into some . . . complications. But the last thing I heard was that they were planning on meeting you at the dock. I told him it wasn't a good idea, but he wouldn't listen," Rick said, his concern growing.

"Well, Captain Ali waited as long as he could, he said he hated leaving them, but if we were to make it over the reef, he had to leave then."

"I don't know what to tell you guys. I was against this from the beginning."

He waited for Amana to regain her composure. "If we don't make our next connection, we may be stranded in Cyprus indefinitely," Amana said, her throat constricting with emotion.

"Listen, Amana, things are getting out of hand here. You need to keep moving and make your next connection as planned. I'm sure Mr. Jared will call you as soon as he can."

"Okay, Mr. Rick, and thank you so much for all you and Mindy have done for us. Someday we will see you again. Good-bye."

"Good-bye Amana."

Rick turned to his wife. "Mindy, Jared and Fatemah didn't make it out."

"I thought they were supposed to meet the captain early this morning."

"They were, but Amana said they didn't get to the boat in time." Rick drummed his fingers on the end table while he considered his options.

Mindy leaned her head against the door frame. "Do you think we should go looking for them?" she asked, eyes unblinking.

Rick shook his head, "This city is in near lock-down. I heard on the news that they are setting up check-points, and the militia is running around all over the place. Pretty soon they'll start arresting any non-Muslim they see. It's not safe."

"I know," slumping back in her chair, "I was just thinking—"

Rick's cell phone rang again. He snatched it up expecting to hear Amana. "Hello?"

"Richard?"

Sitting ramrod straight, Rick blurted, "Jared! Where on earth are you? I thought you'd be gone by now."

"We should have been, but by the time we finished the video and drove to the dock, Captain Ali was gone. I called the captain, and he said to wait it out and call in around one o'clock. So we got a hotel room." He paused and let out a frustrated breath. "We fell asleep and just now woke up. Could you come and pick us up? We were thinking about making a run for it to the Canadian Embassy."

"Forget it buddy. The Canadians wouldn't touch you with a ten-foot pole, not with a fugitive of the law with you, and right now she is a wanted person. Where are you anyway? You sound like you're in a barrel."

"That's another story, but in short, my phone battery died. I'm in the hotel lobby—hold on a minute, something's wrong," Jared paused and cupped the phone as Fatemah came rushing toward him; her burqa torn, her lip bleeding. Breathlessly, she began tugging him.

"Jared, come quick."

"Fatemah, what is it? What's happened?"

She stared blankly at the door. Her lower lip quivered. "They've taken her," she gasped.

Jared stood, trying to comprehend her words, "They what?" Fatemah buried her face in his chest. "Masked men, they kicked in the door and grabbed us."

"They did what? Did they say anything?"

Trembling, Fatemah recalled the images in her mind. "It happened so fast. One man, wearing a red and white checked turban, said something to me in Arabic. They grabbed her and dragged her to a van. I tried to stop him, but he slapped me and threw me to the floor."

Jared pulled her close and thanked the Lord for protecting his wife. In the distance, he heard someone calling his name.

"Jared! *Jared*!" It was Rick.

"Rick, did you hear what happened?"

"Yeah, I heard. By her description, it sounds like Hamas, that's how they dress."

"What would Hamas want with Anita, Rick?"

"I wouldn't know, but if I were a betting man, I'd say they wanted her for leverage, maybe to draw the Ayatollah out of hiding. How should I know?"

"Do you have any idea where they might have taken her?" he asked, not expecting a real answer.

"Good question. I've heard Hamas has been operating over in Syria. If that's where they came from, then that's likely where they took her."

Jared's mouth turned to cotton. "Rick, I know this sounds ludicrous, but I feel responsible for her. She came to us for protection, and I failed her. I need to find her and get her back."

The air crackled with tension. "Jared, that's crazy. You've got no idea who you're dealing with. You'll probably get Anita and yourself killed. These are dangerous men."

"I know Rick . . . I know. But I gotta do something," Jared said, running his hand over his close-cropped hair.

Fatemah tugged at him, her eyes wild as a group of men paraded through the lobby, carrying guns.

"What are you planning?"

"The first thing I need to do is to get Fatemah some place other than this motel. I've ruled out the Harbor House. Leaving her all alone right now isn't a good idea. I may have to think on my feet."

"Look, Jared, we were about to make a run for the Canadian Embassy, but if you want us to come and get you, we will. We can stay another day or so, but then we'll have to get out of here before it all breaks loose. Are you hearing me? But I gotta tell ya buddy, you going off half-cocked is going to get you killed."

Despite the cool temperature, a stream of sweat rolled down Jared's forehead and scalded his eyes. He flicked it aside and tried to concentrate. "I appreciate your concern. This isn't the first time I've gone off half-cocked, but I gotta do something."

Chapter 38

Hamas Headquarters, Syria

Anita sat parallelized between two men as the van sped east on Paris highway, then turned to Rafic El Hariri. They took the right lane, which turned to Fakhredine Highway going south. When the exit to the expressway approached, they took it and got on General Foaad Chehab highway, which led out of the city.

Anita watched as the urban transformed into suburban, from asphalt to concrete, from four-lane to two and then to one. Her stomach knotted at the sight of the Lebanon Mountains looming ahead.

The highway swung south, turned east and cut across the rolling plains. It used to be her favorite place to go when her father toured the country. Now it was all a blur.

When they passed Sofar, Anita felt her heart go into overdrive. *The Bekaa valley, I pray they aren't taking me to the Hezbollah training camp or worse . . . Syria.*

The van, driven by a man wearing a long, straggly beard, slowed as they approached a border crossing. Two men, sporting AK-47's waved the van to a halt. For the next several minutes, the driver and guard spoke in low tones. Not being fluent in Arabic, Anita could only pick up on a few phrases. What she did understand was that she was in deep trouble.

The border guard returned from a red and white building with the clip-board in his hand. After taking one last look at the papers, he handed it to the driver and slapped the side of the van. With a nod, the driver revved the engine and sped across the border into Syria as the armed men closed the gate behind them.

Soon, they were racing north across the desert. An hour later, they sped through the lower Bekaa valley across to the towns of Chtaura and Zehle, going north. By midnight, they left the main highway and began weaving over the rugged terrain though Hermal and Qasr.

Outside the van, a deep veil of darkness shrouded the mountains. The chilled air made her wish she had a coat. After making a stop to refuel and take a bathroom break, they gathered at the back of the van.

"Where are you taking me?" she demanded as a man tied her hands behind her back.

Her driver returned a nasty grin. "You're lucky we haven't killed you and dumped you along the road. Now shut up and get back in the van."

He shoved her with the butt of his weapon, making her stumble and hit her head on the bumper.

"What are you doing you fool?" a second man shouted. "Are you trying to get us all shot?" Lowering his voice, he said, "We were told, 'Intact,' that means no cuts, no scratches, and especially no—"

Bang!

Anita's legs turned to water and she felt the blood drain from her face. With her hand to mouth, she stood, too paralyzed to scream as the man in front of her collapsed in a pool of crimson.

"Now get in or something far worse will happen," her captor snarled.

Stunned, she climbed in and drew her legs up in a tight ball. Visions of the dead man's eyes haunted her. As the next hours of riding passed, her stomach gnawed at her. She tried to not think of food, but it didn't help when the men in the front were munching on pretzels and drinking pop.

Her head bobbed, and she was thrown to the side as the road turned from concrete to a rutted dirt road. One of the guards said something in Arabic, and he pulled a hood from his pocket and shoved it down over her head nearly suffocating her. They bounced along for another kilometer, and the vehicle jolted to a stop.

Outside, Anita heard voices shouting and hands banging on its sides. Someone yanked the doors open, grabbed her by the ankles and dragged her out, kicking. Her foot landed solidly in the man's groin sending him groaning. Men's voices rallied around her, laughing while another man grappled with her flailing feet. Finally, he stood her upright and held her steady until someone cut the rope which bound her hands. With tingling fingers, she rubbed her wrists trying to restore the blood flow.

All around her, male voices chattered wildly as she was pulled through the crowd. With every labored step, she felt the course hands of men touching her body. She fought them off, only to be grabbed by another. The pungent smell of oily canvas cut into her nose, making her gag, and she doubled over. Someone jerked the hood from her head. She rose up and stared into the eyes of her father.

Chapter 39

The Owens House

"That idea is ludicrous," Rick spoke with chopped deliberateness, punctuating every syllable.

So much for that suggestion. Jared ran his hand over his head, after asking his friend to drive him as far as the borders of Lebanon and Syria.

"Besides," he continued, "the military buildup can be seen for miles. Roads are jammed with tanks and APCs, and there are checkpoints at nearly every town and city between here, and Damascus. Getting anywhere is a nightmare."

Jared sat at the small dining room table, nursing a mug of black coffee. Rick had risked his life in bringing Jared and Fatemah back to his apartment, but was unwilling to stick his head out any further.

"Look, I appreciate your concern, but somewhere out there is a frightened, defenseless, fifteen-year-old girl. Who knows what they may be doing to her. What if she were your daughter or sister? As far as I'm concerned, she is family," glancing at Fatemah. "Remember, she's your cousin, and our sister in the Lord."

Rick jumped to his feet sending his chair sprawling. "She's your what?" his mouth gaped open.

"She's my cousin," Fatemah confessed, "I found out about it back in September. When I hired her, she told me her name was Sumara or something. But then she overheard us talking and admitted her last name was Bashera. She is the prime minister's daughter."

Rick slapped his hand on the table, "So that's why she was kidnapped. It was probably her father's men who snatched her." His words came in short, angular phrases.

"All the more reason to get her back," Jared said, not taking his eyes off of the television screen. The news loop played the footage of Anita sitting calmly in front of the camera speaking the truth, speaking to the heart of the nation, putting her life on the line.

Rick took a seat next to his wife who sat rocking, nearly hysterical. "I certainly hope you're not thinking about going with him." she said, her face buried in her hands.

With care, he lifted her chin with his fingers, brushed the hair from her eyes, and kissed her forehead. "I don't know. It would be suicide even to step out of the house, let alone venture across this city."

Fatemah remained quiet, listening to both sides of the argument, stood and walked over to Jared and knelt in front of him. "I think you're right, Jared. She is family. God brought her to us and we owe it to her." Her jaw set, her eyes glowed with determination.

After a long moment, Rick stood and took his place by Jared. He stuck out his hand and pulled Jared to his feet.

"You are either the bravest man I've ever met or the craziest." Rick looked over Jared's shoulder at his wife. "If I could go, I would, but—"

"You needn't make excuses. Your place is with Mindy, mine is to rescue Anita." He'd somehow convinced the others . . . he just needed to convince himself.

"Jared, have you given much thought about how you are going to do that?"

Rubbing his neck, Jared looked up. "I'm working on it, I'm working on it."

"We may not be able to go with you, but we can at least stock you with some supplies. Mindy, remember my hiking gear, let's see if there's something Jared could use."

She stood and glared at him. Her hands curled into two tight balls and she stomped into the bedroom.

Rick pulled an old back pack from the closet and handed it to Fatemah. "Would you mind filling this with some staple goods while we go over this map?"

She took the back pack and went to the pantry. After rifling through their pantry looking for granola bars, beef jerky, bottles of water and some medical supplies, she returned. "Here, you'll need these," she said, her lower lip trembling.

Jared reached out and drew her close. "If I didn't know you would be praying for me, I wouldn't set foot out of that door."

A wry smile preceded her sultry voice. "You had better come back to me with no new holes, or I'll shoot you."

Without thinking, Jared's hand found the scar on his shoulder and began to massage the wound. Memories of the darkened halls beneath the Mosque, where Raleigh and Ahmad fought and died, still haunted him. The bullet which passed through his shoulder nearly ended his life, and he still felt the pain of losing his friends. "I know this a dumb question, but you guys wouldn't happen to have a gun lying around here would you?"

Rick looked up from the map. "Nope. Sorry, we had to leave all that stuff at the point of entry. I do have a nice fishing knife one of my students gave me as a gift a few weeks ago." He went to his dresser and lifted it out."

"What are you doing," muttered Mindy, sitting on the bed, too shocked to move.

"Look, if Jared is willing to risk his life to go after Anita, the least we can do is give him our support."

"But a knife?"

"Yes, even a knife. He might need it to …" he let his voice fade.

Rick returned to the living room and pulled the knife from its sheath. The light danced off its razor-sharp blade. "Are you sure you can handle this thing? I mean really use it, if it came down to it?"

"If you mean, do I have the killer instinct, let's just say, once a Marine, always a Marine. Yes. I can kill if I have to!"

Beep! Beep!

A horn honked outside their apartment, breaking the thick moment. Rick stepped to the curtain and peeked out.

"It's that guy, the taxi driver. He's waving his hand and looking up here."

"Did someone call for a taxi?" Jared asked, looking through a lifted blind.

Rick's face contorted. "Not me, but I think your ride has just arrived."

Jared placed his hands on his hips and shook his head. "I don't know how he does it? Every time I need a ride, he shows up. I never have to call him."

"Where the Lord guides, he provides," Fatemah said, smiling through her tears.

Reluctantly, Jared kissed her and hugged her one last time. He reached down and picked up the back pack, slung it over his shoulder, and made his way down stairs.

Habib jumped out, "Assalamu alaikum y'all," having picked up a little southern vernacular.

Unable to keep from laughing, Jared gave the young man a bear hug. "Assalamu alaikum, to you too, my friend. What are you doing here? And how did Uncle Abbas know we needed him?"

The demure man climbed out of his rickety taxi. His dark, warm eyes bore into Jared's heart. "I heard the voice of God telling me to go to Mr. Rick's apartment and help with a task which the Lord will show."

"Oh? And what task is that?" Jared asked.

"God told me you about the journey you were about to embark on, that you would need the assistance of one who knows the roads. My nephew was, for a short time, a member of Hamas. He knows their ways, knows their hideouts. He will help you to find Anita."

Jared eyed his friend with interest, "Hamas?"

Scuffing the ground, Habib nodded slowly, "It's a long story."

After a moment, Jared released a heavy sigh. "I don't like the idea of putting another person's life in danger, but I sure could use the help."

"Rick, do something," Mindy protested.

Ignoring her, Rick continued "He's right, who better to go with him. I certainly can't. Why not have Habib go? He certainly knows the lay of the land."

Stepping next to his nephew, Uncle Abbas placed a gnarled hand on the young man's back. "The Good Lord has told me to lift up my eyes unto the hills, from there, my help will come. He will not permit your foot to be moved: he who keeps you neither sleeps nor slumbers. He will preserve you from all evil from this time forth, and even forevermore."

A peace washed over Jared. He scanned the faces of his wife and Rick. He knew God had just spoken to their hearts, too.

"Now I can take you as far as the border. Then you and Habib will have to go the rest of the way on foot. That would be best anyway. If I were to drive up in a taxi, they might get a little suspicious." A wry smile brightened his weathered face. "I am sorry that I don't have a weapon to give you, but remember that the weapons of our warfare are not carnal, but mighty through God to the pulling down of strong holds."

"That may be true, but I sure would feel a lot better if I had something better than a sling shot," Jared quipped.

Fatemah drew closer, "Yes, yet I seem to remember what one well-placed stone could do. Now go, before I decide to go with you."

Jared waited until Uncle Abbas and Habib got into the taxi, and paused.

"What are you thinking, Jared?" Fatemah asked.

"I'm thinking that you, Rick, and Mindy are going to have a tough time getting out of the country. Maybe they should accompany you to the *el Labrador,* and let Captain Ali take you to the *Pearl Lady*. I'm sure Mr. Xavier can work out the details as far as their visas are concerned."

Fatemah glanced over her shoulder, "That may take some doing, but I think it's a good idea. I'll talk to them about it. Meanwhile, call me and let me know if, I mean, when you find Anita. I'll be praying for you."

Rick nodded and glanced at Mindy who stood, her fists in tight balls. "It might take some convincing, but I think she'll come around," he said, reaching out his hand. "May God go with you, my friend."

After hugging Fatemah one last time, Jared squeezed into the taxi. A moment later, it sped off, leaving a trail of black smoke.

***

No sooner had Uncle Abbas and his passengers left the suburbs than they found themselves sitting in bumper-to-bumper traffic at a check-point. With time slipping away, Uncle Abbas cut the wheels to the right; jumped the curb, and raced to the next corner, chasing an elderly man, walking his dog, out of the way in the process. A woman screamed and grabbed her daughter moments before the yellow cab skidded past her stoop.

A break in the traffic appeared and Uncle Abbas sped through it. Down an alley he raced, through the narrow passage, knocking over trash cans and sending dogs scampering for safety. Jared grabbed the dashboard and braced himself as the little automobile approached the next intersection. Rather than slowing, the older man gunned the engine, popped out of the alley, and onto the main thoroughfare a block past the check-point. Deep prints in the dashboard marked where Jared's fingers gouged into it, and he released a tense breath.

"Do you always scare the living day-lights out of your fares?"

A smile parted the old taxi driver's rugged face. "No, only when I have urgent business to attend to. And this is most urgent."

Habib leaned forward, "In all the years I've known Uncle Abbas, he has never had one of his passengers die on him."

Hand to his heart, still panting, Jared wiped the sweat from his brow. "Well, I thought I was the first for a moment."

"Not to worry, you were never in any danger, my Son. God is my shield and my buckler."

"Yes, well, I wouldn't push my luck too much," Jared said, still catching his breath. "Why are you going west and not east?"

A pair of unflinching eyes stared back at Jared. "East would take us over the mountains and then north. That would put us on a road which travels directly through the infamous Bekaa valley."

"Believe me," Habib interjected, "you don't want to go there."

Jared's pulse quickened at the thought of him falling into the hands of Hamas or worse, Hezbollah. *If my mama only knew what I'z gettin' myself into, she shoot me for sure.*

Taking the coastal highway, Uncle Abbas drove north as far as Tripoli, and started whistling the Marine's hymn. Jared gave a half smile at the older man's attempt and joined the tune. As they sped north, the road forked and Abbas flicked on his right signal.

"This will put us on Al Minie. It will cut through the narrow mountain pass and take us right up to the Lebanon-Syrian border."

Jared nodded, watching the landscape change.

By nightfall, they'd reached the northernmost border, and Uncle Abbas brought his taxi to a stop. "That will be two thousand American dollars," he said, a wry smile crinkled the crow's feet around his eyes.

Jared wiped his brow, "After the scare you gave me back in town, you should be paying me reparations."

"Touché, my friend, touché."

Like two monarch butterflies emerging from their cocoons, Jared and Habib emerged from the taxi and stretched.

"Thank you Uncle Abbas, we'll need the prayers of your people, if we are to save Anita and come out of this alive," Jared said, leaning over and locking eyes.

The older man's face wrinkled into a smile. "My son, I have been praying for you and your wife ever since the day you saved that young man's life. If you recall, it was I who brought you back to your hotel."

Jared straightened and shifted the weight of the back-pack. His mind replayed those days, and he felt his face brighten. "Yes, yes, I remember now. That was you. You wondered if we had counted the cost."

His eyebrows rose in question. "Have you?"

Placing a hand on the roof of the taxi, Jared peered down. "I seem to remember a story of a shepherd who left the ninety-and nine in search of one lost sheep." Jared paused and took a deep breath. "Yes, my old friend, I have. I can do no less than what the Good Shepherd has done for me."

Uncle Abbas gripped Jared's extended hand. "I will pray that God will send his holy angels to keep you, lest you dash your foot against a stone."

He released Jared's hand and slowly pulled away, leaving them standing on a lonely stretch of road.

Habib gazed up at the January sky. A bank of angry clouds threatened rain. "We'd better get moving before someone spots us," he said, and began a measured pace. "This road will take us to the border crossing. At this time of night, the guards will be in the guard-shack. We should be able to slip past them without being stopped. From there, it will take us deep into the mountains."

"Do you really know the area?"

"I have come through this area many times, I know it well. Once we get across, we should find a place to rest. Tomorrow we can travel by day, but after that, we'd better limit our movements to the night, or the look-outs will spot us and shoot us on sight."

Jared looked over his shoulder, "That's not a very nice way to greet visitors, now is it?"

A flicker of remorse darkened Habib's face. "What can I say? They have a shoot first and ask questions later policy."

***

As dawn broke over the harbor of the Bay of Beirut, a small fishing trawler gently glided through the no-wake zone and docked in its berth. Overhead, sea gulls squawked and plunged headlong into the surf in search of their next meal. Sand-pipers raced each other across the freshly washed sand, hoping to find an unsuspecting snail for breakfast.

A yellow taxi sat along the curb, its engine coughing black smoke. A moment later, three people stepped out and dashed down the gangplank to the boat. After an animated conversation, Captain Ali threw up his hands in surrender.

"Okay, but this will cost your husband another two thousand dollars," he said to Fatemah.

She motioned for Rick and Mindy to board while she fished through her purse. She handed him a wad of money. The old sea captain accepted it with a grunt and began untying the vessel from its moorings. Within a few minutes, they were headed back out to sea.

As the small craft cleared the no-wake zone and entered into the channel, the Lebanese Border Patrol caught sight of them. Not wanting to be boarded, Captain Ali revved the engines and headed for the open sea, and the race was on. Ignoring the repeated calls from the pursuing authorities, the sea warrior refused to yield. With its throttles rammed wide open, the old trawler lunged forward, quickly putting distance between it and the cruiser.

Determined not to let yet another border runner escape, the cruiser came about and gave chase. Its deck crew threw off the canvas cover from its 50 caliber cannon, as the spray from the waves pelted their weathered faces. Flashes lit up the morning sky as the pounding machine gun began firing. The first wave of shells ripped through the wheel house sending shards of wood and glass over the deck.

Captain Ali pulled himself from the wreckage and rolled down the single flight of stairs only to be greeted with another volley. This one cut through the hull, hitting the fuel tanks. A fire broke out in the engine room filling the lower cabin with heavy smoke.

The situation was hopeless, and the skipper hollered, "Abandon ship. Grab something you can use to float on and jump!"

As the boat listed to its side, Captain Ali helped Fatemah to the gun rail where water lapped at their feet. He glanced around. "Where are the others?"

"I don't know. They were right behind me." Fatemah's throat closed from the billowing smoke.

Another blast shattered the portholes below deck severing its spine in two. Fatemah turned. "I've got to go back for Rick and Mindy."

The captain's powerful grip forced her to the gun-rail. He grabbed a life-ring, shoved it in her hands.

"Jump, I'll go back and find them."

With a quick push, Fatemah leaped into the freezing waters, as another round of shells strafed the beleaguered ship's deck. She hit the icy surface and gasped, gulping in a mouth full of the salty brine.

"Captain Ali!"

He ignored her call for help and turned. Another blast sent him reeling over the edge. He disappeared in the foam. Splashing wildly, Fatemah found the bubbling swirl where he'd fallen. She grabbed for anything solid. A moment later, her hand gripped his, and she yanked. He came up sputtering.

"You all right?" she coughed, spitting out salt water.

"I'll make it, now swim before she blows," his voice raspy and tense.

"What about the others?" Fatemah asked.

"Swim!"

***

"Come on Mindy, the ship is sinking," Rick called over the rat-a-tat tat of bullets.

Huddled in a corner of their stateroom, water lapping around her waist, Mindy cringed, too frightened to move. "No! I can't swim." Her voice smothered in fear.

The cabin listed, sending Rick tumbling against the bulkhead. "Honey, if we don't abandon ship now, we'll die."

"No! I won't go, don't leave me." The whites of her eyes flashed in panicked beats.

Hands on the door frame, Rick pulled closer and enveloped his trembling wife in his arms. "It's okay honey. I'm right here."

Another burst of lead ripped through the mortally wounded vessel followed by a flash. Burning debris, and smoke shot into the morning sky as the explosion tore the *el Labrador* apart. The heavy aft section sank first, then the foresail, containing two bodies, disappeared into the black water of the bay.

***

Fatemah watched helplessly as the scene unfolded. "Nooo!" she cried as the realization hit her with the force of a tidal wave.

As she tried to swim toward the burning wreckage, Captain Ali grabbed her. "You can't help them now. They're lost." His words stung like acid. He was right, but the weight of losing her friends overwhelmed her, and she slipped under the surface.

Chapter 40

Bellanca Airfield, New Castle, Delaware

The sun peeked over the New Jersey horizon as if embarrassed to begin another day. Orange rays reflected off the murky waters of the Delaware River, sending up more moisture into the already humid air. Swarms of over-grown mosquitoes gathered, searching for their next victim. Inside the old Bellanca aircraft hangar, shafts of grey light filtered through grungy glass panes, giving it an eerie pallor.

The front door slammed with such force that it sent a wave of shivers throughout the cavernous building. Rajeed's voice rose above the clamor.

"What do you mean, you don't think my plan will work?" he demanded.

Ever since his arrival a month ago, he'd changed his mind so many times, his men lost count. Confidence in his ability to lead waned with every passing day. His temper tantrums became legendary. Already half of the scientists and technicians had bolted.

"Of course it will work. I have designed this schematic to exact specifications. All you need to do is follow my instructions and make five nuclear bombs," Rajeed told Ali Khan, the lead technician.

"As I told Uri and your father, we need more uranium for the size bombs you want."

"That is not possible. This is all we are going to get. To acquire any more will draw too much attention. If you will shut up for five minutes and let me explain my plan, you will see it is much better."

Ali Khan held his stare. "You understand if I don't obey your father what might happen to my family, to the families of my team? He has invested millions of dollars assembling the best mathematicians, chemists, and metallurgists from all over the

Islamic world for one purpose, to cut the head off of the Great Satan. Now you come along with this foolish idea?" he tossed the schematic to the floor.

Shaken by the scientist's insults, Rajeed bent over, picked it up, and stomped into his office.

As he did, Uri drew his sidearm and pointed it at Khan's stomach. "It's not a foolish idea." Then he pulled the trigger.

Ali doubled over as the round ripped through his abdomen, sending him sprawling to the floor.

"Give me a sword!" he hollered as the technician writhed in pain.

A flurry of movement produced a razor sharp weapon. He snatched the sword from a shaken guard's hand.

"This is what will happen to anyone who questions my leadership." He raised the blade above his head and brought it down with a swish.

Ali's head plopped to the floor and rolled.

"Now, get back to work or this will be your fate," Uri said as the veins in his forehead bulged.

The shaken technicians gaped at him as he followed Rajeed into his office.

***

A solitary guard stomped his feet to drive out the bitter cold. He'd kept vigil all night, watching a dazzling display of stars over Mackinaw City pass in review. Now, in the pre-dawn hours, he longed for a hot cup of coffee and a warm bed. One last time, he broke the silence to check in. There was nothing to report.

Teriek Azar, the leader of a Jihadist sleeper cell, watched his men, dressed as waiters and cooks, load the vans with supplies. Earlier that month, having been informed by Amil of the upcoming summit meeting, he and a few of his team broke into the maintenance level of the Grand Hotel and buried a cache' of weapons. Now it was time to put his plan into action.

"Step it up guys, the ferry leaves in twenty-five minutes, and I want to be on it," he said.

If all went well, about this time tomorrow the whole thing would be over, and we will have rendered the Great Satan toothless.

Using falsified documents, Azar and his men infiltrated the Mackinaw Catering Service the Grand Hotel used for special occasions.

"All finished, boss," Kaleel Bashera, known to Azar as Farooq-e-Azam, said.

"Good, get the boys loaded up and let's go," he ordered.

With a quick nod, he ushered the others into the vans. The grim-faced men sat quietly as they headed to the pier where the ferry was moored.

"Farooq," Azar said, calling Kaleel from the back of the van. "When the action starts, be sure to keep me in your sights. I have a man on the inside who will move the moment I give him the signal. It is your job to make sure he doesn't fail."

Kaleel nodded, giving nothing away. "As you wish sir, anything for Allah and the great Jihad," he answered, looking into the faces of the men he'd been training with for the last several months.

Kaleel knew he was dealing with a very dangerous man. Were it not for the fact that the CIA had given him clear instructions, he'd have taken out Teriek a lot sooner. He also knew there was another assassin involved, but didn't know who. Until Teriek made his move, he wasn't sure who to look for. He had to let the game play out. He had to wait, and watch for his opportunity to act.

The two van caravan neared the dock and was met by an army of Secret Service agents. Azar, being in the lead vehicle, slowed and rolled down his window.

"Stop right here sir. No one is allowed to cross over to Mackinaw Island today," the agent said.

Azar produced a clipboard with clearance papers. "Sir, we are with the Mackinaw Catering Service. The management of the Grand Hotel has contracted us for the special event, and we are expected to arrive over there in thirty minutes to relieve the kitchen staff."

The officer scanned the documents and then waved them forward. The security agents swarmed the two vans and began inspecting them using bomb-sniffing dogs and metal detectors. The team of agents opened every box of canned goods and ran their hands through the crates of fresh vegetables.

"Careful of those bottles, sir," Azar said, as the security agents began prying open the cases of liquors. "You might get away with ruining our vegetables, but don't mess with the President's booze."

The young officer smiled and nodded knowingly.

After a few minutes, he returned to the driver's side window and handed Azar the clipboard. "All clear sir, you may proceed to the ferry."

Azar gave him a weak salute, started the engine and pulled forward until he reached the yellow line. Minutes later, the gate closed and they began the slow cruise across the chilly waters of the bay.

Chapter 41

Hamas Base Camp, Syria

"Anita, so good to have you drop in. I hope your ride wasn't too uncomfortable," he laughed.

Narrowing her eyes, Anita bit back her thoughts. *You beast.*

"Now, I don't have long, so I'll get right to the point before I execute you. How did you gain such sensitive knowledge? Your video revealed highly classified information which only I knew." He paused and tried to stroke her face with his thumb.

"Don't touch me," brushing his hand away.

Again his belly jostled in laughter. "By the way, you looked beautiful on the television, like your mother, Allah rest her soul. It's unfortunate that your pretty head will soon be in a basket," his whiskey laden breath enveloped her.

"Shoo, you smell like a brewery."

Smack!

His hand left a welt that burned her soul. Anita's heart leaped to her throat. This was her father, the man who she once adored, who adored her. At one time, she was his world, and he was hers, but not now. Something in him changed. He was not the man she knew. Maybe it was his wealth, his power, his position. Whatever it was, it was evil, and she despised him for what he'd become.

With one glance at the trappings of wealth, opulence, and indulgence, Anita's stomach knotted, and she blushed. *This was nothing more than a brothel.* Women dressed in revealing clothes, paraded around the room with wanton eyes, some as young as herself, while others, like lionesses, lorded over the pack.

"I have nothing to hide Papa," she said, her hand to her cheek, "it all happened quite innocently. You see, I was in your office straightening the curtains when you came in and started talking on

\your private phone. If I revealed myself, you would have shot me on the spot. If I didn't, I feared I would have been discovered, and you would have shot me anyway. So I stayed behind the curtain and waited," she said with the wave of her hand. Her mind raced, trying desperately to think of a way out. "I had to go to the bathroom so bad. You can't imagine."

Despite the seriousness of the situation, her father held her by the shoulders and laughed. "Well, it's an unfortunate and foolish thing you did. Regretfully, I must kill you. I hope you understand."

Abdullah scanned the faces of his men. Some smirked, others bore a dower look. "What? I can't let this type of insubordination go unpunished, can I?"

"Oh, I understand completely Father," she said, shaking off his hands. "Does this mean I don't have to marry that detestable Sheikh Omar whatshisname? I wonder what he will think about your reneging on your deal."

Her father's eyes widened as he broke into laughter.

Looking around, Anita saw that her quick wit pleased all but his most rabid supporters.

After a minute, he regained his composure and eyed her warily, "Tell me a story, and I'll let you live until morning."

Anita searched her memory for something, anything to tell her father. Memories long banished to the past rushed forward as she remembered her mother telling her bedtime stories. Stories like Scheherazade, the beautiful young girl in the story of the Arabian Nights, who told the king a never-ending story to prevent her sister from being executed.

"I remember the story of a Prophet of God." She knew her father would listen if it involved a prophet, she took her chances.

Abdullah clapped his hands, and one of the women brought him a thick pillow on which he sat. "Continue," he said, with the flick of his wrist.

Anita cleared her throat and began pacing as she spoke. "A long time ago, the king of Syria was warring against Israel. He said to his commanders," in a heavy tone, "'I plan on camping in a certain place.'" She lightened her voice. "But the prophet of God sent word to the king of Israel, saying, 'Beware that you do not pass this place, for the Syrians are there'."

By now, Anita knew she had her father's attention. He was hanging on to every word. She continued, "The king of Israel thanked the prophet of God and avoided that area. The prophet did this not once, but on several occasions."

Her father pounded his hand into the pillow, "What? Why did he do that?" he raged.

Anita narrowed her eyes and held a wry smile. "Now the king of Syria was greatly troubled because of this thing. He called his servants and said," then, darkening her tone to match her father's, she moved with animation, accentuating the drama, "will you not tell me who among us is on the side of the king of Israel?' And one of his servants said, 'None, my lord, O king; but the prophet of God tells the king of Israel the words that you speak in your bedroom'. And he said," in an ominous tone, "'go and see where the prophet of God is, that I may arrest him'. They said, 'Behold, he is in Dothan'. So he sent horses and chariots and a great army, and they came by night and surrounded the city. When the servant of the prophet of God rose early in the morning, went out, behold, an army with horses and chariots surrounded the city. And the servant of the prophet said, 'Alas, my master! What shall we do? for we are surrounded.' The old prophet said, 'Do not be afraid, for those who are with us are more than those who are with them.' Then the prophet of God prayed and said, 'O God, open the eyes of my servant that he may see.' So God opened the eyes of the young man, and he saw, and behold, the mountain was filled with horses and chariots of fire all around them. When the Syrians came down against them, the prophet of God prayed again and said, 'Lord, strike this people with blindness.' So he struck them with blindness in accordance with the prayer of the prophet. And the prophet said to them, 'This is not the way, and this is not the city. Follow me, and I will bring you to the man whom you seek.' And he led them to a city in Israel.

As soon as the king of Israel saw them, he said to the prophet 'My father, shall I strike them down? Shall I kill them?' And he said, 'You shall not strike them down. Would you strike down those whom you have taken captive with your sword and with your bow? Set bread and water before them, so that they may eat and drink and go to their master.' So the king of Israel prepared for them a great feast. When they had finished eating and drinking, he sent them back to their master. And the Syrians did not attack Israel again for a long time."

Delighted by her story, her father clapped his hands, and one of her guards appeared. "Wonderful," extending his index finger from a balled fist, he said, "you shall live one more day. Tomorrow we will have a big feast, then I will execute you."

Anita returned a coy smile, thinking of another story.

Chapter 42

Al Mouzeina Mountains

The valley, through which a small estuary cut, was lined with a thick overgrowth and towering trees. With every step forward, Jared and Habib's advance met with resistance. Vines, like a cat of nine-tails, clawed at their exposed flesh. Pellets of crimson dotted Jared's forearm, staining his sleeve. Finally, after hours of hacking, they found a narrow path which skirted the swirling waters of a river.

"I'm sure glad your uncle insisted we wear BDU's and combat boots. I'd hate to think what we'd look like if we didn't," Jared said, pulling yet another vine from his pant leg. "Does he always carry such equipment everywhere he goes?"

Habib stumbled over an outcropping and landed in a bramble bush. He pushed himself up, brushed off the dirt from his knee and smiled sheepishly. "I don't think so, but he seems to always have what he needs, when he needs it. He says it's a gift."

Jared took a swig of water and handed Habib the canteen. After a few minutes, they moved forward.

"This is where we follow the river," Habib said, pointing to the smooth surface of the waters. "We can let the current take us close to Rayak. Then we will need to get out and stick to the road.

The chilled water sent a shock wave through Jared's body as he waded in deeper. Jared caught Habib's eyes. "You didn't mention the water was freezing."

Habib smiled. His teeth chattering, "I didn't mention it because I forgot how cold this river can be. It is supplied with melting snow coming from those mountains," pointing to the horizon.

"Habib, I really appreciate you taking me to the rebel's camp. I just wish I had a wet suit."

He let out a jagged laugh. "Well, I'm not doing it just for you. I'm here to help rescue Anita."

Jared took a halting breath, "You know we could get killed, have you taken that into consideration?"

Habib swished the icy water from his face, "Yes. I knew it before I volunteered, but if you're talking about being ready to face death, I've given it a lot of thought."

"And?"

"And, I'm not ready to decide," he said through purple lips. "So far, I haven't seen the need to make such a radical change in my life, not without compelling evidence."

"Would the testimony of someone coming back from the dead be evidence enough?" Jared pressed.

Habib climbed up the bank, breathing hard and shivering. "That is a good question, one I have never thought of. If we make it through this, I would like to know more about it."

A puff of frustration escaped Jared's lungs. *Lord, open his eyes before it's too late.* Rebuking himself for his reaction, Jared wrung out the water from his pant legs and stomped his feet. "We'd better find some shelter where we can build a fire before hypothermia sets in."

Pointing with his nose, Habib looked ahead, "Rayak isn't that far. Maybe we can find an abandoned building and rest there."

After a few minutes, Habib fell into an even pace with Jared and the two marched along the shadowed road in silence. The light rain filtered through the trees, adding to their discomfort.

"Mr. Jared, did I hear you correctly when you said you built a Mosque?"

Jared, taken aback by the question, nodded, "It's a long story, but for now, suffice it to say, it was my job, and it nearly cost me my life."

Eyebrows raised, Habib held Jared's gaze. "Do you want to talk about it?"

After a few long paces, Jared quickly recounted the events which led up to that moment. "There were some radical Jihadists, who'd taken my pastor into the lower levels of the Mosque and were threatening to kill him. My friend Ahmad, a new believer, insisted on coming along with me to help get him back. Together, we entered the basement. While there, we got caught in a firefight that left me badly wounded." Jared's eyes glistened. "You would have liked Ahmad," pinching the moisture with his fingers.

His friend smiled, "What happened?" His interest clearly piqued.

Jared swallowed the apple-sized lump and continued. "I'd been hit in the shoulder and was a bit dazed when Ahmad stepped up and began firing his gun. I know he killed several men before taking a bullet in the chest." Jared's throat grew thick with emotion, and he paused. The pain was still too fresh.

For a few minutes, the two walked in silence as the scenes replayed themselves again in Jared's mind.

"Do you think it may come to that when we get to where we're going?" Habib's next question jolted him to the present,

After a halting breath, Jared glanced up. "I don't know. I just want you to know we are in this together. We need to back each other all the way."

"Well, I'm not very big, or brave like your friend Ahmad, but I'll do what it takes to get Anita to safety."

"Anita is a special girl, isn't she?"

He nodded, his bluish lips parting in a wide smile.

"I was wondering about that. You only met Anita a few times."

"Yes, well, that's all it took. I am deeply in love with her. I knew it the moment I laid eyes on her. She is feisty, intelligent, opinionated, and beautiful."

"And you learned this in just one afternoon?"

"Yeah, well, it took us quite a while to stock the pantry. And then there was Thanksgiving. Remember it was me who volunteered to wash the dishes along with Anita," he said, the whites of his teeth showing.

"I see," Jared said, knowingly.

"And how does the young lady feel about you, my young friend?"

"I'm not quite sure, she acts like she likes me, but then she would act all stand-offish. I can't figure her out."

"Now there you have it," Jared said triumphantly.

"There I have what?"

"There you have empirical proof that the lady in question definitely likes you."

"How? Why? I mean, how do you know that?"

"Trust me, I should know, I'm married to one of those kind of people. It is an art form, they are born with it. They somehow know how to push your buttons all at the same time, making you think that you are in control. And then they act all kind of detached like 'who me?'"

Habib ran his fingers through his wavy hair and shook it out. "What do I do?"

"She likes you buddy, believe you me . . . she likes you."

Habib had never had a fatherly talk with his dad, and this was the closest he came to having one. He smiled as he let Jared's counsel sink in. "Now I really want to get to know Anita."

***

Long shadows, like barriers, stretched across the road as the evening sun bid the world good night. The familiar chirp of crickets and burp of frogs greeted Jared and Habib as they neared a town. It was Rayak, Syria, a sleepy village made up of a half-dozen huts and a well. A scrawny dog paused, assessed the strange visitors, then tucked his tail and scurried across the dusty street. Nothing else moved.

Jared passed the first of several bombed out houses and wondered what all the fighting was about. To him, the town looked no larger than a whistle stop. By his reckoning, it held no strategic significance. Nevertheless, signs of war surrounded him as evidenced by the bullet ridden buildings and pot-holes left from incoming mortar rounds.

In the distance, muffled cries saturated thick air. Habib raised his hand. Crouching low, he approached a vacant house and peered in. Jared moved closer as the weeping grew louder. Inside, a woman sat rocking the body of a teenage boy . . . it was her son, and he was dead.

Against Jared's protests, Habib pushed past him. Glass and rubble crunched beneath his feet as he stepped through the shattered frame of the door and drew near to her. Jared followed him in and listened as Habib's voice softened. With a tenderness that surprised him, Habib asked, "Can we help you bury your son?"

Vacant eyes held his gaze, too weak to answer.

With great care, Habib gently lifted the body of the boy from her arms and stood while Jared cleared a path to allow him out. Moments later, they stepped from the rubble and made their way to an old cemetery. Using a few primitive tools, Jared and Habib carved out a shallow grave and placed the body of her son in it. Then, with care, they replaced the dirt and laid some rocks on top making a small rise over the grave. No one spoke, no one needed to.

The deafening sound of crickets wafted from across the tree-lined road as they guided the grieving mother back to the bombed out structure she called home.

Looking over his shoulder, Habib asked the woman, "Mother, do you have any weapons around here?"

Without speaking, the grief-stricken woman led them to the back of the structure. She pushed away some timber and rocks, letting them fall to the ground with a thud. Her gnarled hands brushed the remaining dirt from the top of a large box and lifted the lid. She pulled back a piece of tattered canvas revealing a cache of weapons and ammunition.

"This is all there is, but there is no one left to use them. Hamas came here yesterday and took all the men and young men out of town and shot them. I don't know why." Her hand covered her mouth as she began to weep again. After a moment, she continued. "We used to be a proud and noble people, but we have been reduced to nothing. I have no use for these, here . . . take them. May God use them to bring justice upon the murderers who killed my husband and son."

Habib stared, wide-eyed at Jared who moved quickly to fill his backpack with the handguns and ammunition. Beneath an oil cloth lay a couple AK 47s and several magazines. Jared checked the action and slung one over his shoulder, then tossed the other to Habib.

As Jared dug deeper, he uncovered some bricks of C4 and a RPG. "Let's take these, too. We just might need them."

Habib accepted the grenade launcher with an interesting glint in his eye.

"You do know how to shoot that thing, don't you?"

"I uh . . . well, I'll figure it out if I need to," he said, his tone carried a hint of confidence.

Jared's ears perked up at the inflection in Habib's voice. *I wonder if he knows more than he's saying.* He shook his doubts. *This is no time to be questioning your team.*

As they finished, the elderly woman returned from the front of the building. In her gnarled hands, she bore a tray of bread, cheese, and cups for tea. She smiled and set it on the floor. "I have blankets, you will need them on your journey," she said to Habib, who nodded his thanks. Then she receded into the shadows and her grief.

After kindling a small fire, Jared took a seat on an overturned five-gallon bucket and forced down the scant meal the woman provided. The bread was moldy, as was the cheese. One sip of the hot liquid and Jared recoiled, "This tea is thick as mud," he sputtered.

"Be grateful, that was all the old woman had, and she gave it to us." Habib's words stung like fire-ants.

The two men sat in silent contemplation while overhead, thick clouds masked the moon's presence.

"Habib, let's take four-hour watches. I'll start the first one," Jared broke the silence.

"You sure?"

"Yeah, that tea has me so wired, I may not sleep for days," he chuckled.

As the long hours dragged by, Jared couldn't help but think about Fatemah. Questions swirled around in his mind like a dust devil. How was she doing? Did she and the Owens make it to the boat? Did they get across the border? Was this whole thing a set up? And how about John Xavier? Why was he so interested in the Harbor House? Where was all that money coming from? What about Anita, how was she connected? And Habib, how does he fit in?

A soft beep brought Jared to attention, and he whispered, "Habib."

He groaned, "Is it time?"

"Yes, I'm going to walk out the cramps in my legs, and then try to get some sleep," he said, keeping his voice low.

***

The morning broke cold and damp, and grey fingers of illumination stroked through the tall Cedar trees. Jared squeezed open an eye and caught sight of Habib as he hunkered over a roaring fire. A small animal, like a rabbit, was skewered with a stick, and sizzled as grease dropped from it into the flames.

"Hungry?" he smiled.

"Yeah, what is it?"

Shaking his head, "Don't ask."

A whiff of smoke drifted in Jared's direction, and he unfolded himself. Jared stood and stretched giving himself an ample yawn. "Where's the old woman?"

Habib glanced over his shoulder. "I was up at dawn, and she was nowhere to be found. She probably gathered what few belongings she had, and migrated to the next town. I was fortunate to capture this," he nodded at the charcoaled breakfast.

Jared knelt next to him and pulled off a piece of meat. After a quick prayer, he sank his teeth in it.

"Hum, not bad, what is—?" Taking another look at Habib, Jared decided not to press the issue.

"I found a pot and some coffee. I hope you like it," handing Jared a cracked mug.

The steaming liquid rejuvenated his senses as he took a sip. "Um, now that's some good coffee, just like my lieutenant used to make." He propped himself on a concrete block and savored the moment.

For the next few minutes, both men sat and ate in silence. Jared thought about Fatemah and wondered if Habib's thoughts were not on Anita.

After breakfast, Jared finished packing while Habib kicked some dirt over the smoldering embers and prepared to leave. With their blankets drawn around them and held in place by the extra gun belts, they looked like they were a part of the Mujahedeen or a radical militia group. Jared hoped if they ran into the real ones, they could blend in.

Chapter 43

The Grand Hotel

The large grandfather clock in the lobby of the Grand Hotel struck six o'clock p.m. Within a few minutes, some of the guests, having finished dinner, began to filter out. Low conversations between tight-knit groups dissipated as they passed along the carpeted halls. Some made their way to the Jockey Club, one of the many lounges scattered throughout the spacious facility. Among them were the three scientists and a few off-duty Secret Service Agents.

"I can't believe it," one of the security agents blurted as a weather alert scrolled across the plasma screen television. "That lousy weather system is threatening to delay our departure tomorrow."

The other two agents shrugged it off. "Don't worry about it, Nick. It gives us another day to live in luxury," his buddy said. "Now enjoy the ball game."

A burst of laughter from the scientists drowned out his grousing, and he gave them a disgusted look. "All those jerks have done is sit there and tell each other seedy jokes like a bunch of junior high school boys. I ought to go over and shut them up." His bleary eyes glowered at them.

"Ah simmer down, Nick, they don't mean any harm. Heck, some of those jokes are actually funny."

Nick tipped up the last of his drink and brought it down with a smack. Then he stood and headed for the exit. "I'll see you on shift," he slurred as he left the lounge.

Across the hall sat Jimbo Osborne. His security clearance gave him access to all but the fourth floor, so he concentrated his efforts where he thought they'd do the most good. Dressed as a security guard, he kept his boss updated as to the conditions outside. His gut feeling told him Amil was up to no good, but so far, the man had maintained a low profile. He'd only ventured from his room once, and that was to get a take-out from the kitchen. Amil never came near any of the lounges, nor interacted with the other guests. Like Amil, Jimbo did his best to stay away from them as well. He was determined not to repeat the mistake he made a few years ago when he fell asleep doing surveillance on Jared Russell.

Two hours later, the lights blinked for the first time.

The storm, which had been threatening, moved much faster and was worse than expected. By 8:05 p.m., a wall of yellow-gray clouds hit Mackinaw. Trees thrashed violently in the gale-force winds as veins of lightning lit the sky followed by bone-rattling thunder. The atmospheric muscle of the storm punched at the power grid causing the bulbs in the chandeliers to blink. One massive javelin struck an ancient oak tree, igniting its limbs and felling it. A limb fell over the power lines snapping them at a critical junction box. Like huge sparklers on the Fourth of July, the bared wire skipped and danced, setting small fires in the surrounding grass and shrubs. As sheet upon sheet of rain descended, however, the fires were quickly extinguished. The lights throughout the hotel fluttered several times and then went out, leaving the building in a heavy layer of darkness. Shadowed figures moved through dimly lit halls like phantoms from the underworld.

***

Sitting alone in his hotel room, Amil glanced at his watch. The digital read out indicated it was time for the last of five daily prayers. Reaching into his suitcase, he pulled out his prayer carpet and unrolled it. He faced Mecca, knelt, and began reciting a prayer he'd memorized since childhood. When he'd finished, he booted up his lap-top and logged into a secure server. After a minute of waiting, he found the site reserved for encrypted messaging.

Using what is commonly referred to as an "idiot code," he typed in the words, "Best Wishes." Once he was inside the dialog box, he sent his father this cryptic message: "A great day for sight-seeing, caught a glimpse of some sports memorabilia. Will acquire it soon." With that task finished, Amil continued his routine of calisthenics; fifty reps of sit-ups followed by fifty push-ups and fifty squats. Checking the weather, he ruled out an afternoon jog, so he stretched out on his bed. All he could do now was sit and wait. He knew his role backwards and frontwards, yet he played it over again in his mind. Finger to his wrist, he pulled back his sleeve and checked the time. *A little over four hours.* He noted the time.

Outside, a shutter slammed against the window, sending a jolt of adrenaline through his nervous system. It would be treacherous to try to meet his counter-parts in this maelstrom, but if they were willing to hazard their lives to cross the lake, surely he could cross the island and meet them. Again, he checked the time, exactly four hours. With Allah's help, he would rendezvous with his team-mates.

***

An alarm beeped on Jimbo's lap-top as he returned to the Security Office from doing another routine security sweep before settling in for a long night. Someone had just accessed the Internet using an encrypted channel. He made a few key-strokes and began the process of unscrambling the recent missive. After several attempts and failures, he scratched the stubble on his chin. This wasn't as easy as the one he'd cracked open in the Mosque project. That one nearly cost him his life, when a knife wielding Islamist came up behind him. Fortunately, Jimbo was able to get the upper hand on the man and kill him first. This cryptanalysis program might save him a lot of time. After punching in a set of codes and parameters, Jimbo let the computer do its work. Instantly, the screen went black with a myriad of white numbers and letters scrolling past his bleary eyes.

A shadow moved behind him as Belinda Turner, the hotel's head of housekeeping, pressed into his office bearing a tray of hot coffee and a dozen freshly baked cookies. The aroma of the hot liquid mingled with the smell of chocolate chip cookies set Jimbo's senses on high alert.

"Better enjoy it, it's the last of the fresh coffee until the power comes on."

Glancing up, Jimbo reached for a mug. He took a sip of the hot brew, letting its heat radiate throughout his body. It burned his lips but he didn't complain.

"Thanks, how'd you know I like mine black?"

Belinda shook her head in a typical female fashion, "I didn't. When lights went out I couldn't find the other ingredients. I hope I didn't make it too strong."

Jimbo pinched back a grin and swallowed. It was, but he wasn't about to admit it.

The moment lingered and Jimbo caught himself staring. With an artificial cough, he returned to his screen. The rectangular form of a slot machine appeared with vacant boxes. As the decoder tried the many combinations occasionally a letter stopped. After several minutes, a word picture began to take shape.

Belinda leaned closer and stared at the cryptic missive. "What does it mean?"

For a moment, Jimbo held her gaze. *How much should I tell her? She's just another employee, not authorized to know such sensitive information. On the other hand, she's got a good head on her shoulders.* Jimbo released a pent-up breath and rubbed his eyes. "How should I know? It could mean anything." he said, followed by an ample yawn.

Belinda stood and began to pace. "Let me read it out loud. Maybe hearing it will make better sense. 'Best Wishes, a great day for sight-seeing, caught a glimpse of some sports memorabilia. Will acquire it soon.'"

The aged office chair squeaked as Jimbo shifted his weight. "Well we know it didn't emanate from the fourth floor. All their Internet connections are being routed through Langley. This one came from someone here on the ground floor."

"But who? It could have been sent from anyone."

"Not anyone, I know where everyone, except that guy named Amil, is at this moment," Jimbo said, with a smug expression tugging at the corners of his lips.

"Oh? Where are they?"

Pulling out a spiral note pad, Jimbo licked his index finger and thumb and flipped through the pages. A quick peek at his watch, he began; "As of five minutes ago, the three lab rats, I mean scientists, were in the Copula Lounge with the group from NOAA, except for Dr. McMillian. He and that Von Janson guy are in the Billiard room shooting pool."

"What about the people from Greenpeace?" Belinda inquired.

Flipping through his notes, he stopped and read; "Not counting Mr. Amil, there are just the two women, and they are sitting in the lobby."

"So everyone but Mr. Bashera is accounted for. That must mean it was he who sent that message."

Jimbo's eyes held her gaze a moment longer than he thought necessary. With a studied nod, he continued, "That about sums it up. Now on to what he said and what he meant by it."

"'Best wishes' could just mean what it says, greetings," Belinda observed.

"Yes, but today was not at all a good day for sightseeing. So we must surmise it means something else. But what?"

"I don't think he was meaning this hotel, the man hasn't left his room except to come down for a sandwich."

Jimbo adjusted the Coleman lantern so he could read his scribbling better. "Let's see here, who was in the dining room when Amil came down?" Jimbo brought a ham hand down on the desk.

"You'll never guess who I saw come in when Mr. Bashera was there."

"Who?"

"President Ferguson."

Belinda sat, her eyes locked on Jimbo's. "But, but—"

"But nothing. What does this line about acquiring some sports memorabilia supposed to mean?"

Belinda sagged back in her chair. "I don't know and staring at that screen isn't going to help. Let's say we call it a night and start fresh in the morning?"

Jimbo stood and released a bear-like yawn. "Good thinking, I've had it for the day. I just hope after drinking this," he lifted his mug of now cold coffee, "I can sleep."

Chapter 44

Hamas Base Camp, Syria

Dawn broke cold and gray, yet the morning call to prayer cut through the fog like a saber. Within a short time, scruffy bearded men wearing the traditional turbans and loose-fitting clothes assembled in lines and bowed to Mecca, all but Anita.

"I noticed you didn't join us for prayer. You know Allah the merciful will not favor you when you enter his presence later today, don't you?"

Anita, not wanting to infuriate her father even more than she already had, avoided eye contact. She also didn't think it wise at the time to announce her conversion to Christianity, either. Looking at the ropes holding her to a chair, she said, "I found it a bit difficult to kneel seeing as I was tied up at the moment, Father."

The man burst into laughter, "Oh, that's right. You *were* a bit tied up, now weren't you?"

Anita's eyes grew wide as he pulled a large knife from his belt. "Here, let me cut this off so you can pray and prepare yourself for the end."

"Oh, I have already done that, Father, but what I would really like to do is go to the lady's room, clean up, and get something to eat. I'm starved." An impish twinkle danced in her eyes.

He rubbed his fingers through his beard in thought. "I suppose that would be alright, but I will have one of my men with you at all times. One can't be too careful. You understand, don't you?"

Anita lowered her gaze, "No. I don't understand, Father." Her voice rang with an edge to it. "I don't understand how you could kill so many of your own people, or how you are so willing to start World War III. Tell me Father, were those little towns along our southern border just collateral damage? Were they just expendable human lives?"

Smack!

Anita's head spun around with the force of her father's blow, knocking her off balance. Her chair toppled over, and she landed face down in the gritty tent floor. A strong hand grabbed her by the arm and yanked her up. "I ought to kill you where you lay, you infidel pig. No one speaks to the Ayatollah like that and lives. You're lucky your execution is already planned, or I would carry out the sentence this instant. Now finish cleaning up, enjoy your last meal, and prepare to die." His words assaulted her like fiery darts, but she held his stare determined not to give him the satisfaction of seeing her cry.

The guard led her from the tent to a thick bramble. Handing her an unopened bottle of water and a clean wash cloth, he smiled.

"You are a very brave young lady. Allah will honor that," he said, twisting off the cap. He moistened the cloth and handed it to her. "Here, that's a pretty bad scrape on your face. You'd better take care of it." Sheepishly, he bowed at the waist and backed away. "Take your time, I'll see to it that no one bothers you," his muffled voice came from the other side of the bush.

Anita smiled, "Thank you. I appreciate your concern."

After cleaning up, Anita returned to the tent where a couple of hard-boiled eggs, toast, and coffee awaited her. The welt on her cheek still burned like fire, but she had to admit, she pushed him a bit too far that time.

She yearned for her father's love. He was so proud of Amil. He doted over him, nearly worshiped the ground he tread. As for Rajeed, her father endured him. The scar which stretched across his face made him a twisted, bitter man, but at least her father respected him. Not so with Anita. She was a pawn, a bargaining chip, a piece of merchandise to be bought or traded. The arranged marriage between her and Sheik Ismael al Hussar was all about power, about settling a dispute, about political capital. She sniffed back a tear. *If only I could hear him say I love you, I would go to my grave a happy woman.*

Her thoughts were interrupted by her father's gruff voice. He was on the phone with someone. Creeping close to the front flap, she turned her ear.

***

Heat expansion made the rickety shell of the Bellanca aircraft hangar tick like a clock. Indeed, time was running out for Rajeed. He had already lost half of his workers as his constant threats and occasional executions reduced his team to only a dozen.

Rajeed's cell phone rang, interrupting his latest rant. "Yes, Father, is everything alright?"

"No, Rajeed, everything is not alright." He shouted into the phone. "Your stupid sister has turned on us. She overheard my conversation with Iran's President and went to the television station. This is a major set-back."

"Yes, it's been all over the news here as well—"

"I know," the Ayatollah bellowed, "Hours ago, the Zionists made a preemptive attack against Iran's nuclear missile facility. Most of our plans have gone up in smoke."

Anita wished she had rabbit ears.

"Fortunately, we were able to find her. Before I execute her, I am going to make her confess that she is a pathological liar, and that everything she told the press was a pack of lies. Then I will chop off her pretty little head."

Rajeed kicked a stray cat out of his way as he paced. What was left of his team stood gaping . . . not wanting to cross his path. "Well, I was just saying, since I lost so many men, maybe I should come—"

"You must stay focused, Rajeed. Do your job and Allah will reward you. New York City is ripe for the picking. Even if I have failed, you and Amil must not fail. Do you understand? Now are you ready? Because just as soon as I get back to Beirut, I will step up the war effort, and I don't need the U.S. interfering."

"We are prepared to transport the weapon upon your command," Rajeed lied. It wasn't one massive bomb as his father instructed. It was five smaller, more portable ones. His men had stolen an equal number of panel trucks, painted them, and lined each one with a thin layer of lead. Truth was, he was behind schedule and working round the clock to make up time.

"Yes, of course, Father. I will personally see to it the device is in place tomorrow and push the button myself."

A frustrated breath rustled through the connection. "You'd better, or you will burn in Hell for failing to obey Allah and me, his humble servant." He slammed the phone shut and sullied the air with such language; Anita's face felt like it was glowing.

Despite the one-sided conversation, Rajeed continued, "You can count on me, Father. I will not fail you or Allah." A single tear traced the scar which cut along his jaw. Under his breath, he cursed his father, Allah, and all that he held holy. His fist tightened around the whiskey bottle and he tipped its contents into his mouth. Eyes red, he tossed his empty bottle across the room.

Chapter 45

Hamas Base Camp

"That gutless son of mine," he hollered. "He thinks just because some of his technicians bolted on him, he should quit and come home." He mocked his son's voice. "If only I had two sons like Amil. Someone get the girl, we might as well be done with it now," he raged.

A couple of scrawny men, toting AK-47's, pushed aside the tent flap, grabbed Anita and dragged her to the center of camp.

They placed her near a large fire pit, its embers glowed orange and red like a sleeping beast waiting to be fed. Wafts of smoke drifted upward in spirituous circles before dissipating in the afternoon air.

"Before you go chopping off my head," she said lightly, "why don't you let me tell you one more story."

Her father pondered her suggestion a moment. Anita's eyes widened when her father nodded. "Sure, what could it hurt?" Then he laughed and took a seat on an old log. With a wave, he said, "Begin, but it better be good. I'm bored and need a little excitement around here."

After taking a long labored breath, Anita let it out slowly and began, "This is another story about the Syrians. I hope you like it. You see, there was a city encircled by the Syrians, and there were two lepers who sat at the entrance to the gate. One day, as the siege worsened, one of them said to the other, 'Why are we sitting here waiting to die? If we enter the city, the famine is there, and we'll starve to death along with everyone else. And if we sit here, we'll starve anyway. Come, let us go to the camp of the Syrians. If they spare our lives we shall live, and if they kill us, we're going to die anyway.'

So they arose at twilight and went to the camp of the Syrians. But when they came to the outskirts of the camp, they looked around and there was no one there. For God had made the army of the Syrians hear the sound of chariots and of horses, the sound of a great army, and they said to one another, 'Behold, the king of Judah has hired the kings of the Hittites and the Egyptians to fight against us.'

So they arose at the twilight and abandoned their tents, their horses, and their donkeys, leaving the camp as it was, and fled for their lives. When the two lepers came to the edge of the camp, they went into one tent, ate and drank, and carried off the silver and gold and clothing, and went and hid them. Then they came back, entered another tent, and carried off things from it, and went and hid them. Then they said to one another, 'This isn't right. This day is a day of good news. If we keep silent and wait for the morning, punishment might befall us. Now, let us go and tell the king's household'."

Anita saw she not only had her father's attention, but a large group of men had gathered and were hanging on every word. *At this rate, I'll have the entire camp listening to me. Maybe it will buy me some time.*

She continued, "So they came and called to the gatekeepers of the city and said, 'We came to the camp of the Syrians, and behold, there was no one to be seen. The horses and the donkeys were tied, and the tents were as they left them.'"

Then the gatekeepers called out, and it was told within the king's household. Then the king rose in the night and said to his servants, 'I will tell you what the Syrians have done to us. They know we are hungry. Therefore, they have left the camp to hide in the open country thinking when we come out of the city, they will take us alive and capture our city.'"

Then one of his servants said, 'Let some men take five of the remaining horses, and let them see if these things be so.'"

So they took two horsemen, and the king sent them to the camp of the Syrians, saying, 'Go, see if it is true. If it is, report back to me as quickly as you can.'"

And so they went and followed the lepers as far as the Jordan, and behold, all the way was littered with garments and equipment that the Syrians had thrown away in their haste. So the messengers returned, told the king, and the people went out and plundered the camp of the Syrians."

When Anita had finished the story, her father abruptly stood and clapped his hands twice.

"I never did like those Syrians anyway. Now, you will take my daughter and place her in the hold until tomorrow. After breakfast, I will chop off her head."

The two scrawny men fought back snickers, grabbed Anita, and tossed her back into the tent. With all those men wandering about the camp, she shuttered to think what might happen to her were it not for her guards.

Lying on the rocky ground, she let her imagination run wild. How long could she hold off her father's wrath? How many stories could she tell before he figured out her trick? Should she beg for her life? Grovel at his feet? No! She was a Bashera and Basheras never groveled, never begged. Should she offer herself to one of the guards in exchange for her freedom? The thought repulsed her. The Spirit of God rebuked her for allowing such folly to even enter her mind. The verse, "No weapon formed against you shall stand," resonated in her heart. She found herself apologizing to the Lord.

She smiled as if a new day dawned, bright and clear. If only Habib would show up and take her away from all this. She'd marry Habib in a heartbeat. Mrs. Habib Teriek Hanif. She liked how that sounded. She dreamed of having children—lots of them—little brown eyed, black-haired wonders crying out for their Ammi and Abbu. She rolled over and buried her face on the thin blanket and sobbed.

***

Jared and Habib slowed their pace, but kept their guns over their shoulders and hands visible as they approached the outer perimeter of the Hamas camp. Out of nowhere, armed men appeared and pounced on them like a pack of hungry dogs. Jared felt his skin crawling as a dozen guns pointed at his and Habib's heads.

"Who are you and what do you want?" demanded one of the guards.

With his hands locked behind his head, Habib calmly spoke and addressed the man closest to him. "We have just come from mopping up the village of Rayak, we left only one woman behind to spread the word about disregarding the will of Allah, and all the rest we buried. Then, we checked for weapons, we left none."

Habib's answer seemed to satisfy the leader of the guard unit, and he commanded his men to lower their guns.

Speaking more authoritatively, Habib squared himself in front of the main spokesmen and said, "We are on an urgent mission and need to resupply, can we get some provisions?"

The man's eyes scanned Jared, who stood rock solid, not wanting to speak. If he had to, he could carry on a casual conversation, but not for long. Then the man turned to Habib, "You may enter, however, we must blindfold you."

At first Habib tried to protest, but the chambering of the weapons behind him convinced him not to speak another word. He and Jared walked at gun point wondering what they'd gotten themselves into. As they neared camp, the blindfolds were yanked from their heads, and they found themselves in the middle of a bustling militia stronghold. Several jeeps with mounted 50-caliber machine guns were parked along the narrow road Grayish green canvas tents encircled small campfires with a couple of larger tents in the center. Off to the side was a covered area, which to Jared appeared to be the mess site.

Jared nodded to Habib and they casually made their way to the mess tent where they were provided with a scant meal, no questions asked. The rhythm of the camp by mid-day was fairly relaxed; most of the men were either asleep, cleaning their weapons, or playing a game of basketball.

Habib leaned close to Jared, "I'm going to do a little snooping around. Maybe I'll get lucky and hear where they've taken Anita. In the meantime, try not to talk to anyone."

Impressed by his friend's take charge attitude, Jared nodded.

After a few minutes, angry voices broke out on the dirt basketball court as the two teams squared off. The crack of a rifle settled the dispute, and the two teams retired to their respective sides. *I wonder if that would work in America. It sure would keep the fans in line.*

The shadows had moved several more inches, when Habib returned, clearly agitated. Between gulps of air, he drew Jared off to the side so they could speak without being overheard.

"You'd never guess who I saw on the other side of the camp."

"Who?"

"Ayatollah Bashera, the prime minister. He's right here in this camp," Habib's voice was edged with tension. "That makes this place one of the most dangerous places on the planet. If the Syrians, the Mossad, or a US drone find them before we get out, it will be very hard to explain why we are here."

Jared shifted uncomfortably and looked around, "Any sign of Anita?"

"No, but—"

Suddenly, a mortar round exploded in the center of the camp, turning tranquility into mayhem as everyone began diving for cover.

Jared grabbed Habib by the collar and pulled him into a newly formed hole and covered him as 50-caliber machine gun bullets whizzed overhead. Another barrage of mortar rounds fell killing a group of men huddled by a jeep. Within minutes of the attack, the dead and the dying lay strewn over the rocky ground.

"Who is firing at us?" Habib asked, keeping his head low as he peered at the destruction.

"I'm not sure, but they have us zeroed in, if we don't get to cover, we'll be dead in a matter of minutes," his voice was drowned out by an explosion that tore open a nearby tent. Thick, black smoke billowed from the smoldering wreckage providing a momentary hiding place from the withering assault.

Seizing the moment, Jared hollered, "Follow me." Leaping from his foxhole, he ran for cover behind a stand of trees.

Habib jumped up and began running after him. Breathlessly, he dove into a ditch, just as an RPG plowed into a supply truck. Earlier in the day it had been emptied of its munitions, or it would have wiped out half the camp.

***

The ground beneath Ayatollah Bashera's feet shook with the impact of incoming mortar rounds. Leaping from the table, where he'd been sitting, he dashed to the door of his tent and surveyed the situation. He knew instinctively what was happening. The Syrians discovered his hide-out and were looking for him.

"Colonel Jahja, tell your men to dig in and hold off whoever is attacking us until I get out of here. I'll meet you at our secondary camp," he ordered.

Jahja saluted and barked a set of commands, which sent his men scurrying toward the perimeter. Meanwhile, the prime minister and his private security team loaded Anita and a few of his wives into a duce-and-a-half and roared off in the other direction.

***

Through the smoke, a figure appeared. "Look Habib, it's the Syrians."

"Yeah, we are caught in the crossfire between them and the Hamas fighters, and I'm not on either side," Habib said, his breathing coming in short gulps.

For a moment, scenes of Mosul and Fallujah flashed across Jared's mind. He pinched the bridge of his nose with his eyes closed. *You've got to focus, Jared, or you'll never make it out of here,* he chided himself.

Once again, his survival instincts kicked in. As a Lieutenant in the Marines, he was trained in military tactics. He knew where the enemy would take up their positions, and though they had no personal beef with the Syrian National Army, it was they who were shooting at him. He needed to defend himself and Habib if he and Habib were to save Anita. Under withering fire, Jared low-crawled from behind the tree-line to where he could get a better angle on the machine gun bearing down on them. He fired two short blasts with his AK-47 and the enemy gun fell silent. Behind him, he heard Habib firing in short, controlled bursts. *I wonder where he learned to do that.*

Above the din, Jared heard Colonel Jahja, ordering his men to retreat into the rugged mountains behind them. After tossing several hand grenades at the advancing soldiers, Jared and Habib continued to give covering fire for the Hamas fighters. Then they beat a hasty retreat as the SNA began to close in.

"Come on Habib," Jared called in Farsi, "we'd better clear out. *Now!*

Habib nodded, fired a few more rounds, and backed behind the hull of a bombed out truck. "Which way did they go?" he called out, as a cloud of acrid smoke from burning tires engulfed him.

A wave of thick smoke swept over Jared, stinging his eyes and bringing back memories long forgotten. He tried to focus but his vision blurred, and he doubled over, coughing violently.

"Jared," Habib's voice sounded muffled after a large blast. "Catch," he hollered. A bottle of water landed next to him and rolled just out of reach. Ducking beneath a wire fence, Jared grabbed the bottle and squeezed its remnants into his mouth. After washing down the smoke, he cleared his throat and wiped his burning eyes.

"That way," he said, his voice sounded unnatural and felt like sandpaper.

The two men zigzagged through the underbrush, firing behind them as they fought their way along the vine-covered path. Deeper into the forest they plunged further into Syrian territory. Overhead, a helicopter roared, spraying bullets and shell casings around them. Jared fired a few well-placed rounds, and the massive aircraft started trailing smoke. Its engine sputtered as the pilot fought to keep it aloft. Resisting the temptation to admire his work, Jared grabbed Habib by the shoulder and pulled him down as a new round of machine-gun fire strafed the area. Chips of bark, stones, and dirt kicked up from the incoming rounds, covering the two men with debris. Jared lobbed a hand grenade as far as he could and ducked. A moment later the ground shook, and the gun fell silent.

"Run," he ordered, and they fled through a narrow pass.

Still breathing hard, Habib called from behind, "I just hope the Syrian army decides not to follow us. If we're caught, they'll shoot us on the spot."

Ducking behind a large rock, they checked their weapons and reloaded.

"Any movement," Jared whispered.

Habib listened. "I don't think so, but we'd better watch our backs."

Chapter 46

Bellanca Airfield, New Castle, Delaware

Rajeed stood ramrod straight as he nervously watched the few remaining technicians and scientists load the five dirty bombs onto the stolen trucks.

"Easy," he said, his hand outstretched as if he could stop one of the crates from falling.

Uri painted the air blue with an oath, "Get out of the way Rajeed, we can handle it," he barked, sending the young man scurrying back from the forklift.

The crate bumped against the sides of the truck as the driver clumsily maneuvered it around. After several attempts, he got the wooden box which housed the device into place and backed out.

"That's the last of them," Uri said, as he swung the doors of the fifth truck shut, and locked them. "What do you want done with the technicians? Your father said to keep them around just in case something goes wrong."

Nodding his head, Rajeed jammed his hands into his pockets. "I like that idea. Killing them gets too messy and the more bodies we have to bury. I already had to shoot a dog because it was uncovering the last guy you killed. Father gave me over a million dollars to spend, maybe I should pay them double and let them go."

The air crackled with tension as Uri fingered his weapon. "A million dollars, hmm? Maybe I should shoot them, we split the money and disappear."

In a smooth action, Rajeed pulled his weapon from its holster and pointed it at Uri's head. "I don't think so. Now get your men loaded and let's move out."

Nodding, Uri backed away, not taking his eyes off of Rajeed's right hand. He'd learned not to trust the Basheras, especially Rajeed. The man was unstable, and everyone knew it.

With an exasperated huff, Uri nodded and called to his men.

"Okay, let's get moving," he ordered. Several men stood and climbed into the cabs of the stolen vehicles. One by one, they cranked their engines and pulled into position. With their motors running, Uri pushed the button to the corrugated door. It groaned under its own weight and began the long climb upward. As soon as the trucks cleared the door, they pulled out into the bitter night.

Overhead, a blanket of stars sparkled in the thin air. A crescent moon shined upon the earth, bathing the grey building in soft hues. As the last of the caravan cleared the opening, Uri hit the button and disappeared into the building as the door reversed its climb and slammed down, shaking the rickety frame.

Outside, Rajeed sat in the lead truck. Puffs of diesel smoke fouled the air while he waited for Uri to return. Six quick flashes lit the glass panes and he slumped in his seat, and a knot formed in his stomach at such a waste of human life.

A shadow emerged from a side door. Rajeed stiffened as he recognized Uri, still holding his Colt 45. "I told you not to kill them, you fool." His voice was laced with tension, his hand on his sidearm.

"And I did anyway. So what are you going to do about it? Shoot me? I don't think so. You don't have the guts. Think of it this way, I just saved you a million dollars. Let's get moving."

***

Keeping their distance, Jared and Habib followed the Hamas fighters until they reached their secondary camp. The moonless night obscured their arrival, and they slipped into camp unnoticed. An overturned bucket welcomed Jared's weight as he sat and warmed himself by the fire. The sudden feeling of guilt stabbed at his heart when he thought of the Apostle Peter, sitting with the enemy. Jared prayed he wouldn't deny his Lord when the time came.

The few men who'd survived the attack staggered around the camp site like whooped pups. It was obvious to Jared, that the fight had been kicked out of them, at least for a while. One man, his face gaunt, his eyes void of any hope, uncharacteristically offered them some hot coffee, a falafel, and cheese. Habib took it and thanked him, then broke them in half and handed it to Jared.

Habib tore off a piece of bread and dipped it into his mug before eating it. Peering over the rim of his mug, he whispered, "During the fire-fight, I noticed something."

Jared choked down a dry morsel and smiled. "I see now why you dipped yours in your coffee," he said with a crooked smile. "What did you notice?"

Habib wiped his lips with the sleeve of his coat, "Well, it happened so quickly and things were spinning out of control, but I saw some of the prime minister's men pushing a group of women into a large truck."

"So, what's so unusual about that, Habib? He was probably trying to keep his harem safe."

Habib popped a piece of cheese into his mouth and chewed it thoughtfully. "Well, there was just one more thing."

"What's that?"

With his eyes pinched shut, Habib described the snapshots he was seeing. "Like I said, it all happened so fast, but I could have sworn that one of the women had her hands tied behind her back and was gagged. For a moment, I thought it was Anita."

The mug of coffee in Jared's hand jerked sending the hot liquid over the rim and down his leg. He jumped to avoid the volcano, but it was too late. He grimaced and took his seat as unwanted eyes narrowed, then diverted. Jared lowered his gaze, "Anita?" he whispered through pinched lips.

"Yes," Habib said, with a slight nod.

"Are you sure?"

"Well, no, it was pretty chaotic." He paused, letting the scene play out again in his mind.

"What are you thinking, Habib?"

His friend glanced up, "I'm thinking about scouting around. Maybe I'll get lucky and find her. If so, with so few guards, we might be able to rescue her and escape before anyone notices."

Jared ran his hand across the back of his neck. "All right, since you are so fluent, it would be better that you go, but be careful. We don't want to lose the element of surprise."

Habib pulled his blanket tighter around him and stalked off, keeping to the outside of the camp. As he neared one of the quickly assembled tents, he noticed two guards standing on either side of the entrance. Not wanting to draw attention to himself, he decided to hide in plain view. Casually, he stepped into the light of the small fire, took a seat and waited.

Movement, in the corner of his eye, caught his attention as the Ayatollah emerged from a nearby tent. Seeing the big man, and remembering the brutal beating he'd received at his hand, Habib stood up and took a step in the opposite direction.

"You there, stop," the prime minister's tone turned Habib's blood to ice. "Turn around."

The Ayatollah stepped across the open space and stood inches form Habib's face. "Aren't you the young man I caught talking to an American?"

The subtle fact that Rick was a Canadian, eluded the Ayatollah, but it was pointless to correct him, not now, not anytime. Habib's lungs tighten, and he struggled to breath. He tried to speak, but his tongue stuck to the roof of his mouth. To run would be suicide, to stand and fight would have the same effect. *How do you answer a question like that?* Habib's thoughts fluttered in the heat from the Ayatollah's glare.

"Guards, take this man to the center of camp and stake him down," he said, never taking his eyes from him. "You are an American sympathizer. I will deal with you later." Hatred spilled from every syllable.

Before he could move, two men grabbed him, and pushed him into the middle of the campsite.

Hearing angry voices, Jared walked across the camp and stood behind a group of men. His heart nearly leapt from his chest as he watched Habib being kicked and beaten. His mind raced back to the day he caught a group of men from the hardware store beating up Ahmad. Without thinking, his hand reached for the dog leash that was not there. *Raleigh.* He struggled to breath, knowing he was helpless to change the outcome of what was happening. *Lord, please, spare Habib. He doesn't know you yet. Make yourself known to him through this beating.*

When they'd finished, they left Habib on the ground. Blood seeped from his face and hands where he'd tried to defend himself. A soft moan escaped his swollen lips, and Jared fought the urge to rush to his side. For the time being, he had to stand by, watch, and do nothing.

The men yanked Habib to his feet and stripped him to the waist, then staked him to the frozen ground. For the next six hours, Habib lay spread-eagle on the cold, hard earth. It would only be a matter of time before the Ayatollah executed him. If he was going to save him, it had to be soon.

Chapter 47

The Center of the Hamas Camp

By midnight, Habib felt the effects of frostbite upon his exposed flesh. Shivering in the cold, he began to doubt the wisdom of his decision to come with Mr. Jared. A cold wind blew, heightening his discomfort. The more he tried to free himself, the tighter the ropes became, cutting his flesh and leaving it raw. As the adrenaline rush faded and fatigue set in, his thoughts turned to his parents, his siblings, and his new friends Rick and Mindy. He wished he'd had one last chance to thank them, to hug them, to say goodbye. He wondered if Jared knew where he was, and if he did, what would he do, what could he to do?

In a half dream-like state, Anita's face filled his mind. He racked his brain, trying to recall her voice, her laughter, her smile. *Looks like you won't get to hear, 'Oh, Habib, my hero.' No grateful kiss, no hug of gratitude, all because you had to run into her father.*

Looking down at his bleeding body, he began to assess his situation. *This might be a good time to think about Heaven and how to get there.* He squeezed his memory like an orange trying to remember what the evangelist said. A verse came to mind, *"I am the way, the truth, and the life; no man comes to the Father but by me."* Staring up into the heavens, he began to pray, *God, I know I'm a sinner, and I recently learned that you love me and want me to trust in you. So here I am. My friend said you gave your only Son to die in my place that I might be forgiven and rose to life again. And if I trust Him as my Savior I will not perish, but have eternal life. God, I want that. I want that more than anything else. I now reject all I've ever believed about Allah and trust your Son, Jesus Christ to be my Lord and Savior. Thank you, I'll be seeing you in the morning. I'm sure of that.*

***

The last time Jared sat staring into a raging fire was when he and Fatemah were up at John Xavier's cabin. It wasn't like this night, but Fatemah had insisted. It was there they became convinced it was God's will for them to come to Beirut. From that point, they'd never doubted their decision, not until now.

A light wind blew, bringing with it small flakes like fine dust. Within fifteen minutes, however, what began as a dusting soon became a blanket of heavy, wet snow. It fell indiscriminately over sleeping men and machines of war. Wafts of smoke from dying embers filtered up through the trees to join the pregnant clouds which threatened to release their burden. A few lonely sentries moved about the camp leaving dark foot prints. If Jared didn't move soon, escape would be impossible. Even now, with every falling snow flake, his chances were growing thin.

The green LED on his watch flashed two o'clock, and Jared knew it was time. He threw off his blanket and slipped into the forest. After a quick check of his weapons, he began to stalk around the camp perimeter. The handle of the razor-sharp knife Rick gave him fit nicely in his grip. If he had to throw it, he was sure it would find its mark.

Having taken notice where the Ayatollah's tent was, Jared knew which one to avoid and which one held Anita. The two men standing guard told him as much. *That must be the one Anita is in.*

Jared carefully inched his way around the perimeter of camp planting the C4 charges every fifty feet. He set the timers to explode simultaneously at exactly 2:45 a.m. His only fear was that he would run into a major delay. That could cost him his life, a prospect he refused to consider. When he finished, he retraced his steps to Anita's tent.

By now, the wet snow formed wave-like drifts, deep enough for Jared to leave large prints. Thinking quickly, he snatched a branch off a tree and began to sweep his footprints. As he approached, one of the two guards decided to take a bathroom break and stepped behind a thick bush.

Bad decision.

Jared's heart quickened as he moved with the stealth of a leopard. He gripped the handle of the knife and slid it quietly from its sheath. With one quick move, the blade found its mark and the guard fell silently to the ground. A pool of crimson stained the pure white snow.

Quickly, Jared exchanged his blanket for the man's woolen coat and turban, then took his place. For a moment, he and the other guard stood still as wooden Indians. Movement caught his eye as the other guard turned and gave him a wolfish grin. He laid aside his weapon, and reached for the tent flap. Jared knew what was on the man's mind. With lightning speed, he pulled the knife from under his coat and plunged it into the guard's chest. The man squirmed a moment, then fell limp. Looking around and seeing no one, Jared dragged the body into the shadows. When he returned, he knew he had only a few minutes before the C4 would light up the sky.

***

The death struggle which took place outside her tent went unnoticed, as Anita slept soundly on a bed of grass and leaves. With a jerk, the flap parted and she sat up with a jerk. The whites of her eyes glowed like beacons. Anita inhaled a scream when Jared lifted his index finger to his lips. "Anita, it's me, Jared," he whispered through tight lips.

She relaxed her grip on the stone she'd found.

"Mr. Jared?"

"Yes, it's me. Come quickly."

Relief escaped her lips and she threw a thin garment over her shoulders, grabbed a small bag she'd been carrying and followed him out of the tent.

Clasping her by the hand, Jared led her between the tents, stopping occasionally to wait for a sentry to clear the area. As they approached a stand of trees, a shadow moved and the Prime Minister Bashera emerged from behind a tree.

"Papa?"

He was returning from relieving himself when Jared and Anita nearly stumbled into him.

Her breath caught in her throat, every fiber in her being screamed, *Run,* but she didn't. Her feet held fast to the ground as if they were mired in clay. Then he did something she never thought he'd do ... he smiled. The twinkle in his eyes, made her feel like the little girl who once sat on his lap singing songs. He held out his arms and in an instant, engulfed her in a warm embrace. She savored the moment, drinking in the heat of his body, memorizing the rhythm of his heart, but knew it wouldn't last, it couldn't last. Was this a dream or her worst nightmare? Tenderly, he cradled her face in his hands and placed a tender kiss on her forehead. Anita looked into his eyes and saw a dark shadow. *Was it sorrow or regret?*

"Now go, before I change my mind," he said, his throat closing with emotion.

Jared sheathed the knife, clasped her wrist and tugged her away from her father's arms. Tears streamed down her cheeks as Anita watched him turn.

"I love you Papa," she whispered through the falling snow.

He took a step and paused without turning, "I love you too," and was gone.

Jared gave her another gentle tug and led her deeper into the forest. A few minutes later, they reached the place he'd chosen as their rendezvous point.

"Look Anita, they've got Habib. He's staked to the ground in the center of camp. You wait here and don't move no matter what happens. I'll be right back." Then he disappeared behind a large, snow covered bush.

Jared quickly doubled back just as the timers struck 2:45. He waited.

Nothing.

Five minutes passed, and Jared began to wonder if the C4 was faulty, or if he didn't set the timers correctly.

Then the night lit up like New Years as a half-dozen charges exploded. In an instant, the camp came alive with disoriented men shooting wildly at anything that moved. Jared belly crawled to where Habib lay. His purple lips quivered in to a smile as Jared began cutting the ropes.

"Habib, can you walk?"

"No, I can't feel my legs."

"Okay, I'm going to pick you up and carry you."

"What about Anita?" Habib asked, eying the unguarded tent.

"Anita is safe, but we gotta go." Scooping him up, Jared threw him over his shoulder and made for the forest while bullets whizzed overhead.

Deep trenches marked the trail and Jared pushed past the heavy laden branches, and found Anita crouching under a Fir tree. One look and Anita's face lit up like it was Christmas. No sooner had he set Habib on the ground, than Anita leapt into his arms.

"Oh Habib, you came for me."

Jared couldn't keep from smiling, despite the growing danger. "Okay you two. We need to put some distance between us and them before they realize what has happened."

Grasping Anita's hand, Jared tugged her away from Habib's arms. "Habib, here, put these on," tossing him a pair of pants, a shirt and a pair of boots from one of the dead guards.

Habib put them on and shoved his feet into the rugged combat boots.

"If you're ready, we need to get a move on."

"I'm right behind you," Habib said, lacing up the boots, then scooped up the fallen soldier's weapon and stumbled after Jared and Anita.

Chapter 48

The Syrian Wilderness

By the time they reached the first base camp, sun rays danced on the upper branches of the trees. Jared surveyed the carnage now covered by a blanket of snow. The scene was surreal. Some places were undisturbed, while others were desecrated by scavenger birds and wild dogs which snarled over the lifeless corpses.

"Yuck, I can't look," Anita said, holding her stomach.

"We need to keep going. It will be light soon and your father will be hot on our trail," Jared said, moving toward the road.

Great puffs of condensation followed him as he walked through the drifting snow. By midmorning, they reached the bombed out town where they met the elderly woman.

"Those men," Anita paused to sniff back a tear, "those men we were traveling with did this." Glancing around, she pointed to a field. "They assembled all the men and boys in the center of town. Then they marched them out and shot them." Unhindered tears cascaded down her cheeks. "For no other reason," she sobbed, "but that my father didn't want anyone to know he'd passed through here." She buried her face in her hands. "He is the most wicked, evil man on the earth. Do you know he sent my two brothers to the United States to do something terrible?"

Jared stopped and turned. "What did you say?"

"I said, my father sent Amil and Rajeed to America to commit some evil deed."

Keeping his voice down, Jared stepped closer, "What are they planning to do?"

Anita shrugged her shoulder, "I'm not sure, I just heard part of the conversation. He said Amil is a UN Diplomatic Attaché with the Head of the Greenpeace Movement. That's what I tried to tell your Mr. Savior or whatever his name is. I don't know how that would hurt your country, but Father said Amil would make him very proud.

Stunned, Jared held her gaze. "Did you say Mr. Xavier?"

A quick nod, confirmed Jared's guess. *How was she involved with Mr. Xavier, and how did she talk with him? He needed more information.*

"What about Rajeed? What did your father send him to do?"

She bit her lip, eyes searching the ground. "My father spoke to him last night. He was supposed to go to New York City the next day. He said that it was ripe for the picking."

Jared stood, eyebrows knit. "I need to get this information to someone," he said, patting his pockets. "I must have dropped my cell phone back there at the camp."

"Well, we certainly can't go back and get it," Habib quipped, "and they took and smashed mine when they captured me."

Sheepishly, Anita reached into her bag and pulled out a phone. "Here," she said, not letting her eyes meet Jared's

Jared looked at it and her. "Where did you get a fancy phone like that?"

Gulping, "Well, I didn't exactly *get it*. I kinda swiped it."

"You what?" Jared's eyes bulged.

Anita slumped to a log. "It's a long story. The short version is—" she paused and cut her eyes in Habib's direction. "Actually, the first one came from," she paused and shifted uncomfortably. "Let's just say it was connected with the CIA, you know, the Central—"

"—I know who they are." Jared felt his jaw tightening. He jammed his hands into his pockets and kicked an unsuspecting rock forward a dozen yards. "I can hear it now. You're working for the CIA and I'm helping you."

A ragged breath escaped Anita's lungs, "Well, not exactly, working *for* the CIA. You might say I'm keeping them informed. I'm sort of an entrepreneur when it comes to these things." The whites of her eyes refused to be captured by Jared's stare.

"And this one?" holding out the high tech phone.

Anita threw a smile at Habib. He caught it and threw it back. "That phone, I kinda borrowed from your uncle."

Jared stomped in a circle. "This is getting worse by the minute."

Habib took a knee, and watched the two banter back and forth. "That's just great. "I'm not only helping the prime minister's daughter escape, who, I might add, is a traitor, but now I find out that she's a CIA informant as well. If we get caught, they will not only chop off my head, but they will probably chop off my arms and legs," he said, feeling used. "Girl, what are we going to do with you?"

Anita handed him an impish smile. "Better be careful. I might have some juicy information on you."

"Nothing that my government doesn't already know," dialing a number he'd memorized a long time ago.

***

Jimbo staggered to his hotel room bathroom and instinctively flipped the switch.

Darkness.

Using his cell phone for a light, he twisted the cold water spigot and splashed his face, trying to clear his mind. He stared into the mirror. The face looking back at him spoke of loneliness. Something was missing in his life, and he knew it. He just didn't know what. He'd given his best years to the CIA hoping to find fulfillment, but instead he found it to be yet another dead end. His bout with alcohol years earlier nearly cost him his job and left him feeling as empty as the bottles he tossed away.

Maybe I should retire and go back to Daphne. Heck, maybe I should just stay here. His thoughts turned to Belinda.

Returning to bed, he was asleep before the sheets settled around him. Ten minutes later his cell phone chirped cutting his snores in two. He jolted to life and peered bleary eyed at the read-out. Not recognizing the caller, he tried to ignore it, but it insisted.

"Hello?"

"Hello, Jimbo?"

"Yes? Who is this?" His Alabama twang carried across the distance.

"Jimbo, it's me, Jared."

Yielding to the urge, he gave an ample yawn and leaned forward. "Jared, why are you calling me at this time of the night?"

The phone went silent, and Jimbo assumed his old friend was checking the time.

"Sorry if I woke you, but listen. I've got information relative to national security."

"Look Jared, maybe you should call the FBI or the CI—"

"No, Jimbo, you're not listening. All heck is breaking out over here in the Middle East, and I have a young informant who is telling me that Amil and Rajeed Bashera, the prime minister of Lebanon's two sons, are somewhere in the United States plotting an attack."

Jimbo wheezed a long sigh.

"Who's your source and are they reliable?"

Glancing at Anita, "She's the prime minister's daughter, for crying out loud. Of course she's reliable. Her name is Anita Bashera, and she over-heard her father planning this whole thing. "

Silence.

"Jimbo? Are you there?"

"I'm here, but you won't believe it."

"Believe what?"

"It's complicated, but just so you know, I'm on assignment at the Grand Hotel in Michigan, the same hotel where the president is holding a big muckedy-muck summit, and I saw Amil earlier this evening."

***

Jared finished giving Jimbo an update, hung up, then quickly punched in the number for Fatemah's cell, hoping he could reach her.

"Jared, oh Jared, I'm so happy to hear you. I've been so worried. Did you guys rescue Anita? Is she alright?" Her voice circled upward, full of hope.

"Yes, yes, we rescued her before anything happened. I'll tell you all about it when we get back. Where are you?" Jared asked, after a moment's pause.

"I'm in New York City."

"New York," he repeated. "Why New York? I thought by now, you'd be in Seattle with my folks."

"Oh, Jared, something terrible has happened." The pain in her voice resonated across the distance.

Every muscle tensed, and Jared caught himself not breathing. "What is it? Are you all right?"

"Yes, I'm fine; just a few cuts and bruises, a little hypothermia, and some minor burns, but I'm fine—now."

Jared's mind raced. "Why, what happened?"

Fatemah tried to speak, but her throat closed with emotion. He hadn't heard and she hated to be the one to break the news. "You don't know? Do you?"

"Know what? I've been out of contact, up until now, and haven't had time to call. I'm sorry, but what's going on?"

Fatemah sniffed back a tear. "It's Rick and Mindy ... they didn't make it."

Jared ran his hand over his neck.

"What happened?" Habib asked as he and Anita looked on.

Jared shook his head. A raised index finger silenced his questions. "What do you mean, they didn't make it? You guys were supposed to meet Captain Ali and be gone by two o'clock. Didn't they get there?"

"Oh yes, they made the rendezvous," barely able to speak.

"Well then, what happened?"

Sobs punctuated the silence. "Fatemah, are you there?"

"Yes," she whispered. "Their gone, Jared. We were attacked by the border patrol. They fired at us, damaging the boat badly. Captain Ali forced me over the side and was going back for Rick and Mindy when a blast knocked him into the water. A minute later the boat exploded. Rick and Mindy didn't get out in time. She told me earlier she couldn't swim, so I guess they stayed, hoping—" her throat closed, and she buried her face in her hand, sobbing.

Jared held his position, too stunned to speak. The news of Rick and Mindy's death nearly crushed his world. How many more good people are going to have to die in order to stop the advance of radical Muslim fundamentalism? Already Rashad and Ahmad had given their lives, now his friends Rick and Mindy. How many more before this ordeal was over?

"Look! Fatemah, you're got to get out of New York. It's not safe," he said, breaking the silence.

"Why? What's going on?" echoing the tension in Jared's voice.

"I can't talk now, but listen to me. You must leave that city, *now.*"

"No Jared. I want to stay here until you arrive."

"Fatemah, you've not hearing me. Something bad is about to happen, and I need for you to get as far away as possible. Go to mom and dad's house."

"Jared, I can't leave not just yet."

"Why not?"

"I'm still in the hospital."

Nearly dropping the phone, Jared repeated, "Hospital? I thought you were okay."

"I am, but—" her voice trailed off.

"But what?" nearly reaching through the connection as Anita and Habib gaped at him.

"Jared," she paused and blew her nose, "we lost the baby."

"Baby?"

"Our baby," she eked out. "I suspected I was pregnant before all this happened. I was going to tell you on our anniversary, but things began spinning out of control, I just—" her voice melted into a sob.

"Honey, things haven't been spinning out of control. God's still on his throne. It will be all right." Jared said, grasping for something spiritual to say, something that would hold their world together, something to ease the pain he was feeling, that he knew Fatemah was feeling.

Silence.

"Fatemah, are you there?"

"Yes," she said, barely audible.

"Does momma know? Have you told anyone?"

Fatemah sniffed back a tear. "No, I wanted you to be the first."

Breaking the tension, Jared asked, "Fatemah, how soon until they release you?"

"The doctors said I should be strong enough in another day or so. Hopefully, by then you'll be here."

"Yes, I should be back by the end of the week. In the meantime, you try to get some rest. I'll call you as soon as I can. This phone is about to die, so I better go now, I love you."

"I love you, too. Hurry back."

Chapter 49

The Grand Hotel Lobby

Belinda sat staring into the large fireplace as its red and yellow flames licked at the dried wood she'd just tossed in. It was another sleepless night, one of many. For some reason, she'd felt the need to pray, but it didn't seem right. So she made a cup of hot tea, kindled a fire in the hearth, and took a seat. There was something going on in the hotel, and she knew it. She felt it. Her years in the field had given her a sixth sense about these things, but what burdened her most was Jimbo. He seemed so empty, so lonely, so lost. She rebuked herself for letting her mind wander. She'd given up hope a long time ago of ever having a meaningful relationship with a man again. Letting go of a long-held sigh, she muttered, "I guess I'm condemned to a life of widowhood," she smiled at such a silly word; *widowhood.*

A shadow crossed her thoughts, and she looked up.

"Oh hi, Jimbo. Couldn't sleep either?"

He lowered his weight into an over-stuffed seat next to her and stared into the fire. "Nope, I was dead asleep when I got this phone call from the other side of the world."

Clearly interested, Belinda shifted her gaze from the fire. "That important hmm?"

"Yeah, it's important. But I just don't know what to do with the information. You see, this friend of mine told me a wild story about being involved in this whole middle-east conflict thing. Said he'd rescued the prime minister of Lebanon's daughter after she was abducted. That she had credible information about our nation coming under attack by a couple of terrorists."

Belinda held her gaze, "Well, why did he call you? I mean, why didn't he call law enforcement?"

Not wanting to reveal too much, Jimbo lifted his rounded shoulders and let them drop. "I think he was desperate and had no one else to turn to."

"So what are you going to do with this information?" she asked biting back a grin.

Jimbo shifted his weight, "I have a friend in the information business. I need to call him."

Looking over the rim of her mug, she asked, "So do ya think he's up?" letting her Wisconsin inflection give away a long held secret.

"Up, the man never sleeps. He's up alright."

The couch creaked as Belinda leaned back. "I think that's a splendid idea. Can I interest you in a cup of coffee and a slice of pie?"

As Jimbo dialed the number, a broad smile spread across his face, "That's the way to a man's heart."

Belinda shared a smile with Jimbo and disappeared.

One ring and a voice answered full of anticipation. "Hello?"

"John? Have I got some news for you!

Chapter 50

The Syrian Wilderness

Jared pushed the red button and slumped down on a rotting log. "I have got to get back to New York," he said, breaking his silence.

"New York. Why, what's happened," Anita asked.

Jared quickly unpacked the story of Rick and Mindy's deaths and the loss of their baby.

Habib pounded the ground with his fist, "I don't understand. Why would God allow this to happen?"

Jared knew the answer. He knew God was good all the time: that God never allowed evil to triumph, that he was working all things out for His glory and the believer's good, yet, silently, asked himself the same thing.

Anita knelt next to Jared and took him by the hand, Mr. Jared, I remember what your wife told me about God."

Lifting his head, Jared asked, "What did she tell you, Anita?"

"She said, 'God never lets something happen without it passing through His nail-scared hands first'."

A long, thoughtful moment. Anita was right. So was Fatemah. Finally, Jared broke the silence with a deep chuckle. "You're right, Anita. Thank you for sharing that with me." He stood and brushed his pants off. "I guess we'd better get moving. New York's a long way from here."

Habib handed him the back pack. "New York sure is a long way from here. First, we need to get out of Syria, then to Lebanon and then back to Beirut. With all that's been going on, getting out of the country might be nearly impossible."

Jared nodded.

"Yes, and *we* also have the problem of finding and stopping Rajeed before he does something terrible," Anita stood, her small frame barely visible in the shadows.

"What do you mean, *we?*" Jared asked.

"I mean you, me, and Habib."

Jared's eyes switched between the two young people. He wasn't sure if this was her idea or his.

"Anita, you can't come with me to America."

Anita stepped into the morning light, her silken hair glistening with dew. "Yes, I can, you need me."

The idea of smuggling believers out of Lebanon was one thing, smuggling the prime minister's daughter was quite another. "Give me one reason why I should," his voice thick with doubt.

"Well, for starters, Rajeed is very sly. To my knowledge, he has never been photographed. He keeps to himself writing songs, poetry, studying maps, and is an obsessive compulsive on the computer. Father warned him, that if he didn't show more focus, he'd send him into the Lebanese military."

"So you're saying you're the only one who can identify him?"

"Yep, that's right."

Habib stood, arms crossed, smiling at Anita's quick wit.

"Well, what about Amil? I'm sure if he's some sort of diplomat, the authorities would have done a thorough background check on him, correct?" Jared pressed.

"Not exactly," Habib chimed in.

"I happen to know of several of my friends who were recruited from LSU. They had criminal backgrounds and were still hired by companies with ties to America. Once they got their foot in the door, they had a free pass right in through the border. No questions asked."

Jared stepped into the river. His lungs yanked in a sharp breath. "This water is freezing."

"All the more reason to get out of here," Habib said, bracing himself for the bitter chill.

"So how do we stop these guys if we don't know what they look like or where they plan to strike?" Jared asked. A shiver crept up his legs as he stepped deeper into the icy river.

"We don't, but maybe if I can get back into my father's office, I can find something that would give us a lead."

"You mean to say, you're going to add breaking and entering to your long list of misdeeds?" Jared chuckled.

"All those *misdeeds*, as you call them, were washed away when I received Jesus as my Savior." Her eyes narrowed as she shot a glance in Habib's direction.

He shrugged in response, not speaking.

A moment passed and Jared cracked a grin. "Well said, and maybe it's not really breaking and entering, since it is your house, Anita," Jared observed. "Let's just hope we're not too late."

The chilled water swirled around Jared's waste sending icicles through his blood. He felt bad for Anita. Her thin burqa wasn't much to ward off the freezing waters, but she didn't complain. By midday, they crossed under a bridge and climbed up the steep bank. The sleepy village of Haja lay to their right. If they were lucky, by nightfall, they'd be in the eastern territories of Lebanon.

"You guys need a rest?" Jared asked, hoping they'd say 'yes.'

Anita, barely able to put one foot in front of the other, leaned heavily on Habib's arm. "What gave it away?"

Jared smiled, "Oh, I thought you two were just getting better acquainted."

"Acquainted? I practically know him like my—"

"Shush!" Jared said, finger to his lips. "I hear a vehicle approaching."

The three dove for cover in a stand of palm trees. An armored personnel carrier, loaded with soldiers, lumbered along the road as if on patrol. Its slow pace made breathing a strain as the three of them held their breath. After it passed, they let out a unison sigh of relief.

"I wonder if they're on the lookout for us, or my father," Anita whispered peering through the foliage.

"We might as well bed down here, anyway. We have water and a few energy bars my wife packed before we left."

The night closed in around them, and before long, only their soft snoring punctuated the silence. All the while, myriads of stars, like diamonds on a velvet backdrop, paraded overhead. Occasionally a shooting star streaked across the void, but its beauty was lost upon the sleeping trio.

***

The next morning broke cold and crisp. Anita leaned against a rock and shivered beneath the blanket Jared had given her. Habib lay in a tight ball, still as a possum, while Jared watched an orange sphere rise like a phoenix above the Syrian Desert.

Jared stood and stretched, then went over and shook Habib. "Wake up old buddy. We'd better get started, or we'll never make it," he said, staring out over a vast desert. "I just hope we can cross that desert without being spotted."

After passing around the canteen and quickly munching down the last of their energy bars, they slipped from the underbrush. At their feet lay a wind-swept desert dotted with rocky outcroppings.

"Not much to hide us from the sun," Jared quipped.

Taking his place next to him, Habib lifted his hand over his eyes and scanned the horizon. "Or the SNA for that matter. We'd better stay close to the shade of the boulders as long as it lasts."

By afternoon, the sun had reached its apex and blazed down on them like an angry eye. "I sure should have worn a hat and brought along some sunscreen," Jared said looking at an angry red spot beneath his black skin. He wiped his face with the front of his shirt and forged ahead down a narrow path.

Three hours later, after their water was depleted, they reached a stand of Joshua trees. What little shade they provided was defended by mounds of angry fire ants. Jared shaded his eyes and looked toward the horizon. "Another hour and we should reach the foothills—"

"Get down," Habib hollered, as the pounding of propellers grew louder. Out of nowhere, a U.S. made Apache helicopter appeared from behind a small hill. Its Syrian pilot wheeled the gunship around and swooped down upon them, its machine guns firing wildly. A zipper of bullets streaked across the desert kicking up rocks and debris directly in line with Jared. The three scattered like mice, hoping to confuse the pilot.

The gunship hesitated, then trained its guns on the biggest target. The ground shook beneath Jared's feet as he ran for his life. Just before the trail of bullets caught up to him, he swerved and dove behind a large boulder. As he landed, he tried to break his fall with his hands. They hit the dirt with a thud. Shards of angular pebbles dug into his palms sending a sharp pain up his arms. Overhead, bullets, like angry hornets, whizzed past him, striking the boulders and sending down a small avalanche.

Anita huddled close to a bush, too paralyzed by fear to run. Above her stood Habib, a rocket launcher rested on his shoulder. He took aim. A moment later the missile shot from its tube. White hot smoke arced skyward until the missile struck the aircraft. Like some headless beast, the helicopter began to spin out of control. An instant later, the earth shook from the explosion, and the giant bird fell from the sky with a thundering crash.

For a moment, the deafening silence filled the air as Habib stood, admiring his work. The backpack lay open, and the rifle from which the RPG had been fired hung loosely from his hand.

As he gloated, shots rang out as a unit of SNA bore down upon them. Habib grabbed Anita and dragged her behind a boulder.

"Jared, are you alright?" he hollered.

"Yeah, a bit banged up, but I'm okay."

"This is bad, really bad," Habib said between short bursts from his AK-47. "I don't know how long I can hold them off."

"Habib!" someone called.

"Habib, are you alright?" It was Uncle Abbas.

"Yes uncle, but where are you? I can't tell."

"Stay down, I'll come and get you."

An engine roared to life. A moment later, the headlights of an old tattered taxi glared through the smoke of the burning helicopter. It raced over the uneven ground and screeched to a halt yards from the boulders where Jared and the others hid. Uncle Abbas jumped out and was joined by three well-armed men.

"I thought you might need some help getting out of here so I brought some of my children," Uncle Abbas said, a wide smile parting his lips.

Habib looked at the men wearing camouflage, and holding AR-15s. "Are you sure you brought enough men?"

"Oh, I assure you, there are many more where they came from. Now get in." his arms flailing wildly.

Jared pushed Anita and Habib into the taxi, then squeezed in behind them while the three men gave covering fire. As soon as they were a safe distance from the kill zone, Uncle Abbas lifted a walkie-talkie and gave the order. A moment later, his fighters stood up and released a final barrage of RPG's, mortar, and 50 caliber machine gun fire while the taxi sped to safety.

Chapter 51

The Presidential Suite

"What in Heaven's name is going on with these power outages?" demanded the president.

"We are doing all we can Madam President, but the lightning strikes keep blowing the circuits," a nervous adviser said.

"Well, don't we have a back-up system, a generator, something?"

"Yes, ma'am, but—"

A bolt of lightning struck again, sending a charge throughout the power grid, frying the hotel's main buss. The crippled building fell into darkness...again.

"I want all security personnel on full alert, repeat, full alert," Larry Morgan, the head of her security detail, demanded.

"Somebody get a flash light for the president, quick," Andrew hollered.

Within a few minutes, a dozen flashlights flicked on, while aids scrounged around, looking for candles.

"Looks like Mother Nature has pounded us back to the Colonial Days," the president seethed. "Andrew, what's the status with the Israeli attack?"

Andrew Kelly, the president's Chief of Staff, pulled the latest NSA report from a folder. "Madam President, there are mixed reports coming in. The Israelis are denying any involvement in the escalating conflict—" his shaky voice was cut off with a wave.

"Of course they would. But do we have a confirmation that Israeli jets have destroyed two nuclear facilities in Iran?" glaring at his apparent weakness.

"Y, yes ma'am, but—"

"Andrew, are you Jewish?"

He stumbled backward, hand to chest, "N, No, ma'am."

"Then, why are you defending them? Get the UN Secretary on the line immediately."

"Y, yes, ma'am, right away, ma'am," he said, his face turning white as a sheet.

"Madam President," Larry said. "That's not going to happen, at least, not for a while."

Unlike Andrew Kelly, Larry Morgan's tough as nails, no-nonsense approach to problem solving impressed her. He had a way of exuding confidence and for that, she was grateful. Despite the fact she held most men in low esteem: she liked having at least one strong male around. She enjoyed seeing them jump at her every command.

"Alright, for the next few minutes, let's concentrate on the immediate problem. I want the lights back on and us ready for this summit." Her words were peppered with language, which would make a sailor blush.

***

A slight wheeze escaped Jimbo's lungs as he stepped back into the security office. He'd just returned from making the rounds when the lights went out for the final time.

"Do you think we need to let the president's people know we're in the dark?"

Jimbo jolted, hand to his chest. "Oh Belinda, don't scare me like that," wiping his furrowed brow. His fingers found the chair and he relaxed his weight into it. "No, I did that the last time, and about the time I finished, they came back on, so no. I think they can figure it out for themselves. In the meantime, let's see if we can find some candles and or a Coleman lantern."

After a few minutes, the small office was filled with light and warmth to fight off the encroaching cold.

"Okay, so where were we?"

"You were going to tell me about your phone call with Mr. Xavier."

Jimbo lifted his eyebrows a foot. *Now how does she know Mr. Xavier?* He wondered. "Uh, that's pretty sensitive information. Police stuff, you understand." avoiding eye contact.

Belinda returned a slow nod and tried to smile.

Wanting to ease the tense moment, Jimbo asked. "How about you, how'd you get on with these people?" waving his arm around the office.

Brightening, she sat upright. "Oh, now that's a story I enjoy telling. You see, I was hired here after Ben, my husband, God rest his soul, passed away. He'd worked here for years doing lawn care and helping out with the maintenance. We just loved living here on the island. No cars, no buses or trains. It was so peaceful. So, when Ben died, the hotel folks offered me a job. Naturally, I took it. That was about two years ago now." Again, her Wisconsin lilt peeked out.

"Have they been treating you right?"

"Oh yes, Jimbo," she said as she brushed a few strands of hair behind her ear. "They have been more than kind. It's been such a blessing. They're the type of folks that would give you the shirt off their backs."

"I have some friends like that."

"You do? Who?" Belinda asked straightening the knickknacks on the shelves.

"Well, that's who just called me. They're working in Lebanon. They've set up a halfway house or a safe house, something like that, for people who turn from being a Muslim to Christianity."

"That's too bad. From what I've heard, Israel and Lebanon are at war."

Jimbo nodded, not knowing how much he should confide in her. "I just hope they're alright."

"We can do more than that, we can pray," her face beamed in the shadowed room.

Jimbo fingered his coffee cup, "I'm afraid I'm a bit rusty in that department," he admitted.

"Oh, it's never too late. What I've found is, when you have Jesus in your heart, your perspective on life changes, yes sir. Instead of living for yourself, trying to amass wealth and temporal things, you begin living for the Lord Jesus Christ. It's a life of giving, rather than getting." Her voice curled up like smoke.

Up until then, that was how he lived. Jimbo swallowed hard. "You know, that's exactly what my friend, Jared, kept telling me, but I wasn't interested in listening."

"And now?"

"Now that I'm a bit older, I've been thinking what would happen to me if I were to die."

"Jimbo, may I be frank with you?"

"Yeah, sure."

"It's not a matter of *if* it's a matter of *when*. If you haven't placed your faith in Jesus, then you have but one place waiting for you."

"So how do I avoid that, I sure as heck don't want to go to Hell. Pardon the language."

Belinda brushed the comment aside.

"So, what do I have to do to be saved? If that's what you call it?"

Nodding, Belinda smiled, "That's what you call it, Jimbo. Being saved! The answer is as simple as what you did when you sat down on that chair. When you sat down, you put all your weight on it and trusted it to hold you. That's called faith. So it is with faith in Jesus. You simply put your dependence on him to save you."

Elbows on his knees, Jimbo rubbed his chin, "So what do I do?"

Belinda took a seat in front of him, "You simply believe on the Lord Jesus Christ, and you will be saved. It is as simple as that. Jesus did all the work that was required when He died on the cross of Calvary. That alone satisfied the Heavenly Father."

"So how do I do it? You know, get saved and all?"

Leaning back in her chair, Belinda crossed her arms and leveled her gaze. "You know Jimbo, salvation is a lot more than a fire escape. It's realizing you're a sinner before a holy God. When you come to grips with the fact that you have sinned against the holy law of God and are condemned already, it should cause you to cry out for his mercy and grace."

"You don't have to convince me that I'm a sinner. No one knows it better than me. What I need to know is how to have all those sins forgiven."

His honesty made her chuckle. "Well Jimbo, if you admit that to God, he is faithful and just to forgive your sins and to cleanse you of all unrighteousness."

"That's what I want to do. Will you show me?"

"Yes, you start by asking Jesus to forgive you and to come into your heart, and tell him you are now placing your faith in him to save you."

To her surprise, Jimbo pushed the chair back and knelt, his fat hands folded over his heaving chest. A slight quiver echoed in his voice as he bowed his head and began to pray. When he finished, he looked up. Tears rolled down his cheeks and dripped from his chin. "I feel like I just got a new lease on life, like a new man," he said as he stood and stretched.

"Well you can't always trust your feelings, but I'm glad you feel that way. The day will come however, when you won't feel saved. You just need to remember, it is Jesus who is doing the saving and the keeping. The Bible says, 'He is able to keep that which you have committed unto him until that day.'"

"I sure as hec—, I mean, I sure don't understand what that means, but I certainly would like to find out."

"Well, if you plan on sticking around here, I'd be more than happy to tell you. Better yet, I go to a small church over on the mainland, and my preacher would be glad to know about your decision. He could really do some in-depth teaching."

"You know, I've been thinking about retiring from . . . " he paused realizing she knew nothing about him or his background.

"Belinda, this may come as a bit of a shock to you, but I'm here on assignment. You see, I'm an undercover agent with the CIA and I've been sent here to do a job."

"Oh really! And you expect me to be surprised? Who do you think got the order that assigned you here? Mr. Xavier personally called me and sent me your dossier," she said, pulling her badge from her purse, "I'm not just the housekeeper here. I'm your back up! Up to now this whole operation has been on a need to know basis. I run the field office in the northern part of Michigan. I followed your service ever since they shipped you over to Stanford. You did a great job there, and so I personally recommended that the old man assign you here to work with me the next time I needed someone."

"That puts our relationship on a whole new level. I was thinking about retiring and hanging around here, maybe even getting to know you better. Now I gotta call you sir, uh I mean ma'am?"

Belinda slapped her knee, laughing, "No Jimbo, you don't "gotta" call me anything, but please do call me. I'd be happy to get better acquainted."

Chapter 52

Beirut, Lebanon

"I've made all the arrangements with your Captain Ali. He is prepared to take you out of this country," Uncle Abbas said, as he nosed his taxi onto the main highway leading back to the city.

"Why not just send us to America on a commercial flight?" Jared asked.

"Too risky, the Ayatollah has men everywhere. All it would take is for them to spot you or Anita, and you're back in the coup."

Jared nodded and rubbed his aching shoulder from the fall he took, "I think you meant soup. But I suppose you're right. Are the connections still good with Captain Ali? I mean, you know, the cruise ship and all?"

Uncle Abbas smiled, crinkling the crow's feet around his eyes. "If you are referring to the *Sea Queen*, yes, all the arrangements are in place. We simply need to get you to the wharf by two o'clock."

Jared's eyes widened. "Now how in Heaven's name do you know about Mr. Xavier's *Sea Queen*?"

Patting Anita on the knee, "Who gave this young lady a cell phone in the first place? Me. And, I might add, that fancy SAT phone, which Anita has, was provided by me also. I am a lot more connected than you think, my friend."

Anita returned an innocent gaze and clutched her bag close to her chest.

Habib, who'd been listening in the back seat, leaned forward and placed his hand on his Uncle's shoulder. "Will there be any objection if we make a quick stop at Anita's house?"

"What? Did you want to stop and pick up a few things for the trip, Anita?" Uncle Abba asked, glancing over his shoulder.

Her face held a wry smile. "Well, kinda. You see, I think if I can find Amil and Rajeed's plans, we might be able to stop them."

The elderly man rubbed his chin. He glanced at his watch before making a decision. "You know by now the residence has been wiped clean, don't you?"

Anita shook her head, a few strands of hair fell across her eyes, and she shook them aside. "Yes, but aren't you forgetting I took personal care of my father's office. He trusted no one in there besides me and a few of his most trustworthy aids. I know where he hides his closest secrets."

Jared cocked his head around to get a better look at Anita, "Yes, but you can't just go marching up to the prime minister's residence and ask to go snooping around. Not with the new PM there."

An impish twinkle danced in her eyes. "I don't have to. I know all the secret entrances and panels. I could get in and out in fifteen minutes, tops."

"Do you know exactly where that information might be, young lady?" Uncle Abbas pressed.

"Yep, but it's easier to show you rather than tell you."

"Oh, you needn't show me. I'll take your word for it. But if we're going to do it, it will need to be done by midnight, so we'll have plenty of time to get to the boat docks."

"So it's decided?" Anita asked, hand clasp under her chin.

"Not so fast, young lady. Not without a plan. I don't want to have to rescue you a second time. Not that you're not worth it, I mean ..." Jared let his voice trail off feeling his face flush.

"Don't worry Anita," Habib said, taking her by the hand. "I'll come to your rescue any time you call."

Anita's contagious giggle lightened the mood.

"I'd feel a lot better if I accompanied you, Anita," Jared said.

Uncle Abbas ramped off the highway and into the sprawling city. Taking a number of alleys to avoid any watchful eyes, he wove through the seedy side of town until he reached an old, boarded up garage. He beeped twice and an iron slide opened. A set of questioning eyes peered out, then the metal door rolled up allowing the taxi to pull inside. A moment later, the door returned, leaving them sitting in darkness.

Smack!

"Don't touch me." Anita's voice crackled in the air.

"I, I was just looking for your hand." Habib's plaintive voice echoed in the darkness.

Anita chuckled nervously until her eyes adjusted.

"So this is where you hide out when you're not picking up stranded VW owners," Jared observed, looking around. The inside of the garage was devoid of anything significant. It appeared to be just another empty building.

Uncle Abbas opened his door and stepped out. "Follow me. Let me show you something," he said with a wink.

The three piled out, while Uncle Abbas pushed a button which, up until then, had gone unnoticed by the others. Jared's eyebrows knit with interest as the rectangular concrete block dropped out of sight, leaving a black hole. With more agility than he expected, the elderly man bounded down the dark steps, his voice echoing after him. "Come along my children."

With a shrug, Jared followed, Habib and Anita close behind. As the walls closed in around him, a wave of nausea rolled over Jared. Memories of the Mosque gun battle raked across old wounds and he caught himself not breathing.

"Watch your step," Abbas' voice echoed in the dark, jolting Jared back to the present. With some effort, the elderly man pushed on an iron door. Its hinges groaned, but yielded.

Once inside, Jared released his breath as a dozen men and women, dressed in fatigues, sat staring at a bank of monitor screens. No one moved or took their eyes off of what they were doing.

"Come on, follow me," Abbas repeated and clasped Anita by the hand, leading her and the others into a smaller chamber.

After shutting the door, he finally spoke. "This is my headquarters. I have been monitoring the events in Beirut for quite some time," he said, glancing at the other room.

"So that's how you knew when my car broke down," Jared said, rubbing his chin.

A wry smile wafted across the older man's face. "Well, not exactly. However, I will say this, that stunt Mr. Owens pulled when he fixed your VW gave me quite a time until we figured a way around it."

Jared ran his hand over his neck, and shook his head, "You mean to say, you are behind all this?"

Nodding his head, "Most of it," Abbas replied with a twinkle in his eyes.

Anita cut her eyes in his direction and gave him a wink.

"Alright then," Jared said slightly nonplussed, "but I still want to know your plan."

Anita thought a moment, her features darkened as she mapped out a strategy. "Okay," she paused, reveling in the attention, "at midnight, the guards gather in the kitchen for tea and sandwiches."

"Even the perimeter guards?" Jared interjected.

For a moment, Anita held his gaze, thinking, "No, they stay on post, but most of them are located in the front of the house."

Habib faced her, "Most of them? How do you know that they haven't changed protocol?"

She shook her head vehemently, "Because they don't. They've been doing it the same way for years. I should know, I've snuck past them dozens of times coming to Bible study," she giggled.

"So let's just say you make it past the guards, how do you propose getting in?" Jared continued.

"Oh, that's easy. As small as I am, I can squeeze through the dog flap. Then slip into the pantry where there's a secret door. The rest is a piece of cake," she said triumphantly.

"And you know exactly where the safe is?" Uncle Abbas pressed.

"Uh, huh. It's in an anti-chamber inside my father's office."

"How will you get in there?" Habib asked, clearly concerned.

"As I said, the secret door leads to a narrow stairway. Follow it up two flights and it opens right inside the anti-chamber. With a little luck, I could pick the lock and voilà. I'm out of there in under fifteen."

Jared rubbed the back of his neck, "I don't even want to know how you learned to pick locks, Anita."

Her face beamed. "One thing though. I'd feel better if Habib went with me, at least as far as the back door. He could keep watch and make sure the coast is clear when I return."

Jared released a slow breath, "That, young lady, is a great idea. I think it will work. But in the meantime, we need to get you something to wear besides that burqa ... something more fitting for the occasion, like a cat-burglar outfit."

"I think I can help," Uncle Abbas chimed in. "I have a friend—"

"Oh no, you guys are out of this world. First, you manufacture a set of falsified documents, now you have a friend in the burglar business, what next?" Jared's jaw hung half open. "And how did you figure out my connection between Captain Ali and Mr. Xavier?"

The older man tucked his hands behind his back, chuckling. "Oh that's easy. The old captain and I go way back."

Jared stood, shaking his head.

Chapter 53

Administrative Palace

A slivered moon ducked behind a stray cloud as the old taxi rolled to a gentle stop along the curb of France Street. Uncle Abbas shut off the engine and cut the lights, and the street fell silent. Armed with walkie-talkies, Habib and Anita, wearing black, silken cyclist's outfits, stepped from the vehicle. The stately mansions lining the street were dark allowing Anita and Habib to cut through the property without being detected. Like two black phantoms, they circled around behind the Majidyeh Clock tower, an ornate structure guarding the north corner of the Administrative palace grounds. Keeping it between them and the sentries on the roof top, they reached the ten-foot wall surrounding the palace. Breathlessly, Anita motioned for Habib to follow her as she felt her way along its cold surface in search of a seldom used door. In the darkness, she stopped and Habib bumped into her.

"Sorry," he whispered.

The whites of her eyes narrowed. "Be careful."

"I said I was sorry."

Anita snickered.

"Okay, here is the back door to the palace grounds. No one but me knows it's here because it's hidden by a large azalea bush. I use it to sneak out at night. Now follow me."

Habib obeyed without speaking and held her hand as she pushed the door open. Once inside, the palace grounds spread out to their left and right. Straight ahead was the back of the palace buildings.

"Okay, we're inside the compound," she whispered in her walkie-talkie.

"Roger that," came Jared's voice.

Like two spirits, Anita and Habib slipped from the shadow of a tree and dove for the shrubs skirting the porch.

"That's the door with the dog flap. Once I'm in, it's up to you to make sure no one is around when I'm ready to exit. You know what that means, don't you?"

Habib fingered the handle of the nine-inch blade, and nodded. The whites of his eyes flashing in the blackness.

With the agility of a cat, Anita leapt up the steps and through the dog flap before Habib could say what he was thinking.

***

Inside, Anita heard laughter. It was the guards in the other room. Their crude jokes and bad language made her skin crawl. *Focus, Anita, you've got to focus,* she chided herself.

Out of nowhere, a hand reached in and flipped the light. Anita's pulse quickened and she grabbed a rain coat which barely covered her trembling legs. Like a manikin, she held her position, and her breath. Whoever turned the light on was more interested in food than watching for intruders. He grabbed a bottle of wine, flipped off the light and left. Only then did Anita resume breathing. Her heart pounded so loudly that she thought for sure the men in the other room would hear. Before someone else came into the pantry, Anita stepped across the tight space and pulled open the panel. It squeaked, and the voices in the other room paused. Gulping for air, she quickly slipped behind the panel and returned it to its place. After climbing two flights of stairs, she realized she'd not taken a breath since she left the pantry. She expelled a breath of hot air and gulped again. *Breathe, Anita, breathe.*

***

Outside, Habib heard footsteps as two guards and a Doberman Pinscher approached from behind. Scooting further into the shrubs, he hoped the dog didn't pick up on his scent. A moment later, the dog whined as if in pain and tugged at his leash. Its handler, not knowing what was happening, allowed the animal to pull him away from Habib's hiding place.

"What just happened?" he whispered into the walkie-talkie.

"He, he, he, it was me. I got your back, buddy," Jared's voice came in a low tone.

Habib's hand relaxed on the handle of the knife, and he released a tight breath.

***

After waiting for her heart to catch up with her breathing, Anita pushed open the panel at the top of the stairs.

Voices!

She stiffened, not wanting to move, yet knowing time was running out. She glanced at her watch. She'd been inside the prime minister's residence five minutes. If it took her five minutes to crack the safe, she had only five minutes to make her escape. Seconds ticked by, and the voices continued. With the safe just out of her reach, she dared not slip from the safety of the panel and expose herself. Then she heard a chair move, and the voices faded into the distance.

With just minutes to spare, Anita drew a few tools from a pouch she'd tied around her waist and quickly went to work. She pulled on a pair of latex gloves, and removed a false partition revealing a small safe. With the skill of a master thief, she placed a stethoscope over the tumblers, inserted a thin probe and began to push back the inner teeth of the locking mechanism. She smiled as the final tumbler fell away. Then she grabbed the L shaped handle and rotated it. The door yielded to her touch and swung silently out of the way. With a gloved hand, Anita reached in and grabbed a stack of papers not being too discriminating. She unzipped her form fitting top and shoved the documents inside, then zipped it back up. Hearing a door, she quickly closed the safe, replaced the partition and slipped back through the panel just as the light came on.

Knowing that she had only moments to spare before someone discovered they'd been robbed, Anita double stepped it down the stairs. When she reached the bottom, she realized she failed to collect all of her tools. Torn between going back up or making a run for it, she decided to get out while the getting was still good. She squeezed the toggle on the walkie-talkie signaling that she was ready to come through the dog flap.

Static.

She squeezed again and waited. By now, sweat was dripping from her eyebrows, yet she held her position. Seconds stretched into eternity as she waited for the all clear.

Then the walkie-talkie hissed to life. She was in the clear. Anita dashed from the panel in the pantry and dove through the flap just as the alarm sounded.

Her heart skipped a beat as Habib sprang from the shrubs and grabbed Anita by the wrist.

"Run!

With spot lights crisscrossing the lawn, like a prison yard, the two young people scampered between yellow beams. In the distance, Doberman Pinschers snarled and charged after the two fleeing figures. Shots rang out and bullets pelted the ground over which Habib and Anita had just run. The secret gate stood forty feet ahead, but the dogs were closing fast. Thirty feet and the ground shook as heavy vehicles pounded after them. Twenty feet and the dogs snapped at Habib's heels as he pushed Anita forward. Ten feet and the gate, swung open. Jared appeared, waving his arms wildly. The dogs stopped abruptly as the high pitched whistle blew again. In an instant, Anita and Habib leapt through the open gate and Jared slammed it shut behind them. A moment later, a spray of bullets ripped through the wooden obstacle.

Still panting, Jared pushed the two young people forward through the neighboring yards until they reached the taxi. Uncle Abbas sat, gunning the engine. The door slammed, and sped off, leaving a rooster tail of dust and debris.

"Head for the wharf," ordered Jared.

The old taxi groaned as Uncle Abbas pushed it to its limit. Two headlights appeared behind them, and bullets whizzed overhead as a car loaded with the Prime Minister's security team gave chase.

"Faster," Habib hollered, ducking as the back window exploded into a million shards of glass.

A piece of glass nicked Anita's cheek and a rivulet of crimson began to course down it. "I'm okay, I'm okay," she said holding her hand on the wound. "Just hurry, they're gaining on us."

Uncle Abbas' voice cut through the din, "It will be all right, you'll see."

As he spoke, a dump truck lumbered through the intersection only seconds after they cleared it. It broadsided the security team's vehicle, sending it careening out of control. The car flipped on its side, sending sparks and fuel in all directions. In an instant, the vehicle burst into flames making it impossible for another vehicle to squeeze around it.

Uncle Abbas cut his wheels and rounded the last corner. From there, it was a straight shot to the docks.

If only he could get there before the police caught on to where they were headed. Jared prayed for a miracle.

Out of the corner of his eye, he caught movement. It was another taxi painted exactly like Uncle Abbas', then another appeared and another. Within minutes, they were whizzing along Charles Helou Parkway surrounded with old yellow taxis. Above them hovered a police helicopter, but Jared was sure the pilot couldn't tell one taxi from the other. Uncle Abbas slowed his speed and kept pace with the others until they neared Marfaa Street. Then he left the caravan and headed to the docks where a lone figure stood.

It was Captain Ali. As the taxi pulled to a stop, the sea warrior flicked his cigarette into the inky waters and began to untether an old trawler from its moorings.

Chapter 54

Mackinaw Island shoreline

Amil, dressed in all black, slipped from his room. He carefully made his way along the balcony, then down the wide staircase leading to the ground floor. With most of the surveillance teams pulled back, focusing their energy on protecting the president from threats from within the Grand, it made crossing the water-logged lawn easier. Amil knew the general point of egress where his comrades would land and headed directly to the area, stopping only to let his eyes adjust after each bolt of lightning.

A gust of wind swirled, and Amil froze as an upturned table blew past him. He checked his watch. If he didn't find his backup team soon, they'd think the worst and initiate an alternative plan. Instantly, the sky lit up with a thousand fingers of light, and the ground shook sending Amil sprawling. He jumped to his feet and rubbed the mud from his eyes. *Another bolt like that and I'll be fried.*

Between flashes of lightning, Amil saw a lone figure waving his arms. He dashed in his direction and found a group of men, huddled under a small stand of trees. The leader stepped up and greeted him with the traditional kiss on both cheeks. "I was beginning to think you weren't going to make it," the man said, handing Amil a weapon. "It's loaded and here are a couple of extra mags should you need them."

Amil took the proffered gun, ejected the magazine and checked the action. Satisfied, he reloaded it and tucked it in the small of his back.

"Very good. Now, if I'm not back here by 2:30 p.m., that means I failed and you need to implement plan B. Is that understood?"

"Yes sir, and may Allah give you strength to triumph over the infidel president."

Having now established his escape route, Amil was satisfied that the rest of the plan would go smoothly. He returned to his room, changed out of his wet clothes and waited.

***

The cold temperatures from the driving wind penetrated the inner most part of the Grand Hotel like one of the ten plagues. Adirondack chairs and over-sized umbrellas skittered on their sides across the piazza and gathered into a pile against an iron fence with each new blast of air. Inside, Jimbo and Belinda huddled in front of the fire place sipping lukewarm coffee which they brewed using a Sterno burner.

"By the way, now that you know we're on the same team, what did Mr. Xavier say when you called him earlier?" Belinda asked with an interesting glint in her eyes.

Jimbo tossed another log into the fire and stirred the coals with a poker. "Said he knew all about it. Said the phone Jared called me on was one he supplied to his contact. Turns out, she's the same girl Jared rescued."

Clearly impressed, Belinda sat up straight. "You mean his contact is the prime minister's daughter?"

"You got it. And she knows everything, I mean, everything," emphasizing every syllable.

The lights flickered and came back on, and Belinda breathed a sigh of relief. Ten minutes later, a team of drenched, secret service agents clambered in from the cold and gathered in front of the fireplace.

"You guys responsible for the power coming on?" Jimbo chirped.

A weathered agent rang out his CIA parka, "Let's just say, we don't run around outside in the rain if we don't have to."

"Yeah, not like some people," another agent said.

Cocking his head, Jimbo asked. "What do you mean by that? None of us have been outside since the storm hit."

"Maybe none of you guys, but someone was outside. He must be suicidal, he nearly got fried with a bolt of lightning," the agent continued.

"Did you see where he went?" Jimbo probed.

Shaking his head, "No, we were too busy keeping our own heads down. Plus, it was so dark out there I lost sight of him when he rounded the corner."

Belinda eyed Jimbo, "I wonder who it was and what he was doing outside in a lightning storm."

"I don't know, but it must have been very important for him to risk his life. Think we should do a room to room and see what we can scare up?"

Leaning back in her chair, Belinda mulled it over. The old clock rang out four o'clock, and she glanced at her watch. "Yep, right on time. I can't believe in another hour or two, the sun will be up."

Jimbo smirked. "Yeah, but we'll never see it. That storm has us so buttoned down, I'll be jaundiced before this is all over. Anyway, I doubt we'll find out who was outside. By now, I'm sure they're safely tucked in bed like we should be.

"Let's just keep our eyes peeled for anyone acting suspicious." As Belinda spoke, two vans carrying the breakfast crew pulled up.

Teriek and his band of cooks had spent the night in town and were now making their way to the kitchen where they began another day of cooking.

***

The morning broke, cold and blustery, and the occupants on Mackinaw Island hunkered down for yet another brutal day. Inside, the grandfather clock belted out the hour with five deep tones. Soon the aroma of fresh brewed coffee, bacon, and hot-cross buns wafted from the kitchen and drifted throughout the lower level.

Jimbo's stomach growled. He'd waited patiently for hours and was willing to gnaw on a chair leg if he thought it would help ease his hunger. To his relief, a dark-skinned man wearing a crisp, clean waiter's jacket swung the door to the Salle a' Manger dining room open, and began serving breakfast cafeteria-style. Bleary eyed staffers and members of the president's security detail toddled along, pushing their trays, to sleepy to talk. It had been a long night for them as well. After allowing most of the others to go through the line first, Jimbo stood, "After you, my lady."

Belinda gave him a wry smile and moved ahead.

***

For Amil, this was only the second time out in public and it was a bit unsettling. Despite the fact that the men on the serving line were his first strike team, it didn't calm his nerves.

Glancing up, he caught his breath. One face stood out to him. For a moment, he held his gaze, then recovered. *Who is this man?* His mind rifled through the stacks of papers, plans, and pictures. *I don't recall him being on the team.* He lifted his eyes for a second look and the man was gone. Unable to communicate with anyone, Amil took his seat with his back to a window and studied the movements of the room.

***

After a quick visit to the ladies room, Belinda got back in line behind Jimbo. As they moved along Jimbo stopped short. Not noticing, Belinda's tray bumped into his tray spilling his coffee.

"Oh, I'm sorry, I didn't realize you stopped," she said apologetically.

"That's okay, for a moment, I thought I knew someone," he said under his breath, then continued collecting food. By the time he'd finished, he needed a second plate, but was too embarrassed to ask, so he balanced his toast on top of his corned beef hash.

Belinda took her seat next to Jimbo.

"Shall we pray?" Belinda asked.

Looking nervously from side to side, Jimbo nodded, "Why don't you lead us," he said, not knowing where to begin.

Her hand reached out to take his and Jimbo paused. "Come on, hold hands, it won't hurt you."

Sheepishly he complied as Belinda began; "Now, Lord, I know you uphold all things by the word of your power and that nothing happens on earth or in heaven without your knowledge. Give us the wisdom to understand your will and your ways. And, thank you for the food we are about to partake of, in Jesus' strong name, I pray, and we all say; Amen."

Keeping his voice low, Jimbo leaned close, "I'm very concerned about this summit. Something's not right."

Belinda shifted her eyes from side to side. "They're not letting anyone above the second floor, not without top security clearance and we don't have it."

"The meeting isn't being held on the fourth floor, it's being held just off the dining room. After breakfast this whole wing will be blocked off. Only the wait staff will have access to that area."

"I wonder why?" Belinda asked after washing down a bite of toast with a swig of coffee.

Jimbo cut his eyes from side to side, "I'm guessing to keep the booze flowing."

A waiter leaned in and pressed against Jimbo's shoulder as he refilled his cup.

"And that's another thing. The guy with Greenpeace, you know, the Attaché guy? He looks exactly like the waiter who poured my coffee and that bothers me."

Reaching into his pocket, Jimbo felt a piece of paper. He withdrew it and took a sharp breath.

"What is it Jimbo?"

Wide eyed, Jimbo looked up and stared at Belinda. "Did you put this into my pocket?"

Belinda's soft features turned into a question. "Why, no. What is it?"

Glancing around, Jimbo slipped the unfolded note to Belinda. It read, "Stay close."

"What's it mean?" she queried.

"Just what it says, but the question is, 'Close to whom?'"

***

"Mr. Kelly," the president said in a closed door emergency meeting. "How are we handling the news of the Israeli attack on Iran?"

Kelly shifted uncomfortably before answering, "Ma'am, I have already prepared a statement on your behalf asserting your reservations over the wisdom and timing of Israel's action."

She nodded her approval, as he handed her a draft of the speech she was to give later in the day.

President Ferguson prided herself for her ability to speed read. It was a skill she'd learned early in her career. After a quick perusal, she made a few editorial corrections, signed it and returned it to his extended hand.

"Thank you, Andrew. Now about the summit, what is the status? Is everyone here?" Crossing her arms, she tapped her toe impatiently.

"Oh yes, absolutely Ma'am. I have instructed the two groups to make brief opening statements. This will give you room to come behind them, declare your full support of the scientific community, and sign the treaty."

"Very good then, what else do you have for me today?"

"Well, it doesn't look like we are going to be getting off this island any time soon. This storm is setting on us like a hen," Andrew said as he handed her the latest DTB dated January 13[th.]

"There is one new entry which is noteworthy, Madam President," pointing to line 20. "Oil Leak in the Gulf threatens wild life. This may be useful somewhere in your comments."

The president scanned the list stopping at number 20.

"Yes, Andrew, have this oil leak thing included in my speech, would you."

"Yes Ma'am, I'll get right on it."

President Ferguson signed the report and handed it back to her Chief of Staff. "And what about the fuel rods?"

Fully expecting the question, Andrew prepared his answer. "Madam President," his voice stronger than usual, "they are spent fuel rods and they have not been located. I get hourly reports from all the major branches of law enforcement. If there is any change, you'll be the second to know." Their eyes met. His eyes bore into hers with an energy that took her breath away.

For a moment, the air scintillated with electricity. Her hand instinctively clutched her throat as she held her breath. "Why Andrew, I'd no idea you were so," her eyes searched the floor for the right words, "so in touch. Good work," she sputtered.

As the door closed behind him, he let out a long breath. Larry caught his eye and raised his hand for a high-five. "Way to go buddy."

Chapter 55

The Bay of Beirut

The *Sea Queen* bobbed rhythmically against a couple of rubber tires as gusts of salty wind and spray whipped white caps from an unseen source. Captain Ali, his weathered face chiseled by the sea, leaned heavily on the railing and gazed at the gathering storm. With one last drag, he released a trail of grey smoke and tossed his cigarette into the swelling tide.

A set of headlights from an old taxi appeared in the distance, and quickly drew near, its windshield wipers flailing wildly. It screeched to a halt, and Jared jumped out.

"What took you?" the old captain growled, looking at his watch. They were thirty minutes late, and the tide was changing.

"You might say, we were delayed . . . again," Jared answered his eyes searched the man's face for understanding . . . there was none.

"You sure stirred up a hornet's nest whatever you did," the ship's captain said, looking in the direction of the palace. "What did you do? Rob the palace?"

Uncle Abbas shrugged his shoulders and returned a sly grin. "How long before you shove off?"

Ali glanced again at his watch, "Tide is on its way out now. I'd say, we'd better get a move on. Plus, there's a storm brewing out there, and I want to be as far from the breakers as possible when it hits." As he spoke, another gust of wind whipped across the bow of his ship.

With Habib's help, Jared and Anita boarded the *Sea Queen* while the captain made the final preparations.

Uncle Abbas stepped up to the captain, "Thank you my old friend. My children have been through a lot, so take good care of them."

Captain Ali nodded in their direction. "Border patrols have been beefed up. It will be nearly impossible to cross into international waters the usual way. I am going to have to take a circuitous route around the lighthouse. Hopefully then, I'll be able to put some real estate between the border patrol and me. With the storm blowing in, this will be a most hazardous journey."

"Do you think that boat can make it?" Uncle Abbas asked, eying the old trawler.

"This old tub?" The sea warrior said, leaning back on his heels. "She's a thousand kilos lighter and has a hundred more horses in the engine room than the *le Labrador.*"

"It's too bad about the young couple; Mr. Jared took it really hard."

Captain Ali pulled a rumpled pack of cigarettes from his coat pocket, shook one up, and caught it with his lips. After lighting it, he released a long breathe.

"We were fortunate that the cruise ship was nearby and saw it happen. If they hadn't rescued me and that lady when they did, we wouldn't have lasted thirty minutes in these freezing waters."

Uncle Abbas extended a hand, and they exchanged the traditional kiss. "You're doing the Lord's work, my friend. God's speed."

"And to you, too."

The two men parted company; Captain Ali to his duties on board the *Sea Queen*, and Uncle Abbas to his flock.

***

Jared, Habib, and Anita huddled below deck around the chart table studying the papers she'd stolen while the captain shoved off. At first, the gentle rocking of the boat caused them to sway like dancers, but soon, as the trawler broke past the no wake zone, it became obvious that it would be impossible to stand much longer.

"From what I'm reading," Jared said, barely able to hold himself upright. "Amil had been embedded as the U.N. Diplomatic Attaché to the Head of the Greenpeace Movement, but for the life of me, I have no idea how that would harm the U.S."

Just then, the ship lurched to the side as it hit the open waters. "Grab hold of something," Captain Ali called through the speaker system, "it's going to get a little rough."

Habib tightened his grip on the chart table and watched as Anita toppled over and landed on a thread-bare couch. Jared lost his battle with gravity and buckled over, landing on the lower deck.

"I see what he means," he said, pulling himself up. "Maybe we should wait until we get past this storm before we try reading these papers."

Anita, looking rather green, clutched her stomach and doubled over. "I think that's a marvelous idea," she said, hand to her mouth.

Chapter 56

The Conference Center

Waiters — wearing crisp, clean coats, and carrying silver trays above their heads — moved between small clusters of conversationalists unnoticed. The tinkle of champaign glasses and the low conversations among the members of NOAA and Greenpeace were only slightly masked by the piped-in music of Bach, Brahms, and Beethoven.

The long-anticipated summit meeting between President Ferguson and the two parties was about to begin; and the air radiated with excitement. All the planning and preparation for the signing of the Kyoto Agreement came to fruition. Finally, America would fall in line with the rest of the world.

At precisely 1:00 p.m., the president stood and tapped her wine glass. The high-pitched crystalline ring cut through the din, and all conversations ceased.

"Ladies and gentlemen, I now call to order the Kyoto Summit," she paused to allow a round of applause to resonate throughout the dining hall. After a few minutes, the parties took their seats and waited.

"We would like to hear from your esteemed colleagues who have worked so diligently to make this summit possible. So I yield the floor to Dr. McMillan and his team. Following them, we will enjoy a marvelous video presentation demonstrating our progress in cleaning up the environment. And then we'll hear from members of Greenpeace."

***

Amil sat quietly watching the proceedings unfold with passive indifference as the speeches droned on. Unnoticed by all, Teriek adjusted the thermostat up enough to make the already stuffy room a bit warmer. The discussion panel which followed only added to the dulling effects of the drugs Teriek and his men introduced into the beverages before they left the warehouse. Heads began to nod.

At its conclusion, President Ferguson rose to her feet and staggered, catching herself on the podium.

"Whoa, I guess I had a few too many martinis," she said, then collapsed.

"Get Debutante!" Larry Morgan hollered.

A moment later four secret service agents encircled the president while her medical team rushed to her side. They placed her on a gurney and wheeled her to the hotel infirmary.

Amil seized his opportunity and made his move.

So did Kaleel.

The two men converged upon Rachel Anderson, a fifteen-year veteran in the Secret Service, who carried the suitcase which housed the nuclear codes. Her instincts were good! Her reflexes were better. In one smooth move, she drew her side arm, aimed, and pulled the trigger. The muffled pop went unnoticed as one man fell. Before she could wheel around, the other man was on her, smothering her face with a hankie laced with chloroform. An instant later, her knees buckled, and she fell limp, dropping her weapon. The dark suited man picked her up and placed her into a serving cart with a false lid. The action took all of fifteen seconds, but it was enough to get her and the cart across the dining room, and into the kitchen.

***

"Madam President, Madam President, are you all right?" a medical technician asked breathlessly as he jogged alongside the gurney.

"I feel sick," the jaundiced president said as she tried to lift her head.

"Lay still, ma'am," he ordered, placing a cold wet cloth on her forehead.

As the gurney turned the corner and entered the hotel infirmary, Larry Morgan wheeled around, his face paled, "Where's the 'Football?' Where's Rachel?"

"She's right behind us," an agent said as the gurney rolled into the hotel infirmary.

Morgan drew his weapon and bounded for the door, "She's not here, on my six," he commanded.

Half of his team split off while the others stayed with the president, guns at the ready.

***

Larry and the rest of his men burst through the dining room door, guns drawn. Immediately they began to fan out.

"Rachel?" Larry's voice crackled with tension.

"She's gone, sir," one of his men called.

A flash of movement and the door to the kitchen burst open. One of the waiters stood, his Uzi pointed at the ceiling. "Allah al Akbar . . . God is great."

In an instant, the room exploded into gunfire as the agents opened fire. The waiter's white coat turned blood red and he fell to the floor, his eyes still open.

***

Kaleel groaned as the paramedics rolled him over.

"He's alive," the paramedic yelled.

An instant later, three Secret Service agents encircled him, pointing their guns at Kaleel's head.

"Don't shoot, I'm one of you," he coughed, hand to his chest.

"He's wearing a Kevlar vest underneath his waiter's jacket," the medic said, backing away to give Larry Morgan room to maneuver.

With his fingers locked behind his head, Kaleel kicked off his soft-soled shoe. "That's right, now look inside."

One of the agents lowered his weapon, knelt, and followed his instructions. "This guy's got a level four CIA clearance," he said, as he studied Kaleel's ID, identifying him as an undercover CIA agent attached to Homeland Security.

"Scan it," ordered Larry, "Right now, I wouldn't trust my mother without proper clearance."

The agent ran it through a digital scanner and looked up. "Hey, this guy's ligit, he's one of us."

Kaleel tried to sit up.

"Here, let me help you. Let's get you to the infirmary," the medic said as he reached out and pulled him up.

"No, I've got to get to the kitchen. It's the 'Football,' they've taken it," Kaleel sputtered, holding his chest.

Larry holstered his weapon and surveyed the room. "Who's taken her?" His chiseled face grew harder.

With his hand on the medic's shoulder, Kaleel lifted his arm and pointed. "That's what I've been trying to tell you. They've taken her to the kitchen!"

Like the well-trained team they were, the agents followed Larry's lead and charged into the kitchen just as Amil raised a meat-clever to chop off Rachel's right hand.

"Stop or I'll shoot!" Larry ordered, his gun leveled at the man holding Rachel.

The meat cleaver began a quick descent.

Bang!

A shot rang out, and Amil tumbled to the terrazzo floor. The meat-cleaver dropped and skittered in the opposite direction.

In a burst of flashes, the remaining terrorists opened fire. One agent took a direct hit and fell, another spun as a round struck him in the shoulder. He stumbled backward against a hot range. Larry pulled him to safety before the open flame from the stove made things worse.

The agents took cover behind the preparation table and fired with precision. With three of his men dead and one wounded, Larry Morgan doubted whether he could hold the insurgents off much longer.

"Retreat," he yelled and backed out of the kitchen.

"What are you doing? They've got Rachel and the Football. You can't let them get away," Kaleel said, still holding his chest.

Larry checked his ammunition. "I know, but my men were getting ripped apart."

A cloud of acidic smoke wafted from the kitchen and Kaleel let out a frustrated breath. "They'll kill her. You know that, don't you?"

The two men's eyes locked. "Not if I can help it." With a quick glance over his shoulder, he caught the eye of his second in command. "Let's get a flash bang grenade and some tear gas."

"Aye aye, sir," came a crisp answer.

Larry moved toward the other room, his gun held close to his chest. "Where'd they get those Uzi's, anyway?" peering through the round window.

"I don't know, we didn't bring them in with us as we came," Kaleel answered, his gun squeezed into his hand. "That was one of those things I wasn't aware of. We operated on a need to know basis. They must have stashed them here months ago. It was my job to stop the man who grabbed your agent before he got to her. Unfortunately, she shot me instead of him. What is her name?"

"Rachel," Larry said, not taking his eyes from the door.

"Yeah, well. I guess I can't blame her. I didn't realize how closely Amil and I favored each other. Did you know he's my cousin? How 'bout that for coincidence?"

Larry's mouth gapped open, his words lodged in his throat.

"Ready with the flash bang grenade, sir," his lieutenant said, cutting him off.

A quick glance over his shoulder and his face hardened, "Okay, let's give these guys something to think about before they meet their 72 virgins."

With precision, one of the agents yanked open the kitchen door, tossed in the grenade and ducked.

A moment later, the glass window blew out, and the remaining agents rushed the kitchen, their guns blazing. The stunned insurgents fell like bowling pins in a hail of hot led.

"The Football, get Rachel and the Football out of here!" Larry hollered, sweeping the room with his arms extended, gun in hand.

One of the agents waded into the mass of twisted bodies, grabbed her and the suitcase and brought them out.

"Mr. Bashera, check the bodies," Morgan ordered, then turned his attention on Rachel.

Chapter 57

The Sea Queen

The *Sea Queen* crossed over the breakers into the open sea when Anita's phone vibrated. Too sick to move, she reached into her bag and handed it to Jared. He swallowed hard and retook his seat. Outside, the noble craft battled the sea and time. Ten foot waves rolled over the deck from the north and in the distance the border patrol had taken notice of their movements and began turning about.

"Hello," Jared said, still feeling the effects of the rocking boat.

It was Mr. Xavier.

"Oh! Hello, Jared. I'm glad you made it to safety. Is Anita alright?"

"Uh, Mr. Xavier—John, did you set this up?" Jared laid his head back, his jaw clinched.

"Well, no Jared, not exactly. I mean, yes, I set you up in the Harbor House and yes, I recruited Anita, but no, I didn't have anything to do with her getting abducted, or you being attacked by the Syrians."

John," he interrupted, "How'd you know about us being attacked by the Syrians?"

A chuckle echoed across the miles, "I just got off the phone with your Uncle Abbas. He's quite a fellow, isn't he?"

"He's one of your guys?" Jared was incredulous.

"No, not exactly. I'd say Uncle Abbas is an independent contractor. I believe he describes himself as, and I quote, 'Doing the Lord's work,' unquote. Now listen, you guys need to relax, and I'll get you home in a New York minute. By the way, I understand you mentioned to Fatemah that New York is not a safe place. What's that all about?"

"How'd you know about—"

A chuckle on the other end, told him all he needed to know. Jared bit back the bile that crept up his throat. He hated knowing that someone was listening in on his conversation.

"Yes," glancing at Anita, who lay in a tight ball on the couch, "the papers Anita stole from her father's vault seemed to indicate that something big is going to happen in New York, but we haven't had a chance to go over it. The sea is a bit rough."

Just then, the ship lurched to the side and Jared tumbled. He caught himself on a ceiling strap before falling on the couch.

"That's okay. As soon as you board the *Pearl Lady,* have the captain scan it to me. I'll have my team go over it with a fine-tooth comb to see if there's something we can use. I will tell you this, however; we have a situation unfolding on Mackinaw Island as I speak. It involves a couple of people you might know."

"Don't tell me, let me guess, Jimbo Osborne," a smug grin parted Jared's lips.

"Oh, that's right. We intercepted that call, too. Then you know Amil is somewhere on that island—hold on, I just got an intercept."

Jared held his breath, waiting for his boss to come back on the line. "Jared, it looks like this Amil guy just attempted to steal the nuclear codes."

Jared's pulse quickened. "Did he succeed? I mean, did he get them?"

"Apparently not, we had a man working deep throat who tried to stop—wait a minute, I'm getting conflicting reports. Look Jared this is getting complicated. I need to let you go."

"Hold it a minute, John, I need you to level with me, who am I working for, you or the CIA?" Jared asked, rubbing the nape of his neck.

He waited for his boss to answer, "Jared, you work for me. Beyond that, like I said, it gets complicated.

"Well at least tell me the name of the other guy, was it Jimbo?"

Another pause and Mr. Xavier cleared his throat. "Understand this is off the record and very preliminary, but the initial report says that our guys killed a group of terrorists posing as cooks and waiters. As far as the other guy is concerned, his name is Kaleel Bashera, Fatemah's brother.

Jared slumped to the floor, his back against a cabinet. "How—"

"Don't ask, Jared. I'd hate to lie to you, but it looks like he may have been killed in the action. I'll know more in a few minutes."

A wave of nausea swept over Jared. *Not again*, he cried, *not another close friend. Oh God!* He moaned.

Habib rolled over and gave him a weak smile.

"Go back to sleep Habib, we have a long way to go," he said, as he closed the phone.

Jared stood and supported himself on the counter as the ship rocked and reeled. He envied Anita and Habib. *How can they sleep in seas like this*? Bracing himself against the narrow galley walls, he made his way to the forward cabin, opened the door, and flopped on the bed. His shoulders shook uncontrollably under the weight of grief. For unnumbered minutes, he released his emotions until they played out. Then, with a halting breath, he opened a drawer next to the bed and found a Bible. Flipping through its crisp pages, the Twenty-Third Psalm leaped from the ancient tome, and he began to silently read. "The Lord is my shepherd, I shall not want. He maketh me to lie down in green pastures: he leadeth me beside the still waters. He restoreth my soul: he leadeth me in the paths of righteousness for his name's sake. Yea, though I walk through the valley of the shadow of death, I will fear no evil: for thou art with me; thy rod and thy staff they comfort me. Thou preparest a table before me in the presence of mine enemies: thou anointest my head with oil; my cup runneth over. Surely goodness and mercy shall follow me all the days of my life: and I will dwell in the house of the LORD forever."

After closing the Bible, he closed his eyes and a peace rolled over him like an infinite balm.

Chapter 58

The Presidential Suite

Still woozy from the drugs, President Ferguson leaned heavily on the corner of her desk and swore. "How could this have happened? Do you realize I could have been killed? We all could have."

Andrew Kelly stood, hands outstretched, unable to answer the president.

"It will be weeks before the investigators learn how the drugs got here," she continued, "but believe me, I *will* get to the bottom of it. And heads *will* roll." Still holding the cold towel against her forehead, she forced herself away from the desk. "I want a presidential gag order placed on the press corps. I don't want any of this to get out, or we'll have a riot on our hands."

"Yes, Madam President, will there be anything else?" Kelly asked, his lips still white from the ordeal.

Leaning back, she shook her head, "No, I just need to lie down for a few minutes and clear my head. That will be all," she said with a wave of her hand.

Andrew Kelly shut off the lights and started to pull the door closed.

"Oh, and one more thing."

"Yes ma'am?" pausing, he held her gaze.

"I want to personally thank that agent, what's his name?"

"Bashera. His name is Agent Kaleel Bashera."

"Yes, him, tell him I want to see him in about forty-five minutes."

Kelley nodded and closed the door. He looked at the two guards stationed on either side of the door. "No one gets in. No one gets out without my permission. Understood?"

The two men snapped to attention, "Yes sir."

A roach crawled across Amil's hand as he lay motionless under a stainless table. Overlooked by the clean-up detail, he held his position on the kitchen's terrazzo floor, hoping to go unnoticed. The Kevlar vest he was wearing stopped the 9mm round before it punctured his chest. In the confusion, Amil simply rolled under the shelf while the gunfight continued above him.

After hearing Kaleel referred to by his last name, Amil realized who he was dealing with, *No wonder we looked so much alike, he's my cousin.*

A wicked smile came across his face as a new plan emerged. It was risky, and he would have to act quickly, but what did he have to lose? From his vantage point, he watched as Kaleel knelt to identify the bodies. He eased himself out from underneath the shelf, and caught his breath as pain from the bullet doubled him over. Fighting to keep from gasping, he bit back the sparks radiating through his body, knowing to do anything less would get him killed.

Crouching low, he steadied himself on the table and tip-toed closer to where Kaleel knelt. A large frying pan sat on the range, and Amil lifted it high above his head.

A split-second later, Kaleel felt the air move and turned.

Crack!

He crumpled to the floor like a rag doll, unconscious.

A new wave of flames swept throughout Amil's chest and he doubled over, gasping for air. After a minute, he righted himself and glanced around. He released a labored sigh of relief. *Good, no one heard the commotion.* Satisfied with phase one, he made a quick decision. Grasping Kaleel by the wrists, he dragged him to an unlocked freezer and left him there. He was about to leave when another thought occurred to him. He stepped back in and stripped off Kaleel's waiter's jacked and donned it. Then he lifted his Secret Service badge and jammed it over his pocket. Two minutes later, he joined the other agents who'd gathered for a briefing in the dining room.

"Bashera," Amil's stomach knotted. "Yes, sir?" he answered the man leading the briefing.

"Did you get all the bodies ID'd?"

"Yes, and I placed them in the cooler until they can be transported."

Agent Morgan made a note of it on his iPad, "Good thinking. Do you have a list of names?"

Amil's heart pounded so hard, he thought the agents around him could hear it. "Not yet, give me a sheet of paper, and I will make a full report." Not knowing anything else to say.

Morgan pulled a sheet of paper from his briefcase and passed it to him. "Here, and when you're finished, get something for the pain. I know your chest has got to hurt."

Amil fingered the sheet of paper and tried to smile, "Hurts like crazy."

Feeling confident in his ability to meld into any situation, he finished writing the names of his former team and handed it to Agent Morgan, then casually walked down the hallway, looking for another opportunity to strike.

***

A tap on the door awakened President Ferguson from her nap. "I'm awake," she said, her voice still thick.

"Feeling better, ma'am," her personal aid asked.

Susan sat up and brushed the hair from her eyes, "Yes, much better. Thank you, now what's the situation?"

Larry Morgan stuck his head around the aid. "Good to see you're up. Madam, we have Prime Minister Shimer ben Yousef on the line now. Where would you like to take the call?"

"Yes, let me get to my desk. I'll take it there. Thank you."

With her aid's help the president took her seat behind the Victorian, gold leafed desk and lifted the phone to her ear. "Mr. Prime Minister, so good to talk with you." She waited for his response. "I understand you knocked out Iran's nuclear capability as a preemptive strike," not being one to mince words.

"Yes, that is correct. You would have done the same thing to Cuba or another nation that threatened you, Madam President," he said in his defense.

"Oh I concur completely. You don't have to get my permission to defend your country. What's this I hear about you attacking Lebanon though? They were no threat to Israel."

The prime minister cleared his throat, "That's just it, they never were. This is just a ploy, a diversion, to open the door for Iran to attack us. All of that will be disclosed when the UN peacekeepers and investigators finish with their report. It will be revealed that we were infiltrated by members of Hamas. It was they who opened fire on the cities of Lebanon. I gave no such authority."

"Yes, but it is no secret Israel would like nothing better than to establish settlements north of the UN designated border. What if you hired Hamas to infiltrate your own military, just to make it look like you were infiltrated by Lebanon?"

"Madam President, you are talking in circles."

A wicked laugh peculated from President Ferguson's throat, "Stranger things have happened. Remember Iran Contra?"

"Remember Fast and Furious?" he countered.

"Touché."

"So will you stand with us, Madam President?"

"You know there will be massive world condemnation for your alleged actions, don't you?"

"Yes," the Prime Minister admitted.

"And tremendous pressure will be brought to bear upon my country to join the UN backed plan to force Israel to divide Jerusalem. You know that, don't you?"

"Yes, but can we count on you to stand with us, to block any UN sanctions?"

President Ferguson leaned heavily on the desk. Still feeling the effects of the drugs, her mind refused to function at full capacity.

"Madam President, are you there?"

"Yes I am," she paused to dab her brow with a wet wash cloth. "You can depend on America to stand with you."

The prime minister sighed into the phone. "Thank you Madam President. Now I'd better be getting back to my duties. Good-bye, and may God bless America."

President Ferguson, set the phone aside and looked up. "Andrew, I need to get off this island now."

"Madam President, the winds are at 50 knots. We are having to tie down the blades of Marine One, to keep it from being blown off its pad."

"What about one of the Coast Guard ships? Couldn't one of them take us off the island?"

"It would be a rough ride, but the problem is getting you to the ship. They can't get any closer than 300 yards off the coast for fear of rocks. No madam, it looks like we're stuck here for another day."

The president slammed her hand on the desk, making a pencil jump. "Okay, I guess we'll have to. Inform the hotel management that we're spending another night here."

"Yes ma'am. I already have. Is there anything I can get you?"

"Yes, send in Agent Bashera."

"Very good, I'll do it right away," he said, backing away.

Chapter 59

The Presidential Suite

"Agent Bashera," Amil froze in place. Had he been caught? Did they find his cousin? Was he about to be arrested or worse ... shot. He paused, his hand instinctively went for his gun, but stopped.

"The President wants to see you, come with me." Reluctantly, he turned and followed the Chief of Staff without comment.

At the door, two more of the president's security team waited, "You'll need to leave your service weapon here," Andrew said, "standard operating procedures, you understand."

Amil nodded wishing he had another. He handed over his gun and smiled.

Inside the Milliken Suite, Amil stood at attention in front of the president. "Relax Agent Bashera," President Ferguson said, standing with an extended hand. Amil forced air into his lungs and clasped the proffered hand. It was warm and soft, not unlike his wife's, and he imagined himself holding hands with her once again. His breath caught in his throat, and he blinked the memory away trying to act nonchalant. "On behalf of a grateful nation and myself, I want to extend my appreciation for your courageous actions earlier today. What you did not only saved the life of one of my closest friends, but you also kept the nuclear codes from falling into the hands of some very bad people."

Amil stood, staring at the wall behind her. *If only you knew the half of it.*

"Thank you, Madam President and thank you for taking time to speak with me."

Returning to her seat, she signaled him to do the same, "I'm intrigued by the fact that you were working undercover as a CIA operative and our people didn't know about it."

Amil felt heat rising, but remained calm.

"Yes, this was a need to know operation. Only a very few people were let into the loop."

"I see, well, it was good you were in the right place at the right time. I want to officially recognize you for your bravery once we get off of this infernal island and back to D.C."

Amil's face gave nothing away as he nodded. "Thank you President Ferguson. That would be an honor."

"How can I get in contact with you?" she probed. Amil's mind raced.

"I, I'm not sure where my next assignment will be, or when I'll be in the country. How about we let your Chief of Staff get in contact with my handler? I'm sure they could work it out."

"Sounds fine with me. I think Andrew can handle that." Her eyes cut in his direction.

Amil followed her gaze and for a moment caught himself pitying the man for having to dance to a woman's commands.

The president stood, her fingers touching the desk lightly. "Well, again Mr. Bashera, thank you. Oh, and if there is anything you need while we're here, just ask."

Amil held her gaze. "Actually, there is one thing," he said causally.

"And what would that be?"

"Could you arrange a dinner for me and the agent who shot me? I would like to thank her for not aiming at my head." He smiled.

"Why of course, Mr. Bashera. I would be happy to. Maybe she can somehow make up for shooting the wrong guy." She laughed, he didn't.

She buzzed her secretary and conveyed the request.

***

"You did good," Andrew said, as he ushered Amil outside the Presidential Suite. "The president likes you. If you play your cards right, you might even get invited to join her security team."

Wouldn't that be a hoot. Amil smiled at the thought.

As he made his way down the hall, Rachel rounded a corner and bumped into him.

Hand to her mouth, "Oh, sorry, I didn't see you coming." Her face colored, "Look, I can't talk now. I was just summoned, but maybe we can get together later," she said, then hastened on.

Good, she didn't realize I'm not Agent Bashera, letting out a tight breath. A quick glance over his shoulder gave him the all clear, and he made a beeline to the elevator and hit the button. The doors slid shut and he pressed LL, Lower Level.

The doors glided open, and Amil found himself on the Kitchen Service Level, but he needed to go down one more floor. To his left were a flight of metal stairs leading down to the Maintenance Level. After checking to make sure no one was looking, he dashed down them, his leather soles tapping lightly on each step. At the bottom, he was met by a man wearing coveralls with the name Bill embroidered over his heart, sporting a utility belt.

"Son, you don't belong down here, are you lost?"

"Yeah, I'm new here. I must have gotten turned around."

"Well this area is for 'Authorized Personnel Only' so you need to high-tail it back up those stairs," he said with a quick jerk of his head.

Amil's face hardened to a sneer as he brought out the butcher knife he'd picked up on his way through the kitchen. The man's eyes widened as Amil covered his mouth and rammed the knife into the man's abdomen. Bill's lifeless body slumped against the wall, then to the floor. Not wasting any time, He grabbed the man's wrists and dragged him behind a workbench. Still breathing hard, he removed the key ring from the dead man's utility belt. Thumbing through the keys, he continued until the last one appeared. It was stamped with the two letters, EL *Electrical Room*. Amil smiled at his clever wit, and quickly made his way to the door. A quick turn of the key and the door swung open. He flipped the light on and scanned the bank of gray electrical panels with large tubes leading into them. To the side was one main bus and Amil smiled. "Bingo," he whispered.

Fingers trembling from the adrenalin rush, Amil took a hard breath and held it, trying to regain control. After a long, slow exhale, he pulled the main switch. Instantly, everything went black. Using a flashlight he'd gotten off the dead man's utility belt, he illuminated the panel while he removed the main breakers and smashed them on the floor. Knowing the president's security detail would be down within in minutes, he did the same to the extra breakers, then he quietly slipped out under the stairs and waited.

A pair of agents, wielding flashlights, began a careful descent down the metal stairs. Amil held his breath and backed behind a utility cabinet. He just hoped the men wouldn't do any snooping around and discover Bill's body.

"Hey Bill." an agent called into the blackness.

All was silent except for the drip, drip, drip of water.

"I wonder where Bill is?" a voice echoed in the darkness, as two beams cut in crisscrossing patterns around the basement.

"I don't know, better check out the main bus," his partner said.

The lights disappeared into the Electrical Room.

"This looks like it was intentional," one agent said, studying the broken breakers on the floor.

Amil stepped into the dull illumination. "What are you doing down here, Bashera?"

Not seeing his drawn weapon until it was too late; the two agent's eyes widened as Amil lifted it and squeezed the trigger. The muffled report popped four times.

"That's two down," he whispered, then backed out and closed the door.

"Hey guys," someone called, and Amil froze.

Hearing nothing, the agent began a rapid descent. Leather shoes tapped quickly down the steps making them sing with vibrations. Not knowing how many might be with him, Amil slipped into the darkness and held his breath.

As he leaned on a work bench, Amil's hand found an iron pipe. Gripping it tightly, he lifted it above his head. In the darkness, something brushed against his body. Amil's pulse quickened. He could hear the man breathing, felt his heat. *He must be within inches of me,* his mind raced. With one desperate swing, he brought the iron pipe down. He hit something solid, and the agent groaned and fell.

With the flick of a button the flashlight came on, and he quickly assessed his efforts. He jolted backward as two lifeless eyes stared back at him. He'd struck the man right on the forehead, cracking his skull like an egg.

Gulping for air, he waited for his heart to slow before dragging the man's body into the Electrical Room. After closing the door, Amil quietly climbed up the stairs. As he tip-toed through the kitchen, movement caught his eye. He stopped, cocked his head, and placed his hand on his weapon.

"What are you men doing here?" he blurted. It was his back-up team.

"We came on your orders, you said if you weren't back by two-thirty we were to go to plan 'B.' Did you take out the power?"

"Yes," Amil said curtly.

"Good thinking," Teriek said.

Amil glanced at his watch. It was 2:45. "Okay, you stay here, and I'll come and get you when I need you. Until then don't venture out of this area. Those Feds are trigger happy."

Ten men nodded and backed into a walk-in cooling unit to wait.

***

"Mr. Bashera," Rachel said as she passed him in the dimly lit hallway. Sorry for giving you the brush-off. You don't know how badly I feel about, you know, shooting you. Would you forgive me?" Her knees bent slightly as she talked. "I was so relieved when I found out you had a Kevlar vest on."

Amil held her gaze. "Oh that's okay, all in the line of duty," he said, rubbing his chest. "I'll recover, although I am a bit sore. I think one of my ribs is broken."

Amil's mind raced. *This could be my opportunity.* "Is there anything I can do to make it up to you?" her eyes pleaded.

"Well, yes, come to think of it, maybe we could discuss it over dinner."

Rachel's face darkened and she fanned herself, "As a matter of fact, the president just asked me if I could make that happen. Let's say about seven, by then I'll be off duty."

"Oh, okay, that's fine. Are you the one still carrying the 'Football?'" he asked looking at her wrist. A raw wound marked the place where he'd tried to pull it from her wrist.

"No, I did earlier, but not now, I've passed it off to Leah."

Smiling, Amil nodded, "Oh, okay then, I'll see you at seven."

Chapter 60

New Castle, Delaware

Five sets of headlights cut yellowed beams through the fog which crept up from the Delaware River. The musty air hung thick with humidity as Rajeed and his small caravan drove along Frenchtown Pike in search of the main highway leading north. He'd gotten turned around and, not knowing the area, found himself in downtown New Castle, Delaware, one of the oldest towns in the continental United States. Its residents boasted its roots dating before St. Augustine, Florida, but that was of little concern to Rajeed. Cutting his wheels to the left, his rear bumper grazed the fender of a parked car along the narrow street.

"Do you know you hit a car?" the driver of the second panel truck asked through the walkie-talkie.

"No, and I don't care. I just need to get the heck out of this maze," he cursed.

"Go straight and when you get to the light, turn right. Stay on it until you come to the main highway. That will take you to the Delaware Memorial Bridges."

"Where will that take me?" seethed Rajeed.

"To New Jersey."

"I don't want to go to New Jersey. I want to go to New York," he said, after another outburst of milk-curdling obscenities.

"Look Rajeed," Uri said, taking over the comm., "This will get us to New York just as quickly, maybe without as much traffic."

Rajeed relaxed his grip on the steering wheel, "Okay, but it's Sunday, there shouldn't be much traffic anyway."

"You're in America, Rajeed, there is always traffic in America, especially in New York," he chuckled.

"Okay, I see the signs. Stay close," Rajeed said, then set the walkie-talkie down and concentrated.

He hated heights and especially bridges. With the Twin Spans mounting the Delaware River at a height of 175 feet, though not the highest of bridges, it was enough to make Rajeed nearly lose his breakfast. With a quickened pulse and sweating palms, he focused on the vehicle ahead of him. Finally, after five minutes, the New Jersey shore appeared in the distance, and he began to breathe again.

"See, that wasn't so bad, was it Rajeed?" Uri's mocking voice paraded through the comm.

"I'm going to kill that man as soon as he serves his purpose," he muttered through clinched teeth.

Turning north on I-295, the caravan began making their way closer to their prize. Taking I-95 at the split, they continued north to Newark and Jersey City. By the time they reached the Holland Tunnel, golden sun rays glistened off the giant skyscrapers and superstructures.

Rajeed picked up the walkie-talkie, "Okay. This is it. All of you know what to do. As soon as we get through the tunnel, split up. Once you've delivered your packages, meet me at my new headquarters."

Four responses confirmed his orders, and the comm. went silent. The next forty-eight hours would be critical. If all went as planned, New York City would be a nuclear wasteland, and he would be standing before Allah waiting to hear, 'Well done,' something he'd never heard from his father.

The thought of his father made his blood pressure ratchet up. Always demeaning, always picking at him, never a compliment, never a good word. Ever since the chemical fire which scarred him for life, he'd felt his father's distain. It wasn't his fault. After all, he was only following his father's orders. *Hmm, maybe his father wanted it to fail. Maybe his father wanted him and his sister to die. He had no idea it was wrong to possess a small New Testament. It was a gift, for crying out loud. How was he supposed to know Islam vehemently disapproved of him reading anything other than the Quran, especially the Bible?* "I wish I had a Bible now," he muttered under his breath. "Maybe it would give me an answer to the question that's been dogging me. *Does God love me?*

Gritting his teeth, he tromped the gas pedal and sped up. *If he does, he wouldn't allow me to do what I'm planning to do. Maybe, he'll stop me.*

Chapter 61

The Woods Dining Room

As the evening wore on, so did the storm, and so did Amil's frustration. Over a dinner of cold sandwiches and warm tea, he'd listened to Rachel's rant about politics, fashions, and the war. He was sick of it. The thought suddenly occurred to him. *Maybe she is stalling while her friends are doing a background check.*

Amil's heart pounded, his hands slicked, and he was sure Rachel could see him sweating.

Barely able to breathe, Amil stood, hand to his chest, "Please excuse me, Rachel," and made a beeline for the men's room. After filling the sink with cold water, he splashed his face and tried to regain his composure. Standing shakily in front of the mirror, he looked up as two secret service agents entered. His hand instinctively reached for his gun expecting at any moment to hear two weapons shooting at him. As the two men went about their business, a slow release of air escaped his lungs, and he began to breathe again. He finished dabbing his face with a towel, nodded at the man washing his hands, and exited, feeling a sense of relief.

"So sorry, it must have been a reaction to the pain medication," he said, retaking his seat. "You were saying?"

"Oh, I don't remember," she quipped.

Relieved, Amil brought the conversation back to the 'Football.'

"So tell me, aren't you nervous someone might try to steal the codes?"

She wrinkled her nose, "Actually no. This was the first incident in my career. It happened to Leah, not like this time of course, but once someone tried to grab it from her as we escorted the president through a large crowd."

Clearly interested, Amil asked, "Well, what happened?"

"The other agents closed ranks and kept the would-be-grabber away."

"Are you always that close to the president?"

Rachel finished the last of her tea and set the glass on the table. "Oh, not really. We're usually somewhere in the vicinity. If, for example, the president is in the Oval Office, we're just outside in a private security room. If she is on the move, we usually trail her by about ten feet. We are never more than that far away from her at all times."

"Even when she is sleeping?"

"Oh yes! Even when she is sleeping!"

"Hmm, that's interesting."

"What about now, does Leah have the 'Football'?"

Rachel looked at her watch, "Uh, yeah, for another twenty minutes, then I get it back."

Satisfied he'd gotten what he needed from her, he let the conversation drop. "Interested in a walk before duty calls again?"

Taking another glance at her watch, "Yeah, but it'll have to be quick, plus, we can't go far, not in this storm."

The two of them left the dining room, and Amil led her down a darkened hall. A knot formed in his belly. What was wrong with him? She was the enemy. Yes, she was one of the most beautiful women he'd ever met, and yes, it seemed like she enjoyed his company, but that could be a ruse. *So why the hesitation? Kill her and get it over with*, a small voice screamed. It wasn't as if he didn't have blood on his hands already. He did, lots of it.

Making as if he wanted to kiss her, he put her in a choke-hold until she slumped to the floor. Using the keys he'd stolen from the maintenance man, Amil stashed her body in one of the utility closets in the back hallway. Then he was off to find Leah.

Amil knew he had precious few minutes before Rachel's absence would be discovered, and less before the shift change. He needed to find Leah, but that meant getting close to the president . . . again.

He stepped out into the storm.

***

Kaleel rolled over and groaned. A shiver rippled through his body as he lay in the freezer unit. Rubbing his arms, he tried to chase away the goose-bumps.

"Hello?" His voice faded quickly in the chilled air.

"Where am I?" Condensation formed with every word.

Reaching up, he touched the knot on the back of his head and winched, it was wet, and he guessed it was blood. Disorientated and still feeling sick, Kaleel reached for the door.

"Jammed," he muttered, "how original."

His hand reached for his weapon and when he found an empty holster, he cursed his bad luck. "I'm going to get whoever whacked me and stole my gun," His voice sounded thick and heavy. Patting his pockets, he let out a relieved sigh. "At least I still have my cell phone."

He squeezed the side button lighting up the interior and nearly stumbled. He was encircled with the bodies of the terrorist cell. His stomach knotted at the thought of all those sightless eyes, all those souls, all those men suffering in Hell. *And for what? Some radical belief that Jihad was the way to paradise? No. They're not in Hell because of their religious teachings. They were there because they rejected Christ as their Lord and Savior. It's that simple.* He reminded himself.

A quick glance at his phone told him that he needed to act fast. With only fifty percent of battery left, his options were limited so he dialed Larry's number.

The phone rang once, "Larry Morgan."

"Larry, this is Kaleel."

"Yes Kaleel, how did it go with the president? Did she give you one of those 'at-a-boy' speeches?"

Ignoring the comment, Kaleel pushed ahead, "Larry, you've got a big problem."

"Oh? What is it?"

"I wasn't the guy who talked to the president."

A sharp breath let Kaleel know he had Larry's full attention.

"But if you weren't the guy I saw Andrew escort into the president's office, who was it?"

"It wasn't me, that's for sure. Whoever it was, whacked me on the head and threw me into a freezer unit. I'm stuck here right now. You need to know that the guy walking around up stairs is not me. He's an impostor and may be planning on killing the president. Either that or he's still going after the Football."

"I'm not believing this, you, uh, he met with the president not an hour ago and I just saw you or whomever having dinner with Rachel."

"Rachel?"

"Yeah, Rachel, the one who shot you."

"Oh, that Rachel. Where is she now?"

"I don't know, I haven't seen her since then."

"Well, you'd better find her, and fast. She's the only one who could identify him."

"I'm on it."

"Oh, and one more thing, send someone down here and get me out of this freezer," his breath came in short puffs of condensation.

***

Another gust of wind whipped across the island throwing sheets of rain and debris against the window. President Ferguson sat, staring at the cascade of water running down the windows, and wondered what else could go wrong. First, it was Israel, then this infernal storm, the Kyoto debacle, the drugs, and the attempt at stealing the nuclear codes. She'd staked her presidential career on this summit, used up tons of political capitol, not to mention much of her financial war chest, only to see it go up in smoke, or down the drain. *Certainly things couldn't get worse,* she grimaced at the thought.

A knock on her door brought her from her thoughts. "Enter."

It was Larry Morgan.

"Madam President, there is a clear and present danger you need to be aware of," he said in no uncertain terms.

The president, code named Debutante, sat up straight. "Okay Larry, level with me, what is it?"

"I believe both you, and the 'Football' are in grave danger, and we need to have a contingency plan. Do you have a few minutes?"

"Why yes," she said, clearing her desk of some clutter.

"Actually I think we might need an hour to work out all the details."

"Larry, whatever you need." She buzzed the number for Andrew Kelly. "Andrew, assemble my closest aides and security detail, immediately."

Chapter 62

The Security Office

Still huffing and puffing from the long walk back to the Security Office, Jimbo led Belinda back from making a sweep of the facility in search of Amil.

"I need to check on the breaker again. The power has been out for quite a while, especially after those agents got that tree off the power lines," Jimbo said.

As he turned to leave, Belinda's cell phone rang. "Hold it Jimbo, this might be important." Her hand raised in a stop position.

Jimbo filled the doorway and waited for Belinda to code in.

"This is Belinda."

"Is Jimbo nearby?"

It was John Xavier.

Looking up, Belinda's eyebrows rose in question. "Yes, why?"

"Put your phone on speaker, I have something you both need to hear."

That done, Jimbo leaned over the phone and spoke, "Okay, we're here, go ahead. What's this all about?"

"What do you two know about the attack on the president?"

Belinda's jaw dropped and Jimbo nearly fell over. "Sir, we don't know anything. When—"

"Didn't you guys hear the shooting?"

Belinda leaned closer, "No sir, Jimbo saw Amil Bashera, but then he disappeared. We were doing a room to room sweep of the hotel. It must have been when we were on the other side of the hotel. This place is huge. Plus, the security detail wouldn't let us get within ten feet of the conference center."

"Well, that may be so, but I just received credible information that the president is in grave danger, that Amil Bashera is about to make another attempt, and that's not the worst of it."

"Level with us sir, what else is there?" Jimbo asked leaning over the phone.

"Long story short, we've pieced together the thefts of a number of large trucks and some nuclear fuel rods. We believe Anita's other brother, Rajeed is somehow behind it. If you'll remember, he's the one who has never been photographed. We think he is plotting to set off several dirty bombs in New York City, and Jared is about to walk into a mess."

Jimbo let out a long whistle. "John, what's Jared got to do with it?"

"It's complicated, but suffice it to say, he has Anita with him, and she's the only one who can pick out Rajeed in a crowd. I need for you to get things cleaned up there and high-tail it to the Big Apple, pronto. Oh, and by the way, you've got an agent in your freezer unit that needs to thaw out."

Belinda locked eyes with Jimbo. "Have you informed the president?" the tension in the room was palpable.

"We have been trying to get through to the president's people, but I think someone has cut the lines. You need to alert them. *Now!*

***

Teriek, after waiting as long as he could, crept from the Supply Room, found the junction box for the phones and cut the lines. He'd just returned when Amil showed up.

"What took you so long? We have been waiting for hours," he seethed.

"I had to find out where the codes were and eliminate the only person who could identify me."

"So where are they?"

"The codes are within ten feet of the president at all times."

Teriek stroked his chin and paced the small area. His initial plan had failed, costing him all of his A team. Now he depended on his B team to carry the day. This was all new territory. He never planned on killing the president; that would have caused repercussions of global proportions. He couldn't be responsible for starting another war against his country as happened after September 11th, 2001. This would have to be a surgical strike, one that would render the Great Satan impotent.

"All right then," Teriek said, "Here's the plan."

Using a penlight to illuminate the storage room, Teriek drew a schematic of the hotel on a piece of paper. For the next fifteen minutes they leaned over the floor plan, discussing the best way to get at the president. The scuffle of feet outside the door interrupted them.

"Quiet," Teriek hissed.

Peering through the narrow opening of the storage room door, Teriek watched as Jimbo and Belinda led a man from the freezer back upstairs.

"Why don't we kill them?" Amil asked, keeping his voice low.

"Because these guns don't have silencers, and right now we have the element of surprise. We don't need to lose it over three people who aren't associated with the president," he said through pinched lips.

Another hour passed and Teriek was getting antsy. He looked at his watch, "Okay, check your weapons, it's time."

The grandfather clock rang out eleven bells, and they began their climb up the stairs to the fourth floor. All was quiet, and except for an occasional crack of thunder, the dim floors showed no sign of life.

With the second and third floors cordoned off, Teriek and his men slipped up the stairs unnoticed in the dark. His plan was a bold one; half of his men would ascend to the fourth floor, rush the security detail, and take out as many of them as possible, while the other half would repel down from the roof and come in through the windows.

***

Jimbo, Belinda, and Kaleel watched from the darkened Cupola Lounge as six men, dressed in black hooded outfits, crept passed them and up the stairs.

"Let's take them out," Belinda whispered.

Shaking his head, Jimbo cupped his hand next to her ear. "Three against six isn't my idea of a fighting chance, especially if only two of us have guns."

"Here, take this," Jimbo said, handing him one of his back-up revolvers.

Kaleel checked it and made sure it was loaded. "Okay, I'm ready."

Gunfire erupted on the fourth floor and they jumped into action. Belinda and Kaleel led the charge up the stairs. Jimbo followed, his breath coming in labored breaths. Kaleel took aim on several terrorists and fired. After empting one clip, he grabbed a weapon from a dead insurgent and kept firing. They'd caught the terrorists between them and the security detail and began to move in for the kill. Shadowed figures moved through the grey haze, making Kaleel squint. Several of the president's men lay on the floor either dead or dying.

The security detail had fallen back to a secondary position, losing men and ground. It became obvious that the president and her remaining detail would be bottled in a corner.

Kaleel fired, picking off another assailant while Belinda and Jimbo bagged two others.

"That's four down, but where are the other two?" Kaleel hollered through the acrid smoke and haze. Belinda coughed as the air became nearly unbreathable. "I don't know. Jimbo! Can you see the others?" she called.

Two shots rang out. "That's one less," Jimbo called from behind a heavy door.

Then the floor shook from the concussion of a large explosion. Glass and debris flew at them, and the firing intensified.

"Uh oh, I think reinforcements just arrived," Belinda hollered.

Kaleel quickly realized the desperate situation they were in, stood up and sprinted to the presidential bedroom.

"Freeze!" a female secret service hollered.

In an instant Kaleel's life flashed before his eyes.

"It's me, Agent Kaleel, don't shoot!"

"Drop your weapon," she ordered, still pointing her gun at his head. "Now kick your gun over to me, kneel, and don't try doing anything fancy."

Kaleel knelt without saying a word.

All around them, the battle played out.

Without warning, an insurgent jumped into the room firing wildly. The agent took a direct hit and fell, writhing in pain.

Kaleel retrieved his weapon, turned and fired, striking the insurgent in the chest, splattering blood on the wall behind him.

A moment later, Jimbo and Belinda were at his side.

"The agent, she's been hit," Kaleel said trying to catch his breath.

Belinda knelt to attend to her as Jimbo and Kaleel began a room to room hunt for the remaining terrorist.

***

"Where am I," Rachel muttered as the pungent odor of cleaning solutions assaulted her nose. Her head throbbed, and she felt lightheaded.

The sickening realization struck her like a kick to the stomach. "That creep tricked me. I'll get him for that," she spat through clinched teeth.

Hearing gunfire, Rachel's heart skipped a beat as her training kicked into high gear. She knew instinctively what was happening. Reaching for her ankle, she lifted her pant leg and found her back up weapon and flipped off the safety. With the barrel of her gun pointed down, she crept from the storage room and began making her way in the direction of the gun fire.

Chapter 63

The Presidential Suite

The room where the president and her security detail huddled suddenly rocked from an earth-shaking explosion.

Stunned, Jimbo staggered down the hallway, ears ringing. "What happened?" he yelled, but his voice seemed muffled, distant. The air was thick with debris. Acrid smoke stung Jimbo's eyes, nearly blinding him.

Through the haze, Belinda emerged, covered in dirt, her face, streaked with sweat, tears and soot. "I don't know," she said, uncertainly.

Someone groaned

"Quiet, I hear something," Kaleel said, as he climbed out from under some sheet-rock.

"Someone help me, please." The muffled cries brought Jimbo to his senses. He charged into the corner office followed by Kaleel and Belinda, guns pointing in crisscrossing patterns.

"She's gone, the president . . . gone!" Leah cried, half dazed, blood seeping from her arm.

Belinda knelt down beside her, looking into her eyes. Her breathing was shallow and eyes wouldn't focus. "She is fading fast!" she screamed, leaning close. "Hold on honey, help is on its way," she lied, but wanted more than anything to give her a reason to live.

"They've got the Fuutball," her tongue thick. She began to shake uncontrollably as she held up a bloody stump. Her eyes gazed upward and then she relaxed.

Cradling her in her arms, Belinda bit back her tears.

Kaleel assessed the room with a keen eye. "Ropes, they've repelled down the side of the building and are heading for the shore," he said and sprang for the stairs.

Touching Belinda on the shoulder, Jimbo gave her a gentle squeeze, "Come on Belinda, Leah's gone, there's nothing you can do here. We need you."

Belinda gave him a weak nod and pushed herself to her feet. "Maybe it's not too late." She turned and ran for the stairs close behind Kaleel and Jimbo.

As they descended the stairs, they met Rachel coming up.

"They've got the president," Kaleel said, as he raced to the rear of the building. Stopping briefly at the rear entrance, he peered into the night. "They can't get off this island, not in this storm. It would be suicide."

"Don't bet on it," Rachel said, pushing past him and plunging into the storm. Rain soaked and shivering, she wiped her matted hair from her eyes and called into her wrist walkie-talkie, "This is Special Agent Rachel Anderson. We have a Code Red situation. Debutante is fallen, repeat, Code Red, Debutante is fallen."

"This is Captain Joseph K. Cunningham, ma'am. We have been monitoring the scene on our end. How can we assist?"

"Insurgents have penetrated our defenses and have taken Debutante and the Football. They are attempting to get off the island. I repeat they've got Debutante and the codes."

"I copy that, we will alert the task force and tighten the perimeter. Is there anything else?"

"Can you get a helicopter in the air?"

"No ma'am, that's a negative ... winds are too high!"

"Okay, but keep a look out for anything leaving the leeward side of the island."

"Will do, roger that. Out."

***

Teriek pulled President Ferguson by a rope as he and six other terrorists fought their way through the storm. They'd fast-roped from the fourth story window with the president, and when she landed, she sprained her ankle.

"Teriek, just shoot her and leave her, we got what we came for," hollered one terrorist.

"No, we may need her as a bargaining chip if we meet up with any trouble."

The man cursed and slogged toward the place where they'd hidden two inflatable Zodiacs in the underbrush when they first arrived.

Overhead, fingers of lightning splintered the grizzled clouds, and Amil spotted the huddled figures rapidly approaching the shore. Hope of getting off the island faded.

***

"There they are, just up ahead," Belinda hollered over the sheeting rain.

"Get down," Kaleel yelled as a dozen flashes quickened his senses. They dove for cover moments before a wave of bullets zipped past them.

Lightning flashed, and three terrorists appeared in prone positions, firing in their direction. Two others untied a pair of Zodiacs while another shoved the president and the suitcase into the pitching boat.

"Everybody, fan out and try to out flank them. I'm going to take the straight in approach," Kaleel said, wiping his face with his forearm.

Rachel and the others split up and began closing the circle, firing from three different angles. Two terrorists fell leaving one defender and the men in the Zodiac.

Kaleel charged the remaining man, striking him with two well-placed shots to the chest. He paused and rolled him over. It was Teriek. After feeling for a pulse and finding none, he headed for the water's edge.

An engine roared over the crack of thunder. Scanning the shore for its source, Kaleel's heart pounded as a sleek black rubber Zodiac emerged from a thicket and began cutting through the swelling tide. By the time he and the others reached the shore, it was too late. The Zodiac and the president were gone. Large white swells pounded the ragged beach, forcing the other Zodiac to bob up and down with an inane rhythm.

"They're getting away!" Belinda hollered, wiping her face with a soaked hand.

Jimbo stepped close, "Look, about fifty feet off shore. Someone is waving."

Lightning flashed and Rachel pointed, "It's the president. Somebody, help her!"

Without thinking Kaleel plunged into the swelling tide and began making powerful strokes toward the president.

"Hurry, she's not going to make it," Belinda called through cupped hands.

For every two strokes, the waves pushed him back one, yet he battled on.

"I lost them," Belinda hollered to Rachel. "I can't see either of them."

Minutes passed at a snail's pace, while Jimbo, Belinda, and Rachel stood helplessly on shore.

***

"Oh God, save me," the president's words came between gulps of water and air. She'd battled to stay afloat as long as she could, but her arms and legs ached from the freezing cold. Her movements slowed as the effects of fatigue and hypothermia took over, and her teeth chattered uncontrollably. Her ribs screamed in protest with each labored breath, and her throat burned from coughing.

Another wave swept over her, sucking her deeper in the numbing waters. A moment later, a hand gripped her by the wrist and tugged. Her hair swirled around her face as she rose. Unable to see who it was, relief swept over her as her head broke the surface and she gasped for air.

"Madam President, Madam President," a raspy voice yelled.

The dark features of Agent Bashera blurred, and she swiped the hair from her eyes.

"Hold still Madam President or we'll both drown," he said, trying to restrain her flailing arms.

***

"They're not going to make it, Jimbo," Belinda hollered. Taking him by the hand, she led him to the other Zodiac, which was lodged against a tree stump. "Let's go after them."

Jimbo, an old Navy man, hated the water, always had. But he pushed aside his fear and jumped in. "You stay here, I'll go."

Finding the key, he turned it and the dormant engine roared to life. Then he shoved off into the raging surf. The waves beat on the sides of the small water craft, nearly capsizing it several times, yet he plowed through the waves with determination.

Within minutes, he'd reached the couple who were struggling to keep afloat. He grabbed the president and pulled her over the rubber gunwale. She landed on him coughing and sputtering.

"Help me with Kaleel," he yelled.

President Ferguson spit out a mouthful of lake water and complied. A moment later, Kaleel flopped into the well of the boat, coughing, his matted hair partially obscuring his face.

Jimbo returned to the helm, throttled the engines and nosed the watercraft in the opposite direction from the shore.

"Where are you going? The shore's that way," the president demanded, pointing behind them.

"Yes, but the codes are that way," Jimbo hollered over the roar of the motor.

***

Rachel watched Jimbo's boat fade from view, all the while, keeping in contact with Captain Joseph K. Cunningham of the Coast Guard Cutter, Bristol Bay.

"Sir, Debutante is in the lake, repeat, Debutante is in the lake, please send assistance."

"Assistance is on its way," his voice resonated through the walkie-talkie.

Overhead, a bright light appeared momentarily blinding Jimbo as he raced in the direction of the other Zodiac.

Despite the severe weather conditions, the men and women of the Coast Guard risked their lives, as dozens of Hueys lifted from the pitching decks of the Coast Guard Cutters; Mackinaw, Bristol Bay, and Biscayne Bay, and descended on the property surrounding the Grand Hotel.

"This is Captain Joseph K. Cunningham of the Coast Guard Cutter, Bristol Bay. Is this agent Anderson? Over."

"Yes it is. Over?"

"Ma'am, I've got two blips on our radar screen bearing ten degrees off our port bow. They must not know we're here as they are closing on us fast. What's your pleasure? Over."

"Sir the first blip is a bogie. Be advised that they do not, I repeat they do not have Debutante on board. The second blip is friendly. How far apart are the two? Over?"

"Copy that Ma'am, I'd say the first blip is about two clicks ahead of the friendly. Over?"

"Sir, can you guys get a clean shot at it? Over?"

"Yes ma'am . . . wait! They must have spotted us. They are coming about and heading thirty degrees starboard. I still think we can pick him off. Over?"

"Then sir, take your best shot. Over and out!"

Captain Cunningham gave the orders to his XO, who repeated the order and called for a firing solution. Moments later Chief Gunnery Sergeant Stillwell, called out, "We have acquired the target and have a firing solution, captain, sir."

"Fire!"

The XO repeated the order, "Fire!"

Gunnery Sergeant Stillwell squeezed the trigger and red tracers from his 50-caliber deck-gun split the foggy sky.

A yellow ball lit the sky, and Jimbo's breath caught in his throat. He eased back on the throttle and nosed his watercraft in the direction of the explosion. A minute later he brought his boat to a full stop. Floating pieces of wood and rubber lapped in the icy waters.

"Look Jimbo," Kaleel said, pointing at the 'Football'. "Over there."

As Jimbo brought his Zodiac around, a large wave swept over the silver suitcase and pulled it under. Kaleel reached for it, nearly falling over the side in the process.

President Ferguson grabbed him and kept him from toppling over. "Don't, they're not worth it."

Kaleel flopped back in the boat as Jimbo circled the area. "I lost it, it's gone."

Three pair of eyes searched the swells, seeing nothing but murky foam.

"Any sign of the other guy?" Jimbo asked, as the Zodiac crested a wave.

"He's gone," the president said, after she'd regained her strength.

Jimbo pounded the rubber side. "Gone, what do you mean, gone?"

"I mean, the guy that looks just like Agent Bashera, tied a rope around the steering wheel and secured it to the throttle and jumped into the lake. That's when I saw my chance and jumped in too."

"You mean to say, Amil abandoned the boat, hoping the Coast Guard would fire on it, killing you and blowing up the codes?"

The president shook her head, "I don't know about that. All I know is that he jumped in and began swimming away."

Jimbo revved the engines and headed toward the opposite shore, while above them hovered a Huey, its beam covering their every move.

"We'll never make it. I'll bet that guy had someone waiting for him. He'll be half way to Mecca by now," the president said, as the spray of lake water splashed in her face.

"Not Mecca, New York!" That said, Jimbo cut his wheel and headed back to the island.

***

Guided by the powerful beam, he safely landed the rubber watercraft on the shore. Immediately, an army of Marines encircled them providing a thin layer of protection.

"This way, Madam President," said Captain Cunningham, who'd come ashore minutes earlier. "We have Marine One waiting for you, if you will follow me."

"No, don't bother with me, get these folks some medical attention," she said, uncharacteristically.

With a crisp salute, the captain shifted his gaze. "Yes, ma'am." Turning to his XO, "You heard the lady, let's get these people inside before they freeze to death."

A circle of Marines formed around them like offensive linebackers and shielded them as best they could from the howling winds and rain until they reached the lobby of the hotel.

***

The five survivors sat in front of a raging fire, huddled in blankets, sipping hot coffee.

"Madam President, we had a drone hovering above the hotel and were able to monitor the last moments before the terrorists abducted you. Would you like to hear it?"

President Ferguson wiped her face with a towel bearing the monogrammed letters GW the captain had handed her.

She continued to stare into the fireplace as if it would give her the right answer. It had been a long time since she'd not had people around her, advising her, counseling her, making decisions for her. Now it seemed the simplest choice was a chore. She released a long sigh and lifted her gaze to meet his. "Yes, please."

"I have to advise you, Madam President, it's pretty graphic," he added.

Susan steeled herself. "Go ahead, play it."

Captain Cunningham nodded to his XO and he pushed a button on a small device.

"Fall back, fall back," Larry Morgan hollered, followed by gunfire.

"I'm hit," someone yelled.

"They are coming around you, watch out," another secret service agent hollered.

"I'm out of ammo, cover me." The president winched, recognizing Leah's voice.

More gunfire and explosions.

"They are coming in through the windows." It was Larry's steady voice.

An insurgent broke through their thinning lines of defense and pointed a gun at her. As he squeezed the trigger, Larry jumped between the gun and the president. He took the full impact of the slug and fell at her feet. He looked up, gave her a weak smile, and turned the gun on his attacker. He kept firing until the chamber jacked open and he let his arm slump to the floor.

"Fall back to the 'keep.' Get Debutante. Give her a weapon. Put her in the bathtub and lock her in. Don't let anyone get past you." It was Andrew.

Susan bit back the tears that wanted to fall. Her last memory of Andrew was him standing outside the bathroom door with a gun in his hand.

She'd never handled a gun in her life, and he knew it. Nevertheless, he knew it was her last hope.

More shouting. More gunfire.

The lobby resonated as the captain and survivors listened with rapt attention. Susan pressed the towel to her face, trying to shut out the memory of Andrew's final act of courage.

Shouts of Arabic and English curses sounded as the situation deteriorated. It became hand to hand combat as men struggled and died.

A huge explosion caused everyone to jump.

A man shouted, "Allah al Akbar."

The president and the others listened as she fought her captor's attempts to drag her from the bathroom. After a lot of grunting and scuffling, the lobby fell silent.

"I will tell you this," the president said, taking a ragged breath. "When they came for me," she paused, a fire burned in her eyes, "I pointed the gun and fired until it was empty. I don't know if I killed anyone, but I did what Andrew told me to do. I did it for him, for Larry, I did it for all of them." She buried her face in the monogrammed towel and wept.

After a long moment, Kaleel, his head partially covered with a towel, looked up, "Madam President?"

"Yes, Agent Bashera?"

"What about the codes? I'm sorry I lost them."

She let her eyes search the floor, and she hesitated. "Don't be, I'm not."

"You're not?"

"Nope!"

"With all due respect, Madam President," Rachel interjected. "A lot of good people died to save those codes."

The president nodded, a wry smile played on her lips. "Look Rachel, a lot of good people did die today, but not saving the codes, they died trying to save me. And for that I am eternally grateful. But as far as those codes are concerned, they are as safe as could be."

"Why? How? Didn't we see the codes sink to the bottom of the lake?" Kaleel asked.

"No Agent Bashera. We anticipated an attack and so we transferred the codes to the hotel safe and filled the suitcase with laundry."

"Laundry? Who's?"

"Well let's say it wasn't mine," the president said. "We wouldn't want someone finding the suitcase and opening it and begin airing the president's dirty laundry, now would we?"

Postlude

The Grand Hotel Lobby

Captain Cunningham stepped up to the president's side. "Ma'am," the lines in his face deep with concern, "I have some disturbing news."

Four sets of eyes stared back at her. Lowering her chin, she drew him aside away from the warmth of the fire. "Okay, give it to me straight. What is it?" She held his steely gaze.

"The FBI found the stolen spent fuel rods, or at least where they were." He paused to let Susan process the information before giving her more. "They discovered a grisly sight, as well."

A sharp intake. "Oh?"

Captain Cunningham's chiseled features softened, and he let out a slow breath. "They found half a dozen scientists and technicians. They've been dead for a few days."

The president's mind fluttered like a moth to a flame. "I don't get it. Who killed them and why? Furthermore, where are the spent fuel rods?"

The weight of losing her team pressed in upon her, and she sank to the couch. Tears scalded her face as she wept bitterly.

The ship's captain laid a warm hand on her shoulder. "Madam President," Quoting his favorite verse, he said, "Be strong in the Lord and in the power of His might. The nation needs you."

Blankly, she looked up, and the two locked eyes. She inhaled and held it a moment, then let it out.

"Rachel, would you assist me until my full security detail arrives?" her voice gaining strength with every word.

"Of course, Madam President, I'll be right behind you."

The president stood and gave Rachel's hand a gentle squeeze, then with a quick gait, walked away, under the protection of the Marines.

***

Turning to Belinda, Jimbo stood. "I think we'd better call Mr. Zavier. I'm sure I'd like an update. After this mess is cleaned up, he'll probably call me back to Quantico."

Belinda took his proffered hand and rose to her feet. "Not if I have anything to do with it," she quipped. "My orders are to keep you here for a while." Her voice receded as they headed down the hall.

The events of the preceding hours swirled around in Agent Anderson's mind like wind driven snow. First, there was the attempt to drug the president and steel the nuclear codes. It would have worked had it not been for the fast thinking of the man sitting next to her. There was the attack by a second wave of insurgents, killing all but herself and the president. And then there was the race against time as, again, the man sitting next to her, rescued President Ferguson from drowning in Lake Michigan.

Staring into the fire, Rachel knew she had only a minute to say a proper good-bye, but something about Kaleel's movements gave her pause. Why had he not removed the towel from his head? The warmth of the fire dried most of their clothes, and yet he sat, head covered, mesmerized as if in a trance. A quick look at the man's shoes and Rachel's pulse quickened. The man she knew as Agent Kaleel Bashera was a CIA plant who'd infiltrated the Sons of Thunder. In that role, he and a team of insurgents, posing as cooks and servers, slipped into the Grand Hotel, and drugged the attendees of the Kyoto Summit. As such, he was dressed as a waiter, but this man wore a pair of business shoes. Though discolored by lake water, the distinctive markings of a pair of Florsheims were clearly evident.

Catching her breath, she pushed herself upright. The grandfather clock in the lobby gonged three times. As the last tone faded, she broke her trance and shook off the blanket. "Well, I guess I'd better be going. I have a dozen agents to get up to speed before we land in DC, so this will have to be my good-bye," she said, glancing at the man who'd saved her life and the life of the president.

"Mind if I walk you to the door?" Kaleel asked.

Feigning offense, Rachel said, "The last time I went for a walk with you, you knocked me out and stuffed me into a utility room."

Kaleel lowered his voice, "That was a mistake. I shouldn't have knocked you out and stuffed you in a utility room." His hand moved behind his back. "I should have shot you."

With one smooth move, Amil pulled out a pistol with a silencer and fired twice at point blank range. Rachel tumbled back on the couch, eyes staring blindly at the ceiling. Amil, having drowned his nearly identical cousin Kaleel in the lake, assumed his identity for a second time. With the one person between him and the nuclear codes dead, he need only to make his way to the fourth floor, get the suitcase from the hotel safe and disappear.

Without giving it another thought, he threw a blanket over Rachel's lifeless body and dashed up the stairs. Skipping past the second and third levels, Amil crept to the fourth floor, hoping no one was there.

Voices echoed in the distance and he knew he couldn't kill them all. Carefully, he dodged a medical team who were identifying the dead, and made his way to the Millikan Suite. Stepping over the rubble, he found the safe, unguarded. With a couple of well-placed shots, the safe door sprung open. He grabbed the silver suitcase and calmly descended the stairs. With no one to watch the back door, he slipped into the waning storm and made his way across the soggy lawn.

The Zodiac Jimbo returned in, bobbed in the surf not far from where he'd landed. With a quick turn of the key, the engine revved and Amil shoved off. By dawn, he'd crossed Lake Michigan and landed on the Canadian shore not far from where a parked car awaited his arrival. He found the key where he'd hidden it, got in and disappeared in the misty morning.

***

Anita and Habib sat wide eyed in the back seat of a New York taxi cab while Jared anxiously waited for the light to change. It had been a grueling trip from Lebanon to America, but thanks to Mr. Xavier's influence, they passed through Customs without the usual harassment. Within minutes, they'd be at the hospital where Fatemah awaited them.

"Jared!" Fatemah exclaimed, and leaped from her hospital bed and into Jared's arms.

The two embraced warmly while Anita and Habib watched. Seeing them smile, Fatemah reached out, pulling them close. "Anita, Habib, it's so good to see you." Her words morphed into tears as the three embraced.

"Are you ready to go?" Jared asked.

"The doctors have already released me. All I need is to have someone wheel me out."

"Well, we don't have a place to go yet, but that can be resolved pretty quickly. Let me flag down an orderly with a wheelchair and get you out of here. Over lunch, I'll call John and see what he can do to get a hotel."

"Great, I can't wait to eat some real food. This hospital fare just doesn't hold a candle to your mamma's cookin'."

Giving her a quick nod, Jared said, "Well, we may have to pass on mamma's cookin' for a while. We have Anita's brother, Rajeed, running around here planning an attack on New York, and the person who can identify him is Anita," he said, looking at Anita.

Biting her thumbnail, Anita lowered her chin. "I can't believe the things they are saying about him. They can't be true." Her eyes watered and she swallowed hard.

"Comin' through," an orderly said, her Black-American inflection cutting through her two word warning.

Minutes later, the four of them squeezed into a yellow cab, headed for the nicest hotel they could find, compliments of Mr. Xavier and the agency.

***

Like a water-logged tree trunk, Kaleel Bashera's body washed up on the rugged Mackinaw Island shore and bobbed in the gathering foam. Not far from there, two guards patrolling the island's perimeter, noticed something bobbing in the shallow water, stopped to investigate.

"Hey Tom, do you see that?" First Sergeant Rigby said, his arm outstretched, pointing at the shoreline.

SFC Chuck Hudson directed his powerful mag light in the direction of his gaze. "It looks like a body."

Rigby drew his sidearm as the two approached. Cautiously, he rolled the body over revealing an ashen face of what looked like a waiter. He placed two fingers on his jugular vein and held his breath. A moment later his hand jerked back, "First Sergeant, this guy's got a pulse."

Having had CPR training, SFC Hudson knelt in the foamy water. "Here, hold this light," handing his buddy the mag light. He grabbed the body and dragged it higher on shore and rolled it over. His quick thinking and professional training kicked in. Within minutes of pressing on the man's back and mouth to mouth resuscitation, Kaleel coughed up a lung-full of water.

"What happened?" he sputtered, still coughing.

Shining the beam in his eyes, SFC Hudson inspected his pupils and patted him on the back. "Buddy, you are either the luckiest man on the planet, or God isn't through with you yet."

Clearing his throat of lake water, Kaleel blinked the light away, "I prefer to think the latter." A forced laugh brought on another wave of heaving.

"Look man, we need to get you inside. You've got a lot of explaining to do," Hudson said, hoisting Kaleel to his feet.

Kaleel's legs buckled.

Hudson grabbed him to keep Kaleel from falling over. "Hold on now, friend. Try to stand here a minute."

Kaleel bent at the waist and released another round of heavy coughing. Finally, he took a deep breath and wiped his face. "Okay, I think I can make it."

***

"Where is Agent Anderson, I thought she was right behind me with the 'suitcase'?" the president asked Captain Cunningham, the whites of her eyes stabbing a new wave of rain.

"That's what I thought," shielding his eyes as a bright light danced in the hand of an approaching figure.

They'd waited in Marine One longer than they needed to and the president was getting worried.

"There," he pointed. "I think I see someone coming," holding his hand out.

Jimbo's broad girth took shape in the flood lights of Marine One, his face was washed in sweat, rain, and tears.

"What's wrong, Mr. Osborne?" the president's voice was laced with concern.

"Madam President," Jimbo's voice cracked, his shoulders heaved, and he had to support himself against the frame of the helicopter.

Eyes wide, President Ferguson stretched out her hand to comfort him. Taking strength from her touch, he took a halting breath.

"It's Agent Anderson," he paused to choke back the bitterness in his throat. His puppy-dog eyes pled. "You gotta come."

Turning, he dashed into the storm. President Ferguson scrambled from the open door and splashed after him, Captain Cunningham's umbrella barely able to keep up.

Once inside, Susan caught Jimbo by the elbow, "What is it? What's wrong? Is she all right?"

Jimbo returned a slow shake of his head. "No! Something went terribly wrong. She must have seen something about that Kaleel-Amil guy, whatever his name is, and confronted him. She's dead, Madam President. Shot at point blank range." His throat closed and he took a labored breath. "There's another thing, Madam President."

She halted mid-stride, "It's the codes, isn't it?" Her rhetorical question hung in the air like a slow-pitch softball.

Lowering his eyes, Jimbo spoke in a whisper. "Yes, ma'am."

***

Sergeants Rigby and Hudson pushed through the storm and came in through the service entrance. Taking the elevator, they half carried, half dragged Agent Bashera into a hornet's nest of activity. As they neared the lobby, Jimbo and Belinda drew their weapons and pointed them at the man they thought to be Amil.

"Hold it right there, boys," Jimbo barked. "Amil, down on your knees, fingers locked behind your head," his commands coming in staccato phrases. "Belinda, cuff him."

Visions of him and Jared emerging from the basement of the Mosque flashed across his mind giving him pause.

"I'm not who you think I am," Kaleel coughed. Glancing past Jimbo, he saw a blood stained sheet and a group of people leaning over a body.

"What happened?"

Not taking his eyes off of him, Jimbo gave him a quick nod, "You should know, you did this."

"Did what?"

"Killed Rachel, you filthy pig." Jimbo's voice rose as he pulled his arm back to pistol-whip the man kneeling before him.

"Jimbo!"

The president's authoritative voice crackled with tension, stopping his forward movement. "Jimbo, what are you doing?"

Lowering his arm, Jimbo relaxed his stance. "This guy killed Rachel and he's going to pay," he spat through clenched teeth.

"You don't know that. If he did, where's his gun, or the codes? And what was he doing floating in Lake Michigan for that matter?" Hudson asked.

Kaleel's head snapped around, his eyes skipping between the president and Jimbo."

"I, I didn't shoot Rachel, and I certainly didn't steal the codes. I was swimming out to keep you, Madam President, from drowning, and Amil came from nowhere and pushed me under. He held my head down until I passed out. He must have thought he'd killed me. The next thing I know, this guy, glancing up at Sergeant Hudson was leaning over me."

"He's right," interjected Belinda. "Just look at his shoes."

A moment later, all eyes stared at Kaleel's shoes. "See, he's wearing a pair of black soft-soled shoes, the kind worn by nurses."

"Or line-servers," Kaleel added with growing confidence. "We were told to dress like the other cooks and servers. My clothes, including my cell phone are back in the servant's quarters. I can prove I am who I say I am."

"How so?" Jimbo asked warily.

"I got a call from my sister Fatemah. You remember her, don't you, Jimbo?"

Jimbo's resolve began to wane, his gun lowered. "Belinda, would you take one of these fine men and check out his story?"

Cutting her eyes in his direction, "Hey, wait a minute, who's got the rank here?"

"I do." The president's voice sliced through the tense air.

"Yes, ma'am," Belinda replied, holstering her weapon.

As she and SFC Rigby disappeared down the stairs, the president held Jimbo's gaze.

"When did you discover Agent Ander—" her voice cracked and tears splashed down her cheeks. Captain Cunningham extended an arm, and she buried her face in his shoulder.

Parking his gun in its holster, Jimbo helped Kaleel to his feet and plopped him across from the bloody blanket which covered Agent Anderson's body.

"Belinda and I had returned to the security office to discuss our future plans. The grandfather clock had just gonged three times when I heard a couple of pops. At first, we thought it was wood popping in the fire place, so we went on with our conversation. Then, we heard what sounded like feet, running down from upstairs. We knew that was off-limits and so we came out to investigate. By the time we found Rach—uh, Miss Anderson's body, the guy posing as Kaleel was long gone."

As he finished with his narrative, Belinda and SFC Rigby returned from the lower level. She handed Kaleel the phone. "Go ahead, play your last message."

Kaleel gave her a knowing glance. *She obviously knows what it says.*

"I don't have to do this. I—"

Jimbo squared himself directly in front of him, "And you don't have to live another day," he growled.

"Jimbo!" the president's voice warned. "Give the man a chance to finish. You were saying, Agent Bashera?"

Jimbo's eyes cut in her direction, but he bit his tongue.

"Eying Jimbo's looming stature, he gave him a nonchalant shrug. "I was about to say, I can tell you the last message was from Fatemah without looking at it. It said, 'Expecting.'"

Jimbo's face blanched, "Expecting? Expecting what?"

A soft hand came to rest on Jimbo's slumping shoulders, "Jimbo," Belinda said. "If I were a betting woman, and sometimes I am, I'd dare say, she's expecting a baby."

Kaleel's face brightened, "Would it be alright if someone could remove these iron brackets. I'd like to congratulate Mr. Jimbo for being the child's godfather."

A quick nod from the president and SFC Hudson stepped behind Kaleel and unlocked the cuffs. Kaleel brought his hands in front, rubbing his wrists.

"I sure am sorry about Rachel. I was looking forward to getting to know her better." He took a halting breath and began another round of coughing.

"What's next, Madam President?" Belinda's question broke the moment and she looked up.

"Special Agent Bashera, I am giving you full authority to hunt down Rachel's killer and bring the—" She paused before saying something she'd regret. "And bring him to justice." Sucking in a sharp breath, she turned, "Captain Cunningham."

"Yes ma'am," snapping to attention.

"Have your people draft my executive order and have it ready for my signature in thirty minutes."

"Yes ma'am." He saluted, gave her a sly wink and marched off to carry-out her directive.

Fifteen minutes later, he returned and handed the president a sheet of paper. Stepping into the security office, she took her seat behind the small desk and picked up a pen. "I have to say, this is the smallest presidential desk I've ever had the privilege of sitting behind," fingering the pen.

"If my instincts are correct, I think this weekend is all tied to the Lebanon affair and the stolen nuclear fuel rods."

Three sets of eyes widened at the confidential news.

"I had no idea, Madam President," Kaleel sputtered.

"No, no you wouldn't. This is classified information, but I feel you need to know what kind of threat you're dealing with. There are a couple of terrorists on the loose, and I think we haven't seen the worst of it."

The Final Countdown – #25 on Amazon

The clock is ticking and Jared once again finds himself battling against forces beyond his control. Can he and his friends unravel the mystery in time to stop two radical Muslims from perpetrating a horrible crime against our country?
ISBN – 978153297825

Made in the USA
Columbia, SC
28 November 2023